THE COURSER & WALLACE CHRONICLES

A CROSSING IN THE WOODS

THE COURSER & WALLACE CHRONICLES

A CROSSING IN THE WOODS

J. R. McCONNERY

WANDERERbooks

WANDERERbooks

Published by Wanderer Books
Toronto ON, CANADA

Visit JRMcConnery.com for news, updates, extras, and more.

A Crossing in the Forest

The Courser & Wallace Chronicles, Volume I

Designed by J. R. McConnery.
Cover design by J. R. McConnery.
Author Photo © Rx Photography

ISBN 978-09881490-3-8

For my family, my friends, and all the authors who made me want to make this possible.

THE COURSER & WALLACE CHRONICLES

A CROSSING IN THE WOODS

There are no great people in this world, only great challenges which ordinary people rise to meet.

- William Frederick Halsey, Jr.

A PLAN FOR SUCCESSION

Tendrils of smoke stained burnt orange coiled into the air from the ink-laden paper. Flames crept along its borders and inched towards its centre. Aside from the candles burning on the desk across the room, the fire in Jonas Vorley's hand was the only source of light in the room. The window shutters were closed fast against prying eyes. He watched the scrawl melt away and finally let the script fall into the ashy grate of his cold fireplace, where it continued to burn away the signature that offered the permission he'd long sought.

Jonas cocked his head at the rough scraping of footsteps outside, a subtle warning of an approaching knock. Long strides carried him across the dark room to the door. He opened the door as the soldier in the hallway raised his fist. Jonas flashed his teeth in amusement at the man's surprise.

"Serjant," Jonas eyed the double bars on the sleeve of his coat that identified his rank. He took careful note of the intricate hilt of the sword at his hip—a man of noble means. He knew the soldier, but could not recall his name. "Do not waste my time looking surprised. Get on with it." His heart quickened as he predicted the possible contents of the report.

The soldier saluted the Sheryff to hide his discomfort, "Serjant Lauder, syr. Governyr Makkin has requested your presence for an urgent matter."

"What is it?" The impatience was clear in his voice. He already knew what the matter was likely to be, as he knew all things that happened in the region. As Sheryff of the Northern provinces—second only to the Governyr himself—he had to know these things.

"Your traps, syr." Lauder melted under Jonas's striking gaze, which heated with a greater intensity at the confirmation of his suspicions. The serjant hurried to answer the next unspoken question. "Two have been captured."

"Excellent. Take me." Jonas gathered his sword belt and slipped into his riding jacket. The ashes of his letter danced and scattered as he strode past the fireplace to follow Serjant Lauder down the hall.

"Tell me," Jonas said.

"Caught in one of your traps, Headwaters, syr—" Lauder hurried to keep up with his commander's long strides, and felt his words die in his throat as the man cut him off.

"Who?" any would be satisfactory, but a man could dream. Through the nearest window, the night sky was cloudless and lit by a waxing moon approaching its apex. Usually, the military quarter at the southern reaches of the city was quiet at night; there was little unrest so close to the center of power. Now, there was a commotion in the air that heralded the event. The men were awake and buzzing with the capture, even if they did not know its full scope.

"Nagel," Lauder began.

"The elder?" Jonas replied, hoping his luck remained strong.

"The elder," Lauder confirmed. Jonas's chest swelled at the news.

They hurried down sharply hewn steps from the second level and emerged into the fort's courtyard. Militia bustled past, looking busy, but with their peripheral vision trained on their commander, keen to sense his disposition at this latest success. When Vorley was happy, they all could be.

The younger Nagel had harassed him and his operations soundly, but the core of the very resistance rested with the elder. This would sound their final death knell, though the independence front had been dying for months. His scheme to capture them had paid off enormously.

"And the other?"

"His guard. Won't say his name, but I think he's that Barnicke boy, the one that disappeared a few months back."

"Disappeared," Jonas scoffed. Even the boy's father, Lon Barnicke had suspected his youngest son of defecting to the rebellion. They'd had many a discussion. 'If only he'd come back, we would welcome him,' Lon had said. Jonas had agreed as thoroughly as his empty feelings for the boy would allow, having no intention of sparing the traitor.

Jonas stooped under the doorway as they re-entered the fort on the other side of the courtyard. The hallway inside was wide enough for four men to march abreast, allowing a defensive formation in the event of a breach. At the end of the hallway, the governyr paced in front of a heavy oaken door while another soldier stood nervously nearby. This soldier spied Vorley and then Lauder, and visibly relaxed as he recognized the expression of relative ease on Lauder's face.

"What took you?" Makkin asked from down the hall, his voice was weak at the late hour, but his attitude commanded respect.

"Hmm?" Jonas replied firmly as he neared.

"What took you?" the governyr repeated, somewhat less sure of himself the second time.

"I've only just heard."

The two soldiers stood at attention as the two most powerful men in Northern Numyria politely sparred.

"Of course, of course," Makkin accepted the explanation and then changed tack. "You've done it this time Jonas. We've got him."

"Cicero. I've heard."

"And that Barnicke boy... Grian, I think? Grown some shade, but he's got his father's nose."

"Indeed."

"Lucky we caught them," Makkin's corpulent body quivered with excited relief. Jonas never had his doubts, but of late, the endlessly weakening governyr had felt legitimately threatened by the agitators hidden away in the forests to the north. Thankfully, he felt no such feelings of threat from his closest advisor.

"I don't believe in luck. This was hard work and preparation, and foolishness on their part," Jonas flashed his teeth.

"Which one was it?" the Governyr asked.

"Headwaters," Jonas replied. "They were getting very desperate," Jonas replied. He'd fomented a bit of false sympathy in the large town at the Arrowhead River's source. Rich with supplies and young men, the town's sympathetic offerings would have been a bounty to the emaciated independence front. It was simple enough to set up a trap, though he had not anticipated capturing the rebellion's leader. It had to be on its last legs.

"This ends it," Makkin said.

Jonas grimaced. They'd beheaded the snake, but the stuff rebellions were made of—ideas—rarely died so easily. Nonetheless it *was* the beginning of the end. He would simply have to keep up the pressure, a task altogether more manageable once he had the Governyrship fully in his grasp.

"It would seem," Jonas mollified his governyr as his mind turned to the next step in stamping out their enemy. He hoped that particular task would be informed by the coming moments with their captives. "Let's get on with it."

"Just through here, syr," Lauder knocked on the great oaken door and another series of knocks replied. Lauder slid the bar lock against the grain of the wood and opened the door. Makkin hesitated and Jonas strode forward. His footfalls echoed off the stone walls.

In the middle of the room, two men knelt, their hands bound behind their backs and their ankles chained. Both men's eyes rose from the cold stone floor that offered little comfort to their knees.

"What a wonderful surprise," Jonas said, arms wide in false welcome. The younger man, Grian Barnicke, spat at Jonas's feet and sneered. Jonas considered the spittle briefly, then leaned forward casually and backhanded Grian. His face careened into the ground. Jonas ignored the hiss of disgust from Makkin as the Governyr padded into the room after them. With disdain, Jonas turned his attentions on the elder man.

"Cicero Nagel, do you not teach your juniors respect?"

"It is placed where it is earned," Cicero said simply, a calm expression on his face. His lips were thin with discomfort but his brow was relaxed.

Jonas smirked as he reached down to stroke the rebel leader's short and finely sculpted white beard. "This suits you." He recalled that Cicero had kept his face clean shaven in the past.

"Change is good," Cicero replied, "Of course, you know my stance on such matters."

Jonas shrugged and conceded the point, "Perhaps we're not so different." The sort of change he had in mind was less dramatic than Cicero's ideals.

"You're finished now, Cicero!" Makkin bellowed, tiring of the careful banter Jonas was busy constructing. Jonas felt the muscles at the back of his neck tense with annoyance. His patience for the governyr was wearing thin.

Barnicke struggled off the floor back into a kneeling position, leaving behind a stain of blood and spit where his lip had split on the stone. This time, he spat at Makkin, who waddled out of the way too slowly and ended with blood and saliva on his pants and boots.

Jonas backhanded the young man again. "Learn a new trick, dog." This time, the boy seemed to deflate and stayed down.

"I'll have your h—" Makkin started.

"Silence," Jonas hissed, holding up his hand to hush the governyr. It was a rare moment of lost control, but Makkin's posturing had become tiresome. Jonas's patience waned, especially as the secret words of the emperyr's letter echoed at the back of his head, words confirming his pending succession. He ran his hands over his smooth, shortly cropped hair to settle himself. To his surprise, Makkin quieted, and Jonas felt the tension in his neck melt away. "Cicero, we really must come to a compromise on this messy business."

This time, it was Cicero's turn to shrug.

Jonas continued, "We've rooted you out. We've captured your friends, your followers. You're running out of supplies, of supporters. Your capture today is proof enough of that," Jonas slowly paced back and forth in front of Cicero and the prostrate Barnicke boy. Makkin stood out of range of flying spittle, his face red with indignation but his lips closed and, blissfully, tongue still. "Tell us where the rest of you are hiding. If we can put this little thing to rest, we'll spare them. With your help, Cicero, I'm sure my lord—" Jonas indicated to Makkin, "—would be willing to offer you a pardon. A man with your knowledge, your diplomacy... you could be invaluable to the empyre."

"We're past that, Jonas. It's gone too far. *He's* gone too far," Cicero moved to motion with his hands as though making one of his inflammatory speeches, but was reminded he was bound by the rough cord chafing his wrists. "Look out your windows. The people are bound, not such as this," with his chin, he indicated himself and his companion, "but in every way except."

"This is our destiny," Jonas replied. "This land serves the other. That is how it has always been, from the Age of Kings to this Age of Hallows."

"But it need not."

Jonas sighed. Once, in his youth, he'd entertained the very idea, and almost got behind it. But that was a long time ago now. He looked deep into Cicero's eyes and saw there would be no negotiation. The man was set in his ideals. But every man could break. That process started now.

"Very well then." Jonas withdrew a wide blade from its sheath at his side and in two quick movements, pulled Grian's hair to expose his neck, and opened his great vessels onto the floor. Blood spilled out and seeped between the spaces in the stones. "Take him to the dungeon," Jonas motioned for the guards to drag Cicero away. Cicero stared at him, a look of sympathy in the elder's eyes. Jonas turned away. Somehow, he felt that the sympathy was not for the dead boy, but for him.

CHAPTER ONE

A CHANCE ENCOUNTER

Whispering shadows flitted back and forth across the branches above and the brush underfoot; the morning light barely managed to penetrate the forest canopy and cast a green and greyish hue over the subdued life beneath the trees. The air remained eerily silent, devoid of the sort of wild sounds that would have been pervasive in decades past. Yet there was life, evident in the musk of the deer just out of sight, and the rot of last autumn's fallen leaves as they fed the future. Every scent was both distinct and strangely vague.

Thomas Courser felt a wave of apprehension crash over him. He had set out weeks ago to take another shot at making a name for himself, like he had many times before. More modestly, he hoped to at least find the means to feed himself. His circumstances were less than happy, and due to a series of ill-fated events that he would prefer not to discuss with an absolute stranger, he was left alone.

If he could manage to find Ancaster through this particularly thick stretch of forest, he would be trying his luck in the third village he'd visited in the past two months. Word in Clarkstown one week before was that an innkeeper in Ancaster was hiring help, or at least taking on indenture. Likely backbreaking work for a bed and board, but Thomas had worked for far less and for far worse.

Thomas brushed his lengthening hair out of his eyes, his fingers familiar with its coarse dryness. His hair was like hay baked by long forgotten summer sunlight, the ends breaking from the depths of his malnutrition. His eyes, set back in his skull, were a deep and soulful brown. They could tell a story one hundred years long, but even that would fail to explain why his clothes were threadbare, ill-fitting, and dangling off his body. He hitched his pants up and cinched the rope around his waist to keep them there. They seemed to be getting bigger by the day. He fingered the few flimsy spickles left in his pocket and ignored the ache in his midsection that had become routine of late.

Thomas was beginning to lose hope that he'd ever be able to relax or enjoy life. He would scoff at the word 'life' for he was not living; he merely existed, dragging his body through each agonizing day in his short fourteen years in a vain attempt at survival. Sometimes he would answer his own questions optimistically: *Tomorrow will be better, tomorrow all of this pain will end and I will be happy...* but his natural sense of pessimism always told him otherwise. *This won't end until you're dead and gone from here; might as well make it quick.* The future was one of Thom's least favourite subjects. He hated thinking about it, but he was forced to if he was going to survive.

For others, Thomas observed, life was easy. How could the wheel of fate and fortune be positioned so persistently that life should throw every tough break his way, while others got off enjoying the finer things in life? Thomas had stopped trying to understand. It was his lot in life. The constants of fear and hunger, discomfort and loneliness, and an overwhelming sense of hopelessness. He wouldn't be the first Numyrian boy to face such struggles, and he wouldn't be the last. With his next step, the latest setback only added to his discomfort, as his big toe rudely protruded from the corner of his terribly worn canvas shoes.

Of course, the event was an inevitability Thomas was forced to face. He was a growing boy, and growing boys have growing feet. Growing feet need bigger shoes and bigger shoes require money.

Money being a resource that he did not enjoy, one could say that Thomas was out of luck. Thomas would say he'd been out of luck from the moment he'd been born... out of good luck that is. He couldn't give away enough of the bad stuff.

Collapsing in defeat, Thomas Courser lay face down on the mossy forest floor, its earthy scent his only comfort. His big toe was already beginning to feel cold in the chill breeze since it had gone ahead and distinguished itself from its compatriots.

"Them's some mighty nice shoes you got on boy," a voice from above decided. Was Myr finally answering Thom's cries for help? He rolled over with his eyes squinted.

Instead of being blinded by Myr's stunning light, Thomas beheld a hobbled hermit with a toothless grin splayed across his face. If not for the noticeable stoop in his back, the man would have towered over Thom's modest height. He was garbed in similarly ragged clothes, but somehow had the luxury of spectacles; a pair of round, wiry frames with thick, foggy lenses blurred and magnified his startlingly intense gaze. His scholarly character was intensified by the presence of an enormous white beard that, upon closer examination, was actually matted and unkempt.

Suspicion clouded Thom's expression, "What do you want?"

Thomas was not the kind of person who trusted easily; he'd been hurt too many times by placing his trust where it did not belong. He'd made the resolution to be more wary two years before when he had been led into an alley and beaten unconscious by a gang of thugs. He had foolishly been under the impression that he was being offered a warm meal. When he awoke from his beating in the muck, cold and hungry, his disappointment in his own stupidity stung more than the ache in his stomach and the crooked angle of his nose. He'd been lucky to survive. A mistake like that was not going to be made again if he had any say, and he fancied that he did.

"What do I want? I want for nothin'! Look at me, I'm a creature ta be admired if there ever was one!" the man straightened his tattered shirt.

"Well, why are you bothering me then?" Thomas sat up.

"Didn't mean nothin' by it young man, ya just look down on yer luck…" the man explained.

Thomas winced at the word. *Why does it always come back to be rubbed in my face?* He thought.

"Look, I'm fine," Thomas clambered to his feet and began to brush the debris from his front. "I'll just be on my way."

"Do ya know where yer goin'?"

"Well yeah, I mean, Ancaster way, just over…" Thomas looked around aimlessly, and at a loss, pointed in a random direction, "over there! I'm almost there."

"Nothin' but trees that way boy. Yer outta luck an' lost!" the dishevelled man giggled maniacally and began to scratch at his head. Thomas knew what lice were and kept his distance. "Why don't I show ya the way?"

Thomas cocked his eyebrow. This crazy old man was going to guide him through the forest? The hermit would do better guiding himself to his senses before leading anyone anywhere. Still, Thomas began to weigh the options.

On the one hand, Thomas didn't know the man at all, he seemed crazy, and they were by themselves in the middle of a forest known to be home to anti-imperial agitators. Doing anything other than putting distance between him and the elder was a risk. On the other hand, the man seemed genuinely well intentioned. He was old and therefore easily outrun, and, most importantly Thomas was lost. He wasn't happy about breaking his rules regarding the trusting of strangers, but when it came down to it, he didn't really have a choice. He would have to take the risk and let the old man guide him where he would.

"You really know where you're going?" Thomas asked.

"O' course, this is *my* forest!"

"Well all right then, lead the way old man."

"The name's Rawlins," the man replied aloofly.

"Thomas," the boy replied, "pleasure to meet you," he lied.

The newly acquainted pair had been walking for no more than half an hour, but to Thomas, that short period proved to be an endless torment. Not only did the man claim to be an excellent forest guide, he claimed to have been a bard of sorts in a mercenary corps to the far east during his youth. Of course, a claim was to go nowhere without proof, so they passed the time with a private recitation of every song Rawlins could remember. Now, the songs weren't exactly bad—in fact, many of them were classics—it was just the way in which they were sung. In Rawlins's rendition, a timeless ballad became a tone deaf poem passing through the countless gaps in his incomplete smile.

Relief filled Thomas as the singing finally came to a conclusion on the challenging final note of *A Teton Tragedy*. Thomas worried that if if it went on much longer, his ears would begin to bleed. "Wow, that was, um, really good," Thomas felt his right index finger twitching at the lie. "You must have spent days memorizing that one!"

"Well, let me tell ya how I came to learn that song."

"No, really, it's okay, the song spoke for itself, and you truly did it justice."

"Aw, well, mayhaps for the best. 'Tis a long winded tale, and no time now; we're gettin' close."

"Oh really? How much longer?"

"Just a mo," Rawlins smiled.

"We'd surely see the town then," Thomas stopped walking and stared at the man as he continued forward.

"Town? What town?"

"Ancaster. The town you were leading me to."

"Ah."

Thomas threw his arms up in the air in exasperation. The better part of the afternoon was gone, which meant another night in the woods, and another cinch on his belt in the morning. That was what he got for trusting a crazed recluse to lead him out of the woods. Not only a stranger, but one that he knew was crazy from the very beginning. Thomas let out a groan and ground his palms into his eye sockets.

"Well, come on then!" the man said. "I was just showin' ya my home sweet home. Breathe it in through those young lungs."

Thomas peered at the man where he stood beckoning. He began to pick out various signs of life. Rawlins had led him to a small camp that nestled amongst the trees, an area of sparse grass and dirt with a diameter of no more than fifteen paces. A round stone campfire sat in the middle of the clearing with stumps scattered around its circumference. The campfire had a sturdy looking roasting spit constructed above it with a small cast iron cauldron hanging from its central beam. A cord of wood was stacked a few paces from the campfire, with a large chopping block off to the side. Thomas also picked out a ramshackle hut, built alongside a few trees away from the fire pit. Finally, connected between two small trees was a string of clothes dangling above a wash basin. Thomas was surprised by this particular development. *Rawlins actually washes his clothes?*

"Well what do ya think?" Rawlins asked as a look of subtle pride crossed his face.

Not wanting to anger him, as Thomas still needed the man's help to get out of the forest, he quickly came up with a lie. "Um… that's a very nice… house you've got there. Quality structure, really."

"Aw shucks, I built that myself many years ago."

"Hasn't aged a day," Thomas said, examining the shack from a distance. The door looked like it was ready to fall off of its cracked leather hinges, and the four-pane window was missing three panels of glass. The roof was more leaf than shingle, and even had some grass growing out from beneath the few shingles that were visible.

"Can't say the same fer me… can I get ya a drink? Some tea mayhaps?" Before he had a chance to answer, Rawlins lit a small spark that quickly blossomed into a modest campfire.

"I'll have some tea I suppose, but I really shouldn't stay too long. I'll need to be making my way to Ancaster pretty soon."

"Ah you're young, you've got all the time in the world." Rawlins busied himself with boiling some water while Thomas continued to stand awkwardly, unsure of what to do with himself. "Make yerself at home, find a seat. Get comfy," Rawlins suggested.

Thomas flopped down on a stump beside the campfire and massaged his thin calves. The long days of walking were getting harder and harder.

"So what's a young'un like you doin' all by yerse_f in the woods?"

"I'd rather not talk about it," Thomas turned his eyes down.

"Ah come on, maybe I can help ya out."

"Yeah. Sure you can," Thomas scoffed.

"Ya never know."

Thomas hesitated, and then in spite of his better judgment, spoke, "Let's just say I'm on my own, and well," Thomas looked around the spare camp, "times are tough."

Rawlins considered the statement for a moment, and then seemed to have better sense than to ask about the boy's parents. Instead, he replied with a simple, sorrowful nod.

They passed a few minutes in silence as the water boiled and the tea steeped. Rawlins poured some murky brown liquid into a cracked and ancient wooden cup and handed it to Thomas. He did the same for himself and then found a seat on the opposite stump. Thomas sniffed it warily, but deemed it safe and took a tiny sip. Despite tasting stale and sour at the same time, the heat warmed him to the bones and eased his nerves.

"Thank you," Thomas said. The genuine appreciation in his voice surprised him.

"Yer very welcome," Rawlins rooted through his bag and produced a small loaf of crusty bread, which he offered to Thomas. "Help yerself, but don't gorge. Ya look half starved."

Thomas inspected the bread before tearing a piece off and stuffing it into his mouth. It too, was stale, but it was the first thing of substance he'd had in days. He softened the hard bread in his tea. He took the old man's advice and ate slowly while the afternoon light faded to evening. The time passed with more stories of Rawlins past and none of Thom's.

"Look, its gettin' late. Mayhaps yul stay the night n' I'll take ya into town tomorrow. No sense in sleepin' on a dirty doorstep by yerself when ya've got a friend here. An' no sense in gettin' lost in the woods again."

"I suppose that's a good idea," he honestly agreed for the first time since meeting the man. "I'll stay the night and make a fresh go at it tomorrow."

"Just what I thought, make it fresh tomorrow."

Thomas looked around. Night had fallen quickly. "Where shall I sleep?" he asked.

"Well, ya can sleep under the stars, or inside. I was going to do some stargazin' myself. Feel free to join me." Thomas nodded his approval. It was much safer to stay out in the open than in a shack with only one door. Rawlins picked himself up from his seat and entered the shack. He returned momentarily with two ragged but reasonably clean blankets. He tossed one to Thomas, and then laid his own out on the ground before settling onto it. Thomas situated himself close to the fire for warmth and pulled the blanket up to his chin.

Above, through the clearing in the canopy, Thomas picked out his favourite constellations as they sparkled in the blackness of the sky. The practice distracted him from the thoughts nagging at the back of his mind, telling him he was crazy to go to sleep with a stranger so near. The warmth of the tea settled around the bread in his stomach, warming him from the inside as the fire's heat crawled over him. Tomorrow was a new day, and if he could start it feeling well rested and with a belly full of bread and tea, it would have to be a good day. It would have to be.

CHAPTER TWO

THE GLADE

A LONELY PASSENGER JET coursed across the cerulean sky, its white belly difficult to discern as the sun's blinding light warmed the face of a familiar young man laying on the grass. He wondered what it would be like to be isolated from his peers like that cloud, destined to wander a sea of blue for eternity, alone. Life was better with others. That, he decided, was what life was all about, even if you weren't especially good at making friends—even if you were particularly prone to being picked on. He brushed his fingers against the swelling around his right eye. It wasn't bad. Taking the hit from Tyler Nosey in front of everyone had been the worst of it. The laughter and the disdain. The fight wasn't a first, just another in a long line of them spurred on by his insurmountable inability to keep his mouth shut. Oswell Wallace grinned in self-amusement; why hold back when his words brought him such glee? Even if it *was* at the cost of a black eye.

Oswell was shorter than most of the other boys in his class and that was a fact that he hated, at fourteen, he was falling behind the others sprouting up with that wonderful mix of hormones called puberty. Kyle Trillings was shorter than Oswell, so there was that, at least. Oswell was also rather skinny, but he would tell you that he was wiry; and he certainly *could* be considered short, but he would tell you that he was growing. His hair was the colour of fresh hay, healthy in the early summer sunlight and his eyes were a deep chestnut, kind and calm and capable of telling a story one hundred years long.

Blades of grass tickled the bare skin of his legs and arms, bringing him back to reality. He'd been waiting for at least ten minutes, which at fourteen felt like an eternity. Of course, it wasn't uncharacteristic of Grant to be running late. Sure, Oswell liked to sleep in most mornings and skip off on chores around the house, but when Oswell had somewhere to be, he was there on time.

"Hey loser! Get up!" Grant called from across the lawn.

Oswell laughed and jumped up to greet him, "What took you so long? Grab a shower?"

"Yeah, that way I wouldn't be tempted to get sweaty again." Grant sniffed his armpit and grinned meekly.

"You've done me a favour then," Oswell shot back.

Grant stood over half a foot taller than Oswell, and had broader shoulders. His first growth spurt started a few months before, and he was already beginning to look awkward and gangly in his new body. His face was framed by dark black hair, and his eyes were a shocking electric blue. It was the general consensus that Grant Harding was going to grow up into quite the attractive young man. He simply wasn't there quite yet.

"You're most welcome, good sir… I think," Grant replied.

Oswell chuckled. "Walk to the glade? Old time's sake?"

"Walk?" Grant asked.

"Yes Grant, walk," Oswell sensed the contract being signed verbally. There would be no racing.

Grant ground his right foot into the grass and mumbled something to the effect of thinking they were going to play video games.

"What's that?" Oswell urged.

"Fine. Just for old time's sake then."

The pair plodded off into the forest and much to Grant's satisfaction, they did indeed, walk at a leisurely pace.

The leaves above them rustled in the light summer wind, and the rays of sun filtering through them gave everything a warm greenish hue. Oswell and Grant had a mutual enjoyment in the atmosphere of the forest. They walked in silence for a few minutes, a standard ritual as they welcomed the peace of nature. Oswell was the first to break the silence.

"You okay?"

"What?" Grant startled out of a reverie, "Yeah."

"Something's eating you," Oswell said.

"I *am* hungry," Grant smirked sardonically.

"Seriously, what's up?"

"Nothing," Grant reassured him.

Oswell shook his head, disappointed that the forest seemed to have lost its enchanting effect. It was their place, the one spot where they could tell each other everything. Now, it seemed like Grant didn't even want to be there. Something had to be bothering him; he wasn't being his usual self of late.

Oswell honestly didn't know what to make of it. In the past, Grant had always been full of enthusiasm. Oswell fully intended to find out what was bothering him. It was almost as if, in preparation of the following autumn, Grant had shrugged off his childhood in hopes of adopting the mythological 'cool' of a high school student. Yet the pursuit seemed somehow familiar. Had Oswell been subconsciously doing the same? He recalled his conversation with Mandy Wickenhauser a few days before. The attempt to flirt was a pitiful one, but when Grant teased him about it, he had just shrugged.

Oswell and Grant sauntered into the glade. Grant's eyes lit up while Oswell's darkened. Someone had clearly found their treasured hangout. Brown bottles littered the ground and a blackened fire pit sat at its centre. In its better years, the glade had been a place of comfort. It was only a small clearing in the blanket of trees that made up the rich forests of the American Northeast, but it was enough. Fallen limbs and logs made it the perfect place to climb trees, hang around, and talk. Apparently for those exact reasons, it had also become the perfect place to party.

Oswell sighed.

"This is so cool! Why didn't we ever think of this?" Grant exclaimed.

"Think of what? Coming out here to party?"

"Man, this is the perfect place…" Grant peered around with wide, inquiring eyes, "I wonder who was out here. Looks like they had a blast."

"A blast? It's just a bunch of garbage that no one was responsible enough to clean up."

Grant snorted as Oswell wandered about the glade, kicking glass bottles together into a pile.

"This was our place, don't you remember?" Oswell crossed his arms as the last bottle clinked into the pile.

"Yeah, but…"

"But what?"

"Haven't you noticed Ozzie? Just stop and listen. Stop and feel, take it in. Do you notice anything different?"

"Yeah! There's garbage everywhere!"

"I'm serious, do it."

Oswell groaned and scowled at Grant. Grant parried with a sense of impatience and urged him to do as he said, his arms outstretched and palms downward as though hushing a non-existent crowd. Oswell closed his eyes. Breathing through his nose, he listened. Grant joined him in complete silence. Oswell stood still, and waited. And waited.

There was nothing.

"Admit it. You don't feel it either. Do you?" Grant asked after letting the effect take hold. Oswell nodded solemnly. He didn't want to admit the truth he'd already begun to recognize, and had railed so firmly against.

"I don't feel it," he finally said.

"The magic's gone, Oz. I don't know what happened, or why, or how… but it's gone," Grant said, a small part of him sad at the loss as well.

Oswell sank to the forest floor beside the discarded brown bottles. So much of his life had been spent in that forest, devoted to it. Now, without so much as a word, the magic that had kept him coming back was gone. He'd been too naïve to notice it, too comfortable in his denial, but apparently Grant had noticed it and been waiting patiently for his best friend to catch up. Now Grant was the sensible one. He had recognized what it was time to do. Time to recognize that the magic was only in their minds—that magic wasn't real. It was time to grow up.

"What happened?" Grant asked the now silent Oswell.

"I don't know, it didn't hit me until you made it hit me."

"I started feeling it a few weeks ago. The anticipation for summer was gone. I was still excited to have a break, but it was more for the break this time, and less for the adventure."

"If you think about it, what good does adventure do us anyway? It isn't giving us any practical experience... it's just fun and games," Oswell picked up and examined a spent beer bottle, holding it up in front of the distant sun.

"*God*," Grant rolled his eyes, "you sound like such an adult. I still *like* it out here—it's just... different." Grant said. Oswell discarded the bottle back into the pile as Grant continued. "So much has happened in this forest."

"Yup," Oswell replied, eyes closed.

"Do you remember when we started that little brush fire and it almost got out of control?" Grant reminisced, walking the length of a fallen log.

"Of course I do, we nearly singed off our eyebrows putting it out!"

"And remember when we found that magazine?"

"Yeah," Oswell said.

They both sniggered.

"I remember when our dads sat us down for 'the talk' after that."

"Awkward. As if we didn't already know how it all worked," Oswell sat back up and watched his friend balance.

"We didn't know the half of it! You thought babies came from your mom's belly button."

"Shut up," Oswell groaned.

"There's so much history here."

"I feel like I'm losing it," Oswell looked pointedly at his friend, "the history I mean."

"History is a part of you, you'll never lose it." Grant smiled, "Trust me, I have a couple weeks of experience here. You only figured it out a few minutes ago." Oswell looked up at Grant, surprised to be hearing such a sober sentiment from him.

"I guess you're right."

"Of course I'm right! When am I not right?"

Oswell smirked and Grant grinned back. The pair burst out laughing.

Two eyes peered through the low branches of the forest. Laughter pierced through the silence of the forest. Quietly, the watcher passed through the maze of trees towards the source of the laughter.

There they are.

The eyes locked onto two boys relaxing in a small clearing. One sprawled across a log while the other had reclined back onto the forest floor. Both were in hysterics over something. With malicious intent, the watcher crept forward.

Oswell continued to laugh as Grant's hysterics ended abruptly. The hair on the back of Grant's neck stood on end. Oswell stopped laughing and Grant sat up on the log. He looked around warily and Oswell jumped to his feet.

"What's wrong?" Oswell asked.

"Do you feel that?"

"Feel what?"

"Like we're being watched..." Grant peered through the branches surrounding the glade. "Hello?" he called out.

"You're freaking me out. There's no one around."

"I'm telling you Oz, there's someone out there," Grant continued to stare through the branches as Oswell pulled himself up onto his feet and looked in the same direction.

"It's not just anyone," a deep voice warned from behind them. Oswell and Grant both whirled around in fright, Oswell's face blanching, while Grant expelled a blood curdling scream.

"Just me!" a different voice—one much higher—said, as a slender girl emerged from the trees.

Nearly as tall as Oswell, she walked with a certain grace and poise that put her beyond her years. Shoulder-length brown hair framed her freckled heart-shaped face, and the boys could see Claire Drew's mischievous smile accompanied by an entertained glimmer in her eyes. As she came to a stop, her hands rested on her hips, thumbs hooked through the belt loops of her jeans. She laughed heartily, and then demanded, "Had you going didn't I?"

"You practically scared the pee out of me." Oswell exclaimed.

"Practically?" Grant asked.

"I *didn't* wet myself," Oswell replied, "and I *also* didn't scream like a six year old."

Grant sat down on the log, peeved. Oswell followed, delivering a playful punch to Grant's shoulder as he too sat down. Claire agreed with the idea and delivered a similar blow to Grant's other shoulder before squirming in between the two boys.

"Now don't get your panties all up in a bunch," Claire advised, "but seriously, that was hilarious. The look on your face Oz... and that scream Grant. I should have filmed it!"

"Would've been appropriate; we were just acting, anyway," Grant recovered quickly.

"If that was acting, I'd give the both of you an Oscar," Claire jumped to her feet and proffered invisible awards.

"I'll admit it. You got me," Oswell confessed.

"It takes a real man to admit to being a wimp," Claire praised.

"Okay, you got me too," Grant conceded.

"Uh, I think you made that up," Oswell guessed, "In fact, I'm pretty positive that admitting something scared you isn't something that makes you a man."

"You're right, but both of you have confessed now so it looks like I win," Claire laughed.

"Victory is bittersweet," Grant noted.

"It tastes pretty sweet right now," Claire replied, only to have the two boys give her their best sad faces. She frowned, "Oh, there it is."

"Bitter isn't it?" Grant asked triumphantly.

"No, the acting is back. You guys are terrible." The trio of friends all looked at each other and laughed.

Claire's wry sense of humour and wit shone through as she capitalized on every opportunity. It was one of the reasons Oswell liked her so much. Grant was a great friend, but when it came to battles of intellect, Oswell found his conversations—or better yet, sparring matches—more interesting when Claire was involved.

Grant reclined backward, leaning against the fallen trunk. In his favourite position, he propped his feet up on Claire and Oswell's laps. He smiled playfully as Claire gave him a dangerous look, but the stern glare melted away into sudden excitement as her eyes caught movement in her peripheral vision.

Out of the underbrush of the glade's border, a mutt of a dog made its way into the clearing, sniffing about with the occasional glance at the three friends. There was nothing especially extraordinary about this dog, other than the charming smile it seemed to give them every time it looked at them; but as all three of the teens had never had a real pet (Grant had owned a goldfish once that had lived for three days, and Claire's younger brother once owned a hamster that hadn't lasted much longer), they were enchanted.

Claire launched herself off the log towards the dog, which was now sitting proudly with a large stick in its mouth. As Claire approached it, the stick fell to the forest floor, and that brilliant smile beamed up at Claire. This was all Oswell could take, and he too launched himself off the log to greet the dog. Grant, having never gotten over his goldfish trauma, decided it would be better not to get attached.

"Do you think it's a stray?" Claire asked Oswell, her voice high with concern. Oswell knelt down by the dog and picked up the stick. He beckoned for the dog to come closer, and grinned as the animal obliged. A quick look at the dog's neck was all it took to answer Claire's question.

"He doesn't have a collar, and it doesn't look like he's been getting a lot to eat..." Oswell gave the stick a toss across the glade and watched as the dog bounded happily after it. "He's probably just a mutt; I wonder where he came from?"

Claire shrugged and looked over at Grant, who was preoccupying himself with a maple leaf that he'd found. She groaned and looked back at Oswell, "Do you have any food?"

"I don't have anything," Oswell replied, immediately looking towards Grant, who continued to examine his leaf, now with an almost forensic intensity. "Grant, hand it over."

"Hand what over?"

"You've *always* got something," Oswell accused.

"I don't know what you're talking about."

"You always bring food out here. What do you have?"

"Nothing!" Grant maintained. Oswell stomped over to Grant as Claire tossed the stick for the dog. "What're you doing?" Oswell reached out and patted down Grant's front pockets, hearing a faint crinkle as Grant moved.

"The dog is hungry! C'mon man, just give it here," Oswell begged. Grant narrowed his eyelids and held Oswell in an icy stare for a few seconds. Then he grumbled and pulled out a package from his back pocket and handed it to Oswell.

"Beef jerky?" Oswell asked with a tone of disgust. "You actually eat this stuff?"

"It keeps well... are you going to give it to the dog or what? Because I'll gladly have it back."

Oswell rolled his eyes and accepted the begrudged offering. He ripped open the package and crouched down beside Claire, who was busy rubbing the dog's ears.

Oswell held out a piece of beef jerky to the mutt. It sniffed the meat warily and then took it hungrily from Oswell's grasp. The strip disappeared in seconds. Oswell emptied the package's contents onto the forest floor and stood back. Grant groaned in the background and muttered something about fleas.

The malnourished dog devoured the remainder of the beef jerky, and then sat back on its haunches with its tongue hanging out of its mouth.

"Oh! He's so cute!" Claire exclaimed.

"He's so skinny," Oswell added.

"He's so greedy," Grant mumbled. Oswell and Claire both shot icicles over their shoulders. "I said he eats so speedy!" Grant sat back down on his log, deciding once again, that it would be best to remain uninvolved. He'd done enough already.

Oswell and Claire patted the dog eagerly as the dog spun around in circles, trying to get as much attention from the both of them as possible. Abruptly, the spinning stopped and the dog's ears flattened against his skull. Claire startled and Oswell perked his eyebrows in curiosity.

Before either could ask the question out loud, the dog bolted off into the woods and out of sight.

"Oz... I'm getting that feeling again," Grant whispered.

"What feeling?" Oswell asked, distracted.

"Like I'm being watched."

"Oh get over it," Claire said.

"No guys, I'm serious, I want to go," Grant looked guardedly around the edges of the glade once again. "Now."

Claire shot Oswell a look that said: *Is he serious?*

Oswell shrugged and nodded with incredulity.

Grant turned back to Claire and Oswell. His eyes were wide and his lips tight with fear. Recognizing this, Oswell felt the unease in his stomach multiply and rise into his stomach. Claire put her hand on Oswell's shoulder.

"Let's go," Claire agreed. Oswell nodded his assent. The three friends headed back in the direction of their neighbourhood together. Oswell paused at the rim of the clearing and took one last quick glance around the glade before plunging into the forest's depths.

Two eyes stared hungrily into the clearing as the three targets left. There had been too many. His plan would have to wait, but he could sense that it was coming.

Something tugged at him from his very core, a primal instinct that had to be satisfied. Or perhaps it was even deeper than that. An imperative, *a need*. He wanted the girl, but the blonde boy called to him on an almost spiritual level. Destiny had pulled him to this town. He could feel it. It would have to be soon.

CHAPTER THREE

A HOLE IN THE WALL

THE LAND SPREADING out in front of Thomas was a breathtaking sight. The air filled his lungs as he took in the extraordinary feeling of infinity. All around him, the land stretched towards the horizon. Rolling green hills worked their way outward from his position at the centre of everything. It was as if every feature of the landscape had been wiped from the surface with one broad stroke. Not one landmark remained to remind him of where he was and the only distinguishing feature was the presence of one unusual adolescent boy.

Well, I must be on my way, Thomas thought, *but on my way to where?* Faced with a question that currently seemed to have no answer, he closed his eyes, and spun until he felt he would topple over. At that moment, he opened his eyes, steadied his balance, and launched off in that direction.

Beneath him, the grass whipped by. He seemed to be going faster than ever before, almost as though the entire planet had decided to spin in the opposite direction of Thomas, hastening his passage. With that substantial advantage, he found himself traversing the innocuous countryside at a god-like rate.

In the fast approaching distance, Thomas was shocked to see an anomaly in the planet's otherwise unchanging continuity. The green rolling hills appeared to come to an abrupt halt at a towering stone wall. With the obstacle fast approaching, Thomas stopped moving, but the planet had other plans. Its rotation kept him on a steady course for the wall as though the grass were a sea, bearing him onward towards oblivion.

Thom's fear began to rise up in his chest like the swell of the ocean. If he hit the wall at the speed he was travelling, he would be a dead man. He turned and ran.

His legs pounded at the ground to no avail. For every step he took away, he'd travelled bounds and bounds closer to the edge. Thomas felt a spur of terror and pushed himself harder, but he could not escape. Thomas collapsed; his fate accepted.

He peeked at the wall as it flew up toward him. A small black hole was growing in size, as though someone had burrowed through the wall. The hole was the definition of darkness and radiated a cold energy. Everything told him to keep his eyes closed, but something, somehow, forced him to look. With great effort, he pried open his eyes as his body was launched into the hole. Looking around, all he could see was sky. Thomas's fear evaporated, only to be replaced by complete and utter confusion. The hole had seemed so dark, but within, it was cavernous. Unfathomably so. *How is this possible?* He looked up at a shrinking black dot far above that was racing away from him. Turning his attention away from the hole, he looked down. The fear welled back up inside him again as he realized he wasn't flying, but falling.

So this is it, Thomas thought, *this is how I go? I leave this world by some bizarre, impossible accident?* The ground rushed up to meet him. He closed his eyes and made his peace.

Thomas woke up breathless and cursed his vivid nightmares for the thousandth time. He could feel the ground pressing firmly against his body that was, thankfully, anchored securely by gravity. Thomas tossed his blanket aside and pulled himself up off the forest floor.

Spotting the rundown shack, he immediately remembered where he was.

"Rawlins?" he whispered first, voice cracking with disuse. He repeated himself after clearing his throat, but heard nothing in reply.

Thomas cursed himself a second time for trusting the old man. Despite feeling rested after a full night's sleep and the residual effects of his bedtime tea and bread, Thomas was more than annoyed that he had been left in the lurch once again. Feeling betrayed he stomped around the forest clearing for a short time, first kicking at the fire's coals and then at the wood splitting stump. Both assaults hurt his toes, especially the exposed one, and he cursed his temper.

The forest looked the same on all sides: enormous sentries adorned in brown and green, standing guard on the edge of the clearing. Anyone who had been lost in the forest knew that its winding paths and misleadingly familiar trees could form itself up into an enigma that even the greatest philosopher could not extricate himself from. A seasoned woodsman on the other hand, would have little difficulty traversing an unfamiliar wood, as he would be privy to the knowledge and instinct that made it possible to travel from one extreme of a forest to the other.

Unfortunately, at this moment, Thomas was feeling far more akin to the philosopher than to the woodsman. It was in times like these that Thomas felt that Myr was continuing the joke on him that had been played for his whole life. A truly kind god would ensure Thom's safety, not bog him down with countless setbacks all for the sake of a day's malevolent levity.

Thomas folded himself up onto the forest floor and breathed in the earthy scent. It simply wasn't right for Rawlins to leave him lost in the middle of the forest. Of course, it wasn't as if Thomas should not have expected it; the hermit had forgotten in the space of a few minutes that he had promised to lead Thomas to Ancaster.

Thomas sulked in despair on the floor for what seemed like an age to him. In reality, he'd only been there for five minutes when his depression was interrupted by a sharp knock on his head. Sitting up, he was confused to find himself still alone. Again, he felt a slight knock on the back of his head and turned around to find no one.

"Who's there?" he stood and whirled around in an attempt to catch the culprit. He stopped and waited. Sure enough, another tiny knock bounced off his skull. This time, he twisted round fast enough to see an acorn bounce to the ground at his feet. Thomas crouched down to pick it up and whipped the acorn back out into the forest, grimacing at the farce.

Out of the woods, exactly where he'd thrown the acorn, another one rocketed towards him and hit Thomas square between the eyes. Seeing the origin of the projectile's flight, Thomas rushed forward in a rage. He only made it a few feet from the rim of the clearing when he tripped over a large branch on the ground. Lying face down in the dirt, Thomas heard the chattering of a small animal coming from further in the woods. He and felt another acorn bounce lightly off his skull from above. Enraged, Thomas climbed up onto his feet. He looked at the branch over which he'd tripped headlong. It took him a moment to figure out what it was, but when he did, he groaned.

Sitting in a matter-of-fact way on the forest floor was an unmistakeable arrow consisting of one large branch and two smaller ones arranged as the arrow's head. Three feet long, it could only be pointing in one direction. Sitting neatly at the arrow's point was a small parcel. Thomas opened it and smiled profusely at the heel of bread inside. Rawlins had been considerate enough to leave a direction *and* breakfast, without waking him. His frustration with the wild old man melted away and Thomas chuckled at the absurdity of his guide.

Another acorn flew out of the woods. Ready for it this time, Thomas caught it in mid-flight. "I'm going to get you!" he called. He charged off into the forest in the direction the arrow had pointed him.

As he did, one of the forest's giant squirrels chattered in fear and disappeared into the maze that Thomas now hoped to navigate. With a clear direction set out in front of him, and food in his hand, Thomas couldn't help but feel that luck may finally have started to go his way.

Thomas breathed a sigh of relief as he spotted the tree line, but as he broke it, his knees weakened. Before him, a wide expanse of green rolling hills were laid out like a canvas. As in his dream, the land stretched towards infinity. Thomas dropped to the ground and dug his fingers into the soil in a desperate attempt to hold on. His anxiety attacks always came on unexpectedly and were debilitating. He lay there, hyperventilating. Only when he realized that he wasn't being borne unwilling across the land, did he open his eyes.

The hills did not indeed roll on for infinity. Instead, he could easily pick out farmer's crops in the distance, small hamlets, a minuscule river slicing through the landscape, and a town off in the near distance. The town had to be the one he'd been searching for over the past few days. The rolling hills were also bathed in a cloudy grey; quite dissimilar from the idyllic and sunny green hills of his dream. He decided it would be safe to step into the field.

Thomas turned to look back at the forest and grumbled. He'd powerfully overestimated his abilities to navigate it. He'd been told by an old barkeeper that if he were able to find his way, cutting through the woods would save him two days of walking. Instead, it had added an extra two days to his journey. Now, Thomas suspected that the barkeep had been playing a cruel and nearly deadly trick on him. For once, Thomas felt lucky. It *had* to be luck that he'd made it through the forest at all.

Thomas launched himself out onto the rolling hills, feeling the wind coursing through his hair. The breeze was something he had missed over the previous three days. Having been surrounded by leaves and wood, he hadn't been able to enjoy the luxury of fresh air. Thomas watched as the hills rolled past him slowly and the town grew to full size before his eyes.

The closer that Thomas got to the town, the more real it seemed to become. Really, it was more of a city than a town, and indeed, a farmer tilling his field identified it as Fletchery, not Ancaster. He'd gotten totally off track, and any hope of finding employment at the Ancaster Inn was likely missed by now anyway. Some other enterprising (and better oriented) youth would surely have taken the job by now. Fletchery, however, was a city—one big enough to find food and employment. He'd avoided Fletchery over the years, for his experiences as a child in the cities to the south were less than pleasant, but now… he was nearly a man. If he couldn't hold his own now, when would he ever? So he continued on.

By the time he was nearly upon Fletchery's walls, he'd been walking through the city's environs for almost an hour. Poor souls without the protection of the walls but lured by the promise of business in the city. Small children with dusty faces and bare feet frolicked in the weak summer sunlight, while their parents turned eyes from their toil to watch the newcomer with a modicum of suspicion. The scent of manure from the farmers' fields began to fade, replaced by that of crowded humanity. The bustle of the city's market—merchant voices drifting over the modest stone walls—were distantly heard over the relative quiet of the slums. A flashback to Orport, the last southern city he'd visited, immediately paralyzed Thomas. This was nearly the same, less the scent of sea air and rotting fish. Thomas quickened his pace, fists clenched.

Thomas approached a fortified gatehouse that would allow him through the walls. The two guards standing at their posts eyed him suspiciously as he approached. One seemed to be paying extra attention to him. Thomas put on his charming smile and stopped in front of them.

"Good afternoon syrs!" he greeted and offered a deep bow. The two guards looked at each other and one, clearly the leader, stepped forward to speak.

"Whaddaya want beggar-boy?"

"Only to find a place to work, to eat, and to sleep," Thomas replied, coming out of his bow.

"To work? What work could a beggar boy do?"

"Whatever is needed of me syr, I've worked as a stable boy, a merchant's assistant, and even ran errands for a blacksmith," Thomas informed the guard.

The second guard chuckled and the first one grinned. "Well it would seem that we have a regular all-tradesman on our hands."

Thomas nodded in agreement, not picking up on the sarcasm in the guard's voice. "I suppose you could say that."

"Well we've got no need of someone like you in here. What say you find work with your people," the guard indicated the slums Thomas had walked through.

Thom's jaw dropped. He looked up at the guard with a pleading look. "Please syr, I've barely eaten in days, all I want to do is *earn* an honest meal."

"Earn? By the likes of you, it would be more likely stolen. Steal from your own—I'm not going to be the one to let a thief into our midst—Vorley would have my head!"

Thomas threw up his arms in exasperation. "So I suppose I should just move onto the next town then?"

"They won't want you either. I'd suggest you find a hole, curl up, and die there," the guard said, "You're not far off by the looks of ya." Thomas felt the rage building up inside him.

"I could do that, or I could just wait until your mother comes out this way, and then piss on her shoes."

The second guard glared at Thomas, "And what would that accomplish?"

"Well, it would relieve my bladder, it would."

The first guard grabbed Thomas by the arm. Thomas punched him in the groin and darted along the wall. The guard was in too much pain to give chase and the second guard was too stupid.

When he had made his escape good, Thomas slowed down. He continued around the wall to try his luck at the next gate. "Well, there's one more bridge I've burned," he said to himself as he wound his way through the shantytown of shacks and tents built outside the city's walls.

Thomas rounded the corner and spotted a second gatehouse in the distance. He stopped and pushed his toe back through the hole in his shoes. He spit on his hands to wash the dirt from his face and slicked down his hair. Behind him, he heard a voice call out.

"Hey! You there," it whispered.

Thomas whirled around on the defensive, ready to run in case one of the guards had decided to give chase, but no one revealed themselves. "Who's there?" he asked. A few feet away from him, a small child was standing with a rag doll, staring at him with a similar level of curiosity. "Was that you?" he asked the child.

"No you dolt, behind you."

Thomas turned around and noticed a small rundown shack built against the wall.

"Are you in there?" Thomas asked.

"No, I'm in the Emperyr's palace. Of course I'm in here."

"Who are you?"

"A friend, come on in here."

Thomas assessed the situation for a moment. He had absolutely no reason to trust a voice claiming to be his friend. In fact, in Thomas's experience, such claims were more often than not accompanied by less than friendly intentions.

"Why should I trust you?" Thomas asked.

"Uh, the bit about being a friend… that would be it, best I can do," the voice replied.

Thomas groaned. His curiosity was getting the better of him. Balling one of his fists up, he pulled on the door handle only to have the door come right off its hinges into his arms.

He groaned and set the door back in place behind him before turning around to see his so-called 'friend'. Muffled beams of light, filtering through the slats in the walls and roof, lit the room, leaving it in relative darkness. Thom's heartbeat quickened as he picked out the man. He was cast in shadow a few arms lengths away. There was a hiss and then the room was illuminated by candlelight.

Standing before him was a tall and athletic young man a few years his senior. He shone with the inflated confidence of a man that had recently filled out a body that had recently grown tall. His hair was a deep black, and the barest shadow of stubble shaded his jaw in the soft candlelight. He was dressed in clean, tailored clothes. Inconspicuous, but marking him as a man of some means. Thomas wondered what he was doing in a rundown beggar's shack outside the town walls.

"Looks like the old pissers wouldn't let you in, eh?"

"What's it to you?" Thomas was self-conscious in the confined space. His instincts screamed at him to barrel back through the door into the daylight, but his curiosity fastened his feet to the dirt floor.

"Now now, don't get your knickers up in a bunch. I can help."

"And how do you plan to do that? I suppose you've got a ladder to scale the walls?"

"If you're going to give me attitude, I'm not going to help you." The young man took a step forward and began pushing Thomas forcefully towards the door of the shack.

"Wait! Wait!" Thomas dug his heels in, "I'm sorry, I've just...I've been having a bad run of luck... it makes me sour to be around."

The young man stopped pushing him and stood back. "Well, it looks like you do have some manners on you!" he clapped him on the shoulder, "Perhaps there is hope for you yet."

"Yes, plenty," Thomas nodded vigorously.

"Well, let me ask you again, would you like me to help get you into Fletchery?"

"Yes, I would appreciate it greatly," Thomas replied.

"Very well then—follow me," the young man extended his hand, "By the way, my name is Darius, and you?"

"Thomas, but Thom is fine," Thomas shook it before Darius turned and strode towards the wall of the hut. The young man stopped in front of the wall and shoved a rickety shelf aside. Behind it, a small tunnel—no wider than three feet—extended straight into Fletchery's stone wall. Darius looked back at Thomas and smiled.

Thomas looked at the hole in the wall warily. For the second time that day, he was faced with an uncanny similarity to his dream, and once again his heartbeat quickened. It had to be a coincidence. He banished the thought from his mind and took a deep breath to quiet his heart.

"Not a word of this to anyone, Thom," Darius warned.

"Not a word," Thomas agreed.

CHAPTER FOUR

CLOSE TO HOME

Robar Drive sat comfortably on the edge of suburbia. The sleepy road was ordinary in the sense that it looked exactly like every other street near it. Each quaint little road had aging, but attractive, homes flanking the faded and cracking pavement. In places, grass poked through cracks in the asphalt where the Department of Transportation had gotten behind on their workload.

The problem with the small town was how far it was from everything; there wasn't even a mall for the teenagers to loiter obtrusively in. Despite the lack of that particular staple, the Walloway's teenagers found things to do, if not easily, but out of necessity. There was a playground to hang around in, intimidating younger children and new parents alike. There were a few local shops where the high schoolers could find begrudging part-time employment to the delight of their old parents; and the nearest corner store was only a short ten minute walk past the schools, where the limited disposable income of Walloway's youth could be squandered away.

That small town vibe was the precise reason why, at two in the afternoon, Oswell started walking towards the end of Robar Drive towards Moose Bay Road. At the corner, Grant bounced from one foot to another waiting for Oswell, whose expression of pleasant surprise at Grant's punctuality went unnoticed.

"So what did you have in mind?" Oswell asked.

"Barbecue corn nuts," Grant replied.

"Jamieson's?" Oswell asked, deciding he wouldn't be opposed to spending a dollar or two to pass the time.

Grant nodded his head in agreement.

Oswell stroked his chin as he contemplated his choice between the sour gummy bears and the peanut butter candies. The bears were calling for him to buy them. They were delicious in their gummy glory, but Oswell had decided he wasn't hungry after all. As he turned away from the bin, he could swear that a distant voice was calling, *Please, just take one of us!* Oswell rolled his eyes and turned back to the bin. It was the least he could do. He grabbed a plastic bag and, feeling extraordinarily generous, gathered up a small handful and dropped them in. He found his way over to the cash and stood in line behind Grant.

The cashier had the same greedy look on his face that he always wore when Grant walked into Jamieson's. This time was a particularly lucrative visit. Grant was coming away with even more than he usually did. In front of him sat a bag of barbecue corn nuts, honey roasted peanuts, a party mix of some sort, and the experiment of the day: spicy plantain chips. Grant always liked to try at least one new thing when they went to Jamieson's.

The till chimed more loudly than normal as the cashier finished ringing through Grant's four items. In total, he'd run up a bill of twelve dollars and forty-nine cents.

Grant handed over the exact change, as always, and left Oswell wondering two things: where Grant got all of his money, and how in the world he stayed so thin. Oswell approached the counter with his small order and the cashier's eyes sank in disappointment. Ringing him through, Oswell handed over a dollar and got twelve cents back in change. Grant laughed at Oswell's pitiful haul.

Stepping out onto the street, Oswell tossed a gummy bear into his mouth and puckered as the sour coating assaulted his tongue. Grant dug into his barbecue corn nuts by the handful, and the pair began walking back home.

"How're your corn nuts?" Oswell asked, sufficiently bored with their afternoon.

"Perfection..." Grant kissed his gathered fingers between bites, each one punctuated by a loud crunch.

Oswell laughed and shook his head. "Where'd you get all of that money anyway?"

"Mom gave it to me. She felt bad that there wasn't anything to eat in the house."

"Must be nice," Oswell grumbled. He didn't get much in the way of spending money, then again, his father wasn't a dentist. To add to that, Grant had to be exaggerating about his so-called famine. There was always something to eat in the Harding household.

"I guess—" Grant stopped in mid-sentence as a police cruiser raced past them. Both boys stood transfixed.

Oswell looked at Grant eagerly. "Let's go!" he stuffed his bag of gummy bears into his pocket. Grant hefted his bag over his shoulder and joined the chase. It wasn't every day that something police-worthy happened in Walloway.

The squad car roared around the corner and out of sight. Grant and Oswell flew after the car, dodging Mrs. Westhaver and her dirty stare as they too rounded the corner.

"Slow down!" she shouted after them as they ran by.

Neither of them could see the car or its flashing lights anymore, but they continued to run flat out. Oswell easily widened the distance between he and Grant. He'd always been faster, even as Grant started to spurt up in height. They followed the sound of the siren wailing in the distance.

Finally, the sound faded to nothing. Oswell slowed to a walk. Panting, Grant caught up, and stumbled down the sidewalk. With disappointment, they began the walk home. Oswell dragged his candy from his pocket and found that they had already become sticky with the summer heat and from the radiation from his body. He scowled at the waste and tossed them into a nearby bin. Grant looked offended.

They were defeated by their missed opportunity at excitement, and they were too tired to talk. Oswell lagged behind Grant, as they rounded the corner onto Moose Bay Road. Simply watching his feet as they made their way back to Robar Drive. He was day dreaming in every sense of the word when he bumped headlong into Grant and staggered backwards. Grant had stopped just past the corner looking onto Robar Drive.

"The heck?" Oswell asked.

"Man, shut up, look…" Grant pointed. Oswell's eyes followed Grant's gaze to the Drew household, two houses down and across from his own home.

In front of the house was the police cruiser, its lights off. An officer stood with his hat off in front of Allison and Paul Drew, Claire's parents. Paul shook his head and then pulled Allison into his arms. His face was determined, but clouded by fear. In his arms, Allison's face was a mask of pain and sorrow.

The two boys stood in shocked silence and awe, watching the scene. It didn't play out in slow motion like one imagines; it was just real. Raw and real.

Oswell's stupor was shattered by a large hand grasping his shoulder. He turned to look and saw his father. Owen Wallace reeled the two boys in and turned their eyes away from the scene.

Owen Wallace would not usually stand out in a crowd, though at the moment, his face was ablaze with concern. At six feet, and with the soft, round physique of middle-age, he was the definition of ordinary. He had a full head of shortly cropped brown hair, a strong jaw easily mirrored in his son, and what were usually calming hazel eyes. Today, they whirled with concern. He herded the two boys down the sidewalk.

"What happened dad?" he asked, ignoring how childish his voice suddenly sounded. "What happened? Is someone hurt?"

"Come on boys, we need to get home," his father replied. Owen's strong grip guided the two boys down the sidewalk and away from the heartbreaking sight of the Drews.

They were ushered up the concrete steps in front of Oswell's house and upstairs into the living room. They were surprised to see Grant's parents and eight year old sister, Ella in the room. They sat down on the sofa beside Ella who sat quietly, fiddling with a charm bracelet around her wrist. She seemed completely oblivious to whatever was going on. Oswell's mother and Grant's parents stood awkwardly in front of the three children.

From right to left were Owen and Monica Wallace, and Karla and Evan Harding. Each parent's face was clouded by an ominous shadow as they exchanged looks between themselves, unsure of who should speak. Oswell was the first.

"Mom, Dad? Why aren't you *saying* anything?" Oswell's query dramatized the silence; his voice cut the tension, filling the room and replacing the clinking of Ella's charm bracelet with something coherent.

"Something… terrible has happened," Owen began.

"*No*, Owen," his wife warned.

Oswell glared at his mother.

Monica Wallace was petite and looked much younger than her thirty-eight years. She was Owen's lifelong love. At first, it was for her soft brown eyes, slender nose, full lips, and radiant blonde curls. Then, he fell for her intelligence, kindness, and fierce love of her family. In short order, she'd become his wife. Although diminutive, it was easy to sense the power in the woman as she stared down her husband.

Indignation possessed Oswell. His mother had never even pretended that Oswell should be kept out of the loop about anything. The Wallace family had always been one of open minds and honesty. He instantly pepped up to defend himself.

"We know something's happened, we saw the police outside the Drew's—you can't keep this from us. Claire is our friend. We deserve to know what happened to her family." Nobody responded. "This is just as much our community as it is yours."

"But Ella shouldn't hear this either…" Karla finally said, "She's too young…"

"Nick is Ella's friend, she should know too!" Oswell defended. His arm found its way around Ella's shoulder in a protective embrace. She stopped fiddling with her bracelet and started to nod her head in agreement, though it wasn't clear if she knew what she was agreeing to.

"Honey, they need to know. Oswell is right… this is just as much their business as it is ours. They'll find out from somebody else if it's not us—God knows the gossip in this town." Owen said. His eyebrows rose in a bid for permission from his wife, permission she adamantly refused to give him, but a nod from Evan was all it took. "Kids, now I don't want you to worry, everything is going to be fine. We just know it, but…"

"Oh, spit it out," Grant blurted out. Oswell was proud of the outburst, it wasn't often Grant challenged adults. That responsibility was usually left to Oswell.

"Now don't freak out, okay? All of you are safe…" Owen continued. He received an icy stare from Grant once again, prompting him to continue. "Claire and Nicholas are missing. The police think it happened some time this afternoon." A stunned silence fell over the three children. Owen began to ramble, filling the silence, "The boldness of whoever did this, to kidnap two children like that in broad daylight… I just don't know."

Kidnapped? That doesn't happen here, we live in a good neighbourhood, that sort of stuff just doesn't… Oswell's mind raced. The world suddenly seemed huge and he immediately felt insignificant. Claire was one of his best friends. Besides that, Oswell had seen Nick and Ella grow up together; babies from different families, but his brother and sister nonetheless. The Drews were family to both the Wallaces and the Hardings.

"Claire and Nick are gone?" Grant asked, allowing the adults to rectify the error in their words that he so wished they had made. His only answer was a solemn nod from the two fathers. Oswell sat quietly, arm around Grant's younger sister.

Ella began to cry.

- *CHAPTER FIVE* -

A FRIEND INDEED

Thomas couldn't see the outline of his hand in front of his face, let alone Darius's rear end guiding him through the inky abyss. The darkness was stifling and omnipresent and the air of the tunnel was choked with dust disturbed from the craggy walls. Thomas crawled on hands and knees through the murk. He could not see, he could not breathe, and he was beginning to feel anxious. Warm blood from a cut, where a jagged rock had scraped him, dribbled across his hand, painting it and making it sticky where it mixed with the fine powder surrounding him.

"Are we nearly there?" he asked, his voice barely a strangled whisper.

"Quiet," the ethereal voice in front of him reverberated back to him. Thomas didn't know what else to do other than to comply. He hurried to keep up with the shuffling of hands and knees on the rough hewn stone ahead of him.

Thomas bumped headlong into Darius's feet and collapsed onto his belly.

The stone beneath him was uncomfortable and musty. There was no telling how old this tunnel was, but judging by the direction they had travelled, it cut straight through the wall. Thomas wasn't sure he wanted to know what kind of person would think to build such a tunnel—though smugglers and ne'er-do-wells crossed his mind—but he didn't really care. If the opening granted him passage into the city, Thomas would hold nothing against whoever had.

"Okay, we're here. You *will* follow me quietly. Do *not* say a word until we've made it outside," Darius said. Thomas started nodding, forgetting that Darius would not be able to see him, "Do you understand?"

Thomas whispered back that he did and then climbed back onto his knees as Darius moved forward. Thomas followed carefully after him and was welcomed by the scent of summertime straw as they emerged from the wall into a pile of hay. Thom's escape from the darkness could not have come sooner, though he wasn't particularly happy to be buried under the weight of so much animal fodder.

Thomas pulled himself through the strands and poked his head out of the hay behind Darius. Seeing that the coast was clear, he rolled ungracefully out of the pile, stood up quickly, and brushed the debris off his shirt and pants. The scrapes on his hand had congealed through a combination of natural mechanisms and the concrete dust that had set into the blood. He wiped the stains away from the rest of his hand, leaving the makeshift bandage in place.

Darius grabbed a pitchfork and a shovel and handed Thomas the latter. "Let me do the talking," Darius ordered. Thomas nodded. Darius pushed his way through a door and out into the hallway. Thomas trailed behind him. He recognized where he was as soon as he entered the hallway; they had secreted themselves through the wall by way of the stables. Horses were housed in stalls on either side all the way down to the wide barn doors at the end.

Darius set off down the row and Thomas brought up the rear. An older man called out to Darius from one of the stalls as the pair passed by.

"Oi! Rik! Where'd you disappear to?"

"I was showing the new stable boy around," Darius replied. Thomas looked from Darius to the man, shooting him a toothy grin. The man merely scowled in return.

"Aye, well get back to work then," the man said, turning back to the horse he was tending.

"Right away," Darius replied. He continued on down the hallway with the pitchfork resting on his shoulder. Thomas hurried after him.

A moment later, they both emerged from the stable out into the middle of one of the city squares. Beneath their feet, roughly laid cobblestones stretched out to form the open plaza and descend down narrow alleyways bordered by stone buildings. Again, Thomas was struck by its similarity to Orport; it seemed that every city had the same basic features. Somehow, now, it all seemed a little less daunting.

There was a wide berth afforded to the entrance of the stable, no doubt to ensure that no one's property and no people were trampled by exiting horses. However, beyond that radius, the town bustled. His faculties worked to overcome the sensory overload that assaulted his eyes, ears and nose. The smell of the stable's hay and manure had quickly been replaced by the aroma of a nearby vendor's spiced boca nuts, and Thom's ears flooded with the cries of merchants frantic to offload their wares to unimpressed buyers. More striking than those sounds were the colours of every merchant's stall and buyer's garb. Red apples flowed from barrels, as green flags flapped in a brisk wind. Rich nobles perused the market's offerings in their shining leather boots and finely tailored clothes. It was a sharp contrast to the poverty he came from and the poverty he'd walked through in approaching Fletchery. That was the poverty of his whole life, but here, there was wealth, and as nearly a man grown, opportunity. His years working farmlands, and begging through sleepy way-towns were behind him.

Darius watched Thom's awe spread across his face and grinned. "Welcome to Fletchery my friend! Does it suit you?"

"It's so..." Thomas felt around for the right word, "busy!"

"Well if you think the Western Square is mad, you should see Town Centre at noon."

"What time is it now?" Thomas asked.

"Well into the afternoon..." Darius replied. He paused to assess Thomas critically, then said, "Tell me, are you fasting in anticipation of the excesses of Night Life, or is your thinness unintentional?"

"Its been less feast than famine lately," Thomas admitted. He'd seen enough Night Life celebrations come and go without a meal—fasting was never intentional, though he was awfully practiced at it. Night

Life was his least favourite holiday. He hated that everyone else got to eat, have fun, and find love, while he looked on, hungry and alone.

"Well, in a town like this there is no need to go hungry!" Darius said. "Come friend, I will show you the way of the world, and in the process, we shall fill your belly."

Thomas liked the idea of a full stomach, so he simply nodded and smiled, not wondering for even a moment, why he had been chosen for such great fortune. He was certainly due.

"This is Bronson's stand here on your right," Darius told Thomas as they passed a large stand that was tinted red. The banner above it was crudely painted with a chimera: the rear of a pig, the body of a cow, and the head of a chicken. Thomas screwed up his face, appraising the merchant. Looking at the surface of the counter, there was nothing there for purchase. A man had his back turned to them and was fussing over something on another counter.

"What's he doing?" Thomas asked.

"He's a butcher, hence the half pig, half cow, half chicken."

"Three halves?"

Darius ignored the comment, "Oh, and by the way, the stand isn't red with paint." Darius smirked as realization crossed Thom's face. "Needless to say, we don't steal from Bronson, unless you feel like adding your own colours to the mix."

Thomas glanced at the bit of crusty blood still soiling his hand and shivered. He nodded quickly and hurried after Darius down the row of vendors. Darius stopped in front of another, busier stand. Thomas could barely see through the throng of people bustling around the stand. The banner waving high above the crowd was a medley of bright colours.

"This is Peter Prader's produce stand. They say his is the best within a fortnight's journey."

"It's busy!" Thomas rose up onto the tips of his toes in an attempt to catch a glimpse of some of the fruit.

"You've got it my friend. And it's exactly because of how busy it is that we steal from Peter. No one will notice a couple of fruit missing from such a large pile."

Thomas nodded timidly. In his experience, stealing always led to too many bad things. Most of the scars and faded bruises on his body came from failed attempts. Starvation, Thomas decided in the moment, was worse.

"Shall we?" Darius asked, not requiring an answer. He then lithely inserted himself into the crowd, disappearing into its mass. Thomas followed close behind and scrabbled in between two large men near the stand. He looked around nervously and then reached out to grab a round red fruit before melting into the throng.

Moments later, he extricated himself from the mess and found Darius munching on a carrot. No one paid either of the boys a second glance.

"Good stuff... as always, the stories are confirmed," he said between bites of the vibrant orange vegetable. Thomas eyed the carrot and then pulled out his own bounty. Darius' eyes lit up at the sight of it, a flash of mischief flitting across his face. He stopped munching on the carrot and swallowed hard.

"Flog my uncle! I haven't gotten my hands on a mirifruit in weeks. Tell me if they're as good as I remember them."

Thomas, keen to discover what made the mirifruit so desirable, took a generous bite and let the juice fill his mouth. Sweet like sunshine and slightly sour, almost undetectably so. A tingle reminiscent of spice declared itself the moment before he swallowed. Thomas wasted no time devouring the remainder. Darius looked on jealously.

"How was it?" Darius asked.

"Delicious!" Thomas replied, "It was so juicy!"

Darius nodded. "Yes, they say that at this time of year, the mirifruit is at its most succulent, and it's hallucinatory properties are most potent."

Thom's face blanched and then contorted with terror as Darius's face began to twist and deform. His forehead elongated and spread outwards while his chin sucked upwards into his nose. Thomas stared and heard a laugh echoing down the long stone hallways of his consciousness. He whirled around to find the source of the laughter only to have the world close in on him. *Why didn't he tell me?* Thomas thought, horrified.

44

A powerful grip clamped his shoulder and Thomas whirled once again to identify the source. He looked up at an enormous iron triangle, its point reaching down towards him. The creature grasped him with both hands and shook him violently as another triangle-headed creature stood beside it, screeching wildly and pointing spindly fingers at him. He had to be dreaming again—it was a nightmare, and it was only getting worse.

Thomas was turned by the rough grip of his persecutor and pushed roughly down an alleyway. *Where did Darius go?* He felt his feet stumble beneath him, but before he could fall to the ground, the iron triangle righted him and set him back on course. They walked for what seemed like a fraction of a second, time flying by in a haze. His surroundings changed abruptly—they entered a colder, darker place and his heart beat more uncontrollably with every passing moment, amplifying his fear.

The journey came to an abrupt halt as he was heaved through a doorway onto a rough and cold stone floor that seemed to reach up and envelop him. Thomas struggled to hold onto the last vestiges of consciousness as the stone formed around his body. He was being buried alive in liquid rock.

He heard the loud clank of a metal door behind him. A moment later, a figure crept out of the darkness. The body was decrepit, but it moved with a purpose. It grabbed Thomas by the shoulders and shook him. Thomas gave no response except for a moan of terror. An enormous hand reached out from the figure and landed softly on his forehead. Everything went quiet. Peaceful.

Thomas felt a gentle tapping on his back and rolled over. Bathed in darkness, he could barely make out the scene. His sleep-crusted eyes only managed to pick out bits and pieces of his surroundings—primary in his field of vision was an older man crouching over him.

Even in the darkness, Thomas could tell that he was well into his sixties. His face was shrunken from hunger and wrinkled around the corners of his eyes, forehead, and cheeks. Thomas could guess a similar wrinkling would be found around his mouth, although that skin was obscured by a short and rough white beard that extended just past his chin.

His eyes were an elemental blue, and even in the darkness, they sparkled with an intensity matched only by the finest gems. All of this combined into a conspiratorial and intellectual look that failed to match his roughly hewn prisoner's uniform of patchwork canvas.

Looking down at himself, Thomas recognized that he too was clad as a prisoner, but in clothes that were at least a size too small. He squirmed in discomfort and readjusted the fabric at his groin before pulling himself up to his feet. Prisoners clothing. He shuddered with apprehension and fear. A pounding in his head prevented him from concentrating on the man in front of him. The man stood to his full height, at least a foot taller than Thomas, but he was thin with hunger.

Thomas dug his fingers into his temples and squinted at the man wearily. "Who are you?"

The man replied, his raspy voice reflecting the onset of dehydration. "I am a friend."

"A friend? And that is supposed to mean... What?" Thomas asked. "The last person to tell me that is responsible for me being here!" he shouted. His voice echoed off the stone walls.

The man's eyes flashed in the darkness with a seeming sense of hope and recognition. "I apologize for your being here, but I think we may be able to help each other. Where are my manners? My name is Cicero Nagel."

Thomas wasn't sure how a half-starved teenager could help a wholly starved senior, but he offered him his name nevertheless, "Thomas Courser."

"Thomas," he seemed to ruminate on the name for a moment, "Wonderful to make your acquaintance. I have been alone for so very long."

"How long?"

"Weeks."

"I'm sorry to hear that syr, but I really don't see how I can help you," Thomas replied.

"Please, call me Cicero."

"Okay. Cicero then, I don't see how I can help you."

"I have a plan, Thomas. I couldn't do it alone, but now that you're here, it could be possible."

"A plan to do what?" Thomas asked. His damnable curiosity began to overcome his initial distrust.

"A plan to escape, of course."

"You think we can escape? Are you mad?"

"Are you in or are you out?" Cicero asked.

Thomas looked around at the cell, strewn with stale straw and stinking of human filth. The walls crept with greenish moss, intermingling with more than enough mould. The barest light filtered through a narrow slit, cut on an angle at the corner where the wall met the ceiling. His mind flashed to the crime he had committed. He looked down at his hands. For thievery, he would surely lose them, or more likely his life. He looked back at Cicero. If there was one thing Thomas was sure of at that moment, it was that he wanted to live. Facing death—truly facing death—had never made him feel so alive. Thomas had always envisioned the slow and agonizing death of starvation, but the immediacy of the death that lay before him lit a fire within him.

"I'm in," he decided.

CHAPTER SIX

RAINDROPS ARE
FALLING ON MY HEAD

O SWELL WATCHED OUT the window of the car as an airliner lifted off the runway and shrank into the distance.

Everything went so bad, so fast... he thought, groaning and pressing his face up against the glass. Grant and his family had their hesitations about running away from their hometown, but ultimately decided it was too dangerous to stay in Walloway. Perhaps more saliently, they had also figured a vacation to Florida would take everyone's mind off of what was going on. Everyone's mind, of course, aside from the people left behind. Namely, Oswell. Indeed, Oswell was stranded alone in Walloway with nothing to do except worry about his friends.

"Why can't we go with them?" Oswell asked for the umpteenth time.

"You know full well why we can't go," Monica sighed. Oswell crossed his arms and slumped back in the chair, feeling fully justified in playing the role of a moody teenager, for by rights, he was one. They had at least an hour's drive to get home from the airport. Seeing their friends off had them making the trip all the way to Bangor. Now that he was in a sour mood, the ride would seem much longer than it needed to be. Oswell closed his eyes, slid on his headphones, got comfortable, and shut out the world.

Oswell slipped out of the backseat and hurried up to the front door of his home. He dragged his key out of his pocket as his parents sat in the front seat discussing something they didn't want him to hear. Rolling his eyes, he unlocked the door and went inside.

He took the stairs two at a time up to his room and gathered a few things into a backpack: a novel, his music player, and a ball (in case the dog came back and wanted to play). Grant might be envisioning a wonderful time in sunny Florida, but Oswell remained in a dark mood. He needed the outdoors, even if it had lost the bulk of its magic, there was hope that a sprinkle of it could be found here or there, and Oswell intended to find it. Out amongst the trees, he could think and really get to work on the problem that was Walloway's kidnapping. If Oswell was ever going to solve it, he needed the headspace afforded by the forest.

He tramped down into the kitchen, whipped up a jam sandwich and tossed it into his backpack along with a bottle of orange juice. With all of his supplies gathered, he slipped out the back door, into the yard, and kicked his way through the grass to the edge of the trees. With a final look around, Oswell plunged into the woods.

The air was different in the forest. It was earthy, decomposing. A scent that couldn't be found anywhere else. Oswell breathed it in deeply as he wound his way around small and large trees alike. Silence inhabited the forest; unusual, but he didn't mind in this instance; it made it easier for him to think. First of all, was where to start with Claire's and Nicholas's kidnapping? If he played it right, he'd have found every possible clue by the time Grant got back, and the two of them could piece it together (if he hadn't solved it on his own before then). Oswell's heart felt a familiar knife twist at the thought of Claire. A choking sensation rose in his throat as the enormity of the event made itself clear. He would look back on it for his life with the pain that only such an inexplicable crime could conjure. Oswell took a deep breath and exhaled before continuing forward. Though no one was there to see, he refused to cry. Crying would mean he accepted the facts. He didn't. *She is not gone.* They would find her—he would find her. *She's not dead.*

He shook the thought from his head and he stopped at the end of a long stride. He'd mindlessly walked on autopilot for the better part of half an hour, and was well into the depths of the woods. It took him a moment to recognize a few of the trees and to gather his bearings, but even when he did, he couldn't shake the feeling that something was amiss. Amiss, not only in his life, but there was a new strangeness amongst the trees. The forest was not simply quiet, it was *unmistakably* soundless. No birds calling to their juvenile young, warning them not to venture far from the nest. No branches creaking in the breeze that nevertheless sent a chill down his neck. Oswell couldn't even hear that wind, for that matter. He closed his eyes and listened. The mute button on the forest had been pressed. With his eyes closed, someone had also shut off the lights. He opened his eyes and looked to see if anything was moving, but again, there was nothing. He cocked his eyebrow in concern and continued through the woods.

As soon as he began walking, the forest exploded with sound. The animals twittered and chirped and the wind picked back up to whisper across the leaves. It was as if a great hand had pressed the world into silence, and now it had lifted off, allowing the world to breathe. It was a jarring contrast to the stark silence only moments ago, and the effect that pressure had had still seemed to linger as the forest regained its breath.

Oswell scanned the trees and brush around him, seeing nothing out of the ordinary. Grass, moss, dog, trees... Oswell did a double take. Sitting stock still in front of a tree was the mutt that had visited them in the glade. The dog was frozen at first, as if he were a statue, but recognizing that he'd been discovered, he cocked his head and let his tongue loll out of the side of his mouth. Oswell grinned and crouched down, beckoning for the dog to come closer.

"Here boy, come," Oswell commanded. The dog obliged and sauntered over to Oswell.

Oswell gave the dog a good pat on the head much to the dog's enjoyment. "You sure are skinny, aren't you boy?" The dog seemed to understand as he licked his chops and sniffed at Oswell.

Oswell laughed. "You smell my sandwich don't you?" Oswell slipped his backpack off his shoulder and rummaged around to find his jam sandwich. The mutt began to salivate as Oswell unwrapped it. He ripped the sandwich in half and handed one to the malnourished animal. It disappeared in a few moments right before Oswell's eyes. He shrugged and handed the other half of the sandwich over to the dog. Once again, the morsel disappeared quickly.

"You should learn to savour it..." Oswell recommended.

The dog cocked his head to the side again, as if to suggest Oswell's proposal was totally implausible. Oswell laughed at the dog's personality and gave him a rub down his sides, pitying the dog as he felt its ribs. The animal was a magnet for unconditional love. Oswell wanted nothing more than to take the dog home. It certainly would make for a more enjoyable summer, and a distraction from everything else wrong in his life. Oswell figured the dog would oblige; he'd enjoy a regular feeding schedule and the constant attention. Unfortunately his mother had a strangling allergy, and thought dogs were stupid animals, anyway.

This one isn't, Oswell thought. "So where do you come from anyway?" he asked, standing up and looking around. "You know... this is my forest, and *I've* never seen you around here before."

The dog looked up at Oswell, closed its mouth, and pressed its ears flat against its head.

Oswell's arm hairs lifted at the dog's expression of fear.

"What's wrong?"

The dog looked up to the sky and emitted a low grumble.

"What is it?" Oswell pressed again, not feeling silly in the slightest for asking a question of an animal that was obviously not going to answer him.

The dog turned and trotted off towards a pine tree, where he curled up beneath its low branches and set its head between its paws. Oswell recognized what the mutt was doing as a fat raindrop exploded on his head. Oswell groaned. It was the first rain in at least a week, and it had to start when he was in the very middle of the woods. On top of that, a downpour would washout any clues Oswell, or the police were likely to find. Oswell looked over at the dog, and the dog looked back at him. There was a certain knowledge in the dog's eyes.

"So it's true. Dogs do have a sixth sense," Oswell said. "It looks like you're all settled in. If you're still in the neighbourhood tomorrow, I'll bring food for you, okay boy?"

The dog continued to appraise Oswell with an almost professorial air. Oswell returned the stare with a shrug and then turned to leave.

Ten minutes later, Oswell burst into his backyard breathless and sopping wet. Moments after he'd left the dog, the rain crashed to the Earth in torrents. The water easily penetrated the forest canopy and soaked Oswell to the bone.

He nimbly bounded over the wet grass, careful not to slip, and tore up the back steps and through the door into the kitchen. His father was sitting at the kitchen table when Oswell burst through the door. His mother appeared from another room, breathless and telephone in her hand.

Standing on the doormat, dripping water onto the floor, Oswell didn't know what to make of the hard stare coming from both of his parents. Sure, he was making a bit of a mess with all the water he was bringing into the house, but what was he supposed to do? Wring himself out before coming inside?

"Don't worry, I'll mop it up." Oswell said as he slipped out of his shoes and wet socks, and then pulled off his shirt. His parents glared at him. Oswell stopped in his tracks, standing shirtless and barefoot by the back door.

"*What?*" he sensed definitive hostility in the room.

"Where have you been?" Monica asked. An undercurrent of nerves ran beneath her question, electrifying them.

Oswell smiled in spite of this. *As if they don't know where I was.* "I've been to Niagara Falls and back," he said, "the barrel ride was really something!"

"Oswell!" Owen growled.

"What?" Oswell asked, his back raising in defence.

"You *didn't* tell us where you were going," Monica said.

He usually didn't tell them when he was going out. He came and went as he pleased because he always returned at a reasonable time. That was the only thing ever expected of him, and this was no different.

He nodded slowly in agreement, "I never do."

"Well you should have known better," Owen replied.

"Why?"

"Why do you think?" Monica screamed. "Maybe because there's a kidnapper on the loose!"

Oswell killed the smirk that instinctually blossomed on his face, knowing it was the wrong reaction. The kidnapper? "Seriously mom? I think I can handle myself."

"You're *fourteen* years old," Monica shouted.

"Exactly. I'm old enough. You think this guy would be able to threaten me?"

"Are you joking, right now?" Owen's derision was clear. He turned to his wife, "I remember being cocksure at his age, but this is delusional."

Oswell felt his face redden and fury rise up in his chest, "Delusional for wanting to help my friends?" he spat.

"You're not helping anyone by getting kidnapped," his mother fumed as Oswell's chest heaved, ready to rebut. He stopped in his tracks as his mother deflated. "This was a step too far, Oz. We trusted you to think, and you've done nothing of the sort. Go to your room, you're grounded."

Oswell stared at his mother in disbelief. He didn't move.

"Go!" she cried, pointing through the doorway out of the kitchen. Owen found the new meaning of silence, only offering Oswell a firm nod when he looked to his father for some last ditch backup. He'd lost that with his last words to his father.

Oswell scowled and didn't say another word, he strode across the kitchen leaving a trail of water behind him, and stepped around his mother. A moment later, the slam of his bedroom door on the second floor thumped distantly in the kitchen, and Monica began to cry.

Four days later, Oswell's mind was damn near addled. He'd been cooped up in the house for almost the entirety of the four days. He had only left the house once to visit the library with his father. The books he borrowed were all he had. His grounding (as he learned a few hours after beginning) was to include the loss of his television and computer privileges on top of his unjust imprisonment within the house.

Shortly after the grounding, Owen had come up the stairs to talk to him. Owen explained that the grounding was necessary, if not for going out under the circumstances, then for the way he'd spoken to him and to his mother. They had both been extraordinarily worried, and he emphasized that leaving without a note was a dumb move under the current circumstances.

Oswell explained that going without leaving a note was an honest mistake, and that he was very sorry (a genuine apology had to be good enough, right?). It wasn't. He'd earned his sentence, and it was going to stick. He couldn't blame his parents for being consistent. After three days, however, his patience was beginning to wear thin, and by the fourth, it was fraying at the ends.

In the four days, Oswell dashed across the pages of three novels. He also fought battles in his mind to ward off the stress of his friend's disappearance, and in between those active moments, slowly went insane. He had never been forced into confinement for so long; and he thought being trapped in a classroom for an hour or two at a time was bad! When high school started in the fall, Oswell would certainly have a new appreciation for how little time he spent in those educational prisons. Anything would be better than what he was going through now.

Oswell heard a knock on his bedroom door and let the open book fall onto his chest. "Come in."

His father entered the room and sat down at the foot of Oswell's bed; a common occurrence over the past few days. Every time, Oswell felt a surge of hope, and this time was no different. Recognizing the look of query on Oswell's face, Owen shook his head and watched as his son sank deeper into the pillows.

"Your mother and I are going out tonight," Owen said. Oswell's jaw dropped at the injustice. An expert at reading his son's thoughts, Owen nodded. "I know it isn't fair, but I think it's what your mother needs."

"Why can't you just stop this madness?" Oswell asked impatiently. To his father, he sounded like a child that wasn't getting the brand of cereal he wanted.

"You know I can't override your mother. It isn't fair to her. Besides, what you did was really shitty, son. You had to learn someday that there are consequences to your actions. There are only three more days left. You can handle that."

"I've barely managed these four already!" Oswell complained.

"Oh, don't whine like that. You've got the rest of your life ahead of you—it's three more days. When I was your age, I was grounded all the time."

"Fine," Oswell grumbled. "So, what am I supposed to do tonight?"

"Rielle Winters is coming over to babysit you."

Oswell groaned. "I'm not a baby! She's gonna think we're weird."

"You know the rules of this grounding. We need someone to watch you, and to be honest, I'd feel more comfortable if you weren't home alone right now anyway."

Oswell rolled his eyes. He hated to admit it, but in four days without a sign of the kidnapper, or Claire or Nicholas, he was beginning to lose hope, but with that, his parents fear became more and more irrational. That wasn't entirely it though. He was also putting up a because huff Rielle Winters was essentially a goddess. At seventeen years old, she was already the very image of perfection. Oswell knew in his mind that he didn't stand a chance with her, but in his heart, he wished he did. Getting babysat by her, as a young man who could (and had) babysat younger children, didn't help his case.

"Fine. I'll bear the embarrassment for your sake, and Mom's."

"Thanks Ozzie," his father replied gratefully. "Did you want me to pick up anything for you while we're in town tonight?"

"No," Oswell said sullenly, then perked up, "a stay of my sentence?"

Owen frowned. "Rielle gets here at six. We shouldn't be home later than eleven thirty."

"Okay dad, I'm sure we'll both be fine," he worked through in his mind whether it would be better to stay locked in his bedroom or spend time with Rielle.

"I bet you will be," Owen patted his son's thigh. Without another word, he got up and left the room, closing the door behind him. Oswell lifted his book back up and stared down at the words.

He read for at least ten minutes, but after reading the same line five times over, he stopped and closed his eyes.

In the darkness of his own mind, he could see the forest spanning out before him. The trees beckoned to him. Oswell's eyes shot open and he leaped out of bed and stared out his bedroom window.

In the afternoon sun, the trees were a bright green. The scene was ordinary enough, except for one detail. Sitting on the edge of his lawn sat a small dog (*the* small dog), looking right up into Oswell's window. Oswell jumped and ducked below the windowsill. *How did he find me?* He thought.

Oswell peeked out the window again. The dog was gone.

The idea hit him like the shock of a car's power window being unexpectedly wound up into an arm enjoying a breeze. The dog. He'd shown up a day before Claire and Nicholas were taken. That had to mean something. It had been days since the abduction. With every day, the search radius widened as the ground the kidnapper covered lengthened. Unless, of course, he was laying low. Letting them think he was on the run. Letting them think he'd gotten away.

Tonight would be the night. His parents were gone, and Rielle would probably be too preoccupied with her latest boyfriend to notice anything. Oswell would steal back a little bit of his sanity by disappearing into the woods for an hour or two—just for a little bit. Just to make sure that the kidnapper, and his friends, weren't hiding right beneath their noses. His mind touched briefly on his mother's worries about the kidnapper, but he shrugged them off. If there was any clue in the forest that could lead Oswell to find Claire and Nicholas, he would locate it. That started with the dog. Oswell could redeem himself, and if he succeeded, he would become a hero in the process. And if he didn't, at least he could say he tried.

The clock on his nightstand read four o'clock. He had two hours to prepare. It was going to be a long night.

- *CHAPTER SEVEN* -

RESPECT YOUR ELDERS

FOUR LONG DAYS crawled by in the crypt that had become the unfortunate home of Thomas Courser. He wasn't alone in that dank and terrible place, and perhaps that was all that kept him going. His companionship with Cicero Nagel blossomed through the darkness, binding them in a friendship that could have spanned half a lifetime, had it not started only a few days before. They kept themselves occupied with their stories of adventure; Cicero's of glory, Thom's of suffering.

Thomas knelt across the cell from the older man. The cold stones could suck the warmth out of your body in minutes and he had quickly learned that he should either stand, or rest on his knees to minimize contact. Standing made it impossible to sleep, but kneeling afforded that luxury as uncomfortable as it was. They did not sleep often. In near darkness, their sense of time faded quickly. It had taken all of Cicero's wits to determine how long he'd been imprisoned alone. He judged time by the meagre rations provided once daily. To say the least, Cicero weakened by the day, and the hunger pains riddling Thom's stomach were unbearable, even by his standards.

Footsteps in the cold stone hallway outside the door triggered a contortion of grumbling in his abdomen, a response to the morsels about to be delivered. Thomas smiled wanly at Cicero, but Cicero shook his head. It was too soon for another ration. The guard banged on the door, and ordered them to step away. The door scraped open and their guard sneered into the room.

"You smell like death," he said to Cicero, then to Thomas, "How do you bare it?"

"Stop teasing the prisoners," a tall man followed the guard, stooping through the cell's stone doorway.

"Jonas," Cicero croaked.

"Cicero," Jonas replied, his teeth glowing in the dim light of the dungeon. "Captivity does *not* flatter you." His gaze briefly turned to Thomas crouched in the corner, before dismissing the wretch and turning back to Cicero.

"You *could* set me free," Cicero suggested.

"You have information for me then?" Jonas asked.

"Not at this juncture," Cicero replied. Thomas watched intently as the Sherryf squared off with the revolutionary former councillor. Cicero had told him much of what had happened. The rebellion, their motivations and their failings, and finally his capture. Jonas Vorley was the right and left hands of the Governyr, one holding a pen and the other a hammer. According to Cicero, the hammer was the preferred tool of late.

"Out," Jonas waved the guardsman away, and the man hurried out of the room, barring the door behind him. Jonas stepped around a puddle of unknown consistency and crouched down in front of Cicero. "You're dying. I can end your suffering. The offer still stands. I spare your people. You're returned to council… after a much needed rest."

Cicero's blue eyes stared unblinkingly at Jonas. For a moment, Thomas thought he saw his resolve waver. His gaze distant, almost as if he was picturing a long lost memory of those better times Thomas had eagerly heard about. Even though the time he'd spent with the man was short, Thomas knew him well. Facing death, starvation, and darkness together forged friendships of powerful stuff. But this wavering? That scared Thomas. Not once before had Cicero suggested any level of remorse or any desire for cooperation. He was the very definition of recalcitrance.

Jonas smiled.

"I'm retired," Cicero finally said, a small crook at the corner of his mouth belied his mirth.

Jonas growled and stood back up, "You impetuous old man! Don't you understand? We're on the same team."

"Please," Cicero scoffed.

Jonas turned back towards Cicero and hefted him up to a standing position, grasping the breast of his shirt to hold him close. Thomas cried out in surprise, but Cicero held fast. "The Governyr is weak. I *will* replace him. We can work together."

A genuine look of surprise crossed Cicero's face, betraying him for less than a moment. For once, there was a piece of knowledge he hadn't anticipated. Thomas caught his look of surprise. Jonas, somehow, missed it, perhaps distracted by his own surprise at his conspiratorial admission.

"You may be Numyrian, but you're more of the same," Cicero said. "Slavery and disparity for the people of this country. *Your* people, Jonas."

"This is the way of things," Jonas released Cicero's shirt and real shame seemed to occupy the Sheryff's very constitution, if only for a moment. "Better a Numyrian leading us through it."

"I say it's worse. Betrayal over subjugation. First, your own people. Now your governyr? *Jonas,*" Cicero drawled. "Who will you have left to betray but yourself?"

Jonas's eyes narrowed. Ignoring the question, he replied, "You're not long for this place. You have one week to come around, or I'll have to find more creative ways of getting what I need from you."

"You'll not have it," Cicero said simply.

Jonas seethed and then punched Cicero in the stomach. Cicero crumpled to the ground and didn't stir. The Sheryff looked as though he were about to say a final word, then held back. He strode to the door, knocked, and then disappeared through it as the guard opened it. The door slammed shut and bolted after him.

Thomas was frozen where he knelt.

"Today," Cicero croaked from across the cell. "Our window will disappear if we do not act now... my strength... wanes, we must move while I am still able."

Thomas was slow to respond, thinking carefully before speaking. "There is no sense in biding our time any longer." He stood up and walked through the darkness to his friend. Crouching down before him, Thomas struggled to examine Cicero. He was sallow with hunger, and his face still contorted in pain from the assault. Prison was not Cicero's natural habitat. Thomas could scarcely believe the circumstances that had landed Cicero in prison. It sounded too fantastic: an impossibility. Thomas always considered himself an average person. Cicero, on the other hand, was far and away extraordinary. If Thomas could rely on anyone it would be Cicero. He put on a strong act, but now, the man was failing.

Sensing Thom's concern, Cicero put a hand on his shoulder, "do not worry about me my boy. Worry about your role in this design we have constructed."

Thomas nodded and looked to the cell's door. "With the next rations." He heard no reply, but could sense that the older man was agreeing silently. Thomas retreated to his position on the other side of the cell.

An hour later, Thomas heard footsteps approaching from down the hall and saw the familiar orange torchlight slowly filtering into the room. The light brought flickering contrast into the cell. Thomas tried to ignore the extra details. He didn't like to see the squalor of the cell he inhabited.

Heavy, booted footsteps stopped in front of the prison cell.

"Back away from the door," one of the guards commanded as the torch bearer jangled the keys and unbarred the solid oak latch. By now, the prisoners knew the drill, and the command was purely a formality. The food carrier stepped through the door, sliding a tray along the floor to Thomas, who grabbed the food and began to eat greedily. The other tray bounced across the floor and collided with Cicero's prone and motionless body. The guards looked at each other, then at Thomas. Thomas looked up from his food.

"The old bugger died. Punch is wot killed him. Don't worry, I'll make sure the food isn't wasted—" Thomas explained, "By the way, can I get a new cell? This one reeks of piss."

The torch bearer groaned and the second guard stepped further into the cell to approach Cicero's lifeless body. The torch bearer moved into the cell, bringing the light forward. With all eyes on Cicero, Thomas took advantage of the situation. He snapped his wooden tray diagonally across his knee.

The sound echoed sharply in the stone vault, and both of the guards turned to look. Before he knew what had happened, the sharp point of half a tray protruded from the neck of the torch bearer. The grey wood saturated with blood as the torch dropped to the floor in synchrony with the body.

The other guard lunge d at Thomas. Cicero, still very much alive, grabbed the guard's ankle, tripping him and sending him headlong into the floor. The sound of his forehead hitting the stone was sickening. Disoriented and bloodied, the guard attempted to pull himself up, but Cicero delivered a resounding kick to the side of the head and finished the job.

Thomas grabbed the torch, panting, and held it up to examine Cicero. "Back from the dead, are we?" he asked. "Not bad for an old man," he complimented, surveying the unconscious guard.

Thomas handed the torch to Cicero and knelt down to remove the murdered guard's keys and a small dagger from the scabbard at his waist. Blood bubbled out of the man's throat, but Thomas averted his eyes. He had never killed a man before. In this case, it was necessary. Besides, enough cruelty had been visited upon him that the time had come for them to be repaid. Yes, the deed was one that Thomas could live with, especially if it meant he would live.

"Thomas," Cicero rasped, "I'm sorry you had to do that."

"It needed to be done," Thomas replied. Cicero appraised his young friend critically, then decided that Thomas meant what he said.

"We shouldn't waste any time," Cicero said. "Lock the door behind us."

Thomas complied as they exited the cell. The pair turned left and dashed down the narrow corridor with Cicero holding the torch in the lead. The man's apparent frailty surrendered to the speed with which his long legs carried him down the hall—Thomas struggled to keep up.

Moments later, Cicero stopped abruptly and turned around to appraise Thomas. They had reached the stairs that would deliver them from their subterranean underworld and return them to reality. Thomas nodded to Cicero and Cicero nodded back. The pair mounted the staircase and approached the door that granted passage onto the main floor.

Cicero waited as Thomas disabled the heavy lock. A short countdown reached its end in his mind as he pushed the door open and bolted across the threshold. Cicero followed and quickly overtook Thomas. Thomas hadn't a clue in which direction to go as he'd been thoroughly removed from his capacities when he had been brought to the gaol. Cicero, however, knew exactly where he was going. As planned, Cicero navigated the stone corridors and Thomas followed. Nearing the exit, Cicero stopped suddenly, and pushed back on Thomas as the young boy crashed into his back. Breathing heavily, Thomas questioned Cicero with his eyes. Cicero peeked around the corner.

The Warden sat at his desk, leaning his chair onto its two back legs. All that his title really meant was that out of the three guards working the gaol at any one time, he was the one with permission to sit on his rear all day while the other two did the grunt work. The Warden was, however, responsible for keeping prisoner's records, a tedious task that dulled the senses. The escape artists were banking on a certain tedium-induced lethargy.

Cicero turned back to Thomas and held out his hand, requesting the small blade Thomas had pilfered. Thomas relinquished its ownership to Cicero.

"You will go back down the hall and make a noise—call for help. I will take care of the rest," Cicero whispered. Thomas nodded his understanding and retreated down the hall.

Once he'd rounded the first corner, he called out in his deepest voice, "Help!"

Cicero was crouching, waiting for the guard to approach. He heard the chair's legs scrape the rough stone floor as the Warden backed away from the desk. He smiled at the hurried shuffling of feet as the Warden rushed toward the sound of distress. The Warden came around the corner, a hands-breadth from where Cicero crouched. Cicero lunged forward like a spring and his body, blade first, collided with the Warden's. Hearing the tussle, Thomas bolted back around the corner towards the two men. By the time he arrived, Cicero had dispatched the guard.

"You continue to surprise me," Thomas said.

"I'm still spry," Cicero smirked.

Thomas grinned and turned towards the exit. Cicero handed him the blade, having found one of his own on the Warden, "Now, let's get out of this Myr-forsaken city."

Although Thomas had suggested they walk out of the prison to reduce suspicion, the idea had been promptly shot down by Cicero. He rationalized that not just anyone came in and out of the prison, and therefore their exit would surely be noticed. Surprise and speed would be their only option.

Sure enough, a voice instantly called out as the fugitives were newly minted through the front door, commanding them to halt.

The element of surprise that Cicero and Thomas had wagered everything on seemed to pay off as the stunned guard watched in confusion, unsure of what to do. By the time the guard determined why two people would emerge sprinting from a prison, the fugitives had disappeared from his sight.

Weaving in and out of the bustling crowds, Cicero and Thomas traversed the streets of Fletchery with no resistance. Instead, they met confused appraisals by merchants, customers, and other guardsmen. Without saying it out loud, both Thomas and Cicero thanked Myr for the luck they had been blessed with. Thomas recognized one, the guard who'd denied his entry to the city in the first place, and earned a boot to the groin in recompense. The guard seemed to recognize him, but his reaction was not one of surprise. Instead, he tilted his head as if to say 'hello', and allowed them to pass without raising the alarm.

A few blocks later, a deep voice called out, "Stop at once!" They ignored the call, pressing onwards as quickly as their feet could pound the cobbles. This time it seemed their luck had run out. This particular guard required no hesitation in his decision to pursue them through the streets of Fletchery.

With one guard giving chase, their escape became apparent. No longer were they simply running through the streets, they were running from a town guard; a far more incriminating activity regardless of the underlying reason. Thankfully, Thomas had regained his bearings, and recognized the way to the stables.

"Left!" Thomas called as he darted down an alleyway to avoid two town guards ahead of them. Cicero followed swiftly after him. They emerged from the alleyway onto another street, and bolted off in the direction they were originally travelling. Angry voices echoed from the alley as the guards gave chase.

Ahead of them, a guard had his back to them, but hearing the voices in pursuit, he turned just as the fugitives came upon him. His reaction was too late. Cicero and Thomas darted around him and continued their escape.

Nose to the air, a familiar spicy scent filled Thomas's nostrils. They were close. Sure enough, as they rounded a corner, Thomas recognized the Western Square. Across its span were the stables.

With at least ten town guards in tow, Thomas and Cicero dashed across the square much to the amusement of the merchants.

"We need a distraction," Cicero wheezed, clearly beginning to lose his wind.

"I have just the idea!" Thomas replied, also short of breath. With the guards close on their heels, Thomas burst through the doors of the stable, running headlong down the aisle with Cicero right behind him.

"Oi, Rik?" the stableman said, leaning out of one of the stalls.

His jaw dropped in surprise as Thomas sprinted past him unlatching all of the stall doors whilst causing the greatest ruckus he could manage. The commotion frightened the horses and they dashed down the hallway two abreast, making their way for the stable entrance. The pursuing guardsmen turned to run in the opposite direction, stumbling over each other to get out of the way.

Glancing over his shoulder, Thomas grinned at Cicero before diving off to the left into a room full of hay. There he stopped and turned to Cicero. "We'll have to move quickly. Be sure the hay covers the path behind you."

Cicero watched as Thomas dove into the hay and then followed closely behind him. Thomas squirmed into the hole in the wall, and started crawling through the darkness. He could hear Cicero struggling for breath behind him. The air in the tunnel was scarce and stale, and both fugitives were well past breathless.

Moments later, Thomas rolled out of the hole into the shack and picked himself up off the dirt floor. He moved out of the way just as Cicero followed him into the hut. Cicero did not get up. Instead, he lay on his back gasping heavily and clutching his chest. Heaving, Thomas knelt down to help the older man sit.

"I require... a moment..." Cicero said. Thomas nodded and stepped away from the wheezing man.

Thomas rapidly recovered his breath and felt his anxiety begin to take hold. He peeked out the shack's front door, careful not to set it off its hinges. "It will be dark in an hour; we should make our way to the forest while we can still see."

"The cover of darkness will help when we leave the hut," Cicero replied, climbing off the floor and onto his feet.

"They'll find us in here!"

"Thomas, they won't have a clue where to look."

"How do you know?"

"Would you think we escaped through a hole in the wall?"

Thomas did not reply.

"We will wait," Cicero decided with finality. Thomas leaned against the hut's wall and slid to the floor, feeling his anxiety amplify. His heart pounded irregularly and his vision began to cloud at the periphery—it was an all too familiar feeling.

"What have I done?" he whispered to himself. "They'll surely kill me now."

"What do you speak of boy?" Cicero demanded.

"We'll be caught eventually, and now I'm a fugitive... a murderer! They'll kill me, and you!"

"Do not speak in this way!" Cicero reprimanded.

"I'll speak how I please; these may be my last words!" Thomas growled.

Cicero crouched down in front of his hyperventilating young friend, even in spite of his own breathlessness. "Your pessimism is unwarranted. We have not been caught, and I do not intend to allow that to happen." Cicero grabbed Thomas's hands and held them up. "Do you see these? Surely you would have lost them for thievery. How would you live then?" Cicero let go of Thomas. "More likely, you would have lost your life anyway. There is still hope for life. If only you would open your mind to see it!"

Thomas looked up at Cicero, the scared little boy crept from behind his defensive demeanour. He had nothing to say, but he simply nodded solemnly.

"We will make our escape good my friend, you will see," Cicero said. "Steel your nerves. We shall quit this place soon."

CHAPTER EIGHT

MOONLIGHTING

Experiencing a mixture of dejection and awe, Oswell looked on from his spot, less than a smudge on the wall. Rielle Winters arrived shortly after Oswell finished his dinner. The doorbell tinkled in a way that seemed altogether more magical than normal, sounding at exactly six o'clock—it would have been uncharacteristic for Ms. Winters to be anything other than right on time.

Moments after she entered the home, Oswell's parents interrogated her about her progress at school. Oswell was not surprised to hear that all was well on that front. Rielle Winters was a double threat: mind-bogglingly beautiful and intelligent beyond belief. Quite the catch for any boy lucky enough to stumble upon some new way of wooing or impressing her.

Owen jumped into the routine of outlining the details. Rielle had heard them all before, though it had been a number of years since she'd heard them from Owen Wallace.

"And my cell number is—" Owen started.

"On the fridge—got it Mr. Wallace." Of course she got it.

"And you know if there are any problems..."

"I won't hesitate to call."

"And we should be home around eleven."

"Eleven o'clock," Rielle repeated back. Owen smiled, satisfied.

Oswell's mother and father were both dressed for their night out. Monica had her favourite dress on: a midnight blue piece that flowed down from her shoulders to her waist, accentuating her curves, before flaring out and cutting off just below the knee. Owen was decked out in khaki pants, a white dress shirt without a tie, and a tweed jacket, the very stereotype of a middle-aged Caucasian man, though he didn't see any problem with that.

They were going into town for dinner, and had tickets to see the latest live production at the Apollonian Theatre in the nearby town of Foxcroft.

Meanwhile, Oswell stood by awkwardly, transfixed by the young woman smiling eagerly in front of his parents.

Her blonde hair flowed down in straightened layers to her shoulders. Her blue eyes sparkled with youth and her white teeth shone from between two full lips. She wore a simple grey t-shirt and her tight jeans were well worn and had been ripped in a number of places. With little to no effort, Rielle Winters had created a masterpiece.

"Ozzie, you've got all that?" his father asked. Oswell started out of his reverie and felt his face get hot. It was a good thing his thoughts hadn't been out loud.

"Oh yes, every detail," he replied, referring to something entirely different from what his father had meant. Owen nodded.

"All right then, we'll see the both of you when we get back," Owen said as he ushered Monica out the door. "Thanks again, Rielle!" he called out as the door shut behind him.

Standing in the kitchen, Rielle looked at Oswell and smiled. Oswell smiled back thinly, feeling like he didn't belong. He wondered what it felt like to be a goddess among men. His father easily resisted her charms, but any man or boy had to appreciate that level of beauty.

Rielle giggled at Oswell's expression. He was suddenly aware of how short Rielle was. It had been a while since he'd seen her up close, but it wasn't like she had shrunk. Oswell had grown to be just as tall as her.

"So Oz, you're thirteen now?"

"Fourteen," Oswell corrected. His face rose another couple degrees.

"Wow! Remember when I babysat you when you were eight—so cute!" she said. That comment didn't help Oswell's embarrassment.

"Yeah," Oswell laughed, "I guess I was."

"Well, do you want to see what's on TV?" she asked. Oswell was about to remind her that he wasn't supposed to be watching TV, but then thought better of it. He was already enough of a loser being babysat at fourteen, he didn't need to admit he was grounded as well. His parents had been kind enough to leave out that minor detail.

"Yes, let's do that," he agreed and turned to lead her out of the kitchen. He made his way into the family room with Rielle right behind him. There, he flopped down on the couch, reclining against an arm rest, and scooped up the remote. Rielle sat down on the couch beside him. Oswell pressed the power button and began to surf as Rielle sat quietly beside him. Again, Oswell was extraordinarily aware of how tall he'd gotten. Feeling a surge of confidence, he stopped surfing and settled on a movie he had not seen before. It was just starting.

"Oh, I love this movie!" Rielle exclaimed.

Oswell smirked at the lucky choice, "I've never seen it."

"You'll like it. I won't ruin it for you though."

"I don't think you could ruin anything," Oswell said, the words leaving his lips before his brain realized what they'd produced. Rielle turned in her seat to look at him. "I mean, you wouldn't..." Oswell was at a loss for words.

"I wouldn't... what?" Rielle asked. Oswell was distracted by the way her lips moved while she spoke.

"You... you... you wouldn't ruin a movie for anyone," Oswell's words fell flat.

"Is that so?" Rielle smiled and kicked her feet up onto the couch. Her bare feet fell across his lap. "Do you mind?" she asked.

Thoughts raced through Oswell's mind. He didn't know what was going on. Rielle Winters was *touching* him. Her feet felt warm on his thigh. He let his arm fall, draping across her leg. She didn't protest.

"Oh, shush, this is a good part," Rielle hinted as the protagonist joked around with some of his buddies.

"I thought you weren't going to give anything away," Oswell teased.

Rielle giggled, "You're right, but just watch."

Oswell complied and kept his mouth shut. He'd surprised himself and gotten lucky with that line. He shifted in his seat and settled in to watch the movie, managing to steal the occasional glance at the girl of his dreams.

Oswell stretched his arms into the air and looked over at Rielle. The movie had just ended, and the credits were whizzing by on the screen in cable station fast forward. The station was advertising the next movie to follow, but Oswell ignored it, eyeing the clock. It read half past eight.

The movie had been lengthy, extended by advertisements, and Oswell was surprised at how quickly the time had flown. Two and a half hours had passed since his parents left for their night out.

He hadn't really liked the movie—one of those terribly clichéd romantic comedies. The kind that starts with the budding romance, followed by the inevitable mistake that tears them apart, and finally, the redemptive grand gesture that wins back the girl. Nonetheless, he didn't feel as though the time was wasted; he'd watched a romantic movie in the company of Rielle Winters. Such was a feat that the majority of high school boys could not attest to, and he couldn't wait to fill Grant in on the evening.

Looking out the window, he recognized the darkness beginning to settle in. The family room window was hanging open with a simple screen in place to separate the insects outside from everything inside. The scent of the outdoors permeated throughout the room. Noticing this, Oswell breathed deeply and felt the call of the forest. He stole a glance at Rielle. She was looking at him.

"What do you want to do now?" she asked.

Oswell stopped to assess the situation. *She's beautiful...* he thought. *Focus!* Thinking he had a chance with Rielle Winters was merely a foolish, albeit exciting dream. He could spend more time with her, but that would literally accomplish nothing. He had more important things to do.

Letting out an audible yawn, Oswell rolled his shoulders around theatrically and then lazily rubbed his eyes with balled up fists.

"I've had a long day. I think I'm going to turn in."

"Really?" she said. Oswell couldn't be sure, but it sounded like disappointment.

She doesn't want you to go! He thought. Every fibre of his adolescent brain screamed at him in unison, but he somehow managed to stubbornly stick to his plan.

"Yeah, I got up really early this morning," he said.

"Okay... I'll just be down here if you need anything, then," she said and pulled out her cell phone.

"G'night."

"Good night, sleep tight," she said sweetly. Oswell blushed despite his best effort. Everything she said dripped with allure. The words coming from Rielle's mouth conjured distracting images in Oswell's head. *Focus*, he thought again. He quickly banished the images to the far corners of his mind.

He pulled himself up off the couch and stretched his muscles back into working order. He'd scarcely moved throughout the movie, afraid of disturbing her. He gave Rielle a little wave, immediately regretting the awkward gesture, and climbed the stairs to his room.

Once inside, he closed the door and flopped down on his bed, listening intently. There wasn't a noise to be heard except the musical track of the next movie to come on. Staring through the darkness at the ceiling, Oswell waited for five minutes, and then heard Rielle's muffled voice talking downstairs. His heart pined for what it felt he was missing, even as his brain told him he was missing nothing of true significance.

Oswell slid lithely off the bed and gathered the things he'd assembled earlier in the day. Oswell swapped his shorts for a pair of cargo pants and pulled on a long sleeve shirt—the trees' branches somehow became grabbier at night. He pulled on a pair of hiking boots, slid a pocket knife into his pocket, and grabbed the flashlight from his desk. Oswell flipped the flashlight on and off a few times in the darkness of his room to test it, and when satisfied, flicked off the bedroom light and passed through the shadows to the window.

If ever there was a time to be stealthy, it was that moment. Oswell slowly slid his bedroom window up, stopping just before the point where it would creak. It would be a tight fit, but it would have to do.

He swung his leg up over the sill and shimmied his way through the gap, pulling his other foot up and over the sill as well.

Bracing himself against the upper frame of the window and the sill, Oswell clung to the side of the wall, twenty feet above the ground. Removing his right arm from the upper frame, he reached up and grabbed a hold on the roof. The shingles were rough under his hand. He reached up with his left and dangled from the roof precariously.

He worked hand over hand along the edging of the roof, careful to keep his grip. He'd done this only once before, and felt his heart beating rapidly in his chest. The muscles in his arms began to ache, and his shoulders began to sag. He swung by the upstairs bathroom window and finally reached his feet out to pull himself onto the lower roof of the main floor. Oswell tiptoed across the roof and approached the edge where he knew he wouldn't be seen from the family room or the kitchen. There, he swung himself over the lip, hanging as far down as he could, and then dropped the last three feet onto the spongy grass.

Oswell checked himself over to make sure the pocket knife and flashlight were still on him, then he wiped his brow and darted off into the forest.

The branches began grabbing at him straight away as he blindly navigated his way through the darkness. He'd elected not to turn on his flashlight until he was further in. A moment later, he'd had enough of the darkness and pulled out his flashlight. The bright halogen bulb illuminated the life around him: every sort of tree, shrub and fern that could be expected to be found in such a place. As comfortable as Oswell was in the forest, it looked unrecognizable in the artificial luminance. However, the familiar fresh scent of growth filled his nose and comforted him. He was not afraid.

Pressing on with the flashlight, he avoided most of the low hanging branches, and made good time through the woods. He didn't know precisely what he was looking for, but he figured that if he was meant to find it, he would.

Oswell stopped to listen to the sounds of the night, and once again found comfort in the absence of silence. It was as if the forest lived and breathed. It welcomed him there even during its most inhospitable time, and made him feel like he belonged.

He whipped around as a twig broke behind him. Shining his flashlight over the source of the noise, he saw nothing unusual. He let himself relax.

An animal launched from the shrubs in front of him and came to a halt only inches away. Oswell fell backwards in fear, only to recognize the mutt from days past. He crawled onto his knees and scolded the dog.

"You gave me a scare old boy. Don't you know not to jump out of the bushes like that? You'll give someone a heart attack."

The dog looked ashamed for a moment, but then smiled up at him. Oswell grinned at the dog's expression as he rubbed him vigorously on the head. The dog's tongue lolled out of its mouth as it enjoyed the attention even as Oswell's mind worked. This *was* what he was looking for. He just had to figure out how it connected.

"You can't be living out here on your own..."

Oswell stood up and took a step back from the dog. Realization hit him unexpectedly as the pieces of his theory elbowed their way past Rielle in the corner of his mind, and found their way to the forefront. His heartbeat accelerated. Oswell flipped off the flashlight and effectively immersed himself into the darkness. He crouched down and felt the dog come closer to him, nudging his hand for another pat. Oswell complied as his eyes adjusted to the darkness.

It made sense. The dog had only been around for a few days, and he couldn't be wild; he was too used to humans. Oswell's mind raced. He's trying to show me the way. That's why he keeps coming back.

Oswell reached out and held the dog close. "Are you going to bring me to Nick and Claire?" The dog made no reply at first, but then stiffened. Oswell released the dog and leaned away. "What is it?" he whispered.

Oswell remembered stories of dogs having a sixth sense; how they seemed to know when something bad was going to happen. He remembered all of the stories about dogs protecting their owners in times of danger—fighting off bears and mountain lions and sniffing out cancer.

Oswell listened again. If anything was coming, it wasn't a mountain lion or a bear.

Oswell heard a low grumble coming from the dog's throat and he immediately felt terror bubbling in his gut. The familiar sound of the forest had vanished once again—a common occurrence since the dog had shown up.

Out of the darkness, Oswell heard a raspy voice growl.

"Where'd you go you stinkin' mutt?"

Oswell stiffened and dropped down onto his belly, rolling away into a shrub. He heard the dog sprint off in the direction of the voice. Oswell dared not make a sound.

"There you are!" the raspy voice spat. Oswell heard a yelp and winced. "That'll teach you not to run off."

Oswell listened as branches crackled off into the distance. Whomever it was (Oswell had a strong hunch as to whom), was leaving. Once the cracking had subsided, Oswell breathed an audible sigh of relief and rolled out from underneath the bushes. His whole body trembled from the adrenaline pumping through his veins and the fear that gripped his heart. *The kidnapper.* There was no other explanation for him being in the woods. No other explanation for the dog. But why did he stay?

Because they thought he would run...

Oswell somehow managed to gather his wits. Afraid of turning on the flashlight, he pulled himself up to stand and steeled his nerves. The opportunity to find Nick and Claire was not going to come again. This was his chance. His only chance. *Their only chance.*

With a deep breath, Oswell gained his bearings and began to work his way quietly through the trees, listening carefully to identify the man's location in the darkness.

A few painful minutes later, Oswell heard tree branches snapping again. He was back on track. He would find Nick and Claire, regardless of the risk. In this, he would have his redemption.

CHAPTER NINE

ON THE RUN

H IS LEGS WERE consumed by fire. Each one burned so intensely that dread of absolute collapse accompanied each step. His lungs were inflamed and ragged; he could scarcely draw a breath to cool the blaze in his legs. When he'd crossed it days before, the distance between Fletchery and the forest seemed small and manageable. His young soul full of hope, he'd travelled on the wings of optimism. Now, he ran with the winds of fear.

Beside him, Cicero endured a similar state, worse by a degree of magnitude called 'age.' Thomas was astounded that the elder had kept up with him as long as he had.

Things had not gone well from the first moment that they had left the hut on the outskirts of Fletchery. Cicero's suggestion that they leave under cover of night had been one of good intentions, but one cursed by the other side of the argument. By waiting for darkness, the escapees traded one advantage for another. Thomas could not fault his ally for the decision.

"Ready?" Thomas had asked.

"Now or never," Cicero replied.

Thomas poked his head out the door. Clouds oppressed the moon's light high above. Not a soul in sight. Thomas slid into the evening air and Cicero followed close behind him.

"I guess you were right," Thomas whispered, edging along another ramshackle hut. Peeking around the corner, Thomas could see the forest in the distance. "It isn't far," Thomas said, reassuring himself more than informing Cicero.

A loud crash echoed across the slum, followed by frantic screaming and shouting.

"What was that?" Oswell whispered.

"They're onto us," Cicero said calmly. Despite the limited intelligence in the general staffing of Fletchery's guards corps, they'd fail to account for someone capable being at the helm, even though he'd paid a social visit to them that very afternoon. Vorley had clearly recognized that the fugitives could not simply disappear into thin air, and had been prudent enough to send his men into the town's outskirts to search for the prisoners. Cicero's hand found the small of Thom's back. "Make haste!"

Thomas didn't waste any time; he dashed around the corner, intending to navigate the impoverished settlement as directly as possible. His bare feet, hard with calluses, pounded the hard packed dirt. Off to his right, he saw the approaching glow of torchlight, and the oblong shadows it cast.

"You there! Stop!" a guard bellowed. Thomas glanced over his shoulder at Cicero.

"Go!" Cicero cried. Both of them bolted forward, Cicero in the lead. The guards followed in pursuit.

Rounding a corner, Thomas and Cicero were confronted by a lone torch-wielding guardsman. Thomas immediately recognized him as the guard who'd necessitated his pact with Darius, the same man who'd let them pass unmolested immediately following their escape. Cicero's pace didn't slow as they neared the guard, but the guard didn't call out. He didn't even get in the way. Instead, he leapt out of Thomas's path at the last moment, crashing to the ground in a heap with a dramatic cry of exclamation. *Why would he...* Thomas didn't have time to think about it. His legs carried him after Cicero.

Finally, they broke through the slums and into the open field. Thomas heard the guards shouting orders to gather the horses. Thomas and Cicero wouldn't have much time. The guard's failure to capture them in the city would not have gone without punishment. The Sherryf was not a forgiving man, but a second failure was unthinkable. Cicero and Thomas mounted a hill and barrelled down the other side toward the trees. Not too far behind, the clatter of horses was growing.

While their dash across the meadow took minutes, the time stretched on. A gasp of relief escaped Thomas's lips as they burst through the rim of the forest and penetrated its depths with the last few ounces of energy that they could muster from their exhausted bodies.

Branches whipped and grabbed at them as they trampled unceremoniously through the undergrowth. The carelessness with which they travelled would have meant capture if it was not for the darkness that now encouraged their freedom. The shadows of the forest combined with the darkness of night could very well allow them to lose their pursuers.

Cicero stopped abruptly. Thomas stopped a few steps beyond him, confused, terrified and breathing hard.

Now enveloped in silence, Thomas could hear the guards crashing haphazardly through the trees in much the same fashion that he and Cicero had presently abandoned. There was no doubt that the guards were motivated, but the night was a powerful friend for those who did not wish to be found.

"Silence has its purpose," Cicero explained to Thomas. Thomas understood and tried to quiet his breathing. By crashing through the woods, they had been giving away their position with every step. To tread carefully would be akin to being invisible.

Thomas and Cicero walked carefully through the woods, ignoring the fear and the impossibly loud beating of their hearts. At times, guards passed so close that the stench of perspiration pickling beneath their leather armour became overpowering. Indeed, it was in those moments that the fugitives' hearts chose to beat the hardest and the loudest.

It was also in those moments of near discovery that Thomas was fully able to appreciate the friend he'd discovered in Cicero Nagel, and became all the more thankful for his wise companion. Together they were on the brink of accomplishing an astounding feat. It wasn't just anyone who could manage to escape from a prison under the guard of the Governyr's men.

As the fugitives continued picking their way through the brush, Thomas was surprised by a sudden realization. He was no longer afraid.

CHAPTER TEN

THE HUNTED

THE FEAR WAS gone, replaced by the thrill of the hunt. He was exhilarated by the air in his lungs, the stealth with which he stalked his prey, and the delicious obliviousness of the man he followed. Oswell had tracked his quarry, undetected, for ten minutes already. The man moved slowly, but carelessly through the deepening woods making it clear that he did not know he was being followed.

Even with that advantage, Oswell was hesitant at times. *What if I'm caught? What if he's nobody? What if Rielle realizes I'm gone? Where is this man leading me?*

Oswell stopped as the sound of branches snapping disappeared ahead of him. He listened carefully and edged forward. Peeking from behind a tree, Oswell peered through a gap in the trees, and identified where the man had gone. Oswell nimbly approached the ditch and crawled to the top of the steep incline. He watched as his quarry disappeared into the ditch on the other side of the highway.

It's too open; he'll see you, Oswell thought. *You've never been this far before! You have to turn back!* Oswell shook his head. He didn't care about his own safety anymore; he had to find his friends. He had to get to the bottom of whatever was going on, and this was the only chance he had to do it. Oswell couldn't let the man slip away now.

He stood up and dashed across the highway. He carefully navigated his way back into the trees. Oswell felt an itch, a discomfort at the unfamiliar ground. These trees, though physically identical to those on the near side of the highway, set him ill at ease. They were not welcoming. They were formidable, mean... unforgiving. It seemed as though the sleepy woods of his childhood were waxing to reveal their malevolent intentions. He knew, then, that he would find Nicholas and Claire. The forest was alive with evil. Oswell was on the man's ground now. He shivered.

Listening intently, Oswell regained his bearings. His prey was pushing on without him. Oswell couldn't waste any more time. He fell back into pursuit, picking his way carefully, silently through the foliage.

Oswell stopped as silence enveloped the forest, completing the dark shawl with which the trees shrouded themselves. Oswell did not breathe—he had gotten so close. To be discovered now would not only be failure, but the consequences could be terrible. He instinctually grasped the knife in his pocket. Off in the distance, Oswell heard the telltale sound of someone crashing through the woods. Were they coming for him? *No,* Oswell thought with relief. His prey was running.

Two eyes narrowed and glared through the darkness. He was not alone in the forest. The mutt had long since left his side, running ahead towards the camp. To his right, the man could hear someone running carelessly through the trees. In fact, the commotion suggested more than one person. His heart caught in his throat—he'd come too far to be caught now. He'd never failed before.

Turning toward his camp, he began to run lithely and methodically. He could still make his escape.

Oswell bounded over roots and stones, avoiding the darkly hidden perils that populated the forest floor. At any moment, he could sprain his ankle, but in an instant, he could find his friends. His feet guided him through the maze that the forest embodied, and he felt the power of invincibility.

The sound of his prey was getting louder. Oswell was gaining ground. As he neared, Oswell noticed the sounds of hurried conversation. There was more than one voice. Oswell stopped in his tracks to listen, realizing he'd gotten far closer than he had intended.

"Where did they go?" one voice exclaimed.

"They'll have our heads for this!" another voice claimed.

"Not *our* heads! The fools that let them escape in the first place!" the first voice replied.

Oswell crouched down. *There's more than one kidnapper? Have Nick and Claire escaped?* Oswell's heart soared. If Nick and Claire had escaped, there was certainly hope.

Oswell could lead them back to safety. He would be a hero.

Oswell looked up as a blinding orange light came into view. Shielding his dilated eyes from the torch, he flattened himself against a tree.

"There he is! Get 'im!" one of the voices called.

Without a look over his shoulder, he turned and dashed off through the woods as quickly as his trembling legs would allow. The hunter had become the hunted.

* * *

Thomas startled awake from his slumber. Beside him, beneath the shrub, Cicero was still deep in sleep.

When it seemed as though the guards had moved onto another area of the forest to search, both of the fugitives' exhaustion took hold and, finding a concealed place to rest, they stopped. Originally, the plan was to rest, just for a few minutes, but shortly thereafter, both had dozed off. It was still dark, they could not have slept for long.

Feeling drowsy, Thomas stood up and brushed the forest litter off his behind. His back and neck were stiff and he tried in vain to stretch the kinks out of his atrophied muscles.

His stomach growled at him from the depths of his belly, commanding him to eat. Thomas had eaten pitiful morsels once a day while in the prison. Certainly not the sort of food to sustain a young man on the run.

"Cicero?" he whispered, testing the older man's depth of sleep. There was no reply; the older man simply stirred in his unconsciousness and shifted. Thomas ran his fingers through his hair and seriously thought about going in search of food. His stomach grumbled angrily at him again.

"I'm going to find some food... I won't go far," Thomas uselessly explained. Again, there was no reply. He took that as permission.

Thomas spun about to gain his bearings, and then, deciding on a direction, set off into the woods in a straight line so he would be able to find his way back. He wasn't exactly sure what he would be able to find in the forest's darkness, but judging by his hunger, whatever it was that he could find, would do.

He moved slowly, feeling trees and plants as he passed them, testing them for berries. He knew a number of trees whose bark was soft and edible although not tasty. He ripped a softwood branch off a tree and started chewing. Thomas had learned the trick from a drifter in Klora's Wash on the West coast; it tricks the body into thinking that food is on the way, sating hunger.

Ten minutes later, beginning to lose hope, Thomas felt the telltale fruit of a barbleberry bush. Even in the darkness, he could see the yellow, pebble sized berries against the dark green background on which they rested.

He picked them greedily, not bothering to gather them. He ate from the branches to his heart's content, consuming most of the available fruit. The majority of them were well ripened, though a few stung him with a powerfully sour bite. He ignored the occasional shock to his tongue, focusing instead on filling his groaning stomach.

A few minutes later, Thomas was hunched over, vomiting the bulk of the berries onto the spongy floor. He'd eaten too many of them far too quickly. Staring down at the waste in regret, he rubbed his belly. Despite its familiarity with hunger, Thomas's stomach was woefully unprepared to accept the berries. He decided to fill the newly opened space in his stomach with the leaves of the barbleberry bush—an edible, but considerably less palatable foodstuff.

When he'd eaten enough of the leaves to satisfy his stomach, and not enough to retch again, Thomas carefully sank to the forest floor making sure to avoid the wasted berries and bile that slowly soaked into the dry ground beneath a conifer.

Thomas stiffened, perking up his ears to listen. He'd heard someone whisper something quietly. *Too* quietly. He hadn't been able to make out what was said. Nonetheless, the mere possibility that it could be a town guard was more than enough to frighten Thomas. His basic human instinct, hunger, would mean his capture and cost his life, if he did not act quickly.

Without a second thought, Thomas launched himself from the forest floor and fled the scene of his meal as quickly as possible. In moments, two guards were crashing after him, one carrying a torch aloft. In the dim orange light, Thomas vaulted over high roots and dodged sinkholes in the ground. With the food, however meagre, in his stomach, he felt as though he could accomplish anything.

Looking over his shoulder, Thomas could see that he was quickly putting distance between himself and his pursuers. A sigh of relief escaped from between his lips as his feet continued to pound the ground and his rusting legs screamed out in opposition. *I will escape, and I will survive.* Thomas thought, looking around him at the ever darkening trees as the torch light continued to fade with distance behind him.

Off to his far left, another torch was bobbing through the trees and quickly gaining ground on him.

Another patrol of guards must have noticed him, and joined in the chase. They were travelling on an angle to cut him off. He needed to change his course. Immediately, he veered off to the right, hoping to improve his chances for escape.

As he ran through the trees, the second patrol closed in on him, and the first reappeared directly behind him. His exhausted muscles were winning out in their bid to prevent him from running any longer. They'd done enough for the night. The strength was ebbing out of him as he pushed to escape.

Glancing to his left, he nearly fainted. Running alongside Thomas Courser, a few trees over, was another Thomas Courser.

* * *

Oswell lost all confidence in his ability to perceive reality. Moments ago, he'd watched a second torch materialize out of the depths of the forest. His first thought was rather practical: *Who uses actual torches anymore?* The voices called at—no, commanded him to halt. Understanding what capture would mean, Oswell did no such thing.

But now, to top it off, as he glanced to his right, his heart stopped dead in his chest as he saw a mirror image of himself, running right alongside him. *This isn't real,* he began to think, before his stream of thought was cut off by the ground ceasing to exist beneath his feet. His legs flailed through the air as he soared through the darkness. He hit the ground hard and felt a body collide with his own. Oswell tumbled down the hill and finally came to a rest at the bottom of a deep ravine, unconscious. Covered in leaves and forest detritus, he was invisible to the world.

The four guards stopped at the edge of the ravine and looked down. The torches failed to penetrate the depths.

"What do we do?" one guard asked.

"I'm not going down there," the second guard replied.

"Send Shaw down there," a third suggested.

"Why me?" Shaw asked.

"You're the grunt." the first guard replied.

"So are you!" Shaw argued.

"You're the smallest, now get down there before I beat you to death!" the third guard commanded. "Are you afraid of a child?"

"No..." Shaw countered piteously. Shaw heard what the boy had done to Franklin Twain; slashed his neck with a wooden board so deep his head had nearly come off, or so they said. *Yes,* Shaw decided to himself, *I am afraid of the boy, and rightly so.* He grimaced, took a torch, and descended carefully into the ravine.

"Don't let him slit your throat!" the second guard cackled. The first guard chuckled heartily.

A few minutes later, Shaw sighed in relief at the bottom of the gully. He was slightly ruffled, having stumbled three times on the way down and nearly burned himself up in the process. Looking around, he couldn't see anything, even with the torch held high. He stomped through the leaves at the bottom of the hill, failing to find any trace of the fugitive. He turned around and called up the slope.

"He's gone!"

"Get up here then!" one of the guards called.

Shaw took one last look around and, still seeing nothing, shrugged and began to make his way back up the hill. This time, he only fell twice.

Chapter Eleven

RESONANCE

Thomas regained consciousness violently. He didn't wait to gather his senses; like a newborn calf, he stood up artlessly and ran. Without his feet properly beneath him, he stumbled and crumpled to the ground. He wasted no time picking himself up and bolted.

Somehow, the world had been set off balance. The forest seemed to slant back and forth as if the world had decided it was flat after all, and rested precariously on a fulcrum.

Thomas spun off a tree and reeled from the collision, but managed to keep running. Voices echoed in his head. People called him by name, demanding him to stop. He dared not look backwards. It would only unsettle what little coordination he had remaining.

Colliding with another tree, Thomas crashed to the forest floor, unable, or perhaps unwilling to move. He cemented his eyes shut as the world continued to spin around him. The voices were getting louder. He would surely be caught.

Settling on this fate, Thomas took the last breaths he would breathe as a free man. The air was fresh, clean; so different from what he was used to. It expanded in his lungs and expelled itself through quivering lips. He would remember the feeling when they walked him to the gallows. He breathed in, and out. In, and out. In, and out. But no hands grasped him. No spears pierced his flesh. No cries of triumph filled his ears. He would not go out in a blaze of glory. A life of suffering, and Myr taunted him even as he dragged himself towards death. It wasn't fair!

"Get on with it!" he screamed, opening his eyes and flailing about wildly. His cry fell dead, dampened against the green and life around him.

The moment his surroundings came into focus, he recognized his solitude. The woods were silent, almost asleep. The sudden absence of all sound manifested itself as complete relief. Thomas would live. He was shocked by the solace he found in that realization. At least for now, he would live.

- *CHAPTER TWELVE* -

CAMOUFLAGE

A CHILL RAN through Oswell's body. It began in his toes, climbed up his spine, and finally nestled uncomfortably in his brain. He shivered wildly. His entire body ached, restricting his movement, and with all bearings lost, he had no idea where he was. Fear gripped him immediately as he realized that he couldn't see. Smothered in darkness, Oswell was blind.

A voice grumbled nearby as Oswell lay prone on the ground. He could barely make out what the voice was saying, but Oswell could tell that the man was angry. He stomped around as a child with a temper tantrum would. Oswell felt his desire to move melt away.

The scent of rotting leaves filled his nostrils, calming him in a way that only that particular scent could. It filled him with the forest; the forest in which he had had so many adventures and forged so many memories. Realization suddenly hit him and he remembered where he was.

Oswell was in the forest. He felt foolish for not recognizing it immediately. Oswell felt this knowledge calming him, though only slightly. He still could not move for fear of discovery. He wasn't going to be the kidnapper's next victim. In fact, he fully intended that the kidnapper become the victim of the police department. Oswell startled as a voice rang out through the nearly complete silence.

"He's nowhere to be found!"

Oswell stiffened; the man was trying to find him. *That's what the stomping is for...*

Another voice from far above echoed down towards his ears. "Get up here then!"

Oswell did his best not to breathe. He listened intently as the man grumbled about the others being ungrateful and terrible. *Who are the others?* Oswell thought. *How many kidnappers are there?*

Oswell remained in his prone position, completely unmoving as the grumbling voice finally faded away to nothing. The time for that to occur seemed to stretch on into infinity. Even when the voices became completely inaudible, Oswell stayed still. He wasn't going to take any unnecessary risks. The last one had been too close a call. He had good intentions, but his decision not to go for help was a foolish one. He couldn't dwell on that; he'd made his decision. He'd committed.

When at last he felt safe, Oswell rolled over onto his back and sat up. The moment his face broke through the dense patchwork quilt of mouldering leaves, he sucked in a deep breath. The air did little to satisfy him; it almost tasted... stale.

- Chapter Thirteen -

UNDERESTIMATED

BROWN EYES CLOUDED with doubt scanned the trees in search of a sign that the darkness adamantly refused to reveal. Every tree looked the same, though to him, they were strange and foreign. The ground beneath his feet, at least, felt the same, and the patches of sky visible through the canopy stretched on for eternity in the same way as before.

Thomas Courser did not want to admit it, but he was lost.

Listening carefully for any hint at the position of his pursuers, Thomas realized that he was surrounded by silence. Deafening silence. Sound did not travel far in the woods, but he expected to hear *something*. Anything really, except for the dreadful ringing in his ears of course. He reached up to assess a growing bump on the right side of his head, and winced as his fingers lightly brushed the raised bruise. At least his headache could be explained.

What could not be explained, however, was to where the guards had disappeared? Surely, they would not have forsaken their chase because he rolled down a hill. If he'd known it was that easy, he would've done it long ago. But no, the Fletcherian guards were tough, ruthless, and determined. It was their fault that he and Cicero had been able to escape in the first place, and it would be the skin on their backs that would be torn if the fugitives were not recaptured.

Remaining cautious, Thomas climbed back up the ravine in the direction he had come. It would be no use to continue on in the direction he had fled—he had to find Cicero. Luck would have it that Cicero, waking to solitude, would already have started to hunt down his wayward accomplice. By now though, it was quite clear that luck was not something to rely on, especially in the case of Thomas Courser.

Thomas expelled a deep huff of air as he finally crested the ravine. Looking down into the precipitous abyss, Thomas was struck by its depth. He was, in fact, lucky not to have killed himself in the fall. This thought heartened him.

Thomas took a moment to gather his bearings. The thrill of the chase had gripped him soundly and now the excitement of evasion filled him with anxiety-ridden anticipation. If only he could make it to the morning, or through the next hour, or the next minute, Thomas would feel as though he was one moment closer to achieving a feat that, days ago, he would have deemed impossible. Thomas didn't do impossible things; he did less than ordinary things. Things like starving, and getting punched in the stomach, and crying himself to sleep.

As a thoroughly disoriented escapee, Thomas set off through the labyrinth before him, if only to keep moving. In his mind, he was far more likely to find Cicero actively than to let his senior friend find him. And so the woods embraced him, welcoming him into their midst.

They seemed now, to be friendlier than they had ever been before. Not so towering. Not so ominous. When the branches grabbed him, it was a brush, not an assault. A feeling of calm swept over his body as he interpreted the silence around him as peace, instead of his original suspicions of lurking danger. Surprising optimism flooded his very being—the world seemed to have changed fundamentally. There was hope for him. There was possibility for him. There was a man standing stock still, looming in front of him.

Thomas's gut dropped out beneath him as his heart leaped up into his throat. This gave him the curious feeling of being much taller than he actually was. The idea that he was even remotely taller, however, did nothing to calm the fear that promptly grabbed him around the waist and jolted away every sense of peace that had momentarily comforted him.

Thomas turned to run.

"Do not run. I *will* catch you."

Thomas stopped in mid-turn and then slowly faced the enormous man before him.

"Good decision," the man said.

The man was dressed strangely, especially that he was not in a guard's uniform. "What do you want?" Thomas asked, attempting to mask the shaking in his voice. The man chuckled, mocking the facade.

"You think you're brave?" the man took a step forward. Thomas countered with a step backwards. "Look how you cower. You don't even stand like a man." Thomas made no reply, flinching instead as the monstrosity took another step forward. "You'll make a wonderful addition to my family."

"W-what family?" Thomas perked up at the word in spite of the malice lining the man's voice.

"My family. I am *Father*."

Thom's eyes widened. In all of his memory, he could never remember having a family. He had never even had friends—grey solitude and black hardship had been the colours of his life.

Perhaps this man meant no harm; perhaps he knew Cicero and was here to help them. Perhaps Thomas could finally belong to *something*.

The man stared at Thomas hungrily, sensing the indecision. "Yes, you wish to join my family, do you not?" The man took another step forward, making his face fully visible as he emerged from the shadows. Thomas was immediately able to see for himself that he wanted no part in what the man offered.

Although much of it was obscured by a well maintained beard, the man's face was disarmingly handsome. His smile beckoned, expressing care and concern. Beyond that friendly demeanour, what could be gleaned about this man's true intentions came from his eyes. Beady and black, they conveyed hate, violence, and undeniable insanity. Thom's fear coiled back around him, constricting him like a python.

It was clear that this man's family, if he had one at all, was not a happy one.

Thomas took another step back, stumbling over a root and collapsing backwards onto the ground.

"Second thoughts?" Father lunged forward and hefted Thomas into the air with little effort. The man's strength emanated outward, suffocating Thomas. Not knowing what else to do and with the exhaustion of his midnight run, he went limp.

"You submit after all!" Fanaticism illuminated the man's eyes as Thom's flaccid, emaciated body hung motionless in the air. "We'll make a man out of you yet!"

Father's rough hands chafed under Thom's armpits. The man had to be immensely strong in order to hold him in the air as he did. Thomas was not a heavy young man, but there were limits on how light a fourteen year old boy could be.

The grip tightened his already-too-small prisoner's garb. Feeling an unfamiliar form tucked into his waistband, Thomas remembered and reacted. With speed, he unsheathed his stolen dagger. Before the man could counter, a scream of pain pierced through the chilling silence of the forest. The knife extended straight through Father's forearm. Blood drained from the wound like a stream of wine to quench the forest floor. His grip failed and Thomas dropped.

Thom's feet hit the ground and he rolled. He didn't look back as he gained his footing and dashed off through the woods. Thomas could hear groans of agony accompanied by unfamiliar curses. Despite the wound, the man gave chase.

Arms up to protect his face, Thomas ran blindly and haphazardly through the trees. The sounds of pursuit faded quickly, but Thomas did not slow down. His body, apparently, had gotten used to running in the past few hours.

He ran for what seemed like an age. The trees passed by in slow motion whilst his breath came in rapid and ragged spurts. Thom descended into a state of complete concentration. His fear subsided, having been replaced with the singular goal of survival. *I will escape. I will live.*

Thomas's surroundings changed abruptly. He broke the tree line and darted into an endless, narrow corridor between tracts of trees. His feet slowed down as the ground beneath him changed. He crouched down to examine the development.

The surface beneath his feet was hard and rough It was like stone, but perfectly flat... impossibly flat. The stone was continuous and enormous. It was black, but seemed to be painted. Thomas made his way over to a yellow line near the centre of the surface, running his fingers over it. It was smoother there.

"What in the name of Myr is this?" Thomas said. He stood back up and stared off into the perpetual distance, feeling lost in its vastness. The strip of black stretched on for as far as his eyes could see.

The trees on either side of him lightened from black to the darkest of greens. Before his eyes, the green became more and more pronounced. Thomas could not comprehend why, or how.

Behind him, a humming became louder by the second. Thomas turned to detect the source and immediately shielded his eyes. Approaching him at an incomprehensible speed were two round lights. He stood motionless, shocked into a stupor.

In those moments of hesitation, he lost his opportunity. The lights had gotten too close.

- CHAPTER FOURTEEN -

SORCERY

Sitting motionless on the forest floor, the world spun around him as if to make up for his inaction. A high pitched ringing toned subtly in his ears as he watched the treetops high above him revolve like a distant carousel. Oswell Wallace could not make heads or tails as to what had happened. He was just happy that he had not been captured and unaware of how close he'd come to death.

Oswell was bewildered. It certainly wasn't every day that one ran from a kidnapper through a midnight forest alongside a mirror image of oneself, only to tumble down a ravine and plunge into unconsciousness.

As the shock of his fall subsided, Oswell slowly gathered his balance. First, he pulled himself up onto his knees, and then stood up carefully. He was bathed in darkness—his only light was a slender beam of moonlight penetrating a gap in the trees above.

He checked himself over, finding he had suffered no injury save the emerging bump on his head. In his exploration, he also recognized that he had somehow misplaced his flashlight.

Cursing his luck, he fell back to his hands and knees and rifled through the leaves and detritus of the forest floor.

Gone were any reservations about getting dirty—his first priority was to shed light on his situation—both literally and figuratively.

A few frantic moments later, Oswell's probing fingers wrapped around the cold metal hull of his flashlight. He crossed himself and flicked it on. The beam illuminated his surroundings clearly as the white fluorescence of the bulb electrified.

On either side of him were abrupt slopes climbing off into the forest above. He had never explored the forest beyond the highway, and therefore, was completely dumbstruck by the depth of the ravine. Having lost his sense of direction in the fall, he was forced to choose between a few decisions: one, shut off the light, hide, and wait for morning; two, go up the ravine in front of him; three, go up the ravine behind him; four, cry.

Oswell didn't like the inaction of the last choices, and the first choice also wasn't proactive enough. Not only that, but there was no reason for the man (or group of men) that had been looking for him, to stop looking for him. So by simple deductive reasoning, one would assume that Oswell really only had to make a decision between two options. By that token, both options seemed to be equally promising (in that Oswell could not find the difference between the hill in front of him and the hill behind him), so his decision would be one of pure intuition, at which point it would not really be a decision at all.

With that in mind, Oswell decided that it would be best to put his best foot forward, and as that would carry him up the hill before him, he had his bearing.

The hill was steep and rutted; Oswell weaved in and out and up and over countless obstacles. Sinkholes grabbed at his ankles while roots that formed handholds before him tripped him below. On more than one occasion, he nearly toppled back down the hill, saved only by a lucky grasp or a rock that didn't given way. His trek was simplified marginally by his flashlight, but he was nevertheless breathless as he made it to the top of the hill. There, he doubled over and rested his hands on his knees. He didn't like to admit to it, and he wouldn't out loud, but he was out of shape.

When he felt that he'd rested long enough, he scanned the phalanx of trees surrounding him. The flashlight effectively created a tiny patch of artificial daylight wherever it was pointed. Confident in his powerful ally, Oswell began to pick his way through the trees carefully.

With the help of his flashlight, he managed to avoid the protruding branches and concealed roots that seemed to exist purely with the intention of slowing him. He began to feel the edges of worry and fear that had been gnawing at his insides for the past half hour or so, disappear.

"By Myr!" a young guard whispered, "What is that?" The rookie guardsman spotted a bouncing white orb of light off in the distance. It faded in and out, changed shapes and moved up and down in its continual progress forward.

"How'm I s'posed to know?" an older guard grunted back before he'd even glanced in the direction of the glowing orb.

A third guard stopped and examined the light. It seemed to be carrying on completely unaware of its three new observers.

"Sorcery!" the third guard decided, "We've gotta get outta here!"

"We're not goin' nowhere," the oldest guard grunted, "We've gotta investigate."

"I'm not going!" the rookie said, before he could be told to. The older guard looked at the third guard expectantly.

"I'm not going!" the third guard replied. The older guard sighed in disgust at the cowardice of his two companions.

"It's probably a trick of the eye!" the oldest guard grumbled. "I'll check it out, you gutless cowards."

The senior guard set off through the woods in the direction of the bouncing light. He picked his way carefully—if the light was in fact the work of a forest sorceress, he could be in for some real trouble. As a precautionary measure, he loosened his sword in its scabbard and rested his hand on the hilt.

As he crept quietly through the trees, he gained ground on the bobbing light source. By now, his two companions were well removed from his position, and the senior guard felt a bite of wariness grip him.

In the darkness of the forest, the guard couldn't believe his eyes as he silently came within a stone's throw of his prey. A twig snapped beneath his foot and then everything went white.

Oswell heard a snap of a branch behind him and whirled to identify the source. His flashlight whipped around to expose an armoured man bathed in brilliant white light standing with his arms up to shield his blinded eyes. Oswell took the opportunity to do what he did best.

Switching off his flashlight to conceal his position, Oswell dashed through the trees he could barely see and ignored any sense of physical self-preservation other than to simply escape.

He could feel the branches grabbing at his clothes and scratching at his face and arms. He tumbled to the ground, tripping over a root, but managed to roll and recover his escape.

He could hear the damning cries of his newly acquired pursuer, and recognized that two other voices had joined in the chase. Oswell felt a terrible sense of helplessness wash over his body—he'd escaped his pursuers once already. How many more times would he be able to pull that off?

The three hunters were gaining on him. Exhaustion was beginning to grip him, and Oswell could tell that he would not evade his trackers for much longer.

At the very moment he felt as though he would collapse, he did, crumbling to the ground in a piteous pile. A powerful grip gathered him underneath his armpits and Oswell knew it was over. He'd been caught.

- CHAPTER FIFTEEN -

DISORIENTED

A LOUD SCREECH pierced the night as the lights slowed and swerved around Thomas. Thomas stood in the centre of it all, unmoving and dumbfounded. An enormous creature, the source of the lights, skidded past him and came to rest a short distance away.

Another light switched on inside the creature, and Thomas cowered in fear. He could not understand how this night could possibly become any more supernatural.

From within the beast, (a carriage?) a man emerged. The man ran around the front of the carriage, and dashed up to Thomas with his hands up. Thomas didn't move as the man put them on his shoulders.

"What are you doing out here?" the man asked, shaking him gently. "What are you—it's three o' clock in the morning for God's sake!"

Thomas was faced with a decision: fight or flight. The urge to fight gripped him but the lack of power in his limbs, and the absence of the knife he'd plunged into Father's arm placed fighting squarely out of the picture. Thomas had but one choice: run.

Thomas shouted unintelligibly and shoved the man away from him. He darted off toward the forest once again. The man cried out in surprise as he stumbled backward and watched the teenager disappear into the brush.

Thomas did not know where he was going. His eyes were of no use. They were still blinded by the bright lights behind him, so the best they could do was probe futilely into the oncoming darkness.

Behind him, Thomas could (wonderfully) not detect any indication of pursuit. In moments, he was alone in the forest once more. He slowed to a jog and finally to a cautious walk. The forest was silent save his breathing—he had escaped.

Crumpling to the ground and leaning against a tree, Thomas sighed in relief and rolled his head back, knocking it on the rough bark. *Sleep,* he thought to himself, and with that, he did.

- CHAPTER SIXTEEN -

HIDE AND SEEK

HE STRUGGLED HARD against his captor, wriggling violently beneath the grip of his enemy. Oswell was smothered beneath the weight and wiry strength of another man enshrouded in darkness.

"Let me go!" Oswell growled. The words were barely able to escape his mouth. The earthy taste of soil coated his lips, his face pressed into the ground.

"Be quiet!" a struggling voice above him demanded.

"Who the... hell do you... think you... are?" Oswell fought to free his mouth from the suffocating forest floor to speak.

"Who? It's me! Silence, unless you wish to be caught!"

Oswell stopped fighting. He wasn't being taken anywhere, he was being hidden. He tried to relax.

Lying on top of him, he could feel the warmth and heavy breathing of the man concealing him. His unwashed stench permeated the air. Reaching up, Oswell could feel the rough branches of low underbrush. Oswell withdrew his hand as he was pricked by a sharp thorn.

"Who are you?" Oswell whispered.

"Silence," the man hissed. Oswell obeyed and stayed still, scarcely drawing a breath and only listening.

Moments later, feet thundered past the bush within inches of his face. At that instant, Oswell was sure that he had ceased to breathe altogether. When the sounds of the men trailed off into the distance, Oswell squirmed out from underneath his saviour and rolled away.

"Wait—" his protector warned. About to stand up, Oswell felt the man reach out and drag him back in.

A branch snapped as Oswell fell back to the ground, and Oswell immediately noticed what the other man had already perceived. They were not alone.

Rough and calloused hands brushed aside the thorny branches of the bush, reaching out for Oswell. They scrabbled on his skin, scratching him—the terror returned. Somehow, Oswell's saviour came to the rescue once again, grabbing the attacker's ankles and yanking his feet out from underneath him. The aggressor fell to the ground, striking his head against a tree root. The sound it made was awfully wet. In moments, Oswell's protector, an older man, was upon him, strangling the final breaths out of the man.

Oswell watched in horror, amazed at his rescuer's lack of hesitation. He'd never seen a man die before. He looked away as the life faded from the strangled man's eyes.

"Boy! You must listen and do as I say," the older man whispered.

"Boy?" Oswell replied. "Who do you think you are?"

"Who am I?" the man asked, "Have you lost your mind? And have you no respect for the man who has saved your life once again?"

Oswell stared at the man, a mixture of mystification and resentment combining in his expression. "I've never met you before in my life!" Oswell said.

"You have lost it then, Thomas. I thought you were stronger than that. You certainly seemed to be."

"Thomas? Who... who's Thomas?"

"You are," the man replied.

"I'm not Thomas, who are you?"

"Cicero!" the man hissed. "Do you not remember our escape?"

"*Our* escape? I've never met you before old m—Cicero—I've been running all night on my own, thank you very much." Oswell stared defiantly up at the man before him as Cicero wondered at the unprompted rudeness of his young friend.

Cicero stopped and examined the young man before him. He had changed; his face fuller. Somehow he had found new clothes, clothes unlike anything Cicero had seen before. The boy wore a long sleeved shirt and brown pants with countless pockets on them. His garb was fashioned perfectly, and his boots seemed to be sturdy and equally well constructed. Not only had Cicero never *seen* an outfit of such manufacture, he had also never heard of such.

Abruptly, Cicero went rigid, all amazement at Oswell's clothing forgotten. Oswell listened and stiffened as well—more people were approaching.

Cicero sprang into action, dragging the lifeless man's body beneath the thorn bush, and promptly joining the body there. "Come," Cicero hissed.

This time, Oswell did not hesitate. He dropped to the ground and rolled underneath the bush, coming to a stop beside the still warm body of the dead man. He found himself looking into bloodshot and unmoving eyes. Shuddering, Oswell closed his eyes and held his breath as another patrol padded slowly through the forest.

"'As anyone seen Wilkins?" a far off voice asked.

"Negative," a sharp voice replied.

"Probly off pissin' out the last of his evening at Alistair's," a man chuckled, drawing a few laughs from the others.

"He was drunk?" the sharp voice asked.

"Jonas marshalled everyone to rank for this one. 'Twas Wilkin's night off, so yeah, he's bound to be drunk." A few more chuckles issued at this comment.

"He'll find 'is way back in the morn' no doubt."

"Enough jabbering," the sharp voice commanded. "Jonas will tear the hide out of each and every one of us if we don't find that old man."

The other men replied, "Yes syr," and assumed silence.

Oswell lay quietly beside Wilkins's corpse, holding his breath. *Where did all these men come from?* Oswell had entered the forest that night with the belief that if he were to find anybody, he would find one man—not dozens. And what was all this about the old man being a prisoner? As far as Oswell had been able to deduce from the five o' clock news (the one thing his mother let him watch while he was serving his jail time), there was not a manhunt on for a senior citizen. Was his saviour actually a wanted criminal?

The sounds of the patrol faded off into the distance. Beside him, Wilkins's body was still warm. A chill ran down Oswell's spine as thoughts raced through his mind. *How did this happen? I can't be a part of this... I'm an accomplice to murder...*

"Screw this," he whispered. He rolled away from Wilkins and Cicero and dashed off in the opposite direction of the guards. He ignored Cicero, who called after him and started to follow.

Just get away, Oswell thought. *Just get away*. It became a mantra in his head as he crashed through the trees. He ran for as long as he could, falling into an incorruptible rhythm. He wasn't fast, but he didn't stop. He felt like a marathon runner. The trees started to thin and he could sense that he was nearly free of the deep. When finally he saw the sky brightening ahead of him, he knew he'd made it out.

Standing on the edge of the forest, Oswell looked out at the colourless landscape before him. It was nearly morning, and still Oswell Wallace did not know where he was.

CHAPTER SEVENTEEN

MORNING BREAKS

T HE FIRST RAYS of morning light flickered across Thomas's eyelids. He stirred from his shallow slumber. Light sleeping was a practice that had evolved over the past few solitary years on the road. A deep sleep could, and often did, drop you into a bad situation. Nothing was worse than waking up to find that you'd been robbed blind, or Thomas's least favourite, to find yourself surrounded by a gang of thieves looking to do just that, and worse.

The high trill of birdsong jolted him out of his dream world and back into reality. Disoriented, Thomas climbed to his feet and shook the cobwebs from the depths of his brain. Memories of the night before came rushing back to him as his mind cleared itself from the lethargic fog. He could not comprehend how his life had evolved to chaos so rapidly. One moment things had been going practically swimmingly; of course, he'd been hungry, and he'd been homeless for months, but things had been passable… now he was a wanted fugitive, a thief, and a murderer. He was lost, and once again, he was alone. The only difference between the past and the present was that the present included the constant reality that at any moment he could be caught, tried for larceny (the least of his concerns) and murder, and then surely put to death. This was a decided step backwards.

Thomas felt the panic rising in his stomach. It gripped him firmly around the waist and spread across his entire body. His hands began to shake. Within his chest, his heart pumped violently while his lungs drew quick and haggard breaths. Suddenly, his legs gave out beneath him and he collapsed back onto the forest floor. With the birds singing their sunrise sonata, Thomas Courser struggled to breathe as he lay in the dirt certain of his impending death.

Thomas was not inexperienced with anxiety attacks. In fact, he knew them well. He could not remember a time when he hadn't suffered from them. Thomas knew that the reaction was horribly maladaptive, and he knew that he shouldn't allow his mind to carry him to the point of intense, useless panic, but for all that knowing, he could do nothing about it. The only thing that had kept him going in the past few days had been Cicero's assurances and a steady flow of adrenaline. Now both were gone and the attacks had returned.

Five minutes later, his breathing slowed and the panic began to subside. His heart's rapid beating quit its palpitations and he managed to sit up. He was drained; the few hours of sleep he'd gotten through the night hadn't helped.

"Come on, get up," Thomas told himself, urging his legs to function. They twitched hopelessly. Lifting his arms, he reached down and began to massage his legs. He could feel the tightness in his muscles, and winced at the pain brought on by the intense exertion of the night before. Thomas wasn't used to this kind of immobility. He also wasn't used to running for half of the night.

After a few painful minutes of massage, he finally managed to regain his footing. The time had come for him to try to find Cicero. It was no use to stay put—he'd sooner be found by one of the countless town guards than by a single man. He began to walk.

He moved slowly, not really knowing where to go. He'd run through the darkness in fear and completely lost his sense of direction. Surrounding him were the motionless forest sentinels creating an endless labyrinth before him. With every turn and every step the forest remained seemingly unchanged. If he'd been lost the night before, he may as well have been on another planet that morning.

This forest goes on and on, Thomas thought as he forced his near life-less legs through another step. *And yet it ends*, he realized, as he breached the tree line and stared up the incline before him. His heart leapt up into his chest as he recognized the place —the strangest road he had ever seen. It was blacker than any ground he had seen before and made of a material he did not know. Thomas felt his fear growing as he took his first step onto the strange road. A noise in the sky drew his attention up and there, some sort of hovering bird buzzed in the sky far above him. He had to remind himself to breathe.

Suddenly, a commotion began. He stood stock still as a man dressed entirely in blue yelled out. Dozens of enormous carriages hewn from metal surrounded him. Others joined the blue-dressed man; some dressed in blue, others in black, and some in yellow. Two men and a woman ran towards him. He wanted to run, and he willed his legs to do so, but they would not obey him. For the umpteenth time in the past few days, Thomas collapsed, this time into the arms of a stranger.

Thomas did not panic, and he did not cry out. He lay motionless in the man's arms, somehow unafraid. This man did not wish to hurt him, this man wished to protect him. As Thomas looked up into the man-in-blue's eyes, he felt a wave of safety wash over him. He closed his eyes and exhaustion took over once again. One sentence was all he heard before he lapsed into unconsciousness.

"We've got him."

CHAPTER EIGHTEEN

LOST IN TRANSLATION

A LUMP LODGED itself unceremoniously in Oswell's throat. Tears started to well up in the corner of his eyes as he took in what just couldn't be. Maine was gone. The landscape before him consisted of rolling hills speckled with trees, discrete farmlands and huts, and one lone river stretching south around a bend and out of sight. All of this was bathed in a cold grey light. It could have been Maine, but the trees were so... big. And where had civilization gone? Last time he checked, cities and towns were not prone to migration, and he'd never considered his county as farm country.

"There aren't even..." Oswell mumbled, "not even any roads..."

He took a few tentative steps away from the trees behind him and shivered involuntarily. Kids got lost all the time, but he never thought he would be one of them. Everything had gone to hell so quickly. Oswell wrapped his arms around himself and took another few steps.

"Think, Oz, think." Oswell looked around. "What do you know?" He thought for a moment. "You went into the forest at night, and now it's morning. You were chasing the kidnapper, and you got lost. Mom and dad got home hours ago. They'll be looking for you—shit," he threw his arms up in the air. "They're going to be *so* pissed at me. God, what do I do?"

The river, he thought. Somewhere along the line, someone had told him that if he ever got lost, to just try to find a river and follow it. Rivers lead to civilization. Something also told him that when you were lost, you were supposed to hug a tree—stay put—but this forest didn't look very friendly. Besides, that was supposed to be if lost in a forest. He was out of the woods. It would be better to keep moving.

The river was only a short distance away. His exhausted legs carried him across the fields, trudging through tall grass. When he finally reached the river, he let out a sigh of relief before realizing how hungry he was.

"What I wouldn't do for a cheeseburger," he said to himself, patting his stomach. His feet ached in his boots and he was cold. The air had an unseasonable chill for the beginning of July. It was supposed to be warm and sunny. Warm at least. It felt more like fall.

"What's a cheeseburger?"

Oswell whipped around. Standing behind him, a basket on her hip, was a young woman, maybe a year older than him. She wore a long green skirt that disappeared into the tall grass bordering the flowing water. Her clothing was peculiar and unlike the clothes that most girls wore these days—they almost looked handmade. Her red hair was dishevelled as if she hadn't bothered to do anything with it that morning when she woke up. She smiled at Oswell with her green eyes as he took her in.

"Well?" she asked.

"It's a—it's a..." Oswell was struck by the realization that he'd never had to describe a cheeseburger before. "How do you not know what a cheeseburger is?"

"How does a person come to not know things?" she laughed. Oswell stood with his mouth hanging open. This only stood to intensify her laughter.

"It's a piece of meat with cheese on it, between two buns," Oswell finally decided. She nodded, as though it all made so much sense.

"What's your name cheeseburger-boy?" she asked.

"Oswell Wallace," he paused, feeling slightly uncomfortable, "What's your name?"

"Karyn," she replied. Oswell nodded, unsure of what to say. The silence dragged on for a moment, Karyn eyeing him curiously.

"Can you tell me where I am?" Oswell asked.

Karyn laughed again. "How can you not know where you are?" she asked.

Oswell stared at her for a moment. "How does a person come to not know things?" he cracked a grin.

She giggled. "The nearest village is Thane's Hollow... I can take you there, for a price."

"I don't have any money," Oswell replied, feeling woefully unprepared. He had never heard of Thane's Hollow, but it would have to do. His parents would only be a call away.

"I just wanted you to carry my basket," she replied, holding it out to him.

"Oh, okay," He grabbed hold of the handles and took it from her. He was surprised by how heavy it was. "What do you have in here?" Oswell asked.

"Apples." She looked at him plainly. "Follow me," she hiked up her skirt and started following the river. Oswell hurried after her.

"So, where'd you get the apples?" Oswell asked, he appraised the contents of the basket, unimpressed. The fruit were small, waxy-looking things.

"I picked them," she replied. Oswell felt his face warm up. He was bad at small talk, especially with girls.

"Right."

"You can stay for breakfast, if you like," Karyn said, "Since you're helping me bring the apples home."

"I don—"

"You don't have to," she offered quickly. She turned her face away from him. *Is she blushing?*

"Well, I need to call my parents first," Oswell tried to explain.

"Call..." she mused, "Where do they live?"

"Walloway."

"Never heard of it. Where is it?"

"I have no idea where I am, Karyn."

"Right," Karyn replied, giggling. "Maybe father will know where it is—but you'll probably want to stay for breakfast anyway, since you're hungry. I know all the towns that are less than seven days walk from here and Walloway is not one of them." Oswell shifted the basket onto his other hip. What did she mean by that? His parents wouldn't walk to pick him up. They would be worried sick. An idea struck him.

"You don't have a cell phone do you?"

"What's a *cell phone*?"

Oswell rolled his eyes. Had this girl been living under a rock?

"A portable telephone... for... calling people?"

Karyn stared blankly at him.

"You have a phone at home though, right?"

"I don't know what a phone *is*," she replied.

Oswell expelled a huff of air. *Who doesn't have a phone anymore?* "How much farther do we have to go?" Oswell asked, taking a different tack. Karyn seemed to welcome the change of subject.

"Not much longer now," she pointed down the river. "See," she said, indicating some smoke rising behind a stand of trees. "Come on!" she laughed, hurrying ahead.

What am I getting myself into? Oswell thought, hurrying to keep up with her. She led him around a bend in the river and along the edge of a farmer's field. Thane's Hollow came into view and Oswell stopped in his tracks.

Karyn noticed that he had stopped. "What are you waiting for?"

Thane's Hollow was a small collection of sturdily constructed stone buildings, each with a thatched roof. A barely defined dirt path ran down the middle of the tiny village.

"It's like... *Lord of the Rings*," Oswell mumbled. No power lines and no cars, but there was a horse tied out in front of one of the buildings. He wondered if he'd wandered into Amish country.

"Oswell, come on, you can ask my father where Walloway is," Karyn urged. Oswell shook himself from his reverie.

"Are you Amish?" he asked as he followed her down the dirt path into the tiny hamlet.

"I don't know what that is. Here," she said, grabbing the basket of apples from Oswell. She set the basket down next to the door of the modest dwelling.

"Father, I'm back. I found a boy!" Karyn called out as she entered the house, beckoning for him to follow. Oswell didn't like the way she announced his presence, but he followed her in nonetheless.

"I guess he's not home," she said, smiling. She turned around and surprised Oswell by planting a quick kiss on his lips. She blushed. Oswell mirrored the sentiment.

"What was that for?"

"I've never kissed a boy before," she said. Oswell had kissed Cindy Dobblestein when he was twelve, but that was it, and he hadn't learned much; Cindy wasn't a very good kisser. Since then, Cindy had gotten a lot more practice, Oswell had not.

"Well, thank you," Oswell said. Karyn smiled.

"Father must be visiting at Nellin's," she explained. "He should be back soon... want to kiss again?"

Oswell laughed. Karyn was pretty, but the prospect of her father coming back soon did not convince him that such a proposition was a safe one. "Maybe we shouldn't right now." Karyn frowned, but then perked up at a sound outside. "Father's home!" Oswell felt like he'd dodged a bullet.

A tall man opened the front door to the house and ducked inside. He looked at Karyn, standing so close to Oswell, and then turned his attention on the new face.

"Who are you?" he asked. Oswell could sense some hostility in his voice.

"Oswell Wallace, sir," Oswell replied, trying to be as polite as possible.

"I found him by the river," Karyn said. "He helped me carry the apples home."

"Found you by the river..." the man mused, his expression seemed to soften. "Reg Alderon," he extended his hand. Oswell shook his hand, feeling relieved. "Thanks for helping my daughter. What brings you to Thane's Hollow?"

"I- I'm lost. I'm trying to figure out where I am."

"How do you not know where you are?" Reg asked. Oswell glanced at Karyn and they both shared a smile.

"I got lost in the forest," he replied. "Do you know where Walloway is?"

"Walloway..." Reg mumbled, "Walloway, Walloway, Walloway. Nope, doesn't ring a bell."

Oswell frowned. "What's the nearest town?" he asked.

"Fletchery is the closest city," Reg said, "Only about a morning's walk." Oswell had never heard of Fletchery either.

"Any others?" Oswell asked.

"Lots to the south I suppose. Aiken's next down the river, much smaller'n Fletchery though. Maybe half a day by horse or barge."

By horse? This guy doesn't make any sense. Oswell looked pointedly at Karyn and figured it wouldn't be worth asking if they had a phone.

"I need some air," Oswell said. He pushed his way out the door and looked around. "Where the heck am I?" he asked himself again. Nothing made any sense. He'd found houses and people, but they weren't what he was looking for. He needed to get back home; he needed to tell everyone that the kidnapper was still around. He needed a cell phone, and a map. For God's sake, he'd steal a car and drive it home if there was one, and if he knew where to go.

Looking up and down the small dirt path running the length of Thane's Hollow, he spotted another man, seated atop a horse. The man was looking at him with narrowed eyes, as though he recognized him.

"Hey mister?" Oswell approached the man.

"Who are you?" the man asked.

"Oswell Wallace," he hadn't made so many introductions in a long time.

"You look familiar," the man said.

"Do you have a phone I could borrow?" Oswell asked.

"A what?"

Oswell shook his head, "Never mind." He watched as the man's eyes shifted.

"Do you want—" Oswell turned to see Karyn standing in the doorway of her home, she paused as she saw Oswell talking to the man. "Do you want some breakfast?"

Oswell looked up at the man and then back at Karyn. The man didn't look like he was going to be of any help.

"Yeah, that sounds great," Oswell said, his stomach growling at the prospect. He glanced back at the other man, "Hey, thanks anyway mister."

The man frowned, but nodded nonetheless. Oswell walked back over to Karyn and she let him into the house.

"What did he say?" Karyn asked, watching the man ride his horse out of the Hollow.

"Nothing really," Oswell replied, "That I looked familiar. Why? Who is he?"

"Nobody," Karyn said. Oswell cocked an eyebrow and she elaborated, "Jon Locker, just one of the Governyr's messengers. He comes through the Hollow every few weeks."

"First time we've seen Jon in a while," Reg said from his seat at the table. "He rode in this morning from Fletchery, said he was on his way to Orport."

"Going the wrong way then," Karyn mused.

"Hmmm?" Reg mumbled between bites. He motioned for Oswell to sit down and help himself to some bread and jam.

"He was heading back out Fletchery way," Karyn said.

"Odd," Reg agreed.

Chapter Nineteen

FAMILY TIES

H E DIDN'T KNOW what it was, but he didn't really care. He didn't care where he was, he didn't care what was happening, and he didn't care about what he was going to do next. In fact, all Thomas Courser really cared about was savouring the puffy and deliciously round morsel he'd just received.

It was sweet, it was moist, it was soft, and most importantly, it was filling. It was the third 'doughnut' Thomas had consumed in the past twenty minutes, and already he loved them dearly. That is, until he threw them up; all over the woman in blue who had offered them to him.

Too sweet, too much, too soon. He hadn't learned his lesson after the berries from the night before. Constable Sara Webber was not pleased. A man in white stampeded onto the scene and tossed the woman a towel.

"What have you been feeding him? Doughnuts!" the man said. "This boy is displaying classic signs of malnutrition. If he's eaten anything in the past few days, it hasn't been much. He can't be eating doughnuts!"

"I'm sorry, I didn't know!" Sara apologized.

"Are you okay Oswell?" the man asked, peering into Thom's eyes. Thomas merely nodded solemnly. "Sara, can you get him some soda crackers from the cafeteria?" the man asked, "He needs something light to settle his stomach. Clean yourself up first."

Sara nodded in the affirmative and left the room.

"Never leave a cop to take care of someone sick. It's my fault; I shouldn't have left at all. My name's Bryden and I'm the nurse who will be taking care of you until the doctor gets in. We've just called her."

Once again, Thomas was confused. First of all, he couldn't understand why everyone kept calling him Oswell. Second, he didn't understand the words 'cop,' and 'cafeteria,' let alone 'nurse' or 'doctor.' His perseveration on these words was broken as Bryden wiped the back of his hand with a wet, cold cloth. He scrubbed and then repeated the action a few more times until Thom's hand was spotless.

"I'm going to do some bloodwork and start an IV," he said, holding up a small contraption. Thomas shrugged and then regretted his consent as he felt the sharp needle puncture his skin. Thomas looked on in curiosity as blood drained through the hole into a sequence of tubes. He then cringed at the cold feeling in his hand as Bryden connected the 'IV' to a bag of water by way of a flexible tube, which washed away the blood in his line.

"Salty," Thomas remarked on the sensation in his mouth.

"Yeah, some people get that," Bryden chuckled.

Thom's curiosity refocused on Sara as she returned a few minutes later with an unopened rectangular package. She opened it and pulled out a few square wafers and handed them to Thomas. Suspicious this time, he sniffed them warily. Deciding they were safe, he took a tentative bite and then gobbled down the rest of the cracker before beginning another.

"Chill bro, not too fast with the crackers either; that's what got us into trouble in the first place," Bryden warned, grabbing the remaining crackers from Thom's hands and forcing him to eat them slowly. He munched the dry wafers, finding they reminded him of the hard tack he'd subsisted on for many a winter. These were better, salty, and not so difficult to chew. When he finished the handful, he was still hungry.

"Can I have some more?" Thomas asked hopefully.

"Sorry brother, we've got to start slow. We'll get you back up and running in no time," Thomas and Bryden both looked up as another woman, this one in a sterile white coat entered the room.

"And the fugitive is found!" the woman said. Thom's heart skipped a beat at the word, but the look on the woman's face defied the possibility that she was hunting him. "My name is Doctor Grosner, but you can call me Marie. How are you feeling?" she asked as she sat on the bed in which Thomas lay.

"Well," Thomas replied.

"Good, good… thanks Sara, Bryden, I just need some time with Oswell alone," Marie said. They both left the room. "Now, can you tell me a little bit about what happened to you?"

Thom decided it was not in his best interest to tell her about his escape from prison. He stared blankly back at her.

"Okay… can you tell me if anything hurts?" This question, he felt was safe to answer. He shook his head no.

"Good. Now, don't be afraid, it's not going to hurt, but I'm just going to check you over, okay? Make sure you're as healthy as you can be," Marie explained. Thomas settled and allowed her to perform her examination. Over the next ten minutes he was poked and prodded from every angle, but true to her word, none of it hurt him.

"Well this is all very interesting," Marie said to herself at the conclusion of the exam.

Thomas turned to see two adults barrel into the room, exhausted and terrified.

They were on him in seconds. The woman plastered kisses all over his face while the man gripped Thom's free hand, all but crushed the bones in it.

"Mr. and Mrs. Wallace!" the doctor greeted, seemingly unaffected by the adults' entrance.

"Is my baby okay?" Monica demanded, looking to Doctor Grosner for answers.

"Is everything all right Ozzie?" Owen asked Thomas.

Marie answered, while Thomas sat dumbfounded by the treatment he'd received from the strangers.

"There is some good news and some bad news. Unfortunately, there's more bad than good."

"What's happened?" Owen asked.

"It seems Oswell is malnourished, his body is completely exhausted, he appears to be in emotional shock, and he's showing signs of amnesia."

Monica burst into tears.

"Amnesia? How?" Owen demanded.

"Oswell seems to be having difficulty comprehending some aspects of language, and is generally confused. He also does not respond immediately when called by name, and claimed that his name is Thomas. He has a large bump on his forehead, but here is the unusual part—the bump is not significant enough to be causing these sorts of problems."

Thomas remained oblivious by choice to what was being said.

"My theory is that the memory loss may actually be due to acute shock. That's the good news; he may just need to calm down and he'll go back to normal."

Normal? Thomas thought, *nothing about this situation is normal. I'm in a building bigger and shinier than anything I've ever seen before, surrounded by people I don't know, and...* Thomas stopped thinking before he could descend into another panic attack. It was all too overwhelming.

"Well that's good then, isn't it?" Owen hoped.

"He's going to be fine?" Monica chimed in.

"I believe so. I think a good night's rest, and a healthy balanced meal will do him a lot of good, and put him on the right track. However, there is one other thing that doesn't quite add up: his malnutrition."

"He's malnourished?" Owen asked.

"He eats well at home," Monica started, then turning to Thomas, "Don't you Oswell?"

Thomas did not reply.

"Son?" Owen probed, putting his hand on Thomas's shoulder. "Did you hear your mother?"

With his eyes, Thomas followed the hand, up the arm, and into the face of the man that was speaking to him. *Son?* Thomas thought, *mother? These people think they're my parents...* Thomas turned to Monica and looked into her eyes. There, he found concern. *Does she care about me?* They truly believed that he was their son. He certainly saw elements of himself in their faces. His eyes and his hair matched Monica's perfectly, but he saw an older version of himself when he looked at Owen. Thomas shook his head, there was no way. His parents had died years and years ago. He was in some sort of a dream world. It couldn't be real—and yet, who was he to deny the first good dream he'd had in years?

"Yes, father. I eat well at home," he replied. Marie looked at Thomas skeptically, and then at his parents.

"I swear Doctor, I have no idea how this happened. He eats three meals a day. When we left for our dinner last night, he was perfectly healthy!" Owen started explaining.

"You don't think we—" Monica began, a look of horror spreading across her face.

"No, no, not at all; I had just thought maybe an eating disorder... I just think we should monitor his intake for the next few days. Make sure he gets back on track."

"Oh god, for a moment there, I thought that you thought..." Monica whimpered and began to cry again.

"Your family has been through enough lately, I'm certainly not going to add to the stress by making accusations I honestly do not think are true," Marie said. Monica stopped crying, though she still seemed to be on the brink. "Like I said, I think the best thing for Oswell is to get him home, let him get a good night of sleep and a good meal in the morning." Marie turned to Bryden, who had been waiting quietly since Owen and Monica had arrived. "Bryden, can you get everything ready for discharge? It's time for Oswell to go home."

"Home once the bolus is done?" Bryden asked.

Marie nodded.

Bryden agreed and then strode briskly from the room. Marie turned to Owen and Monica.

"Both of you should get some sleep too. I can see the stress in your faces."

"Thank you doctor," Owen and Monica said, slightly out of unison.

"You're very welcome. I'll give the three of you some private time, and I'll have Bryden call on you when everything is in order." With that, Marie cast a last long glance at Thomas, smiled warmly, and then turned and left the room.

"What were you *thinking* sneaking out of the house like that? At a time like this!" Monica cried.

"Honey, he doesn't need this right now. He needs rest, not your interrogation," Owen said.

Monica recoiled, looking wounded, but recovered quickly.

"Of course you're right. Baby, I'm just glad you're okay," Monica planted a soft kiss on Thomas's forehead, he felt the warmth spread out across his face and then through to his very core.

She lay down beside him on the bed, and Owen pulled up a chair and sat in front of him. Thomas smiled. For the first time in his memory, Thomas felt like he was part of a family, and this one *was* one he wanted to be a part of.

CHAPTER TWENTY

LET'S MAKE A DEAL

Oswell patted his stomach, satisfied with breakfast. The bread was gritty and natural and put his mother's whole wheat store-bought bread to shame. The jam was rich with freshness, but not too sweet; again, very natural. He had had no idea there was a Mennonite community so close to Walloway. Karyn beamed with pride as Reg revealed that she had made the jam and baked the bread.

"You liked it?" Karyn asked, resting her head in her hands.

"Yeah," Oswell smiled.

"She's a talent," Reg testified. He put his hand on her shoulder and she smiled at him.

"I learned from the best," Karyn said.

Reg nodded, "She was."

"Who?" Oswell asked.

"Mery, my mother," Karyn said, "She passed about a year ago now, flu took her."

"I'm sorry."

"It's all right, we're making it," Karyn put her hand on her father's where it rested on her shoulder. Reg smiled and nodded. "What did Jon have to say this morning?" she asked.

"He told me he was running a message to Governyr Killam in Orport," Reg said. Oswell recalled the messenger he'd spoken with that morning. "Something about two rebels escaped from the gaol in Fletchery."

Oswell's mind flashed to Cicero, the older man from the night before. He kept his mouth shut.

"They executed one of the guardsmen early this morning," Reg explained.

"Goodness Myr. Why?" Karyn asked.

"Jon said he was responsible for the escape—who knows what that means? Governyr Makkin sentenced him to death by disembowelment," Reg continued.

"What?" Oswell cut in. *Maine doesn't have the death penalty.*

"They killed him," Reg confirmed, "To set an example. Jon says it was pretty bad. Man's wife screamed when they put him down. Said Vorley laughed when he did it, and more when she screamed."

"That's sick," Karyn mumbled.

"Do you expect anything less? We've all heard the stories."

"What stories?" Oswell asked.

"Jonas Vorley's the governyr's man," Reg explained, "has him do all of his dirty work. They say he revels in it."

Oswell grimaced.

Reg took notice of Oswell's discomfort. "Didn't mean to put ya off; m'apologies," he seemed to think for a moment, "Tell us boy, what's your story?"

"Okay," Oswell stalled. The transition was forced, and he felt put on the spot, "Well, I'm from Walloway, and I just graduated from middle school, so I'm starting high school next year."

"High school?" Karyn asked. Oswell cocked his eyebrow again and frowned. This girl didn't know anything.

"What? You've never been to school?" Oswell asked.

"Schools are for the nobles, there aren't any for people like us," Karyn looked at her father.

"Who are you?" Reg worried that he had a noble's son in his home.

"Nobles? I'm not a noble." Oswell said and Reg visibly relaxed, though his confusion remained set on his face. "Seriously, what's going on?" Oswell demanded.

"Nothing is *going on*," Karyn replied. "How can you not know anything? It's like you were born this morning. There's only one school in all of Numyria, and certainly none around here, right daddy?" Karyn asked, and Reg nodded.

"...Numyria?" Oswell said.

"There's a school in Orport," Karyn continued to lecture, "There aren't enough noblemen in Fletchery to warrant one so they send them down south."

"What's Numryia?" Oswell asked again. Karyn threw up her arms in exasperation and Reg stood up. He retreated to a desk shoved against the wall and dragged out a rolled up piece of parchment. He spread it out on the table and placed his finger on a fading map.

"We're here," Reg said, pointing to a small mark on the map, "and this is, well, part of Numyria," he drew his finger around the map. Oswell couldn't recognize it. The map wasn't showing Maine, or anywhere in the States for that matter.

"You're playing a trick on me," Oswell whispered.

"No tricks," Reg said. "I swear."

"I've never seen a map like this before," Oswell said, scrutinizing it.

"You're not from here then," Reg said, "you Myrian?"

Oswell snorted.

"How did you get here?" Karyn whined.

"I don't know!" Oswell exploded. "I don't even know where *here* is! This—this place doesn't make any sense. Horses? *Seriously*? Horses."

"What else?" Karyn cried.

"Cars! Trucks, bicycles, planes! *Anything*!"

Karyn and Reg both stared at their guest. They hadn't a clue what he was talking about. Though they perfectly understood each other, it was like they were speaking in different languages. Oswell couldn't explain himself, and neither could they.

"God," Oswell grumbled, turning towards the door to leave. He'd wasted enough time already. He stopped as three sturdy knocks sounded at the door. Reg stood up and strode across the room. Oswell watched as Reg opened the door. Oswell's jaw dropped. Standing in the portal was Cicero Nagel.

"Thomas!"

"Thomas?" Karyn and Reg said in unison.

"Oswell," Oswell corrected everyone, annoyed.

"Thank Myr I found you," Cicero turned to Reg, "May I come in?" Reg stepped aside and Cicero strode into the room. "Thank you."

"You followed me here?" Oswell demanded. Cicero looked taken aback by the hostility. Karyn and Reg watched on silently.

"I couldn't let you just... walk away. Whether you like it or not, you're my responsibility now."

"I don't think so," Oswell replied.

"You *must* come with me. It isn't safe for you here."

"Why not?" Reg interjected.

"If he's caught, he'll be thrown back in the gaol," Cicero said, ignoring the importance of the answer.

"The gaol..." Reg mumbled. "What did you do?" he asked.

"Nothing!" Oswell cried. "Cicero, you're crazy. Karyn, I don't know this man."

"He knows you," Reg said.

"Thomas—" Cicero began.

"Oswell." Oswell interjected.

"Fine. Oswell. We really cannot waste any time. They will be looking for you. For us," Cicero grabbed Oswell by the arm.

"Get your hands off me!" Oswell shrugged away from Cicero. "I didn't do anything! *You* killed that man, remember? *Not* me!"

"Let us not forget the guard you murdered in the cell," Cicero said.

"Whoa, whoa, whoa," Reg said. "You two are... you two are the rebels..." Oswell and Cicero both looked at him. "Get out of my house. I don't need you bringing any trouble here."

"Father!" Karyn cried.

"Quiet Karyn, you heard the man. Your friend—he's a murderer."

"You believe him?" Oswell asked incredulously. "Do I look like I could kill someone?"

"I've seen younger do worse," Reg set his jaw. Oswell looked at Karyn. She averted her eyes. "*Out.*" Reg finalized.

"Please," Oswell moaned.

"Out!"

Cicero stepped out the front door as Reg pushed Oswell toward it. "And stay away from my daughter!" The door slammed shut and Oswell turned to look at Cicero.

"Look what you did," Oswell grumbled.

Cicero ignored the charge. "Oswell, you need to trust me."

"Why should I trust you?" Oswell asked.

"You saw those men last night. They wanted you. I *protected* you. Didn't I?"

Oswell glared at Cicero. Sure, he had protected him. "Who says they wanted *me,* and not *you*?" Oswell countered. Cicero sighed and gestured around him.

"Does any of this look normal to you?"

"...No."

"What makes you think you're fit to judge what is best for you? The Governyr's guardsmen are looking for two fugitives—Thomas Courser, and me—"

"I'm *not* Thomas Cours—"

"—but by Myr you look exactly like him," Cicero cut him off, "and those men will prosecute you with the exact same prejudice for that reason."

Oswell chewed on his lower lip, thinking hard. Nothing Cicero said made any sense to him. The only thing that seemed to lend any weight to Cicero's argument was the truth that Cicero had protected him, and that the guard had tried to attack him.

Other than that, Oswell had no other reason to believe what Cicero was saying. However, Oswell did not seem to have many options at the moment. He was still in the middle of nowhere, with no idea where to go. Sure, he could stay in Thane's Hollow, but where? He wasn't welcome with Karyn and Reg anymore, thanks to Cicero. If what Cicero was saying was true though, Oswell figured that he would much rather take his chances with Cicero than alone.

Cicero noted the look of doubt on Oswell's face. "Oswell. You will be safest with me; I can guarantee that, if only you will give me the chance to prove it to you."

Oswell stood in silence for a long time, sizing up the man. Cicero did not seem to lose any patience.

"Fine. I'll stick with you for now. What's the plan?"

Cicero furrowed his brow and looked off into the distance.

"We need to get out of here before those guardsmen arrive," Cicero pointed to a cluster of horses, a mile away barreling towards Thane's Hollow.

"You have to help me get back home when we get out of this mess," Oswell said.

"Agreed," Cicero nodded.

"My parents are going to be so pissed," Oswell moaned. They both turned and ran.

CHAPTER TWENTY-ONE

DREAMLAND

H E FLOATED AS if suspended within a cloud. It was an unusual sensation to feel such weightlessness. Not for the absence of gravity, but rather for what seemed to be the absence of a concrete existence. He could not feel his arms or legs, or any part of his body for that matter. Despite his intense desire to wiggle his toes, every ounce of his current understanding reminded him politely that, unfortunately, that was simply impossible. He could not see or hear or smell; he had no eyes, no ears, and no nose; and yet somehow he could feel. Even in the absolute extinction of his body, he knew that he was warm, that he was comfortable.

Is this what death is? All those years of pain and suffering... and I could have had this?

Thomas felt the non-existent hairs on his non-existent head rustle gently, as if they were being blown by the wind. Thom's perception began to change. From the roots of his hair, he could feel the sensation broaden, spreading down his face. The sensation made its way slowly across his body, tingling as the hair on his arms and legs stood at attention in harmony with their cousins on his head. Thomas was not weightless, and his physical existence had not ceased to be. Thomas opened his eyes.

Wrapped around him was the largest, softest blanket Thomas had ever seen, let alone used.

Beneath his head was a fluffy pillow that, combined with the comfortable mattress beneath his body, made his delusional perception of weightlessness perfectly reasonable.

A hand was interminably entwined in the locks of his golden hair. Thomas groggily gazed up at the loving face before him. In this world of excesses, she was one of the most beautiful women Thomas had seen in his short life, and she had his eyes.

Golden light filtered around and framed her face, which was illuminated in the warm morning glow. Her expression lent youth to the gentle lines on her face. Her soft gaze somehow penetrated into Thom's soul, but he did not fight it as her brown eyes set him at ease. A gentle smile formed on her two full lips.

No, this is better. This was worth the years...

Thomas watched in awe as the lips began to move, and stared for what seemed like hours as he floated through silence. He could not remember where he was, what he was doing, or who this beautiful woman was, but the fact of the matter was that he did not care in the slightest.

A look of concern flashed across her expression as her lips continued to move. The warm feeling flooded out of Thomas's body. He was no longer floating in silence, and although the woman above him remained beautiful, he could no longer believe that she was an angel. His fantasy faded and Thomas Courser returned to reality.

"Oswell honey, how are you feeling?" she asked. Thomas furrowed his brow in confusion, wondering for a moment why she had called him Oswell. As she repeated the question, his memory of the night before began to fill in the gaps that had opened up over night. Shortly thereafter, a faint pounding began to beat within his brain. It had not been a dream. Something had gone mad... whether it was him or the world, Thomas hadn't figured out yet.

"I feel fine," Thomas mumbled, rubbing his eyes sleepily.

"Oh good! You slept well?"

"*Very* well," Thomas corrected. They'd put him to bed as soon as they got back from the hospital that morning. It hadn't taken long for him to get to sleep, but he didn't know how long he'd been out.

"And your head? You... you know where you are?" she asked. Thomas had no clue where he was, but he was not looking forward to going back to the huge building he had occupied the night before. Thomas simply nodded the affirmative.

"Oh, my baby is all right!" she exclaimed, wrapping Thomas up in a tight embrace that betrayed her diminutive frame. Thomas failed to hug back, freezing at the word 'baby'. The fact that she thought Thomas was her child rushed back and assaulted Thom's mind, only adding to the pounding in his head. Thomas had spent his entire life —or at least as far as he could remember—on his own. Thomas did not have a mother or a father. He didn't have anyone.

"Monica, don't baby him! The boy needs his space," a man said as he entered the room.

"But Owen, he *is* my baby!" Monica cried.

"Look at him; he's turning red from embarrassment!"

"Actually, I can't breathe," Thomas gasped.

Monica cried out in surprise, relinquishing her constricting grip around Thom's neck and shoulders. He sighed in relief, reclining back onto the bed.

"Look what you've gone and done," Owen scolded.

"I just hugged him!" Monica defended herself.

"I'm fine!" Thomas cut in as he sat back up to examine his surroundings. The room was much larger than the cell he'd spent the last few days in. In fact, it surpassed every home he'd seen; even the furniture was unreal, as if crafted by the finest artisans.

There were a number of pieces scattered about the room and pressed up against the walls. Of the pieces, he recognized the bed on which he lay (which was grand in form; a nobleman's for certain), an unusual looking chair on tiny wheels, a bookshelf, and what looked like a wooden chest pressed up against the wall opposite the bed. Examining the other objects, he took his best guesses at their function, deciding that one piece was a wardrobe, and the other was some sort of glass work surface.

"That's my boy," Owen said, striding over and tousling Thom's hair. Thomas smiled broadly; the feeling of the man's rough hands on his scalp felt marvellous.

"You must be hungry," Monica guessed. She stood up and Owen also jumped to his feet. "The doctor said you needed a balanced breakfast." Thomas perked up at the mention of breakfast. If there was one thing Thomas understood, it was food. He had lost count of how many meals he'd missed. He thought back painfully to every time that he had glumly thought: *I just missed dinner.*

It was a far too common occurrence.

Thomas rolled out of the bed and touched his feet to the immaculately smooth wooden floor. He would have thought it was the deck of a ship, but there was a decided lack of motion to indicate buoyancy on the waves.

Breakfast hadn't usually been a luxury that Thomas could afford; he was always lucky if he was able to find himself a single meal by midday, or for dinner. Thomas did not plan to miss out on an opportunity like this.

"I'm very hungry," Thomas said, rubbing his belly for effect. Monica and Owen gave him enormous smiles in response. Owen opened up the bedroom door and urged him to move through it while Monica squeezed him lovingly on the shoulder and guided him out of the room.

The moment he'd stepped from the bedroom, Thomas had to dropped his jaw. Not only was the bedroom enormous, it wasn't the only room in the house. The house was more like a castle! Stretching out before him was a wide corridor terminating at a staircase.

At the bottom of the stairs, Thomas looked around. He was walking under his own power now, as Monica hurried ahead. Owen was walking at his side. He turned to look at Thomas.

"I hope you're hungry, your mother was up early preparing everything for your '*balanced*' breakfast." Owen gave Thomas a knowing look.

Not sure how else to respond, Thomas nodded absentmindedly as he admired his surroundings. There were many more pieces of furniture at the bottom of the stairs. Off to his left was a large wooden door. Thomas assumed it was the entryway. In front of him was a sitting area, and to his right was a room filled solely with chairs surrounding a long table.

At eight or nine years, Thomas had walked through the front hall of a Nobleman's house as he delivered some packages from the docks. It was probably the best job he'd ever had, if short-lived. The tips from the nobles defined a brief period of time when he'd been well fed and dry for a stretch of greater than a few months. That house has been the grandest he had ever seen. This house was grander, however, it was so *other* that Thomas could not fathom it existing in his world. Nothing was as it should have been.

Owen sat down at the table and urged Thomas to join him there. Thomas obliged, and sat down across from the man who believed he was his father. *Myr, even the chairs look wrong.*

It was at that moment that Thomas noticed the smell. Looking down at his pristine white plate and around the table, Thomas was perplexed to see there was no food around. After all, it smelled like there was a feast about to take place. Owen observed Thomas for a moment and then spoke.

"I'm going to help your mother; I'll be back in a tick."

"Okay..." Thomas replied, beginning to examine the plate and utensils in front of him.

He twirled the fork between the fingers of his left hand. He then grabbed the knife and did the same with the fingers of his right. Although he had heard of forks, knives, and spoons before, he had only ever used a spoon to eat with, and that was a rare occurrence. Thomas's normal utensils of choice—if one option constituted a choice—were his hands.

The fact of the matter was that Thomas rarely ate meals that required a spoon, let alone a fork or knife. Besides, forks and knives were for people with money. In the past, he'd occasionally lucked into a bowl of stew or porridge here and there. Those were sippers (though he did get to use a spoon once). Continuing to twirl the utensils, Thomas sat, happy with the prospect of a hot meal.

Owen chuckled as he came back into the room laden down with plates and trays. "Those aren't toys Oswell, you know that," he laughed heartily.

"Oh, I know, I'm sorry!" Thomas apologized, carefully placing the fork and knife precisely where he had found them. He was slightly embarrassed, but not so much to distract him from the plates piled high with food that had been set before him.

Monica came into the room carrying a large pitcher of some sort of orange liquid and another tray of food, which she promptly set down on the table. She brushed her hands off on her apron and looked at Thomas with an enormous smile on her face.

"The doctor recommended a balanced breakfast. I've interpreted 'balanced' to mean a little bit of everything..." she looked around, and then continued sheepishly, "I guess this looks like *a lot* of everything. I hope both of my men are hungry."

"I don't think you *know* how hungry I am!" Thomas exclaimed, his mouth watering with desire as he surveilled the newly arrived options.

Owen chortled and agreed.

"Well, dig in then!" Monica said. Owen began to dish food onto his own plate.

Thomas observed for a moment, and then began to dish the exact same things onto his plate.

Looking down at the now full plate in front of him, he felt warmth spread through his body once again. He had heard of many of the dishes before him, but he had never tried them.

There were slices of bacon and links of sausage. There were scrambled eggs and pieces of toasted bread. There was a bowl full of fresh fruit that Thomas could not even begin to identify, and another filled with steaming hashed potatoes. Altogether, it was certainly too much to eat. The pessimistic voice in the back of his mind began to nag. *You know this is too good to be true. You know it!*

Thomas ignored the voice and began to dig in. If it was too good to be true, he would enjoy it while he could.

"O.J.?" Monica offered, grabbing the enormous pitcher of orange liquid. Thomas nodded.

She promptly poured the 'O.J.' into the tall glass in front of Thomas.

"Thank you!" Thomas mumbled between bites.

Each bite was different, a new flavour to his mouth with every forkful. Thomas was mixing and matching; trying different combinations as he went. He tried bacon and eggs together, finding that they complimented each other perfectly. He then tried some fruit salad with some sausage, finding that they were best kept separate. When he'd completed a number of different combinations, he tried the 'O.J.' and beamed instantly. It was both sweet and sour with a delightful brightness to it.

Thomas took a break from the food—he'd learned his lesson twice last night and wanted to eat more slowly this time—and looked down the table at Monica. She was eating her food absentmindedly with her eyes on him. Their eyes met and she smiled at him, her expression full of love. A hot feeling blossomed in his face that quickly spread throughout the rest of his body. Monica giggled and turned to Owen. Owen stopped in mid-chew to figure out what was making his wife laugh. Deeming it less important than the food in front of him, he returned to his plate, munching busily.

Thomas averted his eyes and turned back to his plate. He'd put a good dent in the food that he'd dished himself, but there was still at least a third left. Already, he was full. Every survival instinct told him to keep eating; told him to get his fill because there was no telling when he would next get a meal.

He looked back at Monica, who had proceeded to ignore her food completely. She was simply gazing at Thomas. This time, Thomas locked eyes with her and didn't look away. It felt good, and it felt real. Thomas ignored the voice at the back of his mind once again. He was here to stay.

- *CHAPTER TWENTY-TWO* -

POLYTHEISM

O SWELL SHIVERED AS he plunged into the forest behind Cicero. It was the last place he wanted to go, but he didn't have any other choice.

"Wait!" Oswell cried, stopping just inside the tree line.

"What?" Cicero asked, skidding to a halt.

Oswell turned and looked back to Thane's Hollow. The horsemen had arrived and dismounted in the square of the tiny village.

"They're there for you," Cicero said.

Oswell looked up at Cicero. It had to be true. The messenger hadn't known that Cicero would also be there; therefore, they had to have been coming for him.

"You're right," Oswell mumbled. "But why? This doesn't make any sense."

"Of course it does," Cicero said, "You've forgotten who you are. The trauma of last night has affected you—"

"Not this again," Oswell groaned. "Why is it so important for me to be this Thomas Courser guy? He must've been something really special."

"Special? You're actually an ordinary boy, especially considering everything you've been through."

"What have I been through?" Oswell humoured him.

"You're an orphan."

"So… you think that I'm this orphan boy?"

"I think there is no doubt," Cicero maintained.

"No doubt *whatsoever*?" Oswell asked.

"None."

"Look at me Cicero," Oswell plucked at his shirt and pants. "Was Thomas wearing anything like this when you were together?"

"No…" Cicero mumbled.

"And I can't even begin to explain to you the words lost between Karyn and I. Do you know what a cheeseburger is?"

"A cheeseburger?"

"How about a telephone?"

"No, Thomas, I don't know what those are," Cicero said. "What *is* your point?"

"I'm not Thomas Courser."

For the first time, it looked as though Cicero was beginning to lose his patience. About to speak, he stopped and took a deep breath instead. Finally, he said, "Even if I accept that, it doesn't change anything for you."

"Well, it means we can get past what I already know, and get into what I don't: like where on God's green earth I am, and how I got here."

"God?" Cicero asked, transfixed by the word.

"You know, like, the creator, the almighty lord, he said there should be light, and there was. Don't tell me you've never been to church. I thought all old people went to church."

"This *God* you speak of is reminiscent of Myr. However, I have never heard of this '*God*' or '*church*'," Cicero pondered.

"Sure, he goes by many names. 'God,' and 'Allah,' then there's 'Buddha,' and 'Zeus' and a bunch of others I don't really know. 'Myr,' I guess. It all comes down to what you believe in."

The sheer volume of novel material Oswell was coming up with was unbelievable. It was too much for a simple boy like Thomas to conjure up. Oswell's claims were becoming more and more real, but what could that possibly mean? The gears in his mind began to turn.

"Oh God," Oswell shuddered, looking back at Thane's Hollow. He watched as a tall man was dragged forcefully from his home. "Reg!" Oswell cried, stepping away from the trees. Cicero grabbed him and reeled him in.

"There's nothing we can do," Cicero said. Oswell glared up at Cicero, and then looked back at Thane's Hollow.

"He's not going to lie to them Cicero, he'll tell them where we went," Oswell groaned.

"You're right," Cicero agreed. "We need to move. Come."

Oswell plunged deeper into the forest, following Cicero towards whatever the man had in store for him. Oswell didn't like the uncertainty, but he didn't have any other choice. The horsemen galloping towards them mandated a response.

Oswell slowed to a walk and fell into step beside Cicero. His legs were stiff from all the walking, and he was beginning to find the forest tiresome. They'd wandered well into the afternoon. *Why the forest anyway?* Oswell thought.

"So we're not going to hide out in the forest forever, right?" Oswell verbalized his concerns.

"Not forever..." Cicero replied.

"Well good, because I kind of planned to get on with my life eventually."

"In time my boy, in time."

"What do you mean in time? I want to go home, I don't want to wander around this forest with you, even if it isn't forever," Oswell complained. Oswell didn't like this forest; it was colder and darker than his forest. The trees were taller, more imposing and they had an almost greyish hue. Oswell wasn't sure if it was just the light, or if the colour had simply been leached out of them. The only familiar aspect was the smell. Slowly decomposing plant matter had a reasonably constant odour.

"Patience is the key, Oswell."

"I'm a teenager, we're not exactly well known for being patient."

"Myr will guide us in ways we cannot foresee. He clearly wishes to try you in one way or another. As to how long this trial must be endured, I am not certain."

"Well, whatever this Myr guy wants from me, I just want to get it over with."

"You will learn the virtues of patience."

"Yeah, patience, whatever..." Oswell grumbled. Cicero huffed. He had liked Thomas much better. Oswell folded his arms across his chest and the two walked in silence for a while. Cicero stopped occasionally, as if he was looking for something. Oswell attempted to ignore it in spite of his curiosity. *What is he looking for?*

"So what's the deal with this Governyr Macker?" Oswell asked.

"Deal?" Cicero replied.

"Yeah, what's his problem; his M.O., his drive? Why does he do what he does?"

"Ah, I see. Well, first of all, his name is Acer Makkin, not Macker," Cicero began.

"I say ta-may-toe, you say ta-maw-toe. Same difference," Oswell replied. This warranted another look of annoyance from Cicero, this time mixed with a hint of confusion.

"Well, Acer Makkin is the Governyr of Northern Numyria," Cicero continued.

"Yeah, I figured that out already," Oswell said.

"Do you want me to tell you anything at all?" Cicero asked. He was not used to being interrupted.

"Yes, sorry, go on. I'll shut up."

"Makkin was not always the Governyr of Northern Numyria. In order to understand how he came to power, you must understand the history of this world; the history of Myros."

Oswell nodded, saying nothing.

"I will not bore you with the ancient detail; that is for another day," Cicero began.

"Thank you?" Oswell replied. He didn't like the implication that he was going to have to hear the ancient detail, and even worse, that it would be for another day. He didn't want to go home next week, or tomorrow; he wanted to go home now.

"Our world, Myros, is composed of three continents. The first, and oldest, is the continent of Myria. The second was colonized centuries later by Lord Darin, a great explorer; it is where we stand now: Numyria."

"'*New*' Myria," Oswell smirked.

"Yes, Numyria," Cicero agreed. He continued, "The third is the desert wasteland of Narok. All of civilization originated in Myria, but in the age of great exploration, Numyria became a rich supply of resources and…" Cicero paused to think for a long moment, deciding how to proceed. "Greed was a great motivator. Many lesser peoples, my ancestors included, were subjugated into slavery to harvest the bounty of this land. Myria has ruled over Numyria ever since," Cicero paused to make sure Oswell was still following.

"I don't see how this all ties into Governyr Makkin," Oswell began, surprised to find himself absorbed in the story. The pair continued to walk between the trees.

"Patience…" Cicero lectured.

"Sorry, I'm listening." Oswell apologized.

"Now where was I?"

"Numyria: not so hot anymore."

"I said nothing of Numyria's climate," Cicero said.

"Numyria was ruled by Myria…" Oswell sighed. Remembering to avoid his figures of speech was going to be a challenge, but explaining everything he said was becoming tedious.

"Ah yes!" Cicero exclaimed. "Jump through eight hundred years of Numyrian oppression by the *mighty* Myrians and you can imagine that a great deal of turmoil might have been brewing. Despite its subjugation, Numyria became a proud nation with great ambitions, but her pride was never backed by successful rebellion, and even more importantly, it had never been supported by a strong leader. That is, until Saosin Hallows emerged to champion our cause."

"Never heard of him," Oswell said.

"Everyone knows his name now," Cicero said as he dropped to the forest floor and pressed his nose to the moist earth.

"What did he do?" Oswell asked, his interest piquing again.

"He rose up as a voice for our people. He worked diplomatically, forming relationships and alliances far beyond the scope of any common Numyrian before him. Saosin Hallows was no common Numyrian. This became even more evident when he was admitted as council into the court of King Hartlin, Myria's monarch. Shortly thereafter, he further proved that point when he broached the subject of Numyrian Independence."

"Numyrian Independence?" Oswell asked.

"Some eight-hundred years ago, the High Lord in Redefort declared Lord Darin's rule over Numyria illegitimate and subjugated the entire continent."

"I see..." Oswell replied, clearly not understanding. Cicero picked up on this.

"The Myrian government forced the Numyrian people to forsake their leadership, history, and independence. Before, we were poor, but the annexation relegated us to scum in their eyes... a lesser class of the 'superior' Myrian race." Cicero's voice was taking on an electric edge, getting agitated, "Myrians..." he grumbled bitterly. "This ushered in the '*Golden Era*'," sarcasm dripped from his words, "a time of great prosperity for anyone with a few stars to rub together—and the privilege of being Myrian. They say their success was because of their intellectual superiority," Cicero scowled. "They ignored the fact that their success was built on the sweat and blood of the Numyrian people."

Oswell stared at the man before him, surprised by Cicero's passion. Oswell waited expectantly for him to continue.

"When Saosin Hallows brought the issue of Numyrian Independence to the courts at Redefort, he was promptly ejected from the council. In the eyes of the Myrian people, he became a laughing stock; he'd proven himself no better than the low-bred Numyrian scum from which he had risen. However, in the eyes of the Numyrian people, he was the hero they so longed for.

"Hallows was no fool, and he recognized the power he had awakened in the spirit of Numyria. It was in that revelation that Saosin Hallows decided to attempt what had failed so many times in the past: a full-scale military rebellion."

Oswell stumbled over a tree root and nearly lost his footing. He wouldn't admit it (though the redness in his cheeks offered the truth), but he was engrossed in the story. When Cicero did not stop walking or talking, Oswell hurried to catch up in order to stick with the story.

"Over the next two years, Saosin mustered forces secretly on the Numyrian continent. He trained them hard, taking advantage of the strength borne out of their hard labour and honing that blunt weapon into a sharp edge. He called on his alliances to bolster his army's progress, and to keep it secret. Two years was all he needed. On the first of Padren, nearly fifteen years ago, Saosin Hallows began his assault on the nearest coast of Myria. By the following year, he had claimed the lands west of the Villars River, pushing King Hartlin from his seat of power in Redefort to his ancestral home in Harburn. By the end of the next year, he'd surrounded Harburn, and with it, extinguished the final vestiges of Myrian power. To say the least, it did not take long for them to surrender to Hallows's might. It was the end of the Golden Era as the Myrians knew it."

"Sounds like mission accomplished." Oswell decided.

"Not quite," Cicero replied.

"What happened?" Oswell asked.

"Hallows's Myrian friends came crawling back to pay homage to their new leader and promised full political and military support in future, just as Hallows predicted. The Myrians had grown soft in their decadence, and needed a strong leader. Everything had fallen into place for Saosin. Throughout his conquest, his army had grown from the short-numbered but fierce and well-trained Numyrian ranks, to every Myrian soldier that had surrendered and crossed over to Hallows's side. In the recognition of his ultimate power, he forsook the banner of Numyrian Independence, and declared a new age in his honour: the Saosin Era. He deposed every pillar of political or military power in the largest cities and towns of Myria and Numyria. He replaced those positions with allies of his own. One such ally was Acer Makkin."

Oswell looked around the forest. He struggled to comprehend the wealth of information he'd just received. It was a history lesson, but more like listening to someone read a fantasy novel. It was more than enough for him to even get a grasp on the idea that he was in another world, let alone a world with such extensive history and so recently rife with turmoil. There were so many details and so much to consider. In Oswell's mind, there was no way to explain how all of this had happened. There was no way to explain how he had gotten there, no way to explain how he had arrived as a fugitive, and no way to explain why Cicero was so willing to help him. No logical way, at least.

"This is too much," Oswell muttered.

"I know it is a lot to take in, but it's better that you know."

"Better that I know what? That I've completely lost my mind?"

"Not your mind. The more you know now, the better. It is impossible to know what the future holds for either of us. You need to be prepared for anything."

Well with all that information, I guess I'm as ready as I'll ever be, Oswell thought, scratching the back of his head with both hands.

Cicero brushed his hand against a tree, looking at a notch in the bark as a man would watch his lover from afar. He whistled three notes and Oswell watched on in surprise as a bird fluttered down from the branches above and landed on Cicero's outstretched fingers.

"What the..." Oswell whispered. Cicero leaned in close to the bird, nothing more than a slim pigeon, and then tossed it into the air. The bird spiralled upwards and then disappeared amongst the leaves.

"We're safe now," Cicero said, putting a hand on Oswell's shoulder. A rope ladder descended from the canopy. Cicero stepped aside, pulling Oswell with him. The ladder landed where they'd been standing. "I hope you aren't afraid of heights," he climbed onto the ladder and motioned for Oswell to do the same. He did.

CHAPTER TWENTY-THREE

DISCOVERY

THE YELLOWED GRASS stood tall and thick. Hiding within the grass, he was perfectly camouflaged. He picked his way carefully through his natural habitat, feet padding along without the faintest hint of a sound.

Ahead of him, the target remained completely oblivious. She stood in the open, a few feet from the edge of the tall grass, going about her business as usual. There was no reason to suspect anything out of the ordinary; certainly no reason to suspect that she was being watched. It was in this ability to surprise, and to strike with sudden, awe-inspiring force that he gained every advantage. He had the ability to take down his target and do with her what he wished.

Locked on and unblinking, his eyes glowed with the intensity of the hunt. His mouth watered as he imagined the lusciousness of his quarry. His muscles began to quiver in anticipation of the moment that was fast approaching. His stomach ached for its emptiness; it had been days since his last meal. Here, and now he would gorge himself on his target, on his prey. Simultaneously, he would satisfy his hunger and his need for the thrill of the hunt.

The time was upon him. The scent of his prey was powerful in his nostrils and his eagerness to pounce was overwhelming. He was close enough to make his move, and he did.

The Bengal tiger leapt from the grass, landing only inches away from the Chital deer it had been stalking; the chase began. The tiger was fast, but the deer could run longer. He had to make his move before the opportunity was lost. At the last possible moment, he leapt up onto the back of the deer and dragged it down with his powerful forelimbs. Within seconds, the Chital was finished; its windpipe crushed between the Bengal's unrelenting jaws.

Thomas looked on in amazement as the tiger began to drag its meal away to a safe location. He had never seen such a display in his entire life. The only reason that it was now possible was because of the magical screen before him.

It was some magical window into distant lands that could be opened and closed, and according to his adoptive parents, it was called a 'TV'. At first he had been hesitant to sit down as he'd previously had no clue what a television was. Now that he knew, he completely endorsed the decision to sit before the great window and watch what Owen called 'The Discovery Channel'.

Thomas was reclined on the couch (which was an interesting and very comfortable take on the simple wooden benches he had used before). His head was propped up by a pillow and his feet were stretched out towards Monica sitting at the left end of the couch. Owen sat in a recliner off to the right of the couch. Thomas was transfixed by the television and paid no notice to the fact that neither Monica nor Owen were enjoying the quality program along with him.

Instead, they were glancing furtively back and forth between each other and the ignorant Thomas.

The tiger on the television growled angrily at a smaller tiger that made its way onto the scene. It was looking for a piece of the meal. Wisely, the junior thought better of trying to steal and backed off. The larger tiger continued to gorge itself on the carcass.

Monica jumped as the phone rang. The tension in the room had gotten to her. Monica locked eyes with Owen as the phone rang a second time. He tossed his head in the direction of the kitchen, suggesting she take the call in private. She agreed silently, stood up, and left the room.

"Good breakfast huh?" Owen said.

"Yes, it was delicious," Thomas replied as he broke his focus on the television for a moment to answer. Even now, two hours later, his belly was wonderfully full. He had eaten plenty, and could not remember the last time he had been so satisfied. In fact, the only emotion he ever remembered feeling after a meal was disappointment.

Shortly after his breakfast, he'd been ushered into the bathroom and ordered to wash up.

It had taken him a couple of bewildered minutes to figure out how exactly he was meant to wash up. Eventually he managed to get the water running, suffered a painful encounter with scalding hot water, and finally managed to run a bath. He'd emerged from the bathroom half an hour later dripping and naked. Seeing this, Owen quickly ushered a be-towelled Thomas into Oswell's room and ordered him to get into a clean pair of clothes.

After much deliberation, Thomas finally settled on a pair of comfortable blue pants (which required a belt cinched tight to keep them from falling) and a short sleeved shirt (which hung off his lean frame). Now, he was simply glad to be able to relax for a little while, and that was exactly what he had done for the past half hour.

"Well, you know your mother, she never disappoints with breakfast!" Owen exclaimed, his voice disingenuously excited. Thomas cocked his head to the side as he perused Owen's facial expression; something unusual (even within the context of the wholly unusual experience) was happening, but Thomas couldn't figure out what it was.

"Yes, of course, she is rather consistent in the quality of her breakfast preparation," Thomas replied, deciding agreement was the most appropriate response. This time it was Owen's turn to be confused. The awkward atmosphere lasted only a moment, until it was displaced by Monica's hurried return to the room.

Monica jerked her head towards the kitchen. Owen understood her unspoken instruction and stood up to follow her into the other room. Thomas was left alone on the couch and so, naturally, turned back to the TV, which now showed a family of meerkats going about their day. It was less dramatic, but the tiny animals *were* adorable. Thomas zoned out, completely unaware of the conversation taking place in the next room.

"Who was it?" Owen asked impatiently.

"It was the police!" Monica whispered.

"What did they want?" he whispered back.

"They searched the forest that Ozzie came out of—"

"—and?"

"They… they found something."

"What did they find?" Owen asked. Monica sobbed and buried her face in Owen's chest.

"Oh God, please tell me they didn't find Claire and Nicholas."

"No, they didn't find them," Monica said apologetically as she realized what her incomplete explanation and crying had made her husband think.

"Well, what did they find then?"

"They found a knife," Monica began, "covered in blood."

Owen's jaw dropped, but he closed it quickly and began to shake his head in disagreement.

"But what does this have to do with us?" Owen pressed.

"They want to question Ozzie to see if he knows anything about it."

"Why would he know anything about it? He's a fourteen year old boy. Sure they have their faults, but they don't go around stabbing people!" Owen exclaimed. His hand slammed over his mouth as he tried to take back how loudly he had said that.

Out in the living room, Thomas rolled over onto his side, slid his arm underneath the pillow, and buried the side of his face back into it. Only a few minutes in and he was already smitten with the adorable meerkat family and the drama of their lives as it was narrated by a deep voiced gentleman. He paid no notice to the outburst in the kitchen.

"I don't know anything more than you do," Monica hushed, squeezing her husband's shoulders.

"I just don't understand how all of this ties in together."

"Well, if we take him in for questioning, maybe we can find out. He might have found something."

"Well, it doesn't seem like we have any other option, does it?" Owen concluded, looking perplexed.

"No, it doesn't," Monica agreed.

"Let's grab Oz and get this over with." Owen decided. Monica nodded once and followed her husband out of the kitchen and back into the living room where they found Thomas looking very comfortable on the couch.

"Son, we need to go," Owen said. Thomas looked away from the television and over at the two adults.

"Where are we going?" he asked.

"The police station," Owen explained.

"Is that where I was last night?" Thomas asked.

"No, you were at the hospital last night, remember?" Owen said, shooting a concerned look at Monica.

"Well, what do they want at this other place?" Thomas asked, glancing longingly back at the television. He didn't want to leave unless there was a good reason to.

"They want to ask you a few questions," Monica explained softly, "nothing serious though." Monica felt bad for the white lie, but she honestly didn't know if it was going to be serious or not.

Thomas debated with himself as to whether or not he should go. Owen picked up on the indecision.

"I'm sorry Oz, but this isn't really a choice kind of thing. If the police want to talk to you, we need to go and talk to them."

"Oh fine," Thomas said. He eased himself off the couch and stood up. Monica made for the door as Owen shut off the television. Owen placed a hand on Thomas's shoulder and guided him to the door.

It took another minute or so, and some worried looks exchanged between the two parents, but Thomas finally managed to tie his shoes (which was a pretty great accomplishment considering he had never tied shoelaces before) and they left the house.

Thomas perked up considerably after realizing he would get to ride in the great contraption once again. He sat with his head pressed up against the glass, watching things outside whiz by as they navigated to the police station. He didn't care how great horses were made out to be, these things were better than any horse he had ever heard of.

In the front seat, both of the parents were silent, and yet, they were both thinking the exact same thing:

What happened last night?

- CHAPTER TWENTY-FOUR -

THE ENCLAVE

OSWELL FALTERED, MISSING a rung on the ladder as it continued to rise. He was distracted by the sight above him. After passing through the initial canopy, he saw the underside of a wooden walkway. Hanging on for dear life, he closed his eyes as the ladder rose the last few feet.

"Give me your hand," a young voice commanded from above. Oswell grasped the hand gratefully and he was hoisted up onto a sturdy platform. His limbs continued to shake as he looked up at his saviour.

A tall young man, about seventeen years old, stood before him. He had long black hair and soft hazel eyes. He was grimacing as Oswell appraised him.

"You probably want to hit me, but I would advise against that because—" the teenager began. Cicero stood by, a playful smile on his face.

"Why would I want to hit you?" Oswell cut in.

"Don't you remember? I got you thrown in jail," the young man replied, wincing further at his admission of guilt.

"Huh?" Oswell started, but he quickly clued in. "Oh... so it was you who got Thomas, and by extension me, into all of this trouble." The look of complete confusion on the teenager's face was enough to make Oswell chuckle. He was feeling better now that his feet were on the sturdy walkway. He tried not to think about the fact that solid ground was well over a hundred feet below.

"What?" the young man asked.

"Let's start over properly," Oswell offered his hand to shake. "I'm Oswell Wallace, thanks for helping me up here."

"Oswell Wallace...?" Darius mused, still bewildered.

Oswell nodded.

"Darius," he said. "Darius Nagel," Oswell recognized the last name and glanced at Cicero.

"My grandson," Cicero said. Oswell nodded.

"So this is the Enclave?" Oswell stepped around Darius and took in the view. Darius made way, surprised at Oswell's audacity. Oswell wondered at the compound he'd been invited into. They were at least a hundred feet in the air and perched atop a catwalk built directly into the foliage of the trees. Oswell held onto the sturdy railings for support as he looked around.

There were a number of huts rising out of the tops of the trees; some were very short and others were impressively tall. Catwalks connected all of the buildings to each other. Aside from the overwhelming realization that an entire commune had been built above the forest canopy, Oswell found it extraordinary to look out at the leafy sea surrounding the man-made islands of buildings. If not for the grey sky above, which cast a pallor over everything, the sight would be impeccably beautiful.

"Yes, welcome to the Enclave, Oswell," Cicero said.

"This is amazing Cicero... how?" Oswell asked.

"A great deal of hard work, but as you can imagine, it is well worth it. Few know of this place, and none is more secure in the whole of Myros," Cicero said.

"We even have a fire prevention system that I've been working on; it's not fool proof, but every day it gets better," Darius piped up.

"Darius is quite the engineer," Cicero said. Darius beamed with pride, obviously valuing the attention of his grandfather.

Oswell approached the edge of the catwalk and peered down. Through a gap in the leaves he was barely able to see the ground far below him. The location of the safe haven was ingenious. Oswell was awe-struck. As a boy, he'd begged his father to build a tree house for him and his friends, but the dream had never materialized. Instead, Oswell searched for, and found replacements in the forest. He would burrow underneath the roots of large trees, or climb up into the thick supportive branches of others to find his own natural tree houses. The Enclave was like a childhood dream come true, but one that was beyond the broadest scope of his imagination. Recognizing this, Oswell felt another piece of the puzzle fall into place. It was becoming easier to believe that everything happening was real, because there was no way he could have imagined it all. The very unreality of it made an effective case for its reality.

"I want to see more..." Oswell said, still peering down through gaps in the leaves to the ground far beneath him.

"There will be time enough for a tour later," Cicero explained, "as for right now; there is much that you must learn."

"Grandfather is a great historian."

"I think I've already discovered that," Oswell agreed. Oswell turned back to Cicero, "What else is there to know?"

"I'm working on a theory right now that delves into something that I had nearly lost sight of, until you showed up that is," Cicero explained. Darius furrowed his brow as he tried to determine if he knew what Cicero was talking about.

"What do I have to do with your theory?" Oswell asked.

"Come, there is a great deal of material I need to show you," Cicero said. One could practically hear the gears grinding in Cicero's brain. Cicero turned on his heel and strode off in the direction of the largest building that Oswell could see. Oswell glanced over at Darius, and Darius locked eyes with him. They both shrugged simultaneously and hurried to catch up with the preoccupied elder. As Oswell followed, his gaze cast around, amazement filling him aside from the prickling realization that there was no one else in sight.

Darius pushed his way through the door that Cicero had disappeared through, not waiting for Oswell to catch up. Oswell entered the round building and did his best to put aside his amazement. He hurried after Darius and Cicero, both of whom had already made it halfway across the room.

Oswell examined the room as he caught up with the hurried pair. He ran his fingers along the grain of a huge round table in the middle of the room. The table could seat at least twenty around its perimeter and there was a break in the table where one could gain access to the centre of the room. A large observation gallery wrapped around the perimeter of the room, also serving as a modest second floor. Cicero and Darius were already on the gallery as Oswell mounted the spiral staircase.

Cicero climbed up a ladder, closely followed by Darius, and the two disappeared through a hatch in the ceiling. The building was much larger than Oswell had first anticipated. Oswell too climbed up the ladder and emerged through the hatch in the ceiling. He stood up inside a much smaller, but still circular room.

"Come, come, sit down," Cicero invited, "this will be a long story." He was hurrying back and forth between a large desk and a fully stocked bookcase.

Oswell took a seat in front of the desk, and Darius dragged a chair over from the corner of the room to sit down beside Oswell. Oswell noticed the bird from earlier, perched on a rail.

"Bartimaeus," Darius said, catching Oswell looking at the bird. "Grandfather trained him to come at a certain whistle. He can carry messages, but mostly, he just tells us when someone wants to come up here."

"Get a lot of visitors?" Oswell asked.

"Not really. Besides, you have to know the whistle."

Oswell smiled, "Just like a secret password."

"Exactly," Darius replied.

The young pair watched as Cicero rushed back and forth between the desk and bookcase. He grabbed three books, returned two of them, and then slammed the other one down on the desk. This went on for a few minutes. Oswell watched as the chosen stack grew taller. Cicero stood in front of the pile and flipped through each, tossing it aside if it did not suit his needs.

Cicero finally collapsed into his chair with one last tiny book, which he gently set down on the table next to the others. He breathed a long sigh, and closed his eyes.

Oswell and Darius patiently watched the man recuperate, and then he finally opened his eyes and narrowed them at Oswell.

"You said this would be a long story?" Oswell asked, "Looks like a *few* long stories."

"Yes, I have much to show you," Cicero agreed.

"Let's get to it then," Oswell said.

"Grandfather, what is it?" Darius asked, ever eager to learn. Cicero placed his hands on two of the larger tomes on his desk and leaned forward.

"Oswell, you have already learned much of our world's recent history. Do you remember all of the details?" Cicero probed.

"Numyrian oppression. Numyrian Independence movement fails. Some Saosin Hallows guy. Numyrian Independence suggested. No dice. Then Hallows started a war. He won, but Numyria got backstabbed by Hallows. Got it," Oswell rattled off the details. The other two men processed the flow of information, with momentary confusion, then simultaneously decided that he'd adequately followed the chain of historical events.

"You seem to have the gist of it," Cicero decided.

"Let's get to it then!" Oswell rubbed his hands together.

Cicero pulled one particularly thick book towards him and started flipping through the pages. He did so slowly as though he were checking things as he went, but at the same time, he seemed to know where he was going. Oswell and Darius watched impatiently as Cicero gradually made his way to the page that he was looking for. When he finally found it, he nodded, seeming to fight with himself over whether or not he should actually read it aloud.

Darius cleared his throat audibly and Cicero flinched. With that prompt, he finally spoke.

"It is an account of a young man's trial... I have more research to do on this particular point, it can wait," Cicero sighed thoughtfully and then closed the enormous book and shoved it off to the side. He brushed his hands off as though he were done with that line of thinking, and then scanned around the desk in front of him. His eyes lit up as he found what he was looking for and unfurled the scroll theatrically. "This was released to each of the town leaders in Myria and

Numyria," Cicero explained. He cleared his throat and began to read. "Fine citizens of Myria..."

"Notice there is no mention of Numyria," Darius whispered bitterly. Cicero nodded—the comment was pertinent—and then continued reading.

"It is on this day, the first of Numyren, in the first year of the Saosin Era, that I, King Marcel Hartlin, announce my official abdication as supreme leader of all Myrian people.

"Henceforth, the great Emperyr Saosin Hallows—whom has proven himself worthy—will guide the grand Myrian race into the future. He shall rule as he sees fit over all of Myria and Numyria. Allegiance must be pledged to our new leader, or else suffer the pain of death."

Darius rolled his eyes. Something told Oswell that this Saosin fellow was high on himself. Something also told him that a good many Numyrians were unwilling to make such a pledge.

Cicero continued on to the finish. "My signature signifies my abdication and full support of Saosin Hallows as our great new leader and Emperyr. Emperyr Saosin Hallows's signature signifies his acceptance of my abdication and his willingness to succeed me. In the name of Myr, we live, we love, and we die," Cicero looked up from the scroll and scowled. "Affixed are their signatures."

Darius looked sad, even though he scarcely could have been old enough to remember the event, let alone understand it. He clearly understood the ramifications now.

"That sounded like a total load," Oswell decided. Once again, he was met by silence. "Talk about scripted—there was so much ego stroking going on there. That makes me sick."

"Me as well," Darius agreed dramatically, in reference to the sick part, as he did not understand the rest of what Oswell had said. Cicero also nodded his agreement as he rolled up the scroll and set it aside. He set to work finding another scroll in the pile on his desk. When he located it, he pulled it towards him and unfurled it carefully.

"This document was circulated widely. Hallows wanted everyone to know exactly what his dominion would mean." Cicero read the scroll aloud:

"Ladies and gentlemen of the court at Redefort, it is on this day, the twenty-second of Myren in the second year of the Saosin Era, that I, Emperyr Saosin Hallows, present the structure of our new government—" Cicero paused and said as an aside, "Already, these once proud people of the court had become sheep," he shook his head as he continued to read, then summarized.

"Taxes on trade, more funding for his armed forces, and a complete ban on the holy worship of Myr."

"Sounds pretty run of the mill," Oswell said, "what politician doesn't raise taxes and spend more on defence."

"True enough," Cicero agreed.

"But this whole worship thing?"

"*That* was the barb," Cicero said. "What Hallows was declaring in this act changed every facet of our lives, even our faith."

"How can he steal your faith?" Oswell asked.

"He cannot," Darius replied, "but the Cult of Hallows is strong, they worship him as a god, and any accused of honouring Myr, the first god, is punished with death."

"Jesus," Oswell said. "How did he get away with all of this?"

"Notice the special reservation for his army? It was huge, and he kept them happy. He paid them more, taxed them less, and gave them power. They were probably the largest single body of Myrians to pledge their stalwart allegiance to Hallows."

"I guess he was thinking ahead," Oswell figured.

Cicero nodded. "Hallows understands the power of fear, and how to use it," he turned back to the scroll and read word-for-word. "The court at Redefort is now disbanded. All government matters will be handled by the Emperyr, Saosin Hallows, and his Upper Court. The Upper Court shall consist of seven individuals with four levels of authority. Of lowest authority shall be the Governyrs of Numyria whom are responsible for maintaining law and order within their territories of Numyria. Next, shall be the two Vicelords, whom are responsible for taxation and trade. Next, shall be the two Archlords, whom are responsible for military matters including diplomacy and law enforcement. Finally, the Emperyr is the end, representing all power. His word is law, and his rule is divine."

"Pretty serious stuff," Oswell observed.

"Very serious," Darius agreed.

Cicero nodded, "Their signatures are affixed, all seven of them," Cicero handed the scroll to Oswell carefully.

Oswell scanned down the list, reading each name. Only two stood out for him. Immediately, he recognized the name of Saosin Hallows at the bottom of the column. The other name was found at the very top.

"Acer Makkin—Governyr," Oswell whispered.

"Indeed," Cicero mused. Oswell continued to peruse the document, with Darius peering at it jealously from his chair. The silence carried for a few minutes as thoughts ran through Oswell's mind, and his understanding began to shift.

"So," Oswell finally said, "I think I understand the predicament your people are in, but…"

"You are wondering how you fit into all of this?" Cicero predicted, lacing his fingers together beneath his chin.

"Me too," Darius agreed, giving Oswell a doubtful look. Oswell successfully sequestered his disdain.

"The answer, I believe, lies here," Cicero speculated thoughtfully as he unearthed a thin leather bound book from the depths of the enormous pile. Darius's eyes locked on to the words on the cover of the manuscript. Oswell tried to read it. There were two words emblazoned in gold inlay.

"Or-ack-you-low... Vat-ah," Oswell sounded out.

Darius sniggered. Oswell ignored it.

"Oraculo Vata," Cicero confirmed.

"What is it?" Oswell asked.

"This is one of my most prized possessions," Cicero began, caressing the slender spine of the book. "It is a collection of prophecies made by the famed oracle Alvari Vata."

"Don't tell me you believe in fortune tellers," Oswell moaned.

"Vata was no fortune teller. He was gifted with the sacred sight. Many of his prophecies have come true," Cicero looked slightly hurt.

"But..." Oswell began incredulously.

"Do you have any reason not to believe? Have you not already seen things that extend far beyond what you believed to be possible?" Cicero paused for effect. "Everything in life does not reside within the black and the white. Much of what we cannot understand resides firmly within the grey. It is only with an open mind that we can hope to even begin to understand what does not present itself clearly."

Oswell flapped his mouth a few times in protest, but no words came in opposition to Cicero's passion. He was at a loss, and truthfully, he had nothing else to lose. He had already invested a great deal in attempting to believe that his experience on Myros was real. It really was not that much of a stretch to add one more thing to the list.

"Fine," he surrendered, "what does Alvari have to say?"

Cicero smiled and fingered carefully through the thin pages. Each page was home to half a dozen blocks of calligraphic text that Oswell was unable to read upside down. He doubted he would have been able to read them right side up either.

Cicero mumbled to himself as he searched through the pages. He apparently knew what he was looking for, but wasn't exactly sure where to find it. Oswell and Darius watched in anticipation as Cicero seemed to zero in on the correct block. When he had finally found it, he seemed to read it over silently in his head. Cicero nodded and looked up at Oswell and Darius.

"I've found it," he declared, turning the book around so that the two of them could read it. Both of the boys stared blankly at the complex calligraphy as Cicero watched on expectantly.

Darius made a show, nodding thoughtfully as though he understood, but Oswell was far more blunt and honest.

"I can't read it," he admitted, not embarrassed in the slightest.

"Oh, I should have known," Cicero apologized. "Darius, could you read it?"

"Uh, no..." Darius stammered, his face turning bright red. Oswell forced himself not to smile.

"I will read it then," Cicero decided. He flipped the book back around and pulled it closer to him. He leaned in close to the page and began to read.

"One will come, memory astray,
When darkness, death, and sin are found
In hallowed lands of black and grey.
Our world despairs, but hope's abound,
Salvation in a golden way."

Oswell was lost as Cicero set the book down on his desk and appraised Oswell. To Oswell's right, Darius' jaw was slack as he stared at Oswell in awe and disbelief. Taking note of this, Oswell glared at Darius exasperatedly.

"Is there something I'm missing?" Oswell demanded, looking back and forth between the grandson and grandfather. Sure, it was a nice poem, but Oswell had not managed to derive any meaning from it. Cicero did not speak; he simply locked eyes with Darius.

"You don't really think?" Darius argued, shaking his head vigorously. Once again, Cicero did not say a word; he merely continued to stare at Darius unflinchingly.

There was something in the expression on the older man's face that seemed to communicate far more than what words could easily say. However, if one were to paraphrase exactly what Cicero's gaze was communicating, one would say, "I believe it to be true."

Darius seemed to put up a silent fight, first with his grandfather, and then with himself.

After he'd failed miserably in defeating either of them, he seemed to deflate. His eyes closed and he began to mumble under his breath as though he were reasoning with himself. He finally opened his eyes and sized Oswell up. The young man had decided that the truth of it, if that's what it was, would be of greater benefit than it would be hindrance. Oswell was still completely in the dark. He squinted at Darius, waiting for an answer. Darius began to nod slowly. Oswell inclined his head to the side in order to compel Darius towards an answer.

"You, Oswell..." Darius said finally. He smiled reluctantly, and tousled Oswell's blonde hair. "A golden way! It seems you're meant to bring our salvation!"

CHAPTER TWENTY-FIVE

THE USUAL SUSPECTS

THOMAS SHUDDERED VIOLENTLY as he watched a man shove half of a doughnut into his gaping mouth. His recent experience with doughnuts had left an impression on him. He could feel his stomach roiling at the thought of eating even one more of those doughy and sugary morsels. The man, however, clearly had no qualms with them. He'd finished off his first and moved on to a second.

Thomas sat on a hard backed chair between his two adoptive parents. Owen fidgeted nervously on his right while Monica sat stock still on Thomas's left. Thomas played with the belt loops on his blue jeans as he continued to observe the rotund police officer.

A voice rang out through a speaker box above Thomas's head. Thomas was too shocked by the existence of the non-corporeal voice to notice what it said. Both Owen and Monica, however, heard it and stood up. Thomas stood a half second later.

"Would the Wallace family please report to the second floor homicide department? The Wallace family to homicide, thank you," the voice repeated.

Thomas followed the two adults to an elevator across the room while keeping an eye on the now silent voice box on the wall. It failed to sound off again, so Thomas turned his attention to the elevator. He had only encountered an elevator once before and that had been at the hospital. Accordingly, he entered the enclosed space warily.

Thomas observed Owen's expression which rivalled that of a new sailor not yet comfortable with the rocking deck. He was also shifting from foot to foot as if he needed to pee. Monica on the other hand had gone completely white, as though she were afraid of elevators, not of what they were about to discover. The elevator doors closed. Thomas chewed his lip in thought as he stood in the middle of the floor, flanked by the two adults.

The ring of a bell shot through the space as the elevator came to a stop on the second floor. Thomas cringed at the sound and the doors slid open.

Standing on the other side of the doors was a young police officer dressed in plain clothes. In fact, the only thing that really distinguished him from a regular civilian was the badge on his belt and the firearm on his hip. He was tall and gangly with orange hair, large brown eyes, and a face awash with freckles. He avoided eye contact with Thomas, and his arms buzzed with jittery energy.

He focused on Monica, who seemed to be the calmest of the elevator's eligible occupants since Thomas was being excluded by the man for some reason.

"Mr. and Mrs. Wallace, so glad you could make it. My name is Detective Harrison."

"Detective? You look pretty young," Owen said as the three of them stepped out of the elevator.

"I get that a lot sir, but I assure you, I've put the time in, and I've got the badge to prove it," Harrison explained. He seemed to relax a little as he talked about himself. He did, however, return to his original jumpiness with a glance at Thomas.

"What do you want with our son?" Monica blurted out.

"Well, I'm not really the best person to ask..." Harrison waffled. "Please, follow me, Detective Thibault is waiting for the three of you," he explained. Monica huffed, but followed. Thomas and Owen hurried after the two of them.

"You must know something!" Monica pressed.

"Please be patient ma'am," Harrison took long strides down a hallway of cubicles. Monica was hustling in order to keep up with the tall man, but the attempt made her appear frazzled.

"Ah, the Wallaces," an older man droned as he came around the corner. "Detective Thibault," he introduced himself. Thomas thought he sounded like an insect.

"What do you want with my son?" Monica demanded loudly as she stopped inches away from the older man's face.

Thomas examined the man. He was considerably shorter than Owen, standing only an inch or two taller than Thomas. He was balding and had a thick moustache nestled beneath a sharp nose. He wore a grey suit accented with an obnoxious orange tie covered in penguins. He too had a badge on his belt and a sidearm on his hip, but this detective was not nervous in the slightest.

"We want to speak with him about last night," Thibault explained calmly, assessing Thomas as Thomas considered him.

"He didn't do anything!" Owen cried out.

"Guilty conscience? I never suggested he'd done anything," Thibault mused. Owen reddened considerably. "There are merely some details we'd like to clarify with him."

"Clarify away," Monica suggested.

"In private; Thomas, come with me."

"This isn't Guantanamo, buddy. If you want to ask him any questions, both of us will be present," Owen objected. Detective Thibault seemed to hesitate, but recognizing he couldn't do anything without the parent's approval, he caved.

"Very well, all three of you, please follow me," he turned and led the makeshift family through another hallway of cubicles and finally into a private office. He dragged two more chairs in front of his desk, placing them on either side of the single chair that had been intended for Thomas. Thibault sat down behind his desk and appraised the family as they took their seats before him.

"This meeting is being recorded, any objections? No? Then let's begin. We have Mr. Owen Wallace, Mrs. Monica Wallace, and of course, their son, Oswell Wallace," Thibault observed.

Annoyed, Thomas shook his head briefly. Being referred to by this false name was becoming increasingly irritating.

"Well, get on with your questions," Thomas demanded. Thibault looked taken aback, but began his investigation nonetheless.

"The first thing I would like to ask, if I may, is: how are you feeling?"

"Good."

"Just good?" Thibault pressed.

"Just good," Thomas confirmed.

"I see, okay, next question," Thibault declared. "Tell me what happened last night?"

"Sure," Thomas said, deciding to go along with what made sense. "I got lost in the woods, but found the road. I nearly got hit by a—" he paused, searching for the word. Thibault narrowed his eyes in suspicion. "—a car. I ran away, but they found me this morning." He didn't want to reveal too much.

"Just as we thought," Thibault said. He rolled back from his desk and spun around to face a cabinet behind him. He inserted a key, unlocked the cabinet, and removed what appeared to be a large plastic bag. Thomas could not see what was inside of it.

Thibault spun around once again and returned to the desk. Eyes on Thomas, he carefully laid the plastic bag out on the desk for his three guests to see. Resting safely within the confines of the plastic bag was the short knife that Thomas had stolen from the guard. Without hesitation, Thomas jumped up and pointed accusatorially at Detective Thibault.

"That's mine! How did you get that?" he hollered. Monica gasped in surprise and horror, Owen stared icily at the knife, and Detective Thibault smiled.

"That was easier than I thought it would be—I was expecting to have to drag that out of you," Detective Thibault laughed. He flipped open a folder on his desk and grabbed a pile of photos. He laid them down one by one in front of Thomas. Thomas perused the images briefly, seeing nothing out of the ordinary, and then turned back to the detective.

"How did you get my knife?" Thomas repeated.

"Will you shut up?" Owen said, standing up. "What is the meaning of this?" he asked, indicating the photos. Each one of the photos was a different angle of the knife lying in a bed of leaves. The blade was coated in congealed blood.

"The meaning, Mr. Wallace, is that your son has admitted to owning a knife that has *blood* on it," Thibault declared. "All the while, one of his closest friends and her brother have gone missing. The better question is what has he been *doing* with the knife?"

"You're not suggesting that my son— " Monica began.

"I'm not suggesting anything Mrs. Wallace, except that I am curious as to how your son came to possess such a weapon, and how said weapon came into contact with blood," Thibault spat. He turned on Thomas and stared him down. "So what do you have to say?"

"Oswell, you do *not* have to say anything more until we have a lawyer present," Monica told Thomas.

"No, it's okay," Thomas told Monica, unaware that her advice had actually been meant as more of a command. She looked like she was about to protest but she paused as she saw the look on Thom's face. Thomas looked the short man square in the eyes.

"Why do you have the knife, Oswell?" Thibault demanded, jumping on the opportunity. Owen began to protest but Thomas beat him to the punch.

"For self-defence!" Thomas exclaimed, "What else would I have a knife for?"

"I don't know, how about murder?" Thibault insinuated.

"For God's sake, he's fourteen-years-old," Owen cried.

"You think that's too young?" Thibault asked, "*I* don't think so."

"You think I murdered someone with that knife?" Thomas asked incredulously. His mind flashed to the guard he had killed with the broken tray, and to the guard that Cicero had dispatched with the knife. He utilized every skill he had to keep his face straight. He did not want to give anything away that he did not have to. He would have to tell some other truth if he were to avoid the facts about his earlier actions.

"To be honest, I don't know what to think, but the evidence so far has been rather convincing," Thibault ranted. "What else could explain the blood?"

"Self-defence! I already told you. A man attacked me last night, and I used the knife on him," Thomas followed through on his decision to be truthful.

"You're saying a man tried to attack you? In the forest? In the middle of the night?" Thibault asked incredulously. He looked at Owen and smirked sarcastically. "I thought kids were supposed to be good at lying these days."

"I'm not lying!" Thomas protested.

"Why would he lie to you?" Monica demanded.

"To cover his tracks? I wouldn't want anyone to think I killed my friends," Thibault suggested.

"That's enough, I'm not listening to this anymore. We came here to talk to you. Not to hear ridiculous accusations!" Owen fumed.

"You can't pretend the evidence isn't there Mr. Wallace; don't run from the truth!" Thibault exclaimed.

"The evidence?" Thomas snarled, "Are you telling me that if a giant man was threatening to take you, you wouldn't defend yourself? He grabbed me, I stabbed him in the arm, what else was I supposed to do! I didn't want to become the 'next little addition' to his 'family,'" Thomas fumed."

Thibault sat back down in his chair as he put together what Thomas was telling him. Monica and Owen slumped into their chairs, also disturbed. They'd come to the same realization of what had happened. Whatever Thomas said had driven the point home, striking a nerve. Thomas stayed standing, glaring down at the defeated detective.

"Still think I'm lying?" he asked.

"I am so sorry, you're free to go," he apologized. "So stupid," he mumbled as he stood up and gathered the photos and evidence bag containing the knife. He then hurried from the room with a determined look on his face, mumbling something barely audible. "I can't believe I didn't see it sooner... so much wasted time..."

Thomas looked to the two other adults, who were sitting stock still and in shock. He didn't have a clue as to what had just happened, but apparently his story had become far too real for the detective to dismiss any longer.

"Let's go home," Owen mumbled. He stood up, and helped Monica to her feet, then put a hand on Thom's shoulder and guided the two of them out of the detective's office.

Out in the bullpen, the floor buzzed with energy. Officers were running up and down the halls frantically. In the centre of it all, Detective Thibault was shouting madly at the top of his lungs.

Thomas listened as they passed Detective Thibault on the way out. They locked eyes, and Thomas could sense an apology in his expression, but Thibault continued what he was saying.

"The kidnapper may still be in the area! We now have a blood sample! Harrison, send a swab off to forensics, everyone move. He's in the forest!"

Thomas was confused. He had no clue what a kidnapper was, but he was intelligent enough to decide that it must be the man that had attacked him the night before. A satisfied smile gathered in his cheeks at the thought of these men hunting down the 'kidnapper.' Perhaps he would learn a lesson not to bother people in the forest, though Thomas thought proudly, perhaps the stab to his arm had been enough to convince him of that.

A young officer hurrying past noticed the family standing amidst the chaos. "I'm sorry," he said to Owen, "Do you think we could grab a description from your son?"

"Ask him," Owen said, pointing to Thomas.

Thomas smiled at the police officer. "What can I do for you?"

Chapter Twenty-Six

A Solid Argument

Oswell shifted his dubious gaze back and forth between the satisfied Cicero and the dumbfounded Darius. Neither of them relented in their appraisal of him.

"No," he said.

"Yes," Darius replied, smiling slightly.

"Nope," Oswell maintained.

"Yes," Darius said again.

"Enough," Cicero interrupted. Oswell turned to Cicero and opened his mouth in protest.

"We are not going to talk about this any further until you're ready to continue the conversation rationally," Cicero said. Oswell grumbled, rolled his eyes, and then surrendered.

"So a guy writes a poem in this fancy book, and I'm supposed to believe that the poem is, first of all, a prophecy; second of all, about me because of my *hair*, and third of all, that I'm supposed to 'deliver salvation?' Why would I ever believe any of that?"

"We've discussed this already. The 'guy' you speak of is none other than Alvari Vata, a recognized prophet," Cicero began. "The 'fancy book' you belittle is a collection of prophecies, many of which have *already* come true. Granted, many modern people take his prophecies to be the stuff of coincidence and fantasy, but…"

"But nothing," Oswell cut in, "if so many people think it's fantasy, why should I believe it? Why should you and Darius believe it? Majority rules, I always say."

"The reason that most take it as fiction is two-fold: the first is that they have never seen the book, let alone read it. The second is that Saosin Hallows has essentially put a ban on anything of the occult: from religion to fortune telling. We do not live by Hallows's rules, and therefore, we can believe it without suffering the consequences others would," Cicero explained.

Irritated, Oswell scratched the back of his head and put in some thought as Cicero continued.

"Okay, but I'm still going to play the Devil's advocate," Oswell decided stubbornly. "You can't say that it points to me because my hair is golden. I'm as blonde as the next kid, but really?"

"In the first line Oswell, the prophecy speaks of someone who has lost their memory," Cicero replied.

"I haven't lost my memory," Oswell said, smiling triumphantly.

"But to an external viewer like Vata, you would appear to have lost your memory," Cicero explained. "You have no understanding of this world, its people, its customs, or even your own name."

"But that still isn't enough, I mean, unless amnesia never happens here," Oswell said. "That could be anyone."

"...Amnesia occurs, you are correct," Cicero admitted. "However, the 'golden way' is almost certainly a reference to your blonde hair. Anything that you do for our world could be done in a golden way, because it is your way, and you are golden... haired," Cicero interpreted.

"Let's not get too metaphorical here," Oswell advised.

"That is the essence of Vata's prophecies! He speaks in riddle and rhyme. He utilizes metaphor and double meanings. It makes his prophecies specific, yet timeless!" Darius exclaimed.

"Okay, well even if I agree that the poem may be indicating a blonde person that has seemingly lost their memory, you say that these prophecies are specific *and* timeless. I see nothing specific referencing right now," Oswell said. "This prophecy could fit practically anywhere along a timeline of *blonde amnesiac appearances*," he folded his arms across his chest.

"But that is where you are wrong," Cicero smiled.

"Take a look at the second line," Darius suggested.

"When darkness, death, and sin are found," Oswell read. "These things are always around. People die, people sin, and there is always darkness at night..." Oswell thought for a moment, "except during Arctic summers."

"And what does the next line say? It ties directly into the second line for context," Cicero prompted.

"In hallowed lands of black and grey," Oswell read, but stayed silent at the end of reading. "Hallowed... Hallows's lands."

"That would be a direct reference to our time!" Cicero stressed.

Oswell deflated into his chair, defeated. In the context of open mindedness, the interpretations made perfect sense. However, Oswell wasn't sure how he could help solve their problems. Even if the prophecy was true, Oswell did not have the skill or knowledge to deliver the salvation suggested by the prediction.

"How am I supposed to save your world? I'm fourteen years old," Oswell frowned. He played down the fact that he would be turning fifteen in a few months time, although he doubted being fifteen would make even a sliver of a difference in the grand scheme of things.

"I don't know how you are to help us," Cicero admitted as he laced his fingers together, "but obviously, if I knew the answer, I simply would have done it myself. The answers, I am sure, will reveal them-selves in time. That is all that I can promise."

Oswell stared incredulously at Cicero. He was entirely unsatisfied with the answer he had been provided. Sensing Oswell's displeasure, Cicero turned to Darius.

"I think that is enough for tonight. Darius, please show Oswell to his quarters. He has much to think about, and he must be tired."

"Yes grandfather, I agree." Darius stood up and Oswell begrudging-ly followed. "I shall retire as well, good night grandfather."

"Night," Oswell mumbled shortly.

"Good night," Cicero replied. "Both of you know where to find me," he stretched out his arms and indicated the office in which the three of them stood. Apparently, Cicero would not be surrendering to the clutches of sleep just yet.

Darius guided Oswell out of the office, around the balcony, down the stairs, across the main level, and back out into the fresh open air.

"I could give you a tour of the Enclave," Darius offered, "but grandfather is right, you need your sleep. You look like the dead."

The fresh air penetrated Oswell's lungs and the brightness of day widened his eyes. Though his body was exhausted with the effort of his trials, his mind continued to spin uncontrollably with thoughts of home, Claire and Nicholas, his parents, and the wonder of this new world. The prospect of sleep seemed impossible. Yet, Darius watched him expectantly.

"I'll get a rain check on the tour," Oswell decided. Darius looked at him confused. Seeing this, Oswell corrected himself, "We'll do the tour later."

"Okay then, right this way," Darius ushered, glad to have been saved from the embarrassment of asking for a clarification of Oswell's meaning. He quietly mumbled 'rain check' under his breath as they made their way along the catwalks in the grey light. The sun fought its way through the dreary atmosphere, shining bravely from just above the horizon; Oswell felt himself missing the hot sun of Earth. This sun was tepid at best.

"Here we are," Darius offered. He stifled a yawn and conducted Oswell through the door into a small circular hut. There wasn't much to say for the single room. It harboured a small bed, a trunk at the bed's foot, and a desk with a chair off to one side. Darius busied himself opening up the window slats enough to allow a fresh breeze into the room while still keeping it reasonably dark. As Oswell explored the room briefly, Darius continued to speak.

"You can use this room as your quarters for as long as you require. The windows are simple to adjust, if you wish. You should be warm enough but there are more blankets in the chest. I'll bring a change of clothes by before I retire, but don't bother waiting up for me. You'll also find them in the trunk when you wake up. If you wish to use the washroom, simply go the edge of the catwalk," Darius paused and grinned mockingly, "there are plenty of leaves to be had if you need them for... cleaning up."

Oswell listened absentmindedly, picking up on the gist of what he had been told.

"Thank you," he yawned as he sat down on the bed and stretched.

"You're welcome," Darius turned on his heel and left the hut.

The interior of the hut was cool; a breeze blew through the hut, giving Oswell a chill. He crawled off the bed and shut the slats, hoping to find a respite.

Without the breeze, it was markedly warmer. Returning to the bed, thoughts raced through Oswell's mind. He couldn't believe everything that had happened to him, and yet, he was being forced to believe. No matter how hard he tried, he couldn't wake up from the dream.

What would his parents think when they got home to find him missing? Rielle, his babysitter, would be in a state, no doubt blaming herself though this transgression rested firmly in his own responsibility. Owen would be grappling with the sheer force of will that Monica could conjure, his parents would be organizing a hunt with the police, and deep down behind all of the bustle, both of their hearts would be breaking. Yet, here he was, sitting on an uncomfortable mattress filled with—*is this straw?*—on an alien planet that seemed conjured out of the middle ages in which he—*me? Oswell Wallace?*—was expected to save them from some tyrant and plight he didn't even understand? And now, he was supposed to sleep? Oswell scoffed.

He began to pace, his legs tiring further as he attempted to banish the thoughts chaotically racing through his mind, but finally, after the better part of the morning, Lady Exhaustion came knocking. Tentatively, with the smallest measure of welcome and the greatest measure of caution, Oswell welcomed her in.

CHAPTER TWENTY-SEVEN

KNOCK, KNOCK, WHO'S THERE?

THOMAS PRESSED HIS face against the cold glass window of the automobile. Monica was talking rapidly into her cell phone in the front seat of the car. Thomas chose to ignore whatever she was saying. Instead, he watched dark trees whip past him as the car sprinted across the asphalt. They had been on the highway for no longer than five minutes, but Thomas recalled that the journey into town had not been a long one.

The peculiarity of the wide, paved surface cutting through the forest like a great black knife struck Thomas and reminded him of his first encounter with the highway. He shivered violently at the thought. The highway had actually been his salvation, but it was still a reminder of the man he'd met in the forest. The emotions were fresh; after all, it had been less than a day since his encounter with Father in the forest.

Thomas shook his head slowly to relieve himself of the wintry feeling gathering in his gut despite the hearty meal incubating there. After giving the police every detail he could about Father, his adoptive parents had taken him to a 'restaurant,' which, in nature, was an establishment very similar to the inns and taverns of Numyria. That is, the common factor was that they both served food, and you sat down to eat it.

Everything else was entirely different: a person came to take your order (as opposed to shouting at the innkeeper from across the room), you were given nice utensils to eat with (instead of eating with your hands), and the food provided was absolutely delicious (compared to day-old stew and stale bread). The meals came in huge portions, were colourful and fresh, and they smelled as though someone really knew what they were doing in the kitchen. Finally, they paid for their dinner at the end of the meal instead of at the beginning. There were two things odd about that: First, apparently the owners of the 'restaurant' were not afraid of people simply walking out without paying. This would be a very real threat in Numyria. Second, Owen had paid simply by giving a small card to the woman that had taken their orders. At first, Thomas thought the card may have been some form of currency. However, it was promptly returned. This disproved Thomas's theory and left him rather perplexed.

Nonetheless, Thomas had taken another opportunity to eat—an occurrence that was becoming far more common since he'd shown up in this world. His natural instinct to eat had politely suggested to him that he gorge himself on everything that was presented. Thomas had not put up a fight. He'd devoured the gargantuan serving of piping hot 'French fries', and inhaled the enormous 'cheeseburger' Owen had ordered for him. If that hadn't been enough, the waitress apparently knew his situation and promptly served him up a piece of chocolate cake smothered in sugary iced cream. That, he had not been able to finish.

As delicious as the food had been, he now found himself regretting it while his stomach gurgled grumpily in protest of the atrocities done to it. Obviously, his stomach was still not ready for such large quantities of food, a fact he had learned violently, first in the forest, and then at the hospital. He had handled his breakfast easily enough, but apparently (and unfortunately) dinner was going to be another story.

Thomas retched, filling his mouth with the incompletely digested ingredients of his dinner. The combination of potato, ground beef, cheese, chocolate, and cream was not nearly as enjoyable all together as it had been separately. It seemed as though the stomach acid and bile mixed in with the food was one of the main factors contributing to the incompatibility. Hearing his heave, Monica dropped her phone conversation and Owen slammed on the brakes and swerved, skidding to a stop on the side of the road.

"Out, out, out!" he cried, as Thomas did his best not to evacuate the contents of his mouth.

Thomas reached for the door handle but could not find it in his distress. Owen raced around the car and pulled the door open just as another heave forced its way out of his stomach and into his already full mouth. The vomit burst from between his lips, spraying, in order; the seat in front of him, the open car door, Owen's shoes, and finally the gravel on the side of the road.

Being parents, this had a minimal effect on Owen and Monica; it had not been their first encounter with vomit. Monica leapt into action, gathering some napkins from the glove box and her half empty water bottle from a cup holder. Owen had already stepped back and was wiping off his shoes in the grass while allowing Monica access to Thomas.

You've got to stop doing this, Thomas thought. *You're not going to starve; this isn't going away!*

"Rinse your mouth," Monica ordered, handing Thomas the bottle of water. He did as he was told, filling his mouth halfway, sloshing it around in his mouth, and then spitting it onto the ground. The taste lingered, but at least the chunks had evacuated. "Good," she praised. She then splashed some water onto one of the napkins and wiped Thomas's face and shirt clean and then motioned for him to climb out of the car. Once again, Thomas did as he was told and stood beside Owen on the grass off the shoulder of the highway. He felt silly being cleaned up by Monica, as though he were a child. He'd been fending for himself for years, though he had to admit that there was something nice about being cared for.

Monica set to work with her napkins and water, seeming to focus on the fabrics. She wiped up as much as she could with the limited number of napkins she had and then stood up and surveyed her work. It was by no means perfect, but it would have to do until they got home.

"Let's go," she said. She was the effective mother in a crisis and she enjoyed the role; it took her mind off everything else going on. Neither Owen nor Thomas hesitated. Owen returned to the driver's seat and started the car while Thomas took a seat on the other side of the car, as far as possible from the mess. Without further ado, Owen shoulder checked, saw nothing, and pulled back onto the highway.

"I guess we won't eat so much next time," Monica said. She sounded more disappointed in herself for letting him eat so much than she was angry at Thomas.

"And we'll try and get out of the car first next time, right Oz?" Owen asked.

"Yes, I'll try," Thomas replied, checking to make sure he knew where the door handle was.

He leaned back in his chair and closed his eyes, trying to ignore the irritated burn smouldering at the back of his throat and nose. His stomach continued to gurgle, though the bubbling seemed far less threatening now. He bore the discomfort well, and minutes later, they pulled into their driveway.

Thomas found the door handle easily (he wouldn't soon forget how to get out of a car) and hopped out of his own accord. Owen and Monica also climbed out of the car.

Still in her commanding mindset, Monica rushed into the house, disappeared for a moment, and then came flying back out with a bucket, a few rags, and what (after Thomas's observation of its use) appeared to be some sort of cleaning solution.

Owen placed his hand on Thomas's shoulder and squeezed it gently. Glancing up at him, Thomas expected to see anger, or at the least annoyance. Instead, all he found was warmth.

"Honey, I'm going to get Ozzie settled," Owen said. Monica grunted her approval, and Owen grinned at Thomas. Thomas smiled back and the two of them retreated into the house.

"That's one thing I love about your mother: she always takes charge in the event of an emergency," he laughed.

"And she does a good job too," Thomas said.

"Certainly makes my life easier," Owen agreed and then sat Thomas down in front of the television and turned it on to the Discovery Channel.

Thomas buried himself into the couch, received a pat on the chest from Owen, and then turned his attention to the television. Owen disappeared momentarily before returning with a glass of water for Thomas. He took it gratefully.

"I'm going to help your mother," Owen said. Thomas nodded and took a sip of water. Owen smiled warmly and then left through the front door to support his wife in the cleanup of Thomas's dinner.

Looking accomplished, Monica and Owen returned to the living room a few minutes later to find Thomas engrossed in another nature program. Owen sat down with Thomas as Monica disappeared into the kitchen.

The moment of peace was shattered as a frantic knocking sounded on the front door. Thomas jumped in fright while Owen rose to answer the door.

"Allison! Paul!" Owen exclaimed, "Come in, come in!" Owen ushered two adults into the living room. Glancing around the room, they noticed Thomas sitting on the couch. Paul averted his eyes and Allison, eyes still red from crying, teared up again. Owen ushered them into the kitchen.

Thomas shrugged and returned to the television program. In the background, he could hear Allison crying gently, and the other adults doing their best to comfort her. Given Allison's state, he decided it wasn't his place to involve himself in the kitchen's events. He focused his attention back on the television.

A group of enormous fish-like creatures were swimming around quickly. They were very cute, and according to the narrator, were called 'dolphins'. They performed tricks and ate smaller fish in a display that was altogether captivating.

Another loud knock resounded through the house. Recognizing it as someone at the front door, Thomas hurried to answer it. Standing before him was a tall police officer dressed in blue and holding a long flashlight.

"Oswell Wallace?" the officer asked.

"Yes," Thomas lied for the sake of convenience.

"Are your parents home?" he asked.

"Yes we are," Owen said as he stepped out of the kitchen and found his way down the hall and into the entryway. The knocking had also been heard by everyone in the kitchen. Paul appeared in the hallway to see what was happening.

"Mr. Wallace, Mr. Drew, we're calling on the neighbourhood to help in the search through the forest. If you both have flashlights, and are willing, your help would be greatly appreciated."

"You don't even need to ask," Paul said. Owen nodded and then dashed away to the back of the house.

From the sound of it, Thomas guessed that he had left through the back door. Moments later, he returned with two flashlights in tow. He handed one to Paul.

"I told Monica and Allison that we're helping in the search," Owen explained and then turned to Thomas. "You stay here and protect the women," he smirked, trying to lighten the mood.

Paul and the officer chuckled, but Thomas nodded stoically and purposefully made his way to the kitchen. This drew a few more nervous chuckles from the three men. They left through the front door as Thomas disappeared into the kitchen.

Monica and Allison were on him in moments, giving him hugs and pulling him to sit down with them. Allison had successfully gotten herself together. They were both trying to look happy, although there was clear evidence that they had been crying together. Vertical tracks ran down their cheeks through their makeup, and the eyes of both were red and puffy. Their smiles attempted to mask that reality, but they were doing a poor job of it. Thomas's heart went out to Monica again, amazed at her empathy for the other woman.

"Do you think they'll find them?" Allison asked Monica.

"Of course, I do! They've got the whole police force and town on the job. They'll find them," Monica assured her friend.

"I should be helping too," Thomas decided, feeling left out of the effort, and yet very connected to the situation even though he wasn't exactly sure who the townspeople and police were looking for, or why.

He had to guess it was the man who'd attacked him the night before. Thomas would enjoy another crack at him.

"You're helping by staying out of trouble," Monica told Thomas. Allison nodded in agreement and then burst into tears again as she gazed at him.

"I'm sorry, did I do something wrong?" Thomas asked Allison plainly. He felt sympathy for the distraught mother.

"No honey, you didn't do anything wrong," Allison sniffled as she wiped away her tears.

Thomas went to sit down in one of the chairs, but stopped in mid-stride as he heard a knock at the door. He looked towards Monica, who smiled warmly at him.

"The boys must have forgotten something," Monica decided instantly.

"And locked themselves out," Allison added. Owen had a reputation for forgetting his keys and locking himself out of the house. A few years back he had been caught climbing through a second story window to get into the house. A concerned neighbour had called the police when she saw a man scaling the side of the house. Owen had been the talk of the neighbourhood for weeks.

"Ozzie, there. You can help; go let them in," Monica suggested. Thomas hurried out of the room and raced down the hallway to the door as Monica stood and crossed the kitchen to retrieve Owen's keys hanging on the wall.

Monica started digging her way through the keys on the rack. She found the key to the shed, her keys, and the spare key. However, Owen's key was nowhere to be found. Monica furrowed her brow as she picked up the spare key. Her husband couldn't have locked himself out if he had his keys. Monica listened as Thomas opened the front door.

"What did they forget Ozzie?" she called down the hallway from the kitchen, listening carefully.

Thomas heard Monica calling out to him but his reply was stuck in his throat, and only a small squeak escaped. He stared up at the enormous man shrouded in darkness and filling the entryway.

"Ozzie?" Monica called out again as she crossed the kitchen. Her heart pounded against her rib cage, trying to escape, then settled in her throat. Sensing the worst, she felt as though she were about to follow the example Thomas had set in the car, and get the chance to re-examine her own dinner.

Peering around the corner into the hallway, she could see straight to the front doorway. On that particular night, she could also see straight out the open front door, which stood entirely unobstructed. Thomas was gone. Monica screamed.

- *CHAPTER TWENTY-EIGHT* -

THE JOURNAL

AN EAR SPLITTING scream shattered Oswell's unconsciousness. He sat up in his bed, sweating profusely. Oswell recognized the scream easily although he had heard it before only a handful of times. Despite this, he instinctually knew what to do. It was the scream of his mother and he had to help her.

He leapt from the bed and, surrounded by absolute darkness, he rushed to the door of his bedroom. His hands explored the wall, but he could not locate the doorknob. He pushed against the wall angrily as the scream continued to ring in his ears. A groan of frustration parted his lips as he realized he was not pressing up against a door.

He had no idea where he was.

He turned and felt his way carefully along the wall until his grasping fingers clasped onto an iron latch. It was no door knob, but it would do. Oswell wrenched open the door as the screeching in the core of his mind finally died away.

His eyes travelled up along the great shadow of a man standing before him. Another shriek tore through Oswell's consciousness as he intuitively knew who the enormous man framed by the entryway was.

Panicking, Oswell threw his hands up in the air and tumbled backwards onto the floor behind him. His time had come: the kidnapper had found him. Curled up on the coarse wooden floor with his eyes pressed shut, Oswell waited helplessly to be taken.

He never was.

After a few agonizing moments of paralyzing fear, Oswell cracked open his left eye and nabbed a peek at the man. He was gone. Oswell recognized the dark room now that the unhindered light of the full moon could flow through the wide open doorway. There was no one waiting for him… but the scream had seemed so real.

As the room came into greater clarity, everything that had happened came rushing back up to meet him with a sarconic grin, as if to say '*You didn't think it would be that easy to get out of here, did you?*'

The scream continued to sound dully in the farthest corners of his consciousness, but his fluttering heart relaxed as the dream state faded away. The cool night air filled his lungs with life and he stepped out onto the catwalk outside the hut. There, he recognized an entirely new beauty in the moonlit sea of trees. There was a distinctive peace in the dark of the night.

Oswell leaned on the railing of the catwalk breathing, and thinking. Something, however, was doing an excellent job of distracting him. A pressure weighed heavily on his abdomen. He'd been lucky it hadn't evacuated him in his last moments of terror. Oswell recalled Darius's advice.

Simply exit the hut and go the edge of the catwalk.

Not looking forward to the coming experience, Oswell groaned, and began picking leaves off of the trees behind him. The full moon cast more than enough light for him to go about his task. The entire Enclave was illuminated. He gathered a respectable pile, and set them on the floor of the catwalk in front of him. Never before had he realized how much he had taken toilet paper for granted. He dropped his pants, giving the moon a run for its money, and did his business.

It being perhaps one of the most unusual experiences of his life, Oswell closed his eyes and rested his face on his hands and his elbows on his knees. As bizarre as it felt, the cool wind breezing past kept him relaxed. That is, until he felt a leaf brush past his legs.

Opening his eyes, he stared down to discover that the pile of leaves he had collected was gone. The wind had taken every last one of them.

"No!" he whispered, putting his hands on his head in complete disbelief. He had finished his business, but now he was left with a considerable mess to clean up and nothing prepared to do it with. "Couldn't make it easy for me... not even once..." Oswell complained, turning to collect more leaves as his rump exposed itself to the cool night air.

A sniggering rose off to Oswell's left and he stopped mid-pick. He turned slowly to locate the source of the laughter and his face coloured itself crimson with embarrassment.

He could not lift up his pants, or even stand up straight for fear of making a greater mess. The source of the laughter made itself known. Darius came crawling out from underneath one of the catwalks like a spider, and then flipped himself over the railing and landed on his feet with a wickedly joyful smirk that allowed his white teeth to glow in the moonlight.

"I could not have picked a better time," Darius chuckled.

"I kind of disagree," Oswell said. He shuffled backwards away from Darius and began picking leaves at random from behind him.

"I feel like this story is going to stick with you for a while," Darius decided, as though it were now up to him to tell the world of Oswell's embarrassment.

"Show's over, move along," Oswell commanded as he began to take care of his humiliating situation.

"Fine, fine," Darius gave in and hopped back over the catwalk's railing and disappeared underneath it. With the return of his privacy, Oswell finished cleaning himself. Unsure of what Darius was doing beneath the catwalk, he contemplated whether or not to investigate. There were two sides to the argument, he could: One, satisfy his curiosity and see what Darius was up to, but in order to do that, he would have to face Darius and likely more ridicule. Or two, ignore his curiosity, return to his room and go to bed, and in so doing, avoid Darius and further ridicule. Curiosity was a powerful motivator.

Oswell hurried over to the spot where Darius had disappeared, laid down on the catwalk and poked his head over the edge in order to peer underneath. There, he saw nothing but a small gap between the trees below and the boards above. Oswell scanned to the left seeing nothing, and then scanned to the right. Finally, way down the line, Darius crawled upside down along the lengths of the catwalk. Periodically, he would stop for a few moments and then continue.

Oswell hopped up and hurried down the catwalk in pursuit of Darius.

"Coming back for more?" Darius asked.

"No, actually I never finished. I thought I would try this part of the walkway instead," Oswell replied, folding his arms and standing in place with a slight grin on his face.

Below, Darius thought about this comment for a moment and then, realizing what Oswell was saying, scurried out from underneath the platform.

"You wouldn't dare!" he whispered angrily as he rolled up onto the platform with his arms raised in front of his face and his eyes firmly shut.

"What are you doing?" Oswell mocked. Darius cracked his eyes open and peeked around his arms to see Oswell standing before him, fully clothed and clearly not about to move his bowels.

"Oh..." Darius said. He stood up and glared at Oswell.

"Well...?" Oswell probed, grinning defiantly.

"I *was* avoiding a sight I did not wish to see," Darius said, folding his arms across his chest, "however, before I was interrupted by the perfect opportunity to exploit your misfortune for my own personal entertainment, I was busying myself with the fire prevention system. As I mentioned earlier, the system is not yet perfect."

Oswell scratched his jaw and then made his way over to the edge of the catwalk. He lay down on his belly and examined the underside of the walkway. Now that he knew what he was looking at underneath the walkway, he could see a wide trough running along its entire length.

"It's like an irrigation system..." Oswell marvelled as he stood back up to appraise Darius.

"Exactly," Darius beamed, "we've used irrigation to quench our fields for ages. One day, I realized that it would be entirely possible to use that old idea in an entirely new way. I do not believe such a system is employed anywhere else in the whole of Myros."

"So you really aren't just a tough exterior," Oswell said.

"Believe it or not, there is a brain up here," Darius replied, rapping his knuckles on his temple.

"Apparently," Oswell decided. He paused and cocked his head to the side as though he had realized something unusual. "One question," he posed.

"Certainly," Darius replied.

"Why are you working on it in the dead of night?" Oswell asked.

"I'm busy during the day; I do most of my tinkering at night."

"A night owl," Oswell said.

"One could say that." The two young men stood awkwardly before each other for a moment. Oswell cracked a grin, and Darius returned it. "I should be off to bed, as should you," Darius suggested.

"I don't think I could sleep another wink," Oswell told him. The moon was high in the sky, and Oswell had slept fitfully for a few hours. By rights he should have still been tired, but his worry and curiosity had him wired.

"Well, as tired as I am, I won't let you wander the Enclave unaccompanied," Darius decided.

"I should be fine," Oswell said, "Get some sleep."

"Nonsense," Darius decided, "I'll give you the official tour, lest we find you flat as an oatcake on the forest floor tomorrow. Grandfather would never forgive me."

"I don't think I'd like that either," Oswell said, thrown off. It was easy to forget how high up they were. He recovered from the realization quickly, "Where do we start?"

Darius scratched his chin. "Come this way."

Oswell followed after Darius as he set off back towards the hut in which he'd slept. He was slightly confused as to why they were heading back the way he had come, but as Darius walked past the entryway of the hut and skirted around to the right of it, Oswell saw where they were going.

"I like to think of the Enclave as a snowflake," Darius offered as he led Oswell along a new walkway. "We have platforms and buildings constructed around the central hall with these walkways connecting all of them," Darius explained animatedly. "It would have been a lot of work to spread these platforms out, but doing it this way meant each platform could stand isolated from the others; ideal in the event of an emergency." The pair came up on another hut, slightly larger than Oswell's, but not by much.

"What's this?" Oswell asked.

"This is the bunkhouse. There are about twenty beds in there—enough for more rebels—not that we've had a lot of help lately." Darius shrugged as though it were not very interesting, and continued past the bunkhouse. He stopped silently in front of the next hut and held his index finger up to his lips to suggest Oswell follow his example.

"These are Wendell's quarters," Darius whispered. "He's the head guard for the Enclave, of course, he's the only guard... but he would be the head if he had a corps to command." Darius turned his head to the side as though he were listening intently. "You've not met him yet, but you will if we remain here much longer," Darius advised nervously. "He's a light sleeper." Oswell grimaced and with a noiseless motion suggested they move on.

The next hut they came across was large and round, almost plump in appearance with a bulge around the middle. Oswell scoffed at the building as Darius opened his mouth to speak.

"This here is the storehouse. We keep the majority of the Enclave's food supplies in here," Darius explained. Oswell snickered as the appearance of the building became all the more appropriate. In front of the building, Darius motioned down one pathway off to the right.

"That walkway leads back to the main hall as you can see. It is also the main exit and entryway onto the treetops. You may remember that there is a small platform down there onto which I helped you earlier," Darius indicated. Oswell nodded to confirm his recollection. Satisfied, Darius continued on past the storehouse with Oswell close behind. Moments later, they stopped quietly in front of another hut.

"Another man's quarters," Darius informed Oswell, "not such a light sleeper though." Oswell breathed a sigh of relief. "These are the quarters of the Enclave's Deacon, Laurence. As is the custom of most Myrist Deacons, his home is also a place of worship: a Havyn."

"Worship? Like a church!" Oswell whispered.

"Like a Havyn." Darius replied. Oswell sighed, defeated; it wasn't worth the argument.

"Shall we move on?" Darius asked, not waiting for an answer. Oswell hurried after the young man as they progressed around what was, indeed, turning out to be a small, circular web of platforms and connecting catwalks.

Darius didn't bother to stop at the next hut; he merely flourished his hand in the direction of the building as they passed it, "These are my *private* quarters," Darius stressed. "Moving on." Oswell stole a glance at the small hut which was literally bursting at the seams, odds and ends hanging out of the open windows, through which Oswell could not see the barest inch of open floor space. Technical genius, though he may be, Darius was not organized.

"Our tour is nearly complete," Darius advised Oswell as they approached another structure. This one was round and looked rather familiar, though Oswell had a difficult time understanding how it was filled.

"Is that a— " Oswell began.

"Why, yes, it is," Darius replied.

"A water reservoir?"

Darius approached the solid, round structure, located ladder rungs on the side of it and quickly hoisted himself up to a secondary level. "Indeed. This building is the centre of control for my fire prevention system, as well as our supply of drinking water," Darius explained. "Beneath me, there is enough water to fill three times over and then some, every trough beneath every walkway. If ever a fire were to threaten the Enclave, this system would, at the very least, provide us with ample time to evacuate." Sensing the question in Oswell's face, he added, "It's filled by the rain. We get a lot of it here."

"I'm impressed," Oswell decided as he scratched the back of his head. The system, if it actually worked, would be an impressive feat of engineering. Darius beamed at the compliment and hopped back down onto the walkway.

"One more building to see," Darius said. He strode off towards the last stop and Oswell followed. Darius stood in front of the next building proudly, although not as proudly as the last.

"This is the armoury and workshop," Darius explained. "I do much of my work here when it is too big for my own quarters." Darius opened up the door and peered into the darkness. "Of course, there is also armour and weaponry in there," Darius added as though it were of limited significance in his worldview. "Come," he ordered. Oswell followed Darius towards the centre of the circle around which they had just walked. Before them, the central hall rose up out of the trees like a great behemoth.

"Grandfather is probably still in there, buried in a book and trying to figure out how in the name of Myr you ended up here," Darius said. Oswell and Darius stood in silence staring up at the building. Finally, Darius broke the calm. "Well, that concludes the tour. I'm off to bed, and I suggest you do the same."

"I'm not tired."

"I *suggest* you do the same," Darius repeated. "We don't need you falling out of any trees before we figure out if you really are going to be important to us or not."

With a lingering look at the central hall, Oswell groaned and turned. He didn't like being bossed around. Darius smiled and watched as Oswell retreated back to his room. When the sound of Oswell's footsteps in the still night air ceased to be heard, Darius found his way back to his own crowded quarters.

Oswell sat down on his bed and rested his chin in his hands. He had nothing to do except to sit. He couldn't sleep, and being back in the hut reminded him of the dream. *Who is Darius to tell me what to do?* He thought angrily. *I'll do what I want, and I'd like to get to the bottom of all this*, he decided.

Oswell stood up quietly and carefully padded his way to the door. At the threshold, he peered around, and then quietly stepped outside. The breeze had died down and an unusual calm had settled over the treetops. Oswell barely took notice, except to curse the stillness for mandating his complete silence.

He cautiously made his way down the walkway towards the central hall and his destination.

In the hushed night air, Oswell heard an audible sigh.

"You couldn't stay away, could you?" Darius asked disappointedly. Ashamed, Oswell looked at his feet.

"Well, what are you waiting for?" Darius asked. Oswell turned and began to head back to his hut. "No, you fool, come with me," Darius prompted, dashing stealthily along the side of the hall and disappearing around the curve. Oswell stood still for a moment, entirely baffled, and then hurried after Darius.

On the other side of the main hall, Oswell caught up with Darius as he was making his way quietly through the entry. Oswell followed cautiously after him. Not a word was spoken between the two midnight intruders as Darius led Oswell across the room and up the spiral staircase to the second floor observation gallery. Darius was just as curious about Oswell's situation as Oswell.

They padded silently along the floorboards and promptly found themselves crouched at the bottom of the stairs that led up to Cicero's office. A conspiratorial look flashed in Darius's eyes as he pointed to Oswell and then pointed to the trapdoor in the ceiling above them. Oswell understood what was being asked of him, hesitated for only a moment, and then carefully made his way up the ladder.

Oswell took a deep breath and pressed the top of his head against the trap door above him. It moved only slightly. He strained his neck to push it up a little higher and the trapdoor raised another inch. Peering through the gap he had created, Oswell could see that the office was markedly darker, with a number of candles in the room having flickered out. Sitting behind the desk with his head resting comfortably on his hands, Cicero slept soundly. Bartimaeus too, slept with his head nestled underneath his wing.

Oswell let the trapdoor come back down, cast a quick glance and a nod down at Darius, and then pushed up on the trap door with his arm. Stealthily, he climbed up into the office, holding the door open for Darius. He helped Darius up into the office. Darius let the door fall carefully, barely making a sound.

Oswell grinned confidently and began to cross the room. Halfway across, one of the floorboards creaked loudly. Both Darius and Oswell froze in mid-step as Cicero stirred in his sleep and mumbled something under his breath.

The pair stood stock-still for a few moments in order to gauge the safety of moving.

Getting impatient, Oswell decided it was safe enough and moved across the room to the desk. Darius snuck up beside him and stared down at the open book resting on the desk in front of Cicero.

Without hesitation, Oswell snatched it up and examined what looked to be some sort of journal. He retreated across the room to a large armchair accompanied by a tall, three-branched candelabrum with only one candle still alight. Darius followed him and sat down on the armrest of the chair.

Looking over Oswell's shoulder, Darius could see that Oswell had already begun to read in the flickering yellow light.

17th Troden, 799 GE

At various points in history, unusual irregularities in the fabric of our reality have arisen. Although never physically observed, circumstances have encouraged my hypothesis that our reality is not a singular reality, but may in fact be accompanied by many alternate realities.

Through careful investigation, I feel as though I am getting close to documenting proof of a tear in the very material of our world. Theoretically, this tear could prove to be the window through which an alternate reality can be viewed. More radically, the tear could prove to be a doorway through which an alternate reality can be entered. Although I have been most diligent in attempting to uncover physical evidence of what I seek, I have as yet been unsuccessful. However, I feel as though I am getting close.

Only yesterday, I heard tell of a young man who has allegedly lost his mind. Although dismissed by others around him as a madman outside of town, I was intrigued by his situation. Some witnesses tell me that he had an unusual intonation in his words, was harried and confused, and even mumbled words that none could understand. I decided that I would pursue a conversation with this young man, if only for my own personal interest.

Oswell looked up from the text at Darius. Darius, having just finished the entry as well, was also intrigued. He urged Oswell to turn the page. Oswell complied and began to read the text on the next page.

18th Troden, 799 GE

I spent this morning observing the young man outside of town. His behaviour was causing quite a commotion, and I noticed that a number of merchants chose to take the long way around to the other side of town simply to avoid him.

Although he did seem to be quite insane, I managed to work up the courage to go and talk to him. At first, I was nearly frightened away by his attempt to attack me, but once I had assured him that my only intention was to speak with him, he seemed to calm considerably as if that was all he wanted in the first place. I began to ask him questions pertaining to his identity... his name, age, his place of origin. He gladly gave me his age; sixteen years, and name; Colin McLeod. However, his home was a place I had never heard of: 'Bosstown,' I believe. Nonetheless, I pressed on, asking him how he arrived here and the reasons for his distress. There was a great deal of confusion in his explanation of recent events... he genuinely did not know how he arrived near our city.

This answer was just as I hoped; perhaps this young man could be the key to finding what I have searched for so long. I wished to ask him more questions, but much time had passed. I could hear the town criers calling out that the gates would be closing shortly. I thanked the young man for his cooperation and handed him a loaf of bread and a flagon of oatbrew with promises of returning in the morning with more.

Oswell did not hesitate in turning the page this time. Already, he was enthralled with the story of Colin McLeod. Oswell felt a kinship towards the young man. One could say they were in similar situations, although Oswell felt that already, he was faring far better. Cicero grumbled in his sleep as Oswell continued the story on the next page.

19th Troden, 799 GE

> *I returned to the spot where I had met Colin the day before, but he was gone. I was disappointed knowing that I'd let such a promising opportunity slip away. I began a search for the young man... perhaps he had somehow made his way into town.*
>
> *I questioned the guards, and most of them were mute on the subject. I had no success until one of my bribes was successful. A young guard explained to me that Colin had attempted to enter the town, apparently to try and steal some food.*
>
> *In the attempt, he'd gotten into a scuffle with one of the town guards and killed the man in the process. For his crime, Colin was thrown in the Lord's dungeon to await execution. To say the least, I was surprised that Colin had the capacity to kill someone.*
>
> *Through my time with him, I'd discerned that he was simply a scared young boy, in spite of his fiery exterior.*
>
> *Although I gave it my best effort, I have not been able to bribe my way into the dungeons to speak with the young man one last time. I can only hope that Myr has mercy on his soul.*

A sinking feeling gripped Oswell around the midsection and squeezed him so tightly he felt as though his heart had squirmed its way out of his chest. Although he did not know the young man, he felt sorry for him. The same thing could have just as easily happened to him. *If Cicero hadn't come for me...* He thought. Oswell was reminded of Cicero mentioning a trial of a young man. It seemed to line up with what he was reading now. Oswell cast a glance at the slumbering Cicero, wondering what the importance of this information was. Aside from the obvious similarities between Oswell's situation and Colin's, Oswell could make neither heads nor tails as to how any of this was supposed to help them.

He sat in deep thought for a few moments until he was startled out of his reverie by an impatient tapping on his shoulder. Oswell turned his head and looked up at Darius. He gestured for Oswell to turn the page. Oswell did as he was asked and flipped the page. The first thing he noticed was that the next entry was dated three days later than the last, and that the entry was very short. A wave of nerves washed over Oswell as he continued to read.

22nd Troden, 799 GE

I do not know how fortune can be so good to me; I have managed to gain access to the dungeons. I have been told that Colin's final request was to speak with me, and the request was granted. I can only hope that I will be able to provide solace for him in his final hours, and perhaps extract the information I need in the short time I will have.

Oswell flipped the page and began to read the next entry, which was dated on the next day.

23rd Troden, 799 GE

I have been summoned by the township to the south in Aiken. Sadly, Colin will have no friend in the crowd at his execution. I pray wholeheartedly for his soul, and hope that the information he has given me will aid in my research.

Oswell furrowed his brow in confusion. There seemed to be information missing. The writing was hurried, and whoever the author was had left out any detail as to what Colin had told him. Oswell turned the page to find nothing. He flipped through another page, still finding nothing. He rapidly scanned through the rest of the journal, found it empty, and closed it in frustration. Looking up, he jumped.

Cicero was sitting quietly in his chair with his hands folded together on the desk. A look of curiosity and amusement was evident in his face as he appraised the two boys sitting across the room from him.

"I see you've been reading my brother's journal."

Oswell's gaze trailed away from Cicero and found their way to the floor. Darius jumped to his feet, but also appeared to be very interested in the floor's intricate grain. Oswell felt guilty for invading Cicero's privacy.

"Yes, I'm sorry," Oswell apologized. Darius echoed the same sentiment.

"I would have had you read it in the morning," Cicero said.

Oswell sighed in relief.

"What do you think?"

"About the journal?" Oswell asked.

"Yes, about the journal," Cicero confirmed.

"I don't know what to make of it—what does it all mean? Did Colin end up here the same way I did?" Oswell asked.

"One question at a time my boy," Cicero said, "I am not sure exactly what to make of it either. If my brother was correct, Colin may very well have appeared in our world in much the same way you did, although it is still unclear as to how exactly that is," Cicero stroked his chin thoughtfully. "As for if he is from your world; he may very well be. However, my brother, Mathias, hypothesized that there may be many worlds—not just yours and ours." Cicero paused for a moment in thought. "Does *Bosstown* mean anything to you?"

"Boston!" Oswell exclaimed. He hadn't recognized it when he'd read it in the journal.

"Evidently it does," Cicero mused.

"Boston is a city on Earth," Oswell explained.

"Very well, it would seem increasingly likely that Colin came from your world," Cicero decided.

"Did Colin die?" Oswell asked worriedly.

"That is something we can also not know for sure. As you have already discovered, Mathias's journal ends on the twenty-third of Troden, seven-ninety-nine, Golden Era—almost twenty-five years ago. As of yet, I have been unable to verify anything in the journal except for that clerk's entry I mentioned earlier. The dates and details of the execution line up." Cicero pulled another book in front of him and began flipping through the pages as he spoke. "If what my brother says is true, we *could* discover how you got here."

"Well, what are we waiting for? We can ask Mathias for help!" Oswell exclaimed hopefully. Darius coughed loudly as Cicero shook his head.

"My brother disappeared shortly after that last journal entry," Cicero said. "He was a good man, but he left us without answers, only clues. For all we know, he may never have solved it. However, we may be able to figure this out on our own even if he never did. I do believe that you and Thomas have switched places."

"Cicero, I had a dream earlier, and it seemed so real that I believed I was home. I couldn't tell what was going on, other than that I was standing alone at the front door of my home. The door opened, and before me was a huge man. He lunged for me, my mother screamed, and I woke up. Do you think that could mean something?"

Cicero squinted, deep in thought. Looking down, he seemed to realize something and tossed the book before him aside. He then rushed over to the bookshelf and returned with another leather bound book.

"This is more of my son's work. Far less personal," Cicero explained as he flipped quickly through the pages. "Here!" he said, and began to read aloud.

"Although I have yet to find the tear joining these two dimensions, I believe the connection it has created is responsible for the irregularities in our world. People complain of vivid dreams, and many claim to have witnessed apparitions, and even ghosts of loved ones." Cicero looked up, "Vivid dream you say?" He continued to read, "I hypothesize that beyond a physical connection, there is a metaphysical connection as well, linking our worlds inextricably. These apparitions and dreams may actually be the *window* into the alternate reality whereas the physical tear is like the doorway. Perhaps, under the correct circumstances, we would be able to communicate with others in the alternate reality," Cicero finished.

Oswell stood up and approached the desk, "Why do you think he was right?"

"I do not know if he was right, but I *feel* as though he was at least on the right trail. He usually was. If he did figure it out, maybe that's where he went," Cicero pondered.

"You mean—you think he could be alive?" Darius asked.

"Maybe," Cicero said, piercing blue eyes boring into his grandson. "How else does one disappear so wholly?"

Darius looked down and Cicero turned back to Oswell. "Perhaps every person in this world has an analog in the other. You with Thomas, for example. Perhaps you can communicate with your analog and he can communicate with you. That dream, unfortunately, would suggest that he is in a great deal of trouble."

"You think that my dream was real? That it was actually happening back in my world?"

"I don't want to jump to conclusions, but there is the chance. Where else could Thomas have disappeared? After all, it would appear you disappeared from your world into ours. The same thing could just as easily have happened to him."

Oswell did not reply, failing to see any flaw in Cicero's logic. Oswell flopped down onto the squeaky chair in front of Cicero's desk as Darius stood beside him.

"I think we have a lot of work ahead of us," Oswell predicted. Darius nodded, clearly interested in the developments.

"Well, shall we begin?" Cicero inquired.

CHAPTER TWENTY-NINE

VOICES

THOMAS ROSE AND fell with every stride. With each, his ribs collided with the muscular shoulder of the beast carrying him. He cringed at a particularly violent slam; it would be one of those lovely purple and green bruises. If not for the gag in his mouth, he would have cried out.

He could not see due to the canvas sack obstructing his view. Before him, the roughly sewn fibres of the sack scratched at his skin.

The ragged breathing of the giant man carrying him provided a constant, monotonous soundtrack for their escape. He had been running for what seemed like ages, but Thomas knew better. They slowed down as the man flagged under Thomas's weight. As skinny as he was, running with a fourteen year old boy draped across one's shoulder was not an effortless task.

Thomas was struck by the overpowering smell of sweat wafting from the man. Behind that, Thomas noticed the faint aroma of renewing life. He realized exactly where they were. They were returning to the place where it had all begun. The forest. This realization came as Thomas's captor came to a dead stop. Thomas felt his stomach leap up into his throat as he dropped from Father's shoulder.

Thomas crumpled into the ground, the wind knocked out of him, and gasped for air as the sack was removed from his head. Thomas glared up at the man with an intense loathing.

"Ooarrooo?" Thomas tried to speak through the gag. The man bent down and removed the gag from his mouth. "Who are you?" Thomas repeated, his question punctuated with angry venom.

"Don't play stupid," the man replied. He leaned down, bringing his face out of the shadow and into clear view.

Thomas winced as the man's rancid breath occupied his air. Of course, Thomas had known who the man was all along; he just had not been willing to accept it. *Father.* He glanced at the man's arm. A bandage of dirty rags was wrapped around Father's forearm. Thomas hoped it was infected and would fall off. He glanced around subtly, hoping to find a way out of the situation. Seeing this, Father chuckled.

"You won't be getting away with the same trick you pulled last time, will you?" Father asked. Thomas did not dignify the question with a response. "Not so talkative now? We'll fix that. My son will absolutely love you, and my daughter will be so grateful to have someone else her age to play with."

A burning hatred ran through Thom's veins as he glared up at the man from the ground.

"But for now, I don't need you to talk. In fact, I would prefer it if you didn't," the man reached out with his great hands and gripped Thomas's throat. Thomas struggled as the man pulled a cloth from his back pocket.

Father placed the cloth over Thom's mouth and nose and then released his grip on Thomas's throat. Thomas gasped as air flooded his lungs and a sweet antiseptic smell filled his nostrils. The corners of his vision faded away to black, and seconds later he was unconscious.

Thomas awoke to complete darkness. Disoriented and nauseated, with no knowledge of where he was, how he got there, or how long he'd been there. A stale taste lingered in his mouth and a horrid smell stuck in his nostrils. Despite the fact that he could not see, he felt as though the world was spinning uncontrollably. After a few moments, he retched an empty stomach and spat onto the rolling floor beside him before lapsing back into unconsciousness.

When he woke again, he was still nauseous, but the intensity of the world's spinning had weakened. Lying on the cold floor in silence, Thomas clutched his knees to his chest and felt tears moisten at the corner of his eyes. He'd been through worse before. In fact, his history was peppered with plenty of hellish experiences, but the tragedy of the newest one was the cruelty of the circumstances. For once, he'd been happy. That happiness had been a miniature flame lighting his abysmal existence. The fire blossomed from the smallest of sparks with every passing moment in the presence of Monica and Owen. So young in its infancy, the flame had been extinguished. That was why it hurt so much. But Thomas had to do what he always did: *survive.*

The quality of the air told him he was inside, and he was laying on the planks of a rough wooden floor. He sat up slowly and mentally examined his body from head to toe. He was stiff across his chest and shoulders, and could feel the beginning of bruises forming on his ribcage. Darkness surrounded him. He could feel that his left leg was free, but his right leg was shackled. He sat up to try and work his way out of the chains.

They rattled loudly as he pulled at them.

"I wouldn't bother; the locks are solid. If anything, you'll only make Father mad," a girl's voice warned. Thomas acceded to the voice and flopped back onto his back.

"Whe— " Thomas whispered.

"Save your questions for when he's asleep. He could come back any time," the voice advised, cutting him off. Once again, Thomas found himself listening to the voice. "Try to get some sleep; it makes the night more bearable."

The voice died away into silence, and Thomas found himself staring up into the darkness.

He stayed that way for a while, wondering how he had found his way into such a predicament. It seemed as though he had escaped from one prison only to be tossed back into another. Considering the situation, he would have gladly returned to his old life of solitude and poverty if given the chance.

Out of the blackness, a faint whisper seemed to rise up and caress his ear. Thomas strained to understand what was being said, but it was only barely audible. He listened intently as the whispering continued, increasing in volume. ·

It was loud enough for Thomas to be able to discern between this new whispering voice and the one that had advised him only minutes before. The whisper followed a sort of rhythm, as though it were repeating one word over and over again. The volume of the whisper continued to increase.

"Thomas?" the voice whispered, *"Thom?"*

Thomas stiffened. It was the first time he had heard his name since he had last seen Cicero.

It had to be some sort of trick. He decided to honour the first voice's original suggestion, and kept quiet. *I'm not falling for this,* he thought.

"Falling for what?" the voice whispered. Thom's jaw dropped in shock. The voice could read his mind. Terror gripped him.

This trick you're trying to play on me, he thought, collecting himself marginally.

"Thom, I'm not playing any tricks," the voice said.

How do you know my name? Thomas thought, catching onto how the exchange was supposed to take place. He was glad that he didn't have to speak, although the mechanics of the exchange remained a mystery to him.

"Cicero told me," the whispering voice explained.

What?

"Cicero told me."

I heard you the first time! You know Cicero?

"Yes, I know Cicero."

Well, how did you get here?

"Get where?"

I don't know... wherever we are?

"Thom, I'm not with you."

Then how am I talking to you?

"I have no idea," the voice admitted.

Thom's mind began to spin at the implication. Was this why the other person in the room hadn't heard this voice talking. Was all of this taking place inside his head?

"So you have no idea where you are?"

A man... he took me. It's too dark, I can't see anything.

The voice remained silent for a minute, as though it had simply disappeared. Thomas began to feel alone again, and just as he was losing hope, the voice returned.

"You've been kidnapped," the voice decided. *"Are there a girl and a boy with you?"* it asked frantically.

I told you, I cannot see a thing.

"Of course," the voice mused, sounding apologetic.

Actually... I think there might be. Well, at least there is a girl, Thomas thought, struck again by how strange it was to talk to someone without speaking.

"Oh thank God," the voice whispered. *"At least they're still alive."*

Wait, you know these people? Thomas thought angrily.

"I know the boy and the girl, they're friends of mine."

Thomas froze in mid-thought as the sound of someone stirring in the next room cut through the darkness. *Someone's coming!*

Father had returned. Thomas could not see him, and could barely hear him, but he knew by the very malevolent energy that he effused that it was him and that he was close. It seemed as though only a thin wall separated them. In the background, the whispering voice was calling out to him again. He ignored it, forgetting that he could communicate with the voice silently.

In the other room, Father's voice was drenched with rage as he threw things around. Thomas listened fearfully as the rage wore down and the man grew quiet. The whispering in Thomas's ear faded away as Father settled down and seemed to leave the building. Thomas stayed silent and still for many minutes, waiting for safety.

When at last he felt safe, he reached out with his thoughts once again, hoping to reopen communication with the voice.

Are you still there? He asked hopefully. Silence surrounded him and his hopes began to sink.

"*I thought we lost you,*" the voice replied. Thomas's heart soared as the voice returned to him.

Who are you?

"*Oswell Wallace,*" the voice said. Thom's eyes widened in recognition of the name.

Everyone thinks that I'm you!

"*I went through the same thing, but I set them straight,*" Oswell said smugly.

How did this happen?

"*We're not sure how exactly it happened. Actually, we have no idea. But from what we can tell, you and me, we sort of... switched places. You're from Numyria, right?*" Oswell asked.

Yes.

"*I'm from the U.S., and now I'm in Numyria, and you're in the U.S.,*" Oswell explained.

What do you mean we switched places?

"*We aren't sure yet, but right now, it seems as though we... fell through a tear... in the fabric of reality,*" Oswell said, as though he were unsure of what he was saying, and checking it with someone else as he went.

But...

"*Look, I don't know much more than you do. Cicero and I are working on it.*"

Can I speak with Cicero?

"*No, you—*" Oswell said definitively, then paused. "*Well, we don't really know. I don't think you can.*"

Why?

"*I think it is pretty amazing that I'm able to talk to you at all. This is as new to me as it is to you and it's as new to us as it is to Cicero. He says there's a lot we still have to learn before we can say anything for sure, but for now, the fact that I can even talk to you is blowing my mind.*"

Thomas reluctantly followed Oswell's explanation, feeling all the more confused by the end of it.

"*There really isn't anything else for me to say,*" Oswell said. "*I wish there was.*"

You will try to contact me again? Thomas asked.

"I promise, I will. As soon as we figure out more about what is going on. As for you, stay safe, and look out for Nick and Claire."

Who are Nick and Claire? Thomas asked.

"The boy and girl. Please, take care of them for me. We're going to figure this whole mess out, but until then, you need to do what I would've done."

I will take care of them, Thomas vowed without thinking.

"Thank you."

Thomas nodded as the whispering ceased. He lay in silence for what seemed like ages. The stillness of the night was punctuated only by the loud snores of Father in the next room, and the gentle breathing of two bodies that Thomas now knew as Nick and Claire.

In the darkness of the room, Thomas began to feel less alone. The feeling of disorientation was not eased in any way, but he felt as though he was better prepared to face it now. The situation had been so bizarre from the beginning; he couldn't understand how it managed to get worse and worse. At first it had all seemed like a dream, and then it had turned into a nightmare.

His ability to recognize this had given him solace because all past experience told him that eventually he would wake up. Now, all of this was being thrown into question. With the vague explanation that Oswell had provided, Thomas couldn't help but feel conflicted. On the one hand, the explanation *was* impossibly vague and yet bizarre enough that Thomas could easily believe that his current reality was far less than a reality. To him, it was still a nightmare. For all he knew, this world was only a creation of his imagination and it would be over shortly. On the other hand, Thomas had a difficult time believing that any of this could be conjured up by *his* mind. Everything was so new, so novel, and so vivid that the possibility of it being a dream had to verge on near *impossibility*. The thing that really shook him, however, was that either way, Thomas had the eerie feeling that it would be over shortly. If it was indeed real, the ending would have more dire consequences. He wouldn't just wake up. Thomas shivered at the thought, but beyond that, there was little he could do.

He folded his arms across his chest and huddled up for warmth. His exhaustion began to take hold, and carrying the worries and fears with him, he fell into an uneasy sleep.

CHAPTER THIRTY

TROJAN HORSE

A FROWN WORKED its way across Oswell's lips as his brow furrowed up in confusion. Cicero was looking at Oswell expectantly as though Oswell had been holding him at the edge of a cliff for far too long. Of all the possibilities for what Oswell could have just discovered, he felt as though this were both a best and worst case scenario, all rolled up into a crispy egg roll. It was a sticky situation; someone had spilled the plum sauce.

When Cicero told him that he and Thomas had switched places somewhere in the forest, he wasn't willing to believe it. Now, in the short time that he'd been in the Enclave, things were becoming more and more real. Not only had Oswell doubted his ability to establish communication with Thomas, he hadn't even believed the boy existed. Up to that point, the entire situation could have still been some elaborate hoax with everyone in on the scam. Now, however, Oswell was forced into believing. What he had just experienced was no parlour trick; he had literally just read someone's mind across a vast unknown distance, and they had read right back.

As if all of that wasn't enough, now he came to find that Thomas was a captive of the kidnapper; this was where the egg roll situation came into play. Oswell didn't know if he could be confident in Thom's ability to actually help Nick and Claire. In fact, Oswell worried that Thomas could actually be *more* of a liability than anything else by the mere fact that he would not understand how the world worked.

No doubt, Oswell's parents would also be in a frantic state and Oswell did not like to think of his parents going through that. The disappearance of children not biologically their own (Nick and Claire) had been tough on his parents. Monica would be a trembling wreck. Owen was no slouch, but when it came to their child, Monica won the contest for *Emotional Parent of the Year*. Owen could step away from the situation and he also had more faith in Oswell (which Oswell appreciated). His mother, on the other hand, often preferred to see Oswell as her baby—always in dire need of care. Owen would be worried, but he would be putting on a strong face for his wife. Oswell's heart leapt up into his throat.

The only positive thing Oswell could see in the situation was that according to Cicero, Thomas was a very resourceful young man. He had, after all, escaped from prison. If he could do that, why couldn't he escape from *one* man? The other bonus to the situation was that now, Oswell had a direct connection to keep tabs on Nicholas and Claire, and by God, he would do everything he had in his power to help Thomas keep them safe.

Cicero cleared his throat. Oswell jumped and refocused on the older man.

"He didn't really say anything else," Oswell defended his slow response. In truth, Thomas hadn't said anything else important after their brief lapse in communication. Nothing important to Cicero at least. Thomas's vow to protect Nicholas and Claire meant a lot to Oswell. It put him at ease (if only slightly); and if Thomas was willing to help protect his world, then Oswell felt that he had to help Cicero and the people of Numyria, even if he had no idea how he was going to do that.

Cicero eyed Oswell suspiciously, and then recognized the new conviction taking root in Oswell's expression.

"You feel better now," Cicero observed.

"Yes. Thomas promised to take care of Nick and Claire."

"I thought he would. Thomas is a young man of great character. I can assure you of that."

"I would still rather it was me there with them," Oswell muttered.

"You may believe yourself to be better than everyone else, Oswell, but Thomas is more than capable. I hope you will be able to see that at some point. He has much to offer." Oswell felt his face redden at Cicero's assertion. In actuality, Oswell, not infrequently, allowed that arrogant belief to cross his mind. He simply didn't like being called out on it.

Looking away from the older man, Oswell gazed out the open double doors onto the balcony of Cicero's office. Sunlight filtered through the portal, and had been doing so increasingly for the past hour or so. Oswell hadn't even noticed the sun rising, what with the considerable distraction of psychic communication.

Indeed, the sun had risen barely to the height of the trees, giving the leaves a greenish-yellow hue. Oswell began to feel tired. The night had been a long one and the mental exercise of the early morning had been exhausting. He yawned and Cicero smiled benevolently.

"You're tired. Get some rest and then meet me for a late breakfast. You'll need to be alert this afternoon."

"Why, what am I doing?"

"You'll see, don't worry. Get some sleep." Cicero ordered. Oswell began to protest but Cicero put a stop to it. Defeated, Oswell climbed out of his chair, stretched, and then hobbled off to his quarters for another fitful rest.

"What *is* this?" Oswell asked as he lifted a spoonful of the mysterious concoction towards his mouth.

"Porridge. You'll get used to it for breakfast here," Darius whispered. Oswell narrowed his eyes at Darius, but continued to eat all the same. He was much too tired to argue. He hadn't slept well. It seemed though, at least, Darius and Cicero had shared the experience.

A few moments later, an older man crashed into the room with two middle aged men in tow.

The senior had startling green eyes that were magnified by thick spectacles, and an unkempt snowy beard. He had a hand planted on his stooped back, giving him a pained appearance.

The man to the senior's right was tall and thin. He wore a long brown robe with a simple rope tied around his waist - like a monk from an old movie, Oswell thought. He looked underfed, but not hungry, and had a friendly but curious look in his eyes. Oswell caught his gaze and the two locked onto each other momentarily before Oswell looked away.

The man to the senior's left was slightly shorter than the monkish man, but he was well built and athletic. Oswell could sense the energy exuding from the man's stance as he moved lithely across the room in his leather armour. He was bald with rugged features and did not appear to be as friendly as the other. Oswell avoided the possibility of making eye contact with him. The three men each retrieved a bowl of porridge and sat down silently at the round table.

Oswell was about to greet the trio when Darius nudged him in the ribs.

Oswell glared at Darius. "What?" he demanded.

"Silence, I'll explain later," Darius whispered. Oswell was about to protest as he looked around for allies, but shut his gaping mouth as he caught the cold stare of the bald man. Oswell felt icy knives scraping down his back as the man held his gaze. Oswell shivered. That settled it for him; he would wait for Darius's explanation.

"So what was that all about?" Oswell asked as he and Darius hurried from the room. The four other men remained inside, finishing their breakfast.

"We probably should have told you beforehand, so you can be forgiven, but it is Myrosian tradition to break your fast in silence. We treat breakfast as an opportunity to reflect on the mistakes we have made in the past, and decide how we are going to better ourselves for the future," Darius explained. Oswell smirked, it sounded silly to him. "We take our traditions seriously here."

"Okay, okay," Oswell said. "I won't talk next time."

"Good," Darius said.

"So what's the deal with those three? They must be Laurence and Wendell, right? Who's the old dude?"

"Rawlins; he's an old friend of my grandfather, and has been a staunch supporter of Numyrian Independence since—Myr, how old is he? He's been fighting for independence since... King *Lionel* Hartlin," Darius remembered Oswell's lack of knowledge regarding Myrosian history, "So... well over eighty years."

"Keeping up the good fight," Oswell mused.

"Indeed."

"What about the other two?" Oswell asked, figuring he'd already pegged each of them anyway.

"The Deacon is Laurence. He wears that robe *every day*. I hope he has a few of them," Darius mused.

Oswell nodded, "And the other one is Wendell? I'd guessed that much. He didn't look too friendly."

"Right. He's *not* very friendly, and he is also very suspicious. Both are excellent characteristics for someone with the responsibility of keeping the Enclave safe, but not ideal for making one feel welcome."

"True," Oswell agreed, still feeling unsettled by the look that he had been given. "I felt like he wanted to stab me."

"Right again, he probably did want to stab you," Darius laughed.

"What?" Oswell said.

"Wendell doesn't trust anyone until he gets to know them. You; he didn't even know you were here until Cicero told him. Don't worry, we'll set him straight and then you guys will be the best of friends."

"Somehow, I doubt that," Oswell said, then whirled around as the doors to the main hall opened up and the four other men strode down the walkway towards Oswell and Darius.

"Oswell Wallace, Rawlins Normand," Cicero introduced formally, allowing Oswell to shake the old man's hand.

"Nice ta meet ya," Rawlins said, squinting hard at him as though he were trying to decide whether Cicero was fooling him about the young man's identity, and whether or not he could trust his eyesight.

"Yup, you too," Oswell said, appraising the man. He had to be almost a hundred years old. The man grimaced and backed away.

"And this is Wendell Westlake," Cicero continued. "Wendell is our captain and the head of our security."

"Pleasure," Oswell wavered as the large man grasped his hand tightly. Oswell felt one of his knuckles pop as the man released his hand.

"Likewise," Wendell replied. Oswell received the sentiment as insincere, "Captain of nil, but captain nonetheless," he corrected Cicero, who conceded the point before continuing.

"...And, this is Laurence Worth, our Deacon," Cicero continued, once again, allowing them to shake hands. Oswell obliged, feeling much safer shaking this man's hand.

"Nice to meet you," Oswell greeted, feeling more genuine.

"And I, you," Laurence replied pleasantly. "You must come for a visit with me sometime," Laurence began, "I have many questions to ask of you, and Cicero seems to think you need an education in a few areas."

Oswell arched his eyebrow. All he knew about Laurence was that he was a priest, or something like that. Oswell was never one for religion back home, and he immediately felt pressured.

"I never really went to church before; I don't have any interest in your religion. Thanks, but no thanks," Oswell refused. Laurence seemed momentarily taken aback, but composed himself quickly. Laurence turned to Cicero and the two shared a knowing glance before Laurence turned back to Oswell.

"Very well, but I do hope you reconsider," Laurence said, "my door is always open." With that, Laurence bowed his head briefly to Oswell, and then to the others, and took his leave with Rawlins in tow. Oswell was sure he heard Rawlins mutter something under his breath as he walked away. Something along the lines of 'I liked the other one better.'

Oswell glanced at Darius, who shrugged.

"Are you ready?" Wendell asked, his deep voice cutting through the birdsong wafting up from beneath the canopy.

"Ready for what?" Oswell asked, looking to Darius. Apparently Darius had no idea either because he simply shrugged his shoulders again.

"We are going to scout around Fletchery. Just the three of us," Wendell explained, indicating himself, Oswell, and Darius. Darius's eyes lit up. He did not get to leave the Enclave very often. In fact, his recent role in the prison break—secreting Thomas in, and having him confined with Cicero—had been one of the first times in months that he had been allowed to leave.

"May we have a few moments?" Darius asked politely. Wendell nodded solemnly and folded his arms. Darius grabbed Oswell by the arm and dragged him away from Wendell and Cicero. "Come!"

"Where are we going?" Oswell asked, bewildered.

"To the armoury; it isn't very often we get to leave the Enclave. We need to be prepared," Darius explained.

Darius was running now and Oswell jogged to catch up. Moments later, Darius disappeared through a door into the armoury. Before Oswell had a chance to get inside, Darius burst through the door again, carrying a few things.

"We won't need much more than this," Darius outlined as he laid the gear down on the catwalk surface. "Two knife belts, two small blades, two canteens, a length of rope, and an eyeglass," Darius buckled the belt onto his waist and shoved one of the blades into a sheath on the belt. He then slung a canteen over his shoulder. Oswell began to do the same, feeling awkward with a weapon on him. He wondered if it was really necessary.

"You take the rope, I'll take the eyeglass," Darius ordered, handing Oswell the rope.

Oswell sighed, feeling cheated. The rope was much heavier than the eyeglass.

"Do we really need the rope?" Oswell asked, complaining.

"Yes, we need the rope," Darius said confidently.

"No, we do not need the rope," Wendell said, standing in the doorway. Darius jumped in surprise. "Do you think we will be scaling walls? I think not," he said. Oswell smiled and shoved the rope back into Darius's arms.

"Well I'm keeping the eyeglass," Darius grumbled.

"Yes, that may actually be of some use," Wendell agreed as Darius returned the length of rope to a hook on the wall. Wendell didn't speak again until they'd emerged from the armoury. "Come, we mustn't waste any time." Wendell turned and jogged off to the entrance of the Enclave. Darius and Oswell followed close behind the man. At the entrance, Wendell peered down through the trees. Oswell tried to determine what he was looking for, but found he was unable to see through the foliage. Wendell nodded in approval—he could see through the gaps in the leaves, it simply took a trained eye—and kicked the rope ladder off the catwalk and watched it tumble to the forest floor below.

"Go ahead," Wendell ushered Darius. Darius didn't waste any time and started climbing down the ladder immediately. Wendell nodded at Oswell and, taking a deep breath, he reluctantly followed Darius's example.

Oswell dropped to the soft forest floor and made way for Wendell to arrive, but instead, watched the ladder rise back up towards the treetops.

"What's he doing?" Oswell stammered.

"Reeling the ladder back up," Darius said, as though Oswell were slow in the head.

"We can't leave it hanging in the open; that would completely defeat the purpose."

"But I thought he was coming!" Oswell cried.

"He is; now shut up."

Oswell recoiled and did as he was told. He watched as the ladder disappeared into the leaves and then folded his arms across his chest. The only other way down would be to climb down through the trees. Even with his considerable experience from a childhood in the forest, Oswell would not be fool enough to try and climb *these* trees. Everything about Wendell, from the stubborn set of his square jaw to the easy swagger that carried him down the catwalks, told Oswell that the man was not afraid of anything. Oswell was certainly not going to be the one to put it past Wendell to climb down from such a height.

Sure enough, Oswell watched as Wendell materialized into view, leaping from branch to branch, and swinging here and there. It seemed to take him only as long as it would take to climb down the ladder. The man was surefooted and agile. Obviously, he had climbed down from the Enclave countless times before, learning the route and knowing it well. Oswell's jaw dropped in sync with the man as Wendell dropped the last fifteen feet to the ground, landed in a crouch, and then stood up. Wendell smiled at the expression on Oswell's face, but the momentary amusement melted away into his usual look of disapproval almost immediately.

"Follow me and we will find Fletchery in no time," Wendell said. Darius trusted Wendell, and after the display Oswell had just seen, he had every reason to trust Wendell as well. The man seemed more than capable.

Oswell hurried after them, catching up quickly, and then falling into a comfortable jog alongside them. In the forest, it was cool, and Oswell felt like he would be able to maintain the pace for a while. Perhaps the journey would not be so bad. He was starting to like those woods.

"Can we please take a break?" Oswell cried as he puffed in exhaustion. Wendell turned to appraise Oswell, and then slowed to a walk. Oswell took that as his cue and collapsed, arms raised above his head, breathing deeply. So much for an easy journey; Oswell thought he was in pretty decent shape, but Darius and Wendell were clearly in amazing shape. They barely perspired.

"We have work to do with this one," Wendell decided, looking disappointed.

"Certainly," Darius agreed.

"Go ahead, act like I can't hear you," Oswell grumbled.

"Oh, I apologize, are we hurting your feelings?" Wendell chuckled derisively.

Oswell set his jaw with a stubbornness that would match Wendell's most withering gaze, and folded his arms across his chest. Realizing this was not conducive to his breathing, he put them back above his head, defeated and deflated.

"We're close. We will walk the rest of the way," Wendell said, reaching a hand down to help Oswell up. Oswell took it reluctantly and clambered quickly to his feet.

The trio set off in the same direction they were going before they stopped.

"So what's the point of this trip anyway?" Oswell asked.

"I do this periodically anyway," Wendell began, "but this time in particular is so that we can see what's happened since Cicero and Thomas escaped from the jail."

"That's it?" Oswell replied.

"That's it," Wendell said. At that moment, Oswell noticed the trees beginning to thin. A minute later, they were on the edge of the forest, surrounded by sparse trees. The sight was familiar.

Although they had emerged from the forest at a different location than when Oswell had ventured out alone, the scenery was very much the same. Free from the trees, the air was lighter, though the sky was a low and unbroken ceiling of cloud. Oswell felt a chill run down his spine. Hills and farmlands interspersed with smaller, more modest wood stands extended before him to the horizon. A short distance away was a structure Oswell had never seen before. It looked like an enormous stone building, but even from the distant vantage point he held, he could tell it was a wall; a wall surrounding a town. It looked like something out of a fantasy movie, He found it far more impressive and convincing than Thane's Hollow. From their vantage point on high, Oswell spotted a familiar river. It seemed that Reg's claim of a morning's walk from Thane's Hollow to Fletchery could be very accurate. Oswell's mind flashed to Karyn's kiss, and he started to worry about her. He hoped nothing bad had happened to her or Reg for their hospitality. He immediately decided that he had to check on her.

"What do we do now?" Darius asked.

"We get closer," Wendell replied. With that, he settled into a steady jog across the fields. Darius followed as if a shadow, and Oswell, snapping out of his perseveration on Karyn, darted after them.

Oswell dropped into a prone position beside Darius, who lay beside Wendell. They were lying at the crest of the hill with a good vantage point on Fletchery. Darius observed the town walls with his spyglass while Wendell watched the road winding around the hill. Nothing was coming their way. Oswell hoped that the farmer who owned the field they rested in would not mind the trespass.

"There!" Darius whispered and handed the eyeglass to Wendell.

"Yes, looming as usual," Wendell said, absentmindedly handing Oswell the eyeglass. Oswell smiled, feeling included.

"What am I looking at?" he asked.

"On the wall, with the guards, do you see the tall man with the long sword over his shoulder?" Darius asked.

"Yes," Oswell replied, "with the beard?"

"That is Jonas Vorley, sheryff of Fletchery," Darius explained. "And the other man beside him?

Oswell looked away for a moment, finding it difficult to pull his eyes away from the sheryff, as though he commanded visual gravity, before spotting him, "yes."

"That is the Governyr," Darius said. "They do their rounds every day around this time."

Acer Makkin was short and round. His expression was one of decided boredom, though there was a cruel, piggish glint in his eyes that Oswell could see even at this distance. Oswell's overall impression was that Makkin was evil, but benign. Based on that, Oswell couldn't understand why Makkin was in power. The only explanation was the loyalty of the man beside him.

Vorley, was downright frightening. With short cropped brown hair and a thick beard covering much of his face, violence exuded from every pore and his body language was indiscriminating and uncompromisingly hostile. It seemed as though everyone but Makkin cowered away from Vorley, each trying to keep their distance. Oswell eyed the enormous sword resting casually, but menacingly on Vorley's shoulder. The shining blade was complicit in the theft of countless lives (if what Reg said was true).

"Well, what are we waiting for?" Oswell asked. He was honestly afraid of Vorley, but Makkin looked like a piece of cake… literally. With Wendell and Darius's help, they could surely take the two of them.

"What are you talking about?" Wendell said.

"Let's go get 'em!" Oswell whispered, excited. He saw this as his opportunity to go home. If Myr wanted Oswell to help them get rid of Makkin, he'd help them get rid of Makkin.

"Are you mad? We would never get close enough to Makkin to get rid of him, let alone get inside the town walls," Darius scolded.

"We could just sneak in," Oswell said.

"In broad daylight?" Darius wondered.

"You said you made a tunnel," Oswell suggested.

"They found it after the escape," Darius said, "it was destroyed without delay."

"Okay. Ever hear of the Trojan Horse?" Oswell asked.

"No," Darius replied.

"We pretend like we're giving them a gift, like a giant wooden horse, and then we hide inside it. When they bring us inside, we jump out and attack," Oswell explained.

"That is the most foolhardy plan I have ever heard," Wendell said.

"It worked for the Greeks," Oswell muttered.

"It will *not* work for us," Wendell guaranteed.

"How do you know?" Oswell asked.

"Because you know nothing, and besides you're in terrible shape. You wouldn't last in a fight." Wendell said.

Oswell's eyes widened in response to Wendell's overt bluntness. "What is it exactly that I need to know?" Oswell asked, ignoring the jibe at his physical fitness.

"A great deal, that much is clear," Wendell replied "We can't just stride into Fletchery right now, it would be a massacre. Your plan would get us all killed."

Oswell thought about this for a moment, and that moment turned into a few. Finally he softened. His impatience to go home had gotten in the way of everything else, including his own safety. Wendell was right. To do anything immediately *would* be foolhardy.

"I'm sorry, you're right," Oswell averted his eyes from Wendell's intense gaze.

"Thank you," Wendell said. Oswell thought for a moment, feeling his boldness return. If he couldn't do anything to help his cause immediately, then there was no point in delaying the learning of everything Wendell felt he must learn.

"Teach me everything I need to know!" Oswell demanded of Wendell, smiling confidently.

"I can only teach you so much, and there is much more than that for you to know," Wendell replied.

"Well, who else can teach me?" Oswell asked. If he needed to learn how to fight, Oswell was confident that Wendell would be more than apt in teaching him.

"Deacon Laurence," Wendell said, "he can teach you many things that I cannot. Together, we will teach you much of what you need to know."

Oswell sighed in annoyance. He didn't think it was going to be so easy for them to get him to talk to Laurence. Oswell wanted to go home, and now, meeting with Laurence was necessary for that to happen. Who was Oswell to hold his stubborn viewpoint on religion if it was going to get in the way of him seeing his family again? He was pigheaded, but not *that* pigheaded. Oswell nodded solemnly.

CHAPTER THIRTY-ONE

MISTAKEN REUNION

T HOMAS SLOWLY OPENED his eyes, awakening to the scattered rays of morning sunlight filtering through the roof above. Instantly he recognized that he was inside a farmhouse. He hadn't noticed in the middle of the night, but the fact was evident now. Sitting up slowly, he cast his gaze around the room and identified a girl who appeared to be about his age, and a much younger boy, who could not be more than seven or eight. Thomas identified them as the much sought after Nicholas and Claire. Both of them were sound asleep Putting faces to the names was useful. Thomas also confirmed Oswell's knowledge of the brother and sister—they looked nothing like Father.

He must be calling all the children he kidnaps his own, Thomas figured, shivering slightly at the thought. The pair were peaceful in their sleep. He was happy to see that he was not alone in the situation, but he was also mindful that it meant that they too were in a terrible situation they didn't deserve, to begin with. Thomas pictured Father's face and grimaced. Observing Nicholas and Claire, Thomas reasserted his vow to Oswell from the night before; he would do his very best to look after the siblings, and also his very best to fly in the face of their malevolent captor.

At his feet, Thomas was pleased to find a companion that was not asleep. A skinny mutt of a dog was resting his head on his paws and watching Thomas intently.

"Here boy," Thomas whispered, beckoning for the dog to come closer. The dog did as he was told, standing up and stretching before sidling up between Thomas's legs and sitting down with his face only inches away from Thom's. "Good boy," Thomas praised. The dog smiled at him with an expression full of innocence.

"What's your name?" Thomas asked, staring intently at the friendly animal.

The dog cocked his head to the side and then looked away.

"You don't have a name, do you?" Thomas asked, already knowing that the answer was no, he didn't. He rubbed the dog's side gently, feeling each rib of the skinny dog as he went. "I'm going to call you Ribs," he decided, patting the dog on the head.

Ribs looked up at Thomas happily as his tail wagged and brushed against Thomas's ankles. He seemed pleased with the decision. Thomas wasn't sure if the dog was happy about the name choice, or just about having a name at all.

"Well, now that we're acquainted, I'd like to ask you a few questions. Do you mind?"

Ribs's tongue lolled out the side of his mouth and Thomas took this to mean, "Of course I don't mind."

"Do you think there is any way to get out of here?"

Ribs cast his eyes down. Thomas's heart sank. That response was not one that he had been hoping for.

"Don't be so pessimistic," he chided, and then chuckled at this. He was usually the pessimistic one. "Trust me, I'll find a way out," he whispered.

Ribs stared at him skeptically and Thomas grinned at the dog's genuineness. Thomas paused for a moment and wondered at the accuracy of the dog's responses; he wasn't sure if he was just filling in the blanks the way he wanted to hear them, or if the dog truly understood.

Either way, Thomas felt a strong connection to the animal. They were fast friends, and Thomas felt as though he could trust him. Besides, it wasn't like Ribs could tell anyone the things that he said or planned.

"We could just run," Thomas suggested, brainstorming.

Ribs seemed to glance at Thom's shackles.

"Good point," Thomas admitted. He scooted around Ribs and observed his shackles.

They were connected to the floor and made of a heavy, shiny metal. Thomas grappled with it for a few moments and then remembered what Claire had told him the night before. The chains were sturdy, just as she'd said. He gave up.

"They do pose a problem, don't they?" he asked Ribs. Ribs lay down on the barn floor, resting his head on his paws again. The dog's ideas were exhausted.

"I thought I already tol—" Thomas turned his head as the girl named Claire began to speak.

She stared at him slack jawed, "Oz?" she whispered. Thomas thought for a moment, realizing what was going on. Just like everyone else he had encountered, Claire also thought he was Oswell, though it all made more sense now.

"Sorry, Oswell isn't in at the moment, I'm Thomas, but you can call me Thom."

Claire continued to gaze at him incredulously, her expression mixing with a heavy dose of confusion. Thomas knew the expression well; she thought that he was looped. It wasn't the first time that someone had thought that. Thomas had encountered it many times in his travels, though it had happened much more frequently since he'd shown up in Oswell's world.

"Claire, right?" Thomas ventured. She didn't respond right away, as if she were in shock. It looked as if there was an internal conflict spinning turbulently in her mind. She couldn't decide if she was happy or upset that Oswell was there. After an impatient nudge by Thomas, she replied.

"Yeah, you know that."

"Yes, I do," Thomas agreed, missing the inflection in her voice that said he was supposed to know her name for a different reason from why he did. Of course, she couldn't know that Thomas had come by her name telepathically. In fact, Thomas had little desire to tell her that that was how he knew her name. She clearly thought he was crazy enough to begin with. He didn't need to shovel the last few scoops of earth onto his grave; he already felt like he was more than six feet over his head.

A barely audible grumble rattled in Ribs's throat and Thomas glanced over at the friendly dog. He didn't look as friendly as he had before. With his ears flattened against his head and a palpable fear in his eyes, Thomas could barely recognize him as the affable animal he'd conversed with only minutes ago.

Thomas looked back to Claire. She too was transfixed, staring at the dog. Her face blanched as she identified the problem and then turned to shake her brother awake. Nicholas grumbled in protest but dutifully sat up and rubbed his eyes. Claire motioned for Thomas to get away from his shackles. Thomas obeyed her silent command, scooting away from where they attached to the floor just in time.

Father burst through the door and surveyed the young trio. He had a scowl on his face as he slid three trays of food across the floor to them. Father scrutinized Thomas with vicious intent, his grimace deepening, and then eerily turning up into a smile. Thomas had no idea what to make of it. He simply pulled the tray closer to himself as Nicholas and Claire began to eat the food.

Father turned and left the room.

Thomas leaned down and sniffed at the food. It didn't look that bad, a piece of bread and a bowl of what looked like oatmeal. In fact, it looked much better than the worst thing he had eaten, which Thomas tried to forget every day. He wasn't proud of it, but when you were on your last legs, hobbling towards starvation, a half eaten and mostly rotten rat corpse—even with the maggots thrown in—was better than the alternative of death. He'd swallowed every last bite and was sure he'd felt the larvae squirming about in his stomach for weeks afterwards. At times, he found himself regretting that particular meal, but then he always remembered that he probably would not have made it to the next one without it.

This meal, however, was one that Thomas had no interest in. He was not particularly hungry and he had gotten by in worse states. He still had plenty of meat on his own bones (by his standards) and he wasn't going to dignify Father's offering by eating it.

Instead, he motioned for Ribs to come closer. Ribs scrabbled forwards eagerly, but still looked fearful. Thomas pushed the tray towards the dog.

"Go on then," he urged, smiling gently at the malnourished animal. The dog began to dig into it quickly and Thomas snatched it away. Ribs whimpered.

"You can't eat that fast, it isn't good for you," Thomas explained, having learned from experience. He ripped off a piece of bread and dipped it into the oatmeal, and held it out to the dog. Understanding Thom's intentions, Ribs ate the food a little slower, although Thomas still wasn't satisfied with the pace. They'd have to work on it. He chuckled and continued to feed the dog in the same way, happy to do the poor animal a kindness.

Claire looked on as she ate her own food. Thomas caught her glance and she looked away, shaking her head. She didn't seem to approve of Thomas forgoing his meal for the sake of the dog.

Claire, however, did not have the knowledge that Thomas had forgone many meals before. One meal was not so bad, especially considering he had the choice, and he was choosing to donate it.

Thomas patted Ribs on the head as the dog finished off the last bite Thomas had for him. The dog curled up on top of Thomas's feet and closed its eyes contentedly. Thomas looked plainly at Claire. She glanced at the empty tray and then at the happy dog. She smiled thinly and put down her own empty tray as Nicholas played with the spoon in his long empty bowl.

"How did you get here?" Claire asked. Thomas ignored the enormity of the question and instead focused on what she actually meant: how he managed to get in the same position as them.

"Honestly, I don't really know."

"Do your best," Claire urged.

"I encountered... him... in the forest. He tried to take me, but I got the better of him," Thomas began.

"What do you mean you got the better of him?"

"I stabbed him in the arm," Thomas said. Claire's eyes widened with a mixture of shock and understanding.

"That's where he got that from," she mused. She couldn't believe that Oswell, or rather, Thomas as he claimed to be, had stabbed Father. More to the point, she couldn't believe that Thomas was alive after pulling a stunt like that.

"Yes, that was my handiwork," Thomas bragged. "After I escaped from him, I was discovered by..." Thomas reached for the words, "some police officers, they took me to a... a hospital."

"I can't believe you got away," she said, almost to herself.

"Well, it was only temporary," Thomas laughed nervously.

"True," Claire agreed.

"I went with Monica and Owen to their home and it was wonderful," Thomas said.

Claire arched her eyebrows at this description. Oswell never referred to his parents by their first names. They were on a strict 'mom' and 'dad' basis. "That was short-lived," Thomas continued, "Father came to the house and he took me."

"He came to your house?"

"Yes. Owen and Paul were gone with the police, looking for the two of you," Thomas explained. Claire smiled, encouraged by the thought of her father actively looking for her and Nicholas. "There was a knock at the door and the next thing I knew, he had me. Now I'm here," Thomas finished.

"But why you?" Claire asked.

"Probably because I knew he was out there," Thomas postulated, "and maybe because I stabbed him," he added. "Is he the vindictive type?"

"That would fit," Claire agreed.

"How has he treated the two of you?"

"Like prisoners. Not kindly, but he hasn't hurt us."

"Well, let's hope it stays that way," Thomas decided. "Well, the no violence part. We'll put an end to the prisoner thing as soon as possible."

Claire looked skeptical.

"Why is everyone so pessimistic?" Thomas complained. It was one of the few times in his life, but finally he had some confidence in himself. For Myr's sake, he'd escaped from a full blown prison. Why couldn't he do the same here?

Claire was about to answer as the door swung open again. A diminutive and mousy looking woman stepped into the room. She was wearing an old, but clean floral dress that fell about halfway down her calves.

"Father says we're leaving," she informed them, "right away," she added. She then set to work, cuffing Nicholas to Claire and then Claire to Thomas. Thomas's first thought was to resist, but the poor woman was downtrodden and weak, and he couldn't bring himself to do anything that might harm her. He allowed her to cuff him to Claire. She then grasped a key that was dangling from a string around her wrist. She unlocked the shackles that had confined Thomas, Nicholas and Claire to the floor. The three of them struggled, then stood up and stretched.

"Let's go!" Father shouted from the other room. There was a sense of urgency in his voice.

The woman urged the three of them forward, practically pushing the connected children through the door. Thomas had no idea where they were going, or why Father sounded so nervous, but Thomas was pleased that Father was uncomfortable. A small smile crept across his face as they were herded out of the farmhouse and into the morning sun.

- CHAPTER THIRTY-TWO -

CHOICES

LAURENCE HEARD THREE loud, slow knocks on the door. His visitor did not wish to be there. That meant that it was Oswell. Laurence didn't know how Wendell had managed to convince Oswell to visit him, but he was pleased nonetheless. It could have been a simple matter of giving him an order or perhaps it had been a trying discussion to convince Oswell of the merits (although Laurence knew Wendell would not be so patient). The most likely possibility was that Wendell had managed to get Oswell to convince himself that a visit to Laurence was necessary. This was a success in Laurence's books, even if Oswell was coming without any true desire to do so. Laurence always believed that the most difficult part of his job was getting non-believers to come to the table. Now that Oswell was pulling up a chair, Laurence could work his magic.

Laurence crossed the floor and pulled open the door just as Oswell was about to knock on it for a fourth time. Oswell caught himself slightly off balance from the attempted knock, and then righted himself.

"Wendell convinced me that the best way to get through all of this is for me to let you and him help me," Oswell explained. Laurence smirked at the explanation.

"Welcome to my home, and our Havyn," Laurence greeted as he stepped aside to allow the young man entrance to the room. Oswell took one tentative step and then another before breaking into a full stride and finding a seat at a table in the middle of the room. Laurence glided after him and sat down in a chair across from him.

Laurence looked across the table at Oswell. There was a determination in Oswell's eyes that gave Laurence great hope, but before that fire, Laurence could also detect the shield that Oswell had constructed in front of it. Laurence smiled benevolently at his young ward. Wendell had delivered Oswell, or more accurately, Oswell had delivered himself to the lessons that Laurence could offer. It would be Laurence's job now to break down those defences and unleash the true power of the passion that he was only beginning to sense in Oswell.

"I'm very pleased that you have decided to come here," Laurence said.

"Well I don't have much choice, do I?" Oswell replied.

"You *always* have a choice," Laurence said.

"I didn't *choose* to come here," Oswell countered, referring to his unwelcome vacation in Myros.

"Sometimes greater things may seem to be out of our control, but everything is truly based on the decisions we make."

"Don't think so."

"It's true. How did you get here?"

"How should I know?"

"Let me rephrase that: what was the last thing you did before you got here?"

"Oh," Oswell replied, "I went looking for my friends."

"In the forest," Laurence added.

"Yes."

"Was that a decision that you made?"

"Yeah."

"Is it possible, then, that your decision precipitated your appearance here?"

"I guess so..."

"Well you can see then that your choices were involved in at least some small—if not integral—way, in your appearance here."

"Well…"

"Yes?"

"What was I supposed to do? Just do nothing to help my friends?"

"You had every right," Laurence conceded, "but you did not because doing so would is not your nature. You needed to help your friends."

"My personality wasn't my choice."

"I would disagree with that; every decision we make throughout our lives contributes to our experience and therefore to our character." Laurence smiled as he saw a light of understanding flicker in Oswell's eyes, a crack in the armour. "We are guided by fate, but Myr provides us the opportunity to deviate from the Path. Some of our decisions, we were destined to make, but we make those decisions on our own nonetheless. Sometimes, our decisions lead us away from the Path, and Myr is more than happy to adjust his plans for the sake of free will."

Oswell sat silently and in thought.

"Some things are meant to happen, but they do not. Other things were never meant to happen, but they do. This is the fundamental fluidity of our reality. The tides change with the pull of the moon just as our fates change with the influence of our decisions."

Oswell remained silent.

"I wish to assure you, Oswell, that it is not my intention to convert you. Our lives are guided by our decisions. The choice to accept Myr into your life is simply another decision in a lifetime of many. All I hope to do is stand as an advisor, or as a source of wisdom. Ultimately, the choice is yours," Laurence paused, then slid a book in front of him and rapped it gently with his knuckles. "Beyond all the fantasy and religiosity in this book, there are many lessons to be learned from this old tome. I wish to teach you these lessons, and nothing beyond that, unless you so choose. Whatever your choice here, I can also assure you that it remains your choice as to what you do with these lessons."

"Thank you," Oswell replied feeling reassured.

"Splendid," Laurence said, "that will be all for today."

Oswell stared up at Laurence, surprised at the brevity of the meeting. He went to stand up and then, unsure, remained in his seat for a moment, before finally standing up.

"Uh, thanks again," Oswell said.

"Of course."

As Oswell turned to leave, Laurence smiled kindly again. He felt certain that he had chipped away at Oswell's shield. Already, it seemed as though the fire was burning brighter.

Oswell strapped a blade to a scabbard on his waist and buckled another at the small of his back. It was an odd feeling arming himself like a knight. He hadn't a clue how to use a sword—he was a peaceful person by nature. Grant had spent days trying to convince Oswell to throw rocks at crows, and even when he had bowed to peer pressure and gave in, Oswell had made sure that he always missed. What it was, exactly, that Oswell planned to do with the weapons, he was not sure. Having protection, however, felt necessary.

"What are you doing?"

Oswell whirled around, feeling colour rush to his cheeks. Darius stood in the doorway to the armoury, arms folded across his chest.

"Uh—I'm—" Oswell spluttered.

"Use your words," Darius mocked.

"I need to do something," Oswell finally managed.

"And that is?"

"I need to... I need to check on Karyn," Oswell mumbled.

"Karyn?"

"The girl from Thane's Hollow I told you about."

"That one? The one you abandoned to the Numyrian guards?" Darius smirked.

"I have to do what's right," Oswell said. He thought back to his conversation with Laurence, "It's my choice. Y—you didn't see what happened. They came looking for me—"

"Who?"

"The guards, they came—they went to Thane's Hollow. They knew that Karyn and Reg were with me that morning. Jonas—he," Oswell stared into Darius's eyes. "You must know what he would have in store for someone who helped us."

Darius narrowed his eyes and then groaned. "And you were planning on going alone?"

Oswell didn't respond.

"Do you even *know* where you're going?"

"Thane's Hollow," Oswell replied as though speaking the words made the finding of the place easier.

"And I suppose you know exactly how to get there." Darius stared at Oswell who was doing his best to avoid eye contact. "You know my grandfather wouldn't approve." He set his jaw.

"I have to know that she's okay," Oswell thought of Claire and then Karyn. "It's the right thing to do."

Darius's right eye twitched. "Can't believe..." Darius strode across the cluttered room and started outfitting himself, "he's talking me into this..."

"You don't have to co—"

"Shut up," Darius cut Oswell off, "of course I'm coming. But if we get caught, I'm—I am showing you the best way to find the Enclave. In case you get lost."

"Deal," Oswell said, grinning in spite of himself.

Oswell took a sip from his canteen. With Darius in the lead, they'd been walking for close to two hours.

"So you know where we're going?" Oswell asked.

"Like I would rely on you to get us there," Darius scoffed.

"Just asking," Oswell frowned.

"What's your plan anyway?" Darius said.

"I don't know," Oswell put his canteen away. "I just want to check on her."

"Got a thing for her?" Darius chided.

"No!"

"Okay," Darius said knowingly.

"I don't!" Oswell insisted. *Maybe I do,* he thought. When he hadn't been worrying about Claire and Nicholas, or how to get home, he'd been worrying about Karyn. At the start of the summer, Oswell did not think he would find so much to worry about.

Darius smiled, "We're nearly there."

The trees began to thin. They emerged a short distance away from where Oswell had first broken the tree line alone. He immediately recognized the winding river. Looking north, he could imagine Fletchery sitting beyond the hills. To the South, just around the bend, Oswell knew that Thane's Hollow was nestled against a smaller stand of trees.

"Let's go," Oswell said, not wanting to waste any time. They made their way down to the river and Oswell felt his mind wander as he approached the spot where he'd met Karyn. As Darius blabbered on about the improvements he had planned for the fire suppression system, Oswell couldn't help but imagine getting another kiss from Karyn for the valiant act of ensuring her safety.

Darius went strangely silent, setting Oswell on edge. He grasped the hilt of his short sword as they rounded the bend and dashed across the farmer's field into Thane's Hollow.

The village was impossibly quiet, like a great weight subdued its occupants. Two men standing on the porch of the rundown inn spotted them and hurried inside. A woman gathering water at the central well abandoned her task to dash back into her home. Each villager in sight scurried out of view at the mere imposition of two young men with swords. A sense of foreboding gathered in Oswell's gut. Darius unsheathed his sword, and Oswell did too.

"Which house is hers?" Darius asked.

"That one," Oswell pointed to Karyn's home. He started for the door, but Darius grabbed him by the shoulder.

"Are you sure you want to go in there?" Darius asked.

Oswell grimaced in return, reading the dark thought behind his companion's question, but nodded. Darius returned the nod, and followed Oswell towards the front door. He reached up to knock, but stopped as he caught a look from Darius out of the corner of his eye. Oswell listened.

"Do you hear that?" Oswell mouthed to Darius. Darius nodded. Inside the house, someone was whispering, while someone else sobbed quietly.

Oswell pushed the door open with the butt of his sword and peered into the unlit interior.

"Oswell?" Karyn whimpered. Oswell stepped into the shadows, Darius behind him. Inside, he could see Karyn, sitting on the modest pallet that served for Reg's bed, cradling her father's head in her lap. Oswell sheathed his sword and rushed forward to kneel down in front of Reg. His stomach was bandaged, the wound completely obscured.

"W-what happened?" Oswell whispered. Reg could barely speak, whispering something that Oswell couldn't make out.

"They…" Karyn couldn't get anything else out. Oswell knew what had to have happened and looked back at Darius. Darius knelt down beside Oswell and sniffed at the bandages. He cringed and looked back at Oswell, shaking his head. Karyn moaned.

"Reg, I'm sorry," Oswell said. Reg's eyes were cloudy and he didn't seem to notice he was being spoken to. He continued to whisper incoherently. Oswell leaned down and put his ear up to Reg's mouth.

"See… that she's… safe."

Oswell looked up at Karyn. Her eyes were puffy; she'd been crying for hours. Immediately, tears welled up in Oswell's eyes. He'd barely known the man, barely knew Karyn, and yet, he was responsible for Reg's death. He was responsible for Karyn losing her father; losing her father so shortly after her mother. They were happy before he came. Managing. Surviving. He looked back down at Reg and nodded his agreement to the request. A peace seemed to inhabit his dying face, replacing the worried pain that had defined it only moments before Oswell's silent reply.

"Karyn, you need to come with us," Oswell said forcefully, wiping a drop of salty mourning from his cheek. Darius looked like he was about to protest, but couldn't. He stared at the dying man's face and couldn't look away.

"I c-c-can't," she cried.

"You have to," Oswell said again, "It isn't safe for you here." Enough damage had been done already. Karyn could get by on her own, but there was only so much a fifteen year old girl could expect to do—so much she could expect to protect herself from. If Jonas Vorley was any indication, there were evil men in Myros.

Oswell crouched down behind Karyn as a rattling breath escaped from Reg's cold lips. He was gone. Darius reached forward and closed the man's eyes. Oswell rested his hands on Karyn's shoulders. She was shivering uncontrollably. He turned her and pulled her into his chest. She buried her head there and Oswell felt his shirt dampen as renewed tears leaked from her exhausted eyes. They sat like that for a long time, Oswell holding Karyn and Darius waiting patiently. When Darius began to fidget, Oswell could tell they needed to leave.

"Karyn, we need to go," Oswell whispered. She looked up at him with her doe-like eyes, the normally warm brown muted by her sorrow.

"We have to bury him," she said slowly. It wasn't a request.

The sky was dark as Oswell, Darius, and Karyn plunged back into the forest. Oswell knew that Cicero would be angry they'd left. Their cover was blown; with Karyn in tow, there was no way they could convince the others that they had left the Enclave for any other reason. Oswell felt strangely unaffected by the realization. His choices had led him to Karyn, his choices had caused Reg's death, and his choices had led him back to Karyn. Some things were never meant to happen, but they did. Other things were always meant to happen.

Far behind them, a good man was buried behind his home beneath an unmarked stone. Folded across his chest was a single red apple, a farewell from Karyn. One day it would grow to be an apple tree, tall and strong—a provider, like Reg.

Chapter Thirty-Three

ON THE ROAD

COUNTRY MUSIC BLARED through the speakers in the industrial van. Thomas sat in the back, leaning up against the white wall of the vehicle. Ribs was lying on his belly, head motionless beneath Thomas's hand. The dog had quickly grown attached to Thomas and Thomas to the dog. Across the van was a similar scene, with Claire sitting against the wall of the van, looking uncomfortable. Lying down with his back to the floor of the van, Nick rested his head in Claire's lap and she rested her hand on his forehead, mussing the locks of hair that fell there.

In the front of the van, Father was at the wheel trying to sing while the quiet woman—Kelly, according to Claire—sat silently in her seat. They had been driving for longer than Thomas cared to keep track; certainly hours. He liked driving when he could see the scenery flying past him The stark white of the van's metallic walls gave nothing away. He rocked back and forth to wake up his buttocks and then looked up at Claire as she stared at him.

Catching his gaze, she glanced forward, "*Where do you think we're going?*" she mouthed.

"*I do not know,*" Thomas mouthed back.

"I can't see out the window, can you?" Claire asked, using quasi sign language. Thomas sat up straight and stretched his neck as high as it could go.

He could just barely see past the metal divider between the front seats and the cargo area.

Through the gaps in the metallic grid, Thomas could see bits of green trees and the sky, but certainly nothing to help him identify their direction. Even if there was anything, it would be too fragmented, and they were going too fast. Thomas couldn't help.

"I can barely see. There are just trees," Thomas replied.

"Damn it," she muttered, audibly this time. Thomas looked at his feet. Even if he could see something; he didn't know this world. How could he identify a landmark? He was practically useless. Thomas didn't like it, but until such time as he became familiar with Claire's world, they would have to sit in the dark.

Thomas cringed at the uneven twang in Father's voice as the man sang along to the radio. Slow and sad, the music filled the van's cabin with an eerie atmosphere. Father was not a good singer. In fact, he reminded Thomas of Kale Golan, a carpenter Thomas had met in Salty Flats on the west coast. Kale had had dreams of travelling the world on the strings of his guitar. Unfortunately, Kale had more of a fondness for sitting in the brewhouses as a patron rather than as an entertainer. He was all drunken confidence and no natural talent. The strings he plucked and the notes he sang may have sounded good to his own ears but those were the only ears to have such an experience. Kale eventually found his way back to carpentry.

Now, Thomas was wishing that Father would find his way back to being the cold and quiet abductor that he had been before. *At least my ears could stop bleeding.* Thomas sniggered briefly at his own thought.

"What are you laughing at boy?" Father ceased his serenade.

"Something I thought of," Thomas said.

"Care to share with the rest of us?" Father snarled. Thomas struggled, not knowing how to answer the man without inflaming anger. Then it hit him; perhaps that was exactly what he wanted to do.

Thomas braced himself before he spoke and motioned for Nick and Claire to do the same. "I was just wondering how you got into this line of work of abducting children? Singing didn't work out for you?"

The preventative measure was necessary. Father slammed on the brakes and pulled onto the shoulder of the two-lane highway.

The back doors of the van swung open and Father climbed up into the rear. He grabbed Thomas by the scruff of his t-shirt and dragged him to the back of the van. Taking a quick peek around and, seeing there were no cars on the way, he heaved Thomas through the air.

Thomas hit the gravel of the shoulder and rolled before standing up. Seeing Thomas uninjured simply served to infuriate Father more. The huge man leaped from the van and rushed Thomas, shoving him to the gravel and further from the van. There was little Thomas could do to ease that fall. He felt the gravel scrape his back where his t-shirt had ridden up.

Before he could get up, Father lifted him up by the front of his shirt. Thomas communicated no fear with his eyes, only defiance. He glanced away from Father as the man growled at him. Thomas saw what he was looking for; he'd gotten lucky. His eyes flitted back to Father and Thomas returned the glare with added venom.

"You think you're funny boy?"

"Sometimes," Thomas shot back. Father swung his fist into Thom's stomach. Thomas absorbed the blow as best he could, but it still hurt. He cried out in exaggerated pain, hoping it would satisfy Father. As much as he would have liked to give Father a harder time, it wasn't going to do him any good.

Father reeled back again to strike again. Thomas took it as his opportunity and feigned fear.

"Please, don't!" he cried.

Father looked surprised at the sudden fear, and then smiled sadistically. He chuckled and threw Thomas to the ground again.

"Get back in the van," Father ordered.

Thomas picked himself up as Father stood, watching. Thom looked to Father, nodded submissively, and then began his trek back to the van. He took one last glance at the entire reason for the ordeal and then climbed into the van. Father slammed the doors shut behind him and locked them.

"What were you thinking?" Claire whispered. Nicholas quivered in her embrace.

"Sacrifices," Thomas whispered back as Father climbed back into the van.

"No more jokes from the comedian," Father said as he buckled himself in. He pulled the van back onto the highway and cranked the volume up on the radio. He didn't sing.

"*What do you mean?*" Claire mouthed.

"*I know where we're going,*" Thomas replied.

"*You did* that *to find out where we were going?*"

Thomas nodded.

"*You're crazy.*"

Thomas shrugged.

"*What did you see?*"

"*A sign.*"

"*Of course!*" Claire mouthed, recognizing what Thomas had done. The attempt had been a long shot, but it had worked out. Claire shook her head in disbelief. "*Where?*"

"*Canada, 40 miles.*" Thomas gloated.

"*Canada?*" Claire asked, giving Thomas a chance to change what he'd said.

Thomas nodded more slowly this time, unsure of what was giving Claire pause. He stared at Claire, concerned as her eyes darkened and she looked down. She slowly looked back up at him.

"*What's wrong with Canada?*" Thomas asked impatiently.

"*We're leaving the country,*" Claire replied, staring solemnly into his eyes. Thomas didn't know exactly what that meant, but he was beginning to feel as though Canada was not somewhere he wanted to go.

Chapter Thirty-Four

IMPATIENCE

OSWELL CRINGED AS the flat surface of a sword smacked the back of his head. He whirled around to identify his attacker, but the swordsman was nowhere to be found. It sounded as though he was surrounded. The movements of the unseen enemies were everywhere and nowhere at the same time. His opponents were not outspoken in their assault. In fact, they were very nearly silent. However, they were not silent enough for him to be oblivious to their presence. This was how Oswell knew that they were all around him; that and the regular smacks to his head. He could not see them, and he could barely hear them, but he knew with certainty that they were there, and he knew with certainty that there were many of them.

That was impossible though, because Oswell had entered the forest with only one other man. Wendell had guided him into the maze-like forest with the promise of teaching Oswell how to fight. Naturally, Oswell had followed willingly. If he was going to honour his promise to Reg, as well as help the people of Myros, he needed to know how to fight.

Oswell had only been in one fight before. It was three years before, and his opponent's name was Tyler Nosey. Tyler was bigger and stronger than Oswell, but Oswell had had about enough from the other boy. Oswell seemed to remember the reason for the fight having to do with Tyler showing a less-than-kind interest in Claire. Oswell and Claire were like brother and sister, and as Claire's pseudo-brother, Oswell was bound to stick up for her (even if Claire wasn't interested in him sticking up for her). According to Claire, and she maintained it to the day, Tyler was not being mean to her, but rather, trying to get her to like him. Before the fight, she'd had a small crush on Tyler Nosey, but following the fight, she'd been obligated to ignore him. As much as she had liked Tyler Nosey, she couldn't like a boy that fought and beat her best friend. Especially considering the rough shape Oswell found himself in following the fight. It took a while for Oswell to recover from his two black eyes, split lip, and bruised ribs (not to mention his bruised ego). His parents hadn't been happy with Oswell's decision in that situation. Following the fight (and a lecture from his parents), Oswell had been sure to take a more peaceful stance on controversial matters.

Learning how to fight from a powerful, athletic, and capable man like Wendell sounded like the perfect opportunity. Oswell had barely been able to contain himself at the thought of using all the tricks Wendell would teach him. Tyler Nosey had gotten bigger and stronger over the years, but with Wendell's training, beating him would be child's play if it ever happened again. Oswell, however, hadn't realized the training might be Wendell's opportunity to punish him for visiting Thane's Hollow and bringing Karyn back.

He learned quickly. The seeds of doubt had been sown, grown, and quickly reaped with the initiation of Oswell's training. As he stumbled around the forest he could feel the skin on the back of his head rise up and redden beneath the hair and he couldn't help but feel as though this training was not going to be of any use in fighting Tyler Nosey, let alone keeping Oswell alive in Myros.

Oswell whirled around again hoping to catch a glimpse of an incoming blow. He found there was nothing to be seen. Frustrated, tired, and in pain, he backed into a tree, closed his eyes, and slid down to the forest floor defeated.

"What do you think you did wrong?" Wendell asked, emerging from the shadows in front of Oswell. Oswell opened his eyes and groaned in frustration. Even facing Wendell's direction, the man had been invisible. The last twenty minutes had been an ordeal he did not wish to repeat.

"I've got no idea," Oswell grunted.

"Were you confused?"

"Yes."

"Did you feel anything else?"

"Other than the smack of your sword on the back of my head?" Oswell muttered. Wendell gave Oswell a dark look and Oswell reassessed the question. "I was as good as blind," Oswell decided. Wendell nodded in affirmation.

"Yes, perhaps even worse," Wendell confirmed. "Stand up."

Oswell groaned, but climbed to his feet nonetheless.

"Step towards me."

Oswell took a slow step away from the tree behind him.

"I want you to close your eyes and spin around 5 times, and then try to locate me."

Oswell rolled his eyes impatiently, but did as he was told. As he spun, Wendell melted into the trees.

Oswell opened his eyes and looked around. Wendell did not make a sound. Now Oswell was not only blind, but deaf.

"How am I supposed to find you now?" Oswell demanded, only seconds into the exercise. Wendell emerged from the trees to Oswell's left and Oswell turned to him, expecting the man's disappointment. "What do you expect? I got all turned around!"

"I did not think you would find me. You would never have," Wendell hissed. Oswell recoiled back from the man. "You have hit on one problem exactly: you got turned around. In this forest, your orientation is of the utmost importance. You must pick a course, and you must stick to it." Wendell explained. "The same principle can be applied to battle. You must stand your ground. Be aware of your surroundings, but do not let your surroundings overcome you. Remember this: your surroundings *surround* you. Own them and use them to your benefit. Failing to take your every advantage, this one included, could be a fatal mistake."

Oswell nodded slowly, beginning to understand.

"Your second mistake was your impatience. It took all of twenty seconds for you to give up. In battle, patience is of utmost importance. Do not rush your opponent. Let him come to you. Be patient. Allow your opponent to make the mistake, and when he does, take advantage of it. His mistake will come long before yours if you give it the time to develop."

Oswell's cheeks flushed at the acknowledgment of his rapid failure, but then he set his jaw and paid closer attention to Wendell's lesson.

"Now, I want you to brace yourself. Stand your ground, and focus on something about this tree," Wendell began, running his fingers down the side of a large pine tree. Oswell widened his stance and picked a spot where some white sap was oozing out of a knuckle in the tree. "Close your eyes and turn around five times, then try to locate me."

Oswell closed his eyes and Wendell melted into the trees. Oswell turned five times and then opened his eyes. First, he focused on the white sap and gathered his bearings. He did not move from the spot. Instead, he closed his eyes once again and listened.

All around him, the sounds of the forest were clear. Oswell hadn't noticed them before. He opened his eyes and scanned the trees, blinking slowly. Taking his time, he searched his surroundings. They no longer felt like an obstacle, but rather, an extension of him.

The soft mulch beneath his feet was springy, offering a lightness to his stance. The wind whistling calmly through the forest painted a picture of his environment. Each tree began to look like an individual, rather than a clone in the greater whole.

Oswell's arm slowly rose, pointing into the trees.

Wendell emerged slightly to the right of Oswell's decided location. The man was smiling. "Amazing!" Wendell complimented. He hadn't expected Oswell to catch on so quickly.

Oswell beamed. "Now, let's do it again," Wendell laughed. Oswell closed his eyes.

"You've made great progress today Oswell," Wendell praised as the pair wound their way through the trees back to the Enclave. Oswell felt more comfortable in the forest, and thoughts of the futility of the lesson that Oswell had confronted only an hour or two before, had long faded from his mind.

Oswell stopped as Wendell motioned. Wendell then ran towards a tree, clambered up the first ten feet easily, and then, using the branches, climbed off into the green ceiling. Oswell shook his head in wonderment. Why didn't he just call Bartimaeus?

A few minutes later, the ladder dropped through the canopy and landed lightly on the forest floor. Oswell grabbed a hold of it and started climbing as the ladder reeled upwards, hastening his ascent. When he emerged at the top, he stepped onto the platform and stood up beside Wendell.

"You're going to have to teach me how to do that sometime," Oswell envied.

"Perhaps one day," Wendell agreed, "but you've learned enough from me today. Let's find some lunch."

"I want to check on Karyn first," Oswell said. Karyn was resting in Oswell's former quarters, tended to by Laurence. Oswell had forfeited the hut so Karyn could have her own place of refuge, and Laurence had kindly offered to keep an eye on her.

"Very well, I wanted you to visit with Laurence again anyway."

Oswell gauged Wendell's expression. He could tell that Wendell was still upset about Oswell leaving the Enclave without warning him, and worse, bringing an outsider back to the Enclave. It had been a risky move, but one done out of kindness. Wendell would have to forgive him eventually.

"I'll talk to him," Oswell agreed, deciding it was easier than arguing. Besides, his last meeting with Laurence hadn't been so bad.

"Good," Wendell nodded. He started towards Karyn's hut.

"Where are you going?" Oswell jogged down the catwalk after Wendell.

"I also need to speak with Laurence," he knocked gently on the door to Oswell's former quarters.

"Come in," Laurence said. Oswell followed Wendell into the cool confines of the hut. Oswell rushed over to the bed and got to his knees in front Karyn. Laurence stood up and followed Wendell out of the hut at Wendell's indication. Oswell was happy to get some private time with her.

"How are you doing?" Oswell asked. She stared back at him. He could tell from the look in her eyes that she'd come a long way in the short time she'd been there.

"Getting better," she said. "I—I meant to thank you for..." she paused for a long time. "For coming back for me."

"I had to," Oswell replied. Karyn stared at him unabashedly and he felt his cheeks warm.

"No you didn't," she said.

"We'll have to agree to disagree," Oswell finalized, standing up. He brushed a piece of hair off of her face and behind her ear, and feeling bold, he kissed her forehead. It was her turn to blush.

Oswell looked up and jumped as Laurence came back into the hut. He glanced at Karyn and felt his face reach a sweltering level of redness. Laurence grinned knowingly.

"Laurence, Wendell wanted me to talk to you."

"Of course," Laurence said. He turned to Karyn, "is there anything else I can do for you right now?"

"No, I'm fine. Please, go. Thank you."

"I'll come back and check on you after," Oswell said. She smiled again and then closed her eyes. Oswell and Laurence stepped out of the hut.

Outside, the air was brisk. Oswell was beginning to grow impatient with the weather; he'd long anticipated a hot summer, and now it had been stolen from him. The climate of northern Numyria was frustratingly tepid. Admittedly, it made his exercises with Wendell more bearable.

"I'm glad you decided to come back for a talk," Laurence said as he led Oswell towards his quarters.

"I'll do *anything* to get home," Oswell replied. Besides, Oswell had indeed learned something last time; the talks were not a total waste. That lesson had been integral to saving Karyn. Oswell shuddered to think what could have happened if Reg had died before he got there.

"Hmm, yes," Laurence noted, "I thought you might say that."

"What do you mean?" Oswell asked, surprised as he sat down across from Laurence.

"Tea?" Laurence offered, pouring himself some.

"No thank you," Oswell replied, caught off guard. "What do you mean?" he repeated.

Laurence set a cup of tea down in front of Oswell nonetheless, and then sat down with his own cup. "After our first conversation, I already had the inkling that you were impatient, but now I am sure of that, after hearing about your training this afternoon." Oswell's brow furrowed as he realized what Wendell must have wanted to talk to Laurence about. He felt like he had been tattled on.

"This is about my patience?" Oswell asked incredulously. "I'm working on it!" *These guys are obsessed,* he thought.

"Perhaps in battle you will be patient, at least we will hope," Laurence conceded, "but patience is a virtue that you must exhibit in all aspects of your life."

"Why?"

"You yearn to return to your world, and I understand that you miss it," Laurence explained. "It may not have been your explicit choice to come here, but come here you did."

"Yeah, I guess that's what we said."

"The time for you to return to your world will come."

"When?" Oswell demanded.

"You should know better than to demand that of me. I do not carry all of the answers."

"Sorry."

"Just as you learned today that you must be patient in battle, you must also be patient in life. After all, you battle for your life, among other things."

Oswell nodded, understanding.

"Just as you must wait to seize your opportunities in battle to win, you must wait to seize your opportunities here. Open your mind to the possibilities."

Oswell couldn't help but feel like Laurence was referring to Karyn. He continued to nod, understanding the connection between what Wendell had taught him, and how Laurence was trying to extend it.

"You have great potential Oswell," Laurence decided, smiling benevolently from behind his cup of tea.

"Thank you," Oswell replied.

"You just have to allow that potential some room to breathe. Urging your return to Earth will only distract you from the tasks set to you here."

Oswell nodded slowly, and then stopped. "You say I just have to wait for my opportunity—what if it never comes?"

"Your opportunity will come," Laurence assured Oswell. "It could be tomorrow or it could be years from now." Oswell's eyes cast down. "One day, you will be given the opportunity to make a choice, but when it comes, you must be aware that the choice is there. If you are patient, you will not miss it."

Oswell felt as though the confidence of his success with Wendell was wearing off, hastened by the honesty in Laurence's words. In that humility, Oswell could see that Laurence was right. There was no use in rushing to do anything. Everything would come with time if only he would wait for it. Still, learning to be patient was not going to be easy. Coming from a world of instant gratification, adjusting his expectations would take practice.

"Okay, what do you want me to do?" Oswell asked slowly.

"Wait," Laurence whispered.

Oswell reached for the cup of tea and took a sip. He sat in silence, watching Laurence as the older man watched him back. They sat as the sun embarked on its slow descent towards the horizon. Laurence finally stood up a few hours later.

"Excellent work," Laurence said. His voice was soft as it gently punctuated the silence that had inhabited the room for the past few hours. Neither Laurence, nor Oswell could believe that the young man had managed to sit in patient silence for so long. It had been difficult at first; Oswell had fidgeted and fought back complaints for the first half hour, but following that, it had been closer to what one would call manageable.

Sensing that the lesson was over for the night, Oswell stood up. "Good night," he replied.

He then turned and walked slowly from the hut, looking forward to getting some sleep, if he could manage.

Laurence sat back down in his chair, gazing at the door Oswell had disappeared through. He stayed until the fading light crept from the room, leaving him in darkness.

CHAPTER THIRTY-FIVE

SOMETHING IN COMMON

THOMAS JOLTED OUT of a daze as the ground beneath the moving van began to crunch. He glanced at Claire. Her chest rose and fell rapidly with stuttering breaths.

The tires of the van rolled slowly along the gravel road. It was an obvious change from the smooth pavement that Thomas had grown accustomed to and fallen asleep to. They had not been driving for very long and Thomas found it difficult to believe that they had arrived in 'Canada' so quickly.

Glancing back at Claire, he mouthed the word to her in inquiry, but she shook her head. They had not crossed the border yet.

If we're not in Canada, where are we? Thomas asked himself. Unable to see anything but trees out of the front window, Thomas pressed his back up against the wall of the van and gave up.

It didn't look any different from before, they were just going more slowly.

Father took another turn off of the first gravel road and Thomas felt the ground under the tires shift yet again. It didn't sound like gravel anymore, but rather, it seemed they were no longer on a road at all. The ride was bumpy as if they were driving along a grassy dirt path.

The van rolled to a stop and Thomas stood up, stooping to fit. Claire did the same, pulling Nick up with her as Father climbed out of the front seat. Kelly unbuckled herself and followed and Thomas listened as she made her way around the van. She pulled the rear doors open as an engine fired up just out of sight.

"What are we doing?" Thomas asked.

"We're going to stay here for the night," Kelly said quietly, avoiding eye contact. Thomas took note of the guilt in her tone. "Come."

Father dragged a tarp off of a small green sedan parked nearby. He popped the trunk and dragged out two large bags. He then set to work building two tents. Thomas watched as the man grunted and groaned and finally managed to get both tents constructed.

"In," he said. Thomas, Claire, and Nicholas stared at him. The look on his face hardened and Thomas put his hand on Claire's shoulder.

"Come on," Thomas said, guiding his charges into the tent. Father chucked a bag of potato chips and three bottles of water into the tent.

"Get some sleep," he said. "Big day tomorrow."

Thomas woke to the sound of their tent rattling. He hadn't slept well. He let go of Claire—they'd been huddling for warmth—and sat up.

"Up and at 'em," Father laughed. His cheeriness made Thomas feel nauseous. Claire and Nicholas woke up as Thomas climbed out of the tent. They followed him out quickly. "Break it down, boy," Father commanded, motioning towards the tent. Father's was already disassembled and packed into the trunk of the green sedan.

Thomas raised an eyebrow and looked at the tent. *Break it down?* He thought. Thomas turned back to Father.

"What do you mean?"

"Don't play stupid," Father growled. "Take the tent down!"

Thomas did his best to reverse the process Father had carried out the day before and with Claire's help managed to get the tent stuffed into the bag.

Father leaned out the window of a small green sedan and slapped the door excitedly. "We'll be ridin' in style now!" he shouted. "Pile in!"

"Why are we changing cars?" Thomas asked, eyeing the sedan warily as he shoved the tent bag into the trunk and slammed the trunk shut.

"You ever try to cross a border in an unmarked white van?" Father asked.

"Ummm…" Thomas began.

"Rhetorical question dumbass." Father motioned for them to get in once again. "Kelly, you get in the back; Nicky's ridin' shotgun with me."

"Okay," Kelly mumbled, eyes locked on her toes which were poking out of her sandals.

Nicholas looked to Claire but Claire simply stared at Father with a burning hate in her eyes.

Nicholas shrugged and then jogged around the side of the green car. He climbed into the front seat with Ribs hot on his tail as Kelly climbed into the back. Thomas grimaced and then placed his hand on Claire's shoulder and guided her towards the car. She shrugged out of his grasp and slid into the middle seat of the car. Thomas sat down beside her.

"Buckle up!" Father ordered. Thomas struggled to get his belt on as Claire tightened hers. There wasn't much room in the back seat. Nicholas and Ribs looked comfortable in the front.

"Off we go!"

Father spun the car around and rapidly returned to the main road. Thomas didn't feel any better as the tires climbed off the gravel road and back onto the smooth asphalt. It wasn't motion sickness that was giving him a queasy feeling; it was the depth with which Father had planned every one of his moves. Even the photographs he'd taken of them a night before must have had some purpose. Thomas started to think this wasn't the first time Father had done this.

Up front, Nick had his hand hanging out the window, using his arm as a wing against the wind. Father hummed peacefully along to the music on the radio. Thomas gave a quick and silent thanks to Myr that he wasn't singing. Thomas was confused—he still didn't understand what was so bad about going to Canada. He decided that if he was going to find out what was going on, he really only had one option since open conversation with Claire was out of the question.

Oswell? Thomas reached out. He sat, concentrating for a few minutes, and heard nothing.

Oswell? he repeated, *are you there?* Thomas sat back and focused.

"*Thom?*" Oswell's voice whispered back. Thomas looked around and saw that no one else had heard Oswell. More confirmation that the connection was solely in his head. He was free to talk.

Yes, it's me.

"*What's happening?*"

We just switched cars.

"*Why?*"

We're going to Canada.

"*Canada?*" Oswell's voice expressed his confusion.

Claire says we're going to Canada.

"*Oh no... no, no, no...*"

So it is *as bad as Claire made it seem.*

"*Yes.*"

Why?

"*It's another country, Thomas. Everyone looking for you is going to have a much harder time doing it. How are they even going to know where you went; they're not going to know where to look!*"

That explains why Claire is so worried.

"*You're damn right it explains her worry! Damn it!*"

Well what can I do about it?

"*The same things you've been doing. Protect Nick and Claire and wait for your moment.*"

What moment?

"*It'll come. Maybe at the border... damn, that's a risk he's taking. Cicero says you're resourceful, you'll have to figure it out.*"

I don't understand.

Oswell paused for a moment, as if in thought. "*If you are patient, your chance will come. You have to get Nick and Claire out of there.*"

I'll do my best, Thomas pledged solemnly. He did not feel very confident about fulfilling the vow. Though Oswell's words calmed him slightly, they were still only words.

"I hope that will be enough," Oswell replied. The situation was becoming more and more difficult for Thomas, and Oswell was becoming more and more worried. He focused on what he needed to do, and tried to calm down. *"Good luck Thom. I'm here for you when you need me."*

Thank you, Thomas thought, feeling only slightly reassured. He would have preferred a good knife and the opportunity to slide it across the front of Father's meaty neck. Given his track record though, Thomas didn't even think that would work out in his favour. He turned his mind away from the futile thinking and focused back on the car as he sensed Oswell's consciousness slip away from him.

Claire nudged him in the side and gave him a demanding look as if to ask 'what were you doing?'

Thomas half-shrugged; he wasn't sure exactly how to explain it and, further, was unwilling to explain it in front of Father. The first was based on his own ignorance regarding what he'd just done, and the second on his instinct for self-preservation.

He glanced at the digital clock on the dashboard, then looked out the front window of the car. Ahead, a building sat in the middle of the road. He felt the car beginning to slow, and then come to a stop. A man in uniform was leaning into the window of a red car in front of them. *Is this the opportunity Oswell meant?* He thought. His mind immediately began working, but was interrupted by Father's voice.

"Not a word from any of you," Father hissed. He stared down Thomas, and Thomas felt an icy chill run down his spine. "Nicholas, ear muffs," Father ordered. Nicholas put his hands over his ears. "You could try to get this man to help you," Father motioned to the man conversing with the occupants of the vehicle in front of them. "Just remember: he isn't going to react faster than I will. You two might survive," Father said, glaring at Claire and then lingering on Thomas. Father then whispered, "But Nicholas won't."

Thomas understood what Father was saying. The man ahead of them was some sort of officer, much like the police Thomas had met on his first night on Earth. He could help them, but if they tried, Father would kill Nicholas. He'd sooner go down swinging than let the three children escape unharmed. The risk was too great; Thomas would have to wait for another opportunity.

Father took a deep breath and exhaled as the red car in front of them rolled away from the stop and Father lightly pressed the gas to bring his car forward to replace the previous one. He rolled down the window and smiled up at the man in uniform.

"Hello, Bonjour," the man said.

"Hello!"

"How are you today?"

"Good, and yourself?"

"I'm fine, thank you. Where are you all coming from?" the man spoke with an unfamiliar accent.

"Concord, New Hampshire."

"Ah, I see. Passports, please," the officer said.

"Nicky, pass me the travel folder please."

Nicholas followed Father's direction and grabbed the folder from the glove box. He handed it over to Father.

"Here you go," Father passed it on to the officer.

"Thank you." The man began perusing the identification as Father drummed his fingers on the wheel. The officer's gaze lingered on one of the passports for an extended period.

"What is the purpose of your visit?" he asked, without looking up from the identification.

"Family vacation."

"And where will you be staying, and for how long?"

"We're camping as we go, and we'll be visiting for two weeks," Father informed the officer. The man finally looked up from the identification and placed them all on the roof of the car. He took a step back from the vehicle and appraised it, then retrieved the documents from the roof and handed them back to Flynn.

"Thank you sir, have a nice visit."

"Thank *you*, officer," Father replied as he shifted the vehicle into drive. They began to pull away.

Thomas looked at Claire. A tear rolled down her cheek and Thomas put a hand on her hand to comfort her, feeling powerless to offer anything more. She gave him an unsure smile, and he returned one of his own to her. Thomas glanced outside as a sign whipped past at the side of the road. The words were unfamiliar and he did not understand what it said:

Bienvenue à Québec.

CHAPTER THIRTY-SIX

IN CONFIDENCE

O SWELL RAISED HIS sword in a defensive position that was little more than a slight angle and locked elbows. Wendell clucked his tongue at his young pupil and shook his head.

"Stay calm."

"I'm trying!" Oswell cried.

"What is it that stops you?"

"The man standing in front of me with a very large sword!"

"You've nothing to fear; be confident in what I am teaching you."

"We just started!"

"And we must start somewhere," Wendell said. "You must be re-laxed. Your body must flow like the air you breathe. It is simple to strike a steadfast rock, but impossible to strike at the wind." Wendell's blade slashed through the air with a whistle. "You will be here, and you will be there," Wendell explained, motioning about. "You must remain one step ahead." Wendell slashed his blade through the air again.

"Do you have to do that?" Oswell asked nervously. The sword looked dangerously sharp.

"Of course not, but it adds to the effect, no?" Wendell laughed. Oswell chose not to answer. Wendell grinned impishly and relaxed. "Look at your stance. You're as tense as a bowstring." Wendell sheathed his sword and approached Oswell. "Look," Wendell began, kicking at the insides of Oswell's feet. "Take a wide stance and bend your knees."

Oswell widened his stance just beyond shoulder width and relaxed his locked knees. He bounced slightly to make sure he was doing it correctly.

Wendell narrowed his eyebrows. "You're still too taut," Wendell said. "Release the tension in your shoulders and in your arms."

Oswell rolled out his shoulders and let his arms fall to his side, the tip of his sword nearly touching the ground at the angle he held it.

"Now, starting from here, we build up," Wendell explained.

"Okay, just tell me what to do."

Wendell took a few steps back from Oswell and mirrored his student's stance.

"Grasp the sword firmly," Wendell said. "Too tight," Wendell corrected. Oswell loosened his grip slightly. "Good. Now, bend your elbows and bring them in close to your body; from here, we can strike rapidly and with full force." Oswell did as he was told.

"Look around you Oswell. Gather your surroundings; where is the ground that will afford you the greatest advantage? How many opponents do you have and how much room do you have to move? What is there in your environment that can be used to your advantage? The sun? A rock? See the opportunities."

Oswell scanned the area around him. It was mostly trees with uneven ground. He could not see an advantage in any particular position.

"You see no advantage," Wendell observed.

"Am I supposed to?" Oswell asked.

"Unlikely," Wendell replied. "Sometimes, the environment offers us nothing. It is in such a situation that we must look for advantages elsewhere."

"Where?"

"Your opponent."

"Uh, I don't think my opponent is going to give me an advantage for no good reason."

"No good reason, certainly. However, in battle, good reason comes in the form of mistakes."

Oswell nodded slowly.

"Patience is the key in every match, even in one that has afforded you great advantage to begin with," Wendell explained. "You must be careful and remain focused. Take full control of your body, as I hope you are doing now. Attain balance. Your opponent will attack and you will evade him. You can parry and you can sidestep, but you cannot make a mistake. Mistakes belong to your opponent."

Oswell nodded again, setting his jaw.

"Some opponents will be less challenging than others, but all deserve your respect," Wendell glared at Oswell. "Understood?"

"Yes, Wendell."

"Good. By respecting your opponent, you cannot be caught off guard by your overconfidence. Overconfidence was the folly of many a dead man."

Oswell set himself in his stance and nodded in recognition of Wendell. Oswell had no intention of being one of those dead men.

"And always be prepared for the unexpected," Wendell added, smiling mischievously.

Oswell looked confused; how could you prepare for something you weren't expecting? He smiled at the absurdity, but his grin disappeared as the sound of a sword cutting through the air startled him. He spun around and raised his sword in defence. The attacking blade clanged off of Oswell's, and Oswell stumbled backwards.

Darius had a stern look on his face as he set his stance against Oswell. Oswell gathered his bearings and melted into the pose he'd just been taught. It didn't feel right, but he tried to remember exactly what Wendell had taught him.

"Respect, relaxed, ready," Wendell preached.

Oswell raised his sword and took a step towards Darius. He carefully gauged his footing, ensuring he had balance and control. Darius appeared to be achieving the exact same thing.

Oswell advanced slowly against Darius, who was side stepping gradually to Oswell's left.

Oswell glanced around, attempting to identify any particular reason for his opponent's manoeuvre. Unable to identify anything, Oswell took a swing at Darius. His sword cut through thin air, barely missing a tree as Darius lithely avoided the attack.

Oswell turned around and resettled himself. His cheeks burned in embarrassment and Darius's eyes laughed. Oswell rushed at his opponent again, connecting only with thin air as Darius dodged the sword once again. Oswell was beginning to get frustrated.

"Relaxed," Wendell said from the sidelines. Oswell took a deep breath and felt the blood flow out of his cheeks. He advanced more slowly this time, not attacking. He would wait for Darius to make a mistake.

The two circled each other, both trying to spot some sort of weakness and at the same time, attempting to goad the other into attacking. Both were stalwart in their restraint, though Darius seemed to have an easier time of it. Darius feinted towards Oswell, and Oswell turned rapidly, just like he'd seen in the movies, swinging his sword around in a wide arc to catch his opponent. As he spun, Oswell felt the wind rush through his hair and across his teeth. He felt like a rock star. The feeling, however, was short lived.

Oswell felt his sword connect with the forged steel of Darius's blade. Oswell's sword rattled out of his hand and to the forest floor as Darius pressed the tip of his own sword into Oswell's back. Oswell did not move an inch.

"Good work Darius," Wendell congratulated. Oswell felt the tip of the sword pull away from his back. He relaxed imperceptibly, still on edge. "Last but not least," Wendell chuckled, "never show off, and never turn your back on your opponent."

Darius sheathed his sword as Oswell sheepishly reached down to grab his own.

"Somehow you managed to break both of those rules in one foolish move," Wendell reprimanded.

"I'm sorry," Oswell apologized. Wendell shrugged.

"How else would you learn such a valuable lesson? I'd rather you learned it at the cost of your pride than at the cost of your life," Wendell brushed his hand over the stubble on his chin. "Now, let's see you two at it again."

Oswell turned towards Darius and gathered himself, relaxing into the proper stance. Darius fell into an identical position.

"Begin!" Wendell shouted.

"Tired?" Wendell asked, smiling.

"Very," Oswell and Darius replied in unison.

The trio were making their way through the forest back to the Enclave. Oswell had sparred with Darius for the better part of the afternoon, and the two of them had ended with a humbling two-on-one match against Wendell. Needless to say, the pair had a lot of work to do, but Wendell had admitted that Oswell learned quickly.

Oswell was also smarting from a number of bruises, welts, and cuts all over his body. He had wanted to ask why they didn't use wooden swords to learn, but he had held back for fear of sounding a coward. Now, he was glad that they had practiced with real swords; it gave him a real incentive not to mess up, and perhaps that was why he had picked up the basics so quickly.

"I must say Oswell, you do have some natural talent," Darius said.

"Thanks," Oswell grinned.

"You learned much faster than I did," he added.

"Although *you* were no slouch," Wendell said to Darius before climbing a tree and disappearing into the green ceiling.

"Why doesn't he call Bartimaeus?" Oswell wondered.

"Bartimaeus hasn't been around forever," Darius said.

"...And he won't be around forever either," Oswell finished, seeing where Darius was going with the thought. "I wonder how he does it..."

"Practice, confidence, and a general lack of fear," Darius said, chuckling.

"That last one sounds important," Oswell agreed, joining in the laughter. The two young men stepped out of the way as the rope ladder unfolded through the leaves and hit the ground.

"Go ahead," Darius offered. Oswell grasped onto the first rung he could reach and began pulling himself up. He climbed the first few rungs, allowing Darius to climb on behind him, and then gave silent thanks that he did not have to climb the whole way. His arms were dead tired from the swordplay all afternoon. At that moment, the ladder's crank system was his salvation.

"I. Am. Starving," Oswell groaned as he pulled himself up onto the catwalk of the Enclave. He hurried out of the way so that Darius could climb up as well. Standing at the ladder's crank, Wendell grunted his agreement. Oswell wondered at the fortitude of the huge man. Even after a long day out in the forest, he was still fully capable of climbing a tree a hundred feet into the air and then hoisting two young men across the same distance. The man's strength was unfathomable for Oswell. Oswell's father, Owen, seemed almost frail by comparison.

"Let's see what Laurence has cooked up today," Darius said.

"You won't hear any argument from me," Oswell agreed, patting his belly. The three strode across the catwalk to the main hall and burst through the doors. Inside, Laurence and Karyn were enjoying the raucous conversation carrying on between Rawlins and Cicero. Before each of them was a bowl of stringy brown meat and a mixed assortment of what looked like carrots and potatoes floating in a rich broth.

"Stew's on," Laurence said, glancing up, "help yourselves," and then immersed himself back into conversation. Oswell hurried across the hall and picked up a bowl, happy to see that Karyn was up and about. He scooped some stew into it and began to walk away, then turned and handed the bowl to Darius. Darius smiled and nodded his head, then found a seat at the table. Oswell served another bowl to Wendell, and then finally one for himself. Feeling, for the first time in a long time like he had truly earned a meal, Oswell sat down at the table beside Karyn, and began to eat.

"This is delicious," Oswell said.

"We don't have much to work with, but Laurence knows how to season everything perfectly," Darius replied.

"No kidding," Oswell mumbled between bites.

"Actually, I made it," Karyn piped up.

"Oh?" Darius asked.

"It's really good!" Oswell reiterated. Karyn smiled confidently.

Oswell stole a glance across the table and noticed Wendell had diverted Laurence from his previous conversation. The two of them had their heads together. Oswell couldn't make out what it was they were whispering about. He smiled at the thought that Wendell was probably bragging about how fast a learner Oswell was, and how much natural skill and talent he had. With that thought, Oswell perked right up and continued on eating.

After dinner, Laurence approached the two young men and placed a slender hand on each of their shoulders.

"Oswell, if you would be so kind, I'd like to continue our conversation from the other night," Laurence smiled gently. "Darius, your grandfather has some things that he would like you to do," he added. Darius nodded quietly, and delivered a light-hearted jab to Oswell's shoulder. He then grabbed his empty bowl and jogged across the room towards Cicero.

"Did Wendell tell you how amazing I am?" Oswell asked proudly as he stood up.

"…He told me that you are progressing quickly," Laurence replied. Oswell's brow furrowed at the tone with which Laurence answered him. Oswell didn't like the hidden message behind Laurence's correction. "Come, we have much to discuss."

Oswell cast a long glance at Karyn before leaving the hall with Laurence. He would have to tell her about his day as soon as he finished with Laurence. He found himself longing to talk with her.

He walked the catwalk with Laurence, not a word being said. Once inside Laurence's quarters, Oswell found his way to the chair he'd inhabited at their last meeting. Laurence sat down across from Oswell, neglecting to offer him tea this time.

"You are a confident young man," Laurence observed. Oswell did not reply. "Are you wondering why I say this?"

"Yes."

"Wendell told me about your progress," Laurence began, "And although impressive in its rapidity, I am disturbed by one detail."

"What's that?" Oswell asked, folding his arms across his chest. Oswell thought the lecturing would be over after the sermon on patience.

"It is good to be confident. It offers poise, allows calm in the face of adversity, and inspires those around you. But Oswell, it is not a virtue to be overconfident. I am afraid that it is this that I see in you."

"Overconfidence?"

"Yes, overconfidence; you experienced it today in your first match with Darius."

"How so?"

"You believed in your own ability to such an extent that you felt as though you could not make a mistake. Overconfidence breeds complacency, and that is what happened when Darius beat you."

"Wendell wasn't even finished teaching me yet!"

"And yet you felt as though you were good enough to beat Darius? He is a seasoned and well-trained opponent."

"What's your point?"

"Confidence is a powerful tool. It conveys your skill to your opponent, even strikes fear, and it empowers you. However, overconfidence is foolish. It leads to mistakes, and in our field of work, mistakes lead to death. I am sure that is not what you want."

Oswell unfolded his arms and slumped in the chair. He had always been very confident, that was true. As a kid, he'd been shorter than most of the other boys, but he'd always excelled on the soccer field and in the classroom. He didn't like to admit it, but the success he'd had in those areas had allowed his confidence to develop into cockiness.

Oswell looked down, ashamed, "You're right."

"Thank you. I do tend to be accurate with such things... oh, and there goes my overconfidence. Don't depress yourself over this, Oswell. Hubris is a central to our human nature. Overcoming it is a constant challenge, and harnessing it in others can be a great advantage."

"I'll try my best," Oswell vowed.

"And that is all that I can ask for," Laurence smiled. "Now, is there anything else you wanted to talk about?"

"Laurence… I'm worried about Nick and Claire."

"The two children with Thomas, correct?"

"Yeah," Oswell said.

"Cicero told me about your psychic communication. It is a phenomenon I am rather unfamiliar with. In fact, I haven't a clue as to how it works," Laurence looked up to the roof of his quarters and closed his eyes. "However, I suppose it does not matter how it works; only that it does." Laurence focused back in on Oswell. "Explain to me why you are so worried about them."

"Well, we live in the United States, which I guess you could say is like Numyria… a country. Canada is another country and so I'm pretty sure the police… or guards, on either side of the border don't work together exclusively. Or at least, not well," Oswell paused, worried that his analogy might be confusing Laurence. Laurence appeared to understand. "I'm just worried that now that they've crossed the border, the police who *are* looking for them won't know *where* to look, while the police who would be able to look for them, won't *know* to look."

"I believe I understand your worry," Laurence mused, resting his chin in his right hand.

"However, I trust Cicero, and he says that Thomas is a boy of great internal strength. If anyone can help your friends, I believe Thomas can."

Not reassured, Oswell stared at Laurence and wondered if perhaps, everyone was being a little *overconfident* in Thomas, and, as Laurence had just pointed out, overconfidence gets people killed.

CHAPTER THIRTY-SEVEN

ROAD TRIP

THE PIT IN Thom's stomach widened with every intermittent whimper that escaped Claire's mouth. Every time they passed one of the large, green highway signs Claire let one slip.

The bold white lettering was perfectly readable to Thomas, but the names of these places meant nothing to him. He knew of towns like *Oland*, and *Tallgrain*; towns like *Saint Georges*, and *Saint Jerome* were unfamiliar to him. Even more amazing to Thomas was the enormous concrete city they had driven through. A sign before entering the city had read *Montréal*. Prior to this, the largest town he had seen was Fletchery. The buildings in Montréal made the hospital near Walloway look like a mushroom house, and the city itself was enormous; it took them nearly an hour before the buildings started to shrink to comprehensible sizes again.

Helplessness began to wash over Thomas. The car they drove in made the world so much more accessible. The distance they had travelled was unfathomable to him. He'd heard of record travelling speeds on the fabled Quarter Horses, but to Thomas, they were practically legends. Thomas was an orphan, and a poor one at that. He'd never ridden a Quarter Horse, let alone seen one. In fact, he'd never even ridden a normal horse. Thomas walked. Everywhere.

Now, they travelled great distances in a car with no observable effort. Thomas could not gauge how far they had gone, but he knew it was probably further than he'd walked in his whole life. Every hour put the three of them further away from the people who were looking for them.

The weight of his responsibility was beginning to crush him.

Even with the confidence of Cicero and Oswell, Thomas felt woefully inadequate. As a young, skinny teenager, he was no match for the considerable height and weight of Father. To Thomas, Father was an enigma. Thomas didn't know what the sadistic man's intentions were. For all he knew, Father could be thinking of the best way to dispose of him at that very moment. Oswell had promised him that an opportunity for escape or salvation would come, if only he waited for it. However, Thomas was beginning to doubt whether he had that sort of time to play with. The necessity to come up with something, and fast, was becoming all the more real to Thomas.

Snapping out of his destructive self-demoralization, Thomas peeked over at Claire.

Saying she looked worried would be a terrible understatement. She was crying silently with hot tears rolling down her cheeks like translucent tendrils of a flame. Despite the fact that Thomas had only known her for a short time, he was really beginning to like Claire. Seeing her cry was tearing Thomas apart. He couldn't stand it, and yet, there was nothing he could do to ease her pain. Just thinking about it made him feel more hopeless. He tried to snap out of his pessimism again, and focused his eyes on the road ahead.

As the next green highway sign approached them, Thomas was surprised that Claire did not whimper. Looking over at her, she certainly did not look happy or any less scared than she had moments ago, but the fact that she neglected her involuntary whine for once set Thomas to thinking. He nudged Claire and raised his eyebrows, wondering what was up. He watched as the sign flew past them. *Ontario.*

Claire stole a glance at Father. He was busy singing along (badly, at that) to a twangy country song. Apparently he'd gotten over Thom's stinging criticism in the white van. Thomas had learned to try and block out the lyrics. It had gotten to the point where he could almost imagine Father wasn't singing at all.

Claire looked back at Thomas and whispered a single word, "English."

Thomas nodded, understanding the hint. He'd learned from Claire that Québec was predominantly French-speaking. As Claire and Nicholas could not speak French and Thomas could certainly not *parlé*, they would likely be out of luck if they ran into anyone who may have considered helping them. Now they were entering Ontario, which, according to Claire was English-speaking. He could deal with that. The pit in his stomach seemed to shrink ever so slightly. Somehow, this tiny reduction in discomfort was enough for Thomas. That relief, mixed with the drowse-inducing heat of the car put Thomas to sleep moments later.

Chapter Thirty-Eight

Moonlighting... Again

Oswell rolled over onto his side away from the hand on his shoulder. "Will you frig off?" he grumbled.

The hand continued its attempt to shake him awake.

"Darius, I'm trying to sleep here… later…" he moaned.

The hand ceased its assault. Oswell smiled in his stupor.

"Thank y—" Oswell felt a firm smack resound off the dome of his skull. "What the hell!" he shouted as he fell out of his bed, reeling from the strike.

"Get your things together," Wendell ordered. Oswell looked up at the huge man, surprised to find that it was not Darius. He then looked around the darkened barracks.

"Where are we going?" He shivered; Oswell didn't like sleeping alone in the space filled with so many beds. He did, however, prefer that he slept there, instead of Karyn.

"Training. Pack light. We're moving quickly," Wendell said sharply, then turned on his heel and left the room. As soon as the door closed after Wendell, Oswell clumsily jumped to his feet and rushed towards his trunk.

He lifted the lid and retrieved his some canvas trousers—eschewing his trusty jeans—and the plain, light cotton shirt he'd opted for over the t-shirt that had been ruined on his first night in Myros. The cotton shirt was full sleeved and fit his form with room to breathe. The dark brown material made him feel like he belonged in the woods. He would be camouflaged well. Oswell looped his sword belt around the waist of his pants and slid a short sword into the sheath he had affixed to it. He pondered for a moment as to whether or not he should bring his flashlight. This time, he opted to forget it. If Wendell wanted to train him in the middle of the night, it was likely that the darkness had something to do with it.

Without grabbing his bag—he *had* been told to pack light, after all—Oswell hurried out of the barracks and out into the moonlight. Up on the catwalk, the entire Enclave was illuminated.

Once again, Oswell was struck by the beauty of the scene. The night revealed the forest's natural beauty while the day's unnatural grey pallor only masked it. He felt a curious nagging at the back of his mind, wondering why the climate in Myros was so different from his own. His predominant thought, however, was wondering if the sight of the Enclave perched atop the trees would ever get old. He was struck by the realization that it was the lack of city lights that made it all possible; the night was clean and clear and the moon's light shone through a sky devoid of pollution. Oswell wondered at the inherent splendour of nature, and mourned for the loss of it in his world.

He traipsed down the planks of the catwalk and sidled up beside Wendell. Wendell turned and looked Oswell up and down. He nodded his approval and Oswell smiled. Wendell was decked out in similar attire, sans blue jeans, of course.

"Where's Darius?" Oswell asked.

"Not coming," Wendell replied.

"Oh," Oswell said, wondering why. He didn't have long to ponder this enigma, as Wendell threw the rope ladder down through the trees and motioned for Oswell to climb on.

"I want to climb like you do," Oswell proposed, feeling bold.

"Not yet," Wendell replied.

"But—" Oswell began.

"And you will certainly not learn in the dead of night," Wendell added, cutting Oswell off. "Now, climb down the ladder." Oswell ignored the instinct to be indignant. Instead he did as he was told.

Moments after his feet touched down on the padded earth, the ladder began to rise back up into the trees.

Closing his eyes, Oswell listened to the forest. He stood in near silence, waiting for Wendell to join him on the forest floor. Oswell did not have high expectations of hearing his agile guide, but he knew that if he focused, he would have a better chance. Oswell decided that this would be a good test for his developing perception.

"Nice try," Wendell chuckled a few moments later as he tapped Oswell on the shoulder.

Oswell opened his eyes to see the dark shade of Wendell. Although it was bright above, beneath the dense forest canopy it was closer to inky black with only the occasional ray of moonlight adding a contrast to the monotonous forest floor.

"You're too good sometimes," Oswell complained.

"You can never be *too* good," Wendell corrected. Oswell stubbornly didn't reply.

Wendell's white teeth shone in the darkness. He crouched down and Oswell fell to one knee beside him.

"So what's the plan?" Oswell asked.

"I'm going to teach you how to read the forest."

"At night?"

"If you can make it through the forest in the middle of the night, you will be able to navigate it during the day. We use the exact same principles for both, but we have more to distract us during the day," Wendell began. The thought process seemed counter intuitive to Oswell. "I'd prefer that you don't use knowledge of the forest as an excuse to go ranging without clearance," Wendell added.

"Deal," Oswell said sheepishly. Last he checked, he didn't owe a debt to any other beautiful red-headed girls. "So these principles... what principles?" Oswell asked.

"The first rule is something we've been working on since you started your training with me: focus."

"It's becoming a common theme."

"A short attention span is a great weakness; focus gives you clarity of thought and action."

"I *was* trying to focus so that I could hear you coming down."

"Think of focus as a knife, and practice a whet stone. Over time, you will sharpen your focus. Right now, your blade is dull," Wendell explained.

"I'll take that as sage advice, rather than the insult it sounds like," Oswell said.

"Are you ready to learn?"

"Yeah," Oswell replied.

"Now, we need to utilize our focus to maintain one thing, and one thing only."

"What's that?"

"Your direction."

"Easier said than done," Oswell replied.

"It is done easily when you have no distraction. This is why we learn at night. It is quieter, and there is less to see. When your focus has improved, you will be able to do it during the day."

"Because I will be able to block out the distractions."

"Precisely. Once you have acquired this basic skill, you will recognize two things—" Wendell said. "First, you will notice that this forest comes more easily to you. You will know every tree and every root, every twist and every turn. With practice, you will be able to navigate this forest with immeasurable ease and use its features to your advantage. "

"Sounds good to me," Oswell replied. "What else?"

"Second, you will be able to utilize your focus in any situation; find your way through any forest, overcome any adversary, and solve any problem."

"So you're saying if I learn how to move through the forest, I'll also be learning how to kill people?"

"Not exactly," Wendell sighed, "I give you this goal as a stepping stone to greater control. I'm simply giving you the opportunity to hone your focus to a fine point. With that focus, everything else will follow."

"Sounds like a lot of work," Oswell said.

"If you'd like to quit, be my guest," Wendell replied, spreading his arms wide. Oswell said nothing, knowing that he had to do whatever Wendell said if he ever wanted to go home. In the back of his mind,

Oswell could hear his father, Owen, reciting his favourite lesson: *nothing in life comes easy.*

"I thought as much," Wendell said. "Now, we will begin our exercise."

Oswell nodded. His eyes had adjusted to the darkness and he could see his teacher more easily.

"Where are we?" Wendell asked.

"Beneath the Enclave," Oswell replied.

"Correct. In which direction am I facing?"

Oswell thought hard. He closed his eyes and imagined where he would be if he were above the trees. Establishing himself on the catwalk by the ladder, Oswell pictured the horizon and imagined the sun rising up from beneath the sea of trees. *Sun rises in the East,* Oswell thought. Maintaining his orientation, Oswell opened his eyes and observed Wendell.

"You're facing east."

"Correct. Why might I be facing east?"

"Because... there isn't much else but trees west of here."

"Excellent reasoning," Wendell congratulated. "That was the easy part; you figured out which direction we need to go."

"East is towards Fletchery," Oswell said. "Let's go then!"

"Not so fast," Wendell grabbed Oswell by the shoulder. "You have your bearings now, but unless you maintain your focus, I can guarantee you will lose them. What do you do if you lose your bearings?"

"Well, we use the North Star to keep our bearings back home—do you guys have something like that?"

"Navigation by the stars is a preferable option; we will use it when we can. Our navigating star is called Aldus, come." Wendell stood up and strode forward, kneeling down again in a broad ray of moonlight. "This is easier in the winter," Wendell laughed.

Oswell crouched down beside Wendell and gazed up through the dense canopy of leaves. He could only see a fraction of it, but in that fraction, there were countless stars.

"Which one is it?" Oswell asked.

"Aldus is one of the few blue stars in the sky. Do you see it? It's in the centre of *the Tree.*" Wendell pointed up into the sky. Located at the crux of a constellation in the shape of the letter 'Y' was a bright star with a slightly blue tinge.

"I see it," Oswell confirmed.

"Aldus never moves though *the Tree* rotates about it. If you point at Aldus and draw a line to the ground, you are pointing due south. It's a useful tool if you ever get lost."

"Good tip," Oswell said. He pointed at Aldus and drew a line to the ground. "So that's south, this is east; let's go." Wendell nodded and followed after Oswell as the young man began to work his way through the trees.

"Focus, and use the trees to guide you," Wendell said as they walked slowly. "Imagine a straight line between two trees and follow that line."

Oswell did as he was told, making up an imaginary line between two trees that pointed east. After reaching the next tree, he created another line and followed that. Wendell said nothing to correct his charge.

Falling into a rhythm, Oswell continued the exercise, making good time. His mind did not wander as he applied his full attention to making sure he did not deviate from his path. Obviously, he would be unable to maintain a perfectly straight path, but for once, he felt as though he knew where he was going. That is, until a noise off to his left distracted him.

Oswell turned as a shadow leapt at him from behind a tree. Drawing his blade, Oswell parried the blow. He cried out in surprise as the two pieces of metal glanced off of each other.

His assailant launched at him a second time, and Oswell parried the blow successfully again.

Thinking back to his training, Oswell tried to calm down. He wouldn't admit it if someone called him on it, but his heart pounded rapidly with fear. In the back of his head, he was wondering to where Wendell had disappeared, but he banished the thought and focused on his adversary. He could barely see the man, dressed in all black. It took everything he had to keep track of his movements, however, the glint of moonlight off of his shining blade gave Oswell a clear indication of what to avoid.

Launching forward, Oswell slashed at the man, fighting the terror in his heart. It was all too real. Still, his improvement was encouraging. Days ago, he would have probably been dead already.

"Who are you?" Oswell gasped, parrying another blow. His opponent did not respond.

The two rushed back and forth violently a countless number of times, and Oswell felt his arms and legs beginning to tire. He was surprised he hadn't tripped over anything yet and he thanked God (or Myr?) for that.

"Enough!" Wendell's voice boomed. Oswell and his opponent stopped on the spot.

"Where were you?" Oswell asked still on guard, but feeling more at ease now that an ally was close by.

"Watching," Wendell replied in a matter-of-fact manner.

"What?" Oswell asked, incredulous. He shot a glance back at the shadow of a man.

Reaching up, the assailant unravelled the wrap from around his head, allowing his unkempt black hair to fall around his smiling, but sweaty face.

"Darius?" Oswell exclaimed.

"At your service," Darius grinned.

"You... could have gotten yourself killed!" Oswell shouted, sheathing this blade.

"Aren't we cocky?" Darius chuckled. Wendell laughed heartily, and Oswell glanced at the older man, feeling his face redden.

"For good reason," Oswell shot, trying to move past his embarrassment, "I almost had you there at the end."

"Almost?" Darius replied, not convinced.

Ignoring the rebuttal, Oswell turned to Wendell. "So finding my way through the forest wasn't the only thing you had planned for tonight?" Oswell asked. "Any other surprises I should be aware of?"

"If I told you, they wouldn't be surprises," Wendell said.

Oswell relaxed a little more, and glanced up at the sky. He located Aldus and regained his bearings.

"Good work," Wendell praised Oswell. The test had been ongoing. He'd successfully regained his bearings after a thorough disorientation.

"Thanks," Darius said, grinning, before Oswell could reply.

"Yes, Darius, you as well," Wendell added.

"So, can we attack Makkin now?" Oswell asked brazenly, sensing Wendell's increasing confidence in him.

"Not a chance," Wendell chuckled. Oswell found himself caught off guard once again by the man's laughter. Wendell was in uncharacteristically good spirits. He was rather proud of Oswell. The young man had held his own against a surprise attack in the dark of night against a larger opponent. Still, Oswell deflated visibly with the denial. Despite what Laurence wished, Oswell wanted to get whatever was needed of him done as quickly as possible, in order to satisfy Myr's plan and get home. Now, however, he neglected to voice this motivation. Could his disappointment be something else? Maybe he was too distracted by everything Wendell had him doing. Of course, it was also possible that his patience was improving after all.

"Acer Makkin is too well protected and we are too few. We wouldn't stand a chance in battle," Wendell said.

"Well, how are we going to do it then?" Oswell asked, still curious.

"That, my young friend, I do not know."

Oswell thought for a moment, and then came to a dead end. He knew there was an answer somewhere, but it certainly was not making itself easy to find. Oswell paused at that thought and looked back to Wendell.

"So... that's east," Oswell pointed, remembering his bearings, "and that is north."

"Correct," Wendell agreed.

"But... how do we find the Enclave?" Oswell asked. Wendell nodded as though he was expecting the question sooner or later.

"Yes, that is a more difficult task," Wendell admitted. "Let me show you."

CHAPTER THIRTY-NINE

CONFLICT RESOLUTION

IT FELT GOOD TO be back. Beneath Thomas's feet, the occasional twig snapped and his step was light with the spring of moss. For some reason that he could not explain, he felt more at home in the forest than ever before. In truth, Thomas was simply happy to have gotten away from Father. He didn't care where he was or why, just that his captor was not there.

The forest looked the same to all sides, but he was not worried about being lost. The trees were filled with life and the sounds of that life filled the air. It was where he belonged, and Thomas was sure of that. There was only one thing he *was* unsure of: the persistent stabbing on his right side.

He'd noticed it at least half an hour ago, a gentle sensation at first. Like someone had brushed past him on a busy road. In fact, Thomas had chosen to ignore it the first couple times it happened.

Now, however, the sensation had increased. It was as if someone was now jabbing a finger between two of his ribs. He cringed with each beat.

Thomas shouted in surprise as the intensity of the assault increased. He stumbled sideways. Thomas couldn't see anyone, but he had just been pushed. Gathering himself, he whirled around, trying to identify his foe. Without warning, he was launched sideways again, and much harder this time. He lay sprawled on the ground and before he could get up, Thomas began to roll, propelled by the drive of his attacker. Pressed up against a tree, he could go no further. He felt himself begin to bend around the tree. The pain in his back began to rise to an almost unbearable level and then abruptly, it was gone.

Thomas jumped awake, breathing raggedly. He felt a gentle hand on his side and a slender finger across his lips. He'd been sleeping. Claire was trying to wake him up. She slowly removed her finger as Thom's breathing slowed. Claire looked troubled.

"What's wrong?" Thomas whispered.

"You mean besides the fact that we're trapped in a tent in a forest in Canada by a kidnapper who thinks that we're his children?"

Thomas paused, unsure of what to say. "You just... you look worried."

"I *look* worried?" Claire whispered, "I *am* worried. You better get used to this face, because it's going to be making a lot of appearances."

"Okay," Thomas breathed. "Well, what's going on then?"

"The sun is starting to come up," Claire whispered, "Father's still asleep in the other tent. I thought this would be a good opportunity to talk."

"You're probably right," Thomas replied, glancing at the peacefully sleeping Nicholas. They'd stopped and camped out after a long day of driving.

There was no need to scare the poor kid with their talk. Besides, he probably needed the sleep.

"How can you be so calm?" Claire asked him.

"I've been through worse than this."

"When?" she asked, trying to think of the last time Oswell had been kidnapped or worse. "Oh, right," she corrected, remembering that the boy in front of her wasn't Oswell Wallace.

"I've killed for my survival before, I won't hesitate to do it again," Thomas said.

Claire seemed to withdraw from him, looking frightened. It was hard to believe that such a young man could be capable of that, but the tone of his voice told Claire that he was telling the truth.

"Do you have a plan?" Claire asked.

"Not yet, but it will come to me eventually." Thomas said, hoping that Oswell was right.

He honestly had no idea how he would ever get them out of their situation. His escape with Cicero had been one born out of a great deal of planning and preparation. It had been carried out by two capable individuals who, on that day, were blessed with a great deal of sheer, dumb luck.

Now he was supposed to pull an escape plan for himself and two others out of thin air. This time, however, he couldn't expect much help. He had only the help of two frightened children and an emaciated canine. Thomas was not naive either, he was also barely more than a child and his adversary was a massive, fully grown man practiced in the field of child abduction. Escaping from Father would be no easy feat without help, and a generous serving of luck.

"I hope it comes soon," Claire replied, lying down. Thomas too lay back down, hands behind his head to prop it up.

"All we can hope to do now is survive. We need to hold on and wait for the right time. I'll see it when it comes, I promise," Thomas spoke with the confidence of his supporters from another realm. Claire nodded, and then rested her head back onto the thin pillow. Thomas smiled reassuringly and did the same. Side by side, the pair tried to sleep.

Thomas jolted awake as Father ripped the zipper of the tent door open. The man was in a rage, but Thomas had no idea why.

"Get up," the man ordered. He grabbed Thomas by the scruff of his neck and heaved him outside the tent. Nicholas started crying inside. "Shut up boy!" Claire stumbled out of the tent with Nicholas grasping onto her hand as tears continued to flow from his eyes. "I said be quiet, Nicholas," Father repeated, trying to put on a show of serenity. The small boy continued to cry. Father strode towards him and raised his hand.

"Leave him alone!" Thomas shouted, standing up. Father glanced at Thomas in surprise and let his hand fall back to his side. He then turned towards Thomas.

"Or what?" Father asked, "I hope you've got something to back up an order like that."

Thomas found himself at a loss for words.

"Well?"

"Wouldn't everything go a lot smoother if you were nicer?" Thomas asked, deciding that diplomacy might be the best course of action at the moment, considering his situation.

"Maybe, but it wouldn't be so damned fun!" Father lunged towards Thomas. Thomas instinctively dodged out of the way and Father lurched past him. A snicker inadvertently escaped Thom's lips.

"You'll regret that," Father growled. He rushed at Thomas again. Thomas attempted to recreate his first avoidance technique; this time, he tripped and fell to the ground. Smiling evilly, Father stopped his bull rush and advanced on Thomas.

"Not so lofty now, are you?" He delivered a brutal kick to Thom's ribs.

Thomas cried out in agony, feeling the pain burn across the entire right side of his body.

"Now get in the car! All of you." Father demanded. "And no more talking!" He set to work demolishing the tent as Claire and Nicholas climbed into the backseat.

Thomas glared at Father's back through the tears that betrayed him by flowing from his eyes.

He turned his gaze on Kelly, who was awkwardly standing off to the side. She looked sleepy, as though nothing unusual had happened. Thomas shot her a pleading look, but she seemed to take no notice. Kelly was numb.

Gathering his strength, Thomas ground his teeth through the pain and climbed to his feet. Holding his side tenderly, he limped towards the car and slid into the backseat beside Claire. Kelly sat down in the front passenger seat as Father stuffed the poorly packed tent into the car's trunk.

Thomas glanced over at Claire. She stared back at him, his pain seemingly reflected in her eyes. She didn't say it out loud, but Thomas could read what she was saying loud and clear.

Thank you so much, and... I'm sorry.

Thomas hoped his return message was equally as clear. *I might as well be good for something.*

Father slammed the trunk and entered the car. Turning in his seat to look back at his young passengers, he directed a message at Thomas.

"No more funny business." Without waiting for a reply (as he no doubt did not wish to receive one), Father started up the car and pulled away from the temporary campground. Thomas stared ahead as the car rolled onto the highway and sped across the asphalt. He had no desire to look back now. He only wanted to look forward. There were opportunities in the future, and now Thomas felt a greater resolve to seek them out. He would keep his eyes forward and look for those opportunities, because he was not going to miss any chances. He was sure of that. Looking forward was also convenient because his bruising ribs were making a very persuasive argument to keep him from turning around.

The steady hum of tires on pavement and the warmth of a body sandwiched beside him had a way of putting Thomas to sleep. He groaned in pain as he shifted and woke up. Claire was shaking him gently on his shoulder. She had learned quickly not to nudge him in the ribs, but he felt the pain nonetheless.

Thomas scanned around trying to determine the reason for Claire waking him. The highway they had been on had shrunk down to one lane in either direction. Trees sat relatively close to the side of the road. Wherever they were was a lot smaller than the places they'd been.

He hadn't a clue as to how long he'd been out, but he felt refreshed, and that was a good feeling, despite his pain.

Watching the trees slide past the window, Thomas realized they were slowing down. Perhaps this was why he was woken up.

Father spotted a sign coming up on the right. He slowed down even more, and then turned off the highway onto a dirt road. The wooden sign looked old, but well kept. Thomas read the emblazoned lettering carefully.

Cahill Campground.

Thomas looked at Claire and she stared back at him. Not once did Thomas actually think that Father was taking them camping. He figured the tent was a temporary measure due to the long distance they had to travel. Thomas was surprised that Father had not lied to the border officer. Regardless of the surprise, Father's honesty did not afford Thomas any degree of comfort.

The fact that did afford Thomas comfort was that a campground, as he had come to understand from Claire, was likely to have people. Those people would surely be able to help him, Claire, and Nicholas. Thomas simply had to figure out the best way to get their help without endangering his two charges.

The gears in his brain began to work out the solution to this problem. Ahead, Thomas could see a middle aged man sitting in a small folding chair in front of a small cottage off to the left of the dirt road.

Seeing the car approaching, the man stood up and appeared to be eyeing Father's vehicle warily. Suddenly, a look of recognition lit up the man's face. He waved happily to Father, and as their car passed the man, he waved to the children in the back as though he were expecting to see them there. Thomas felt his hope drop like a boulder down a hill, tumbling downward, shocking him with every crash.

CHAPTER FORTY

THE TIES THAT BIND

OSWELL LEANED HIS head back against the wall of the hut and laughed. "I can't believe you did that!"

"What was I supposed to do?" Karyn asked, joining him in laughter.

"Well, you didn't have to tie him up like that," Oswell said.

"He needed to pay for his crimes," she maintained about the young thief she'd once caught breaking into their home.

"It seems you're pretty resourceful," Oswell complimented. She giggled. It had only been a few days since her father's passing, but when she was occupied, Karyn seemed like the same, happy young woman he'd met by the river.

"I *do* know my way around a blade," Karyn ensured him, She eyed Oswell's short sword, which sat in its scabbard by the door.

"Is that so?" Oswell goaded, "Let's see what you can do!"

"My pleasure," she dashed over to the door and grabbed the sword. Oswell watched as she dragged the sword from its sheath and started to trade blows with an invisible foe.

She is good, Oswell thought. She glanced at him and smiled.

As she executed a precise thrust, an intense pain like a hot knife being wrenched around blossomed in Oswell's side. He felt the pain intensify beyond tolerance and fear spread across his face as he grasped at the site of his inexplicable agony. The sword clattered to the floor as Karyn jumped. She ran forward and put her hand on his.

"What's wrong?" she asked.

"My... my side is..."

"What?" Karyn demanded, worry clouding her expression.

Oswell failed to respond. He felt the pain begin to subside and then disappear altogether.

He let out a sigh of relief and slumped back in his chair. Feeling his ribs with his hand, he couldn't find anything to suggest he'd been injured. Oswell stood up and lifted his shirt to examine his ribcage.

"What happened?" Karyn asked. Oswell ran his fingers along the arches of his ribs. Karyn's fingers trailed after his and Oswell shivered involuntarily with pleasure.

"I'm not completely sure," Oswell admitted, trying to fight back the heat in his face.

"We should ask Cicero," Karyn decided, still examining his side.

"You're right," he agreed. She grabbed his hand and dragged him out of the hut.

Cicero looked up from the book he was reading as Oswell and Karyn emerged through the door in the floor. "How may I be of service?"

"Something weird happened," Oswell said.

"What?" Cicero asked, standing up and stepping around his desk.

"I'm not entirely sure," Oswell admitted, still breathless.

"We were just talking, and then he had a horrible pain in his side... he could barely speak," Karyn explained for him.

Cicero returned this explanation with a blank stare.

"Right here," Oswell mumbled, "a sharp pain started right here," Oswell pointed at one of his ribs. "It spread out from there, and then disappeared." Oswell let his shirt fall back down into place.

"Perhaps you've been overexerting yourself with your training," Cicero thought.

"I don't think so..." Oswell replied. "I've never felt anything like that before. The pain was so real, and so intense, and now it's just... gone." Oswell paused to think. He took a moment, and then shook his head. He couldn't explain it, but he knew Cicero was wrong.

"Maybe it was in your head?" Karyn suggested. Cicero seemed to agree and Oswell started to nod.

"Maybe you're partly right," Oswell figured, "maybe I've been overexerting myself trying to talk to Thom." Something about the hypothesis left Oswell unsatisfied.

"Or perhaps," Cicero mused, "it is not an overexertion at all…"

"What do you mean?"

"Perhaps your connection with Thomas exists on levels other than a verbal one. It could be possible that you've actually felt Thom's pain."

"No, that can't be," Oswell groaned.

"Why not?"

"Well, it could," Oswell admitted, "but if Thomas is hurt… maybe…"

"Maybe Nicholas and Claire are as well?" Cicero finished Oswell's sentence, seeing where Oswell's thoughts were going.

Oswell felt his heart beat faster in his chest as he worried about his friends. He didn't say a word in reply to Cicero.

"Might it be a good idea to check in on Thomas?" Cicero suggested. Karyn looked like she was interested to witness the psychic communication she'd heard about. Oswell nodded, hoping that Thomas would have some good news for him. Or at the very least, he hoped that Thomas would not have any bad news for him.

"You know what?" Oswell decided, trying to lighten his mood, "we really should think of this connection thing before anything else."

Cicero nodded in concurrence, and remained silent so Oswell could concentrate.

Thomas? Oswell reached out. His thoughts stretched out into the depths of his mind, trying to send the message beyond by going deeper. *Thomas?* He repeated. Oswell tried again and again and again, and then, exhausted, he gave up.

"A break, perhaps?" Cicero proposed. Oswell nodded, using the back of his hand to wipe away the beading of sweat collecting on his forehead. Cicero set a glass of water in front of Oswell and Oswell drank it thirstily. A few minutes later, Oswell indicated to Cicero that he would try again.

He focused deeper this time. Closing his eyes, he descended into the darkness, and forced out the sounds around him with his palms over his ears.

Thomas?

"*Oswell? I thought I heard you a few minutes ago.*" Thomas responded almost immediately this time.

Yes, it's me. Oswell replied. It seemed that his first attempt had been more successful than he'd thought, or perhaps they simply both needed to be receptive to the exchange if it were to be easier.

"*Glad you tried again,*" Thomas replied.

Oswell discerned a clipped tone in his voice. *Are you okay?*

"*I've been better.*"

Did someone—did he hurt you?

"*Yeah, the bastard kicked me in the ribs,*" Thomas growled. Oswell nodded in immediate understanding. Cicero was right; Oswell could feel Thom's pain—at least to a degree.

That explains it.

"*Explains what?*"

I felt a pain in my right side about ten minutes ago.

"*You* felt *my pain?*"

Yes, I did.

"*But how...?*

We have no idea. What happened to you?

"*Father was about to hurt Nicholas—I stepped in.*"

Thank you, Oswell replied gratefully.

"*What else was I supposed to do? The little bugger is growing on me—ouch.*"

Are you sure you're going to be okay?

"*I'll pull through,*" Thomas replied, "*I always have before.*"

Where are you now?

"*Claire says we're in Ontario.*"

Oswell let out a groan of disappointment. They had to be hours past the border.

"*Oswell?*"

Yes?

"*I've no idea how we are going to get out of this.*"

You'll get out of it with my help. We will *find a way,* Oswell half-heartedly assured.

"*I'm going to believe you, but only because that's all I really have.*"

Believe me—just keep your eyes open for the right opportunity.

"*I don't have much of a choice do I?*"

It's beginning to look that way, Oswell replied honestly. *I'll keep in touch. Look after yourself.*

"*I will. You too. Until next time,*" Thomas bid farewell.

Oswell opened his eyes and released a sigh. It was a mixture of frustration and anxiety. He felt as though he was beginning to lose control. It was not a feeling he relished.

"I can't keep doing this Cicero. *I* need to be there for them."

"We've been through this already—you will return when Myr deems it. Thomas is more than capable; you need to trust him."

"How can I trust him? I barely know him."

"*I* know him."

"You've only known him for a few days."

"Together, the two of us have been through the gravest ordeals of his life. In dire situations, one reveals more about oneself than one would ever do on one's own. Already, I know more about you than you would believe."

"How much could you possibly know about me?" Oswell asked, regretting the invitation immediately. He hoped Cicero wouldn't say anything bad about him in front of Karyn.

"I know you're stubborn to a fault," Cicero replied. "You're headstrong and overconfident, but passionate and determined. You're impatient and blunt with your words, but you're also honest and, to put it directly: talented. Oswell... you have a lot to learn, and you also have a lot to offer. You walk a fine line, with some of your greatest weaknesses contributing to your greatest strengths. But your greatest strengths sometimes feed your greatest weaknesses. In that, you are human. You're a good man with good intentions, even if you falter along the way. I know you Oswell Wallace, and I believe in you."

Karyn was smiling as Oswell sat in stunned silence. He didn't know what to say to the older man. He grasped for words, and unable to find an appropriate response, he found himself in silence.

CHAPTER FORTY-ONE

ABOUT-FACE

THOMAS GAZED AT Claire long and hard, thinking about what she had just said to him. They were whispering so quietly that he was almost able to pretend that what she'd said had not been said at all. Even though he wanted to believe that Claire's observation was wrong, he knew that what she had seen was true, because he had seen it himself.

"You're right," Thomas admitted. The expression on Claire's face shifted from concern to desolation. Claire's hopes were exactly the same as Thomas's; she hoped that she was wrong and that Thomas would have been able to convince her otherwise. Now she knew that she was not.

"They all know him," Claire repeated, rolling onto her back and staring up at the roof of the tent. It was getting brighter, which meant they would not have much longer to talk.

"They're acting as if this is all normal. Not only do they know 'Flynn', but they're acting like they know us." Thomas felt revulsion stirring in his stomach as he said Father's last name."

"It's creepy," Claire cried, "they just stare at us... smiling."

Thomas nodded his agreement. The other campers hadn't said a word to any of them except for Father since they had arrived. They didn't act like the children did not exist, in fact, they did the exact opposite. Even when speaking with Father, their eyes were locked on his children.

Thomas wasn't sure what to make of that, but he knew one thing for sure; it made him uneasy.

Thomas too rolled onto his back, and then glanced over at Nicholas. The young boy was still sound asleep, looking content. The expression was becoming less uncommon.

"Nicholas seems almost happy," Thomas observed.

"As soon as we got here," Claire whispered back. "The moment he got out of that car, he's barely stopped smiling. Father doesn't frighten him here."

"For good reason, I suppose," Thomas admitted. Claire nodded her agreement reluctantly.

Father had changed fundamentally the moment they'd arrived at Cahill Campground. In the short time since they had gotten there, Father had made no threats. In fact, he had been relatively pleasant and kind to each of them. Even Ribs was experiencing the benefits. He'd had his first actual meal since Thomas had known the dog.

"That doesn't make me feel any better about it," Claire maintained. "I'm worried about Nicholas. This isn't normal... it's like he's forgotten mom and dad completely."

Thomas nodded absentmindedly. He was worried about Nicholas just as deeply as Claire, but he had other things on his mind as well. His primary worry was the complication created by the campground's inhabitants. If it was a normal campground, Thomas could simply keep his eyes open for an opportunity to get help. However, from what he'd seen so far, the other campers would have little to offer in the way of help. This meant even more of his plan was going to rely on him. Not that he had a plan yet. That was the first hurdle he had to overcome.

Thomas looked back at Claire. She was staring at him, waiting for a reply. He decided that he would not add to Claire's distress by telling her what he was thinking. He simply shook his head.

Claire's brow furrowed. She knew he was hiding something from her, and she didn't like that. Claire never liked being left in the dark about things. It made her feel like a child, and she felt she deserved more than that.

"What is it?" she demanded.

"Nothing."

Claire scowled at Thomas, wrinkling her nose. He noted this and frowned, but it wasn't changing anything.

"Let me in," Claire pleaded. Her pleading to be included made Thomas more aware of the weight he'd volunteered onto his shoulders. It was itching to be shared. He tried to readjust it, but it only felt heavier. Thomas appraised Claire and decided that he wasn't giving her enough credit. His job had become much more difficult. Claire was capable, and Thomas was fallible. He could use her help.

"It's just… I don't have a plan yet," Thomas admitted. "And things just got a lot more complicated." Claire's nose unwrinkled and she smiled as Thomas opened up to her. Thomas was surprised that his admission didn't have a negative effect on Claire. She actually seemed less worried.

"We'll figure it out. Together," she said.

Thomas warmed at the thought.

In the tent next to them, Father groaned. Thomas shot Claire a cautionary grimace and then reclined backwards to rest his head on the thin pillow he'd been provided. Claire did the same, and closed her eyes, pretending to sleep. Thomas's eyes stayed wide open, fixed on the opening to the tent.

He listened as Father moved about inside his tent, and then finally unzipped the door and stepped out into the morning air. Thomas pictured Kelly following after Father silently.

Their tent flap was unzipped slowly and Father poked his head in through the door. His eyes locked on Thomas, who stared back at him defiantly. Always defiant. Thomas did his best to shoot icicles at the man.

Father simply shook his head in disbelief and chuckled lightly. The young man had a fire in him. Still, it was nothing that couldn't be beaten out of him, if necessary.

"You'll learn not to be so hostile young man," he warned in an almost singsong voice.

Thomas kept a stiff upper lip and refused to acknowledge. "Wake your brother and sister up. We're having breakfast in fifteen."

Thomas redoubled his efforts to will Father into spontaneous combustion as the tall man backed his head out of the tent and disappeared. He left the flap of the tent open. With the man gone, Thomas shivered inwardly at Father's words. He acted like they were actually a family. Thomas had always dreamed of having one, but not like this.

He rolled over and nudged Claire. She peeked at him from one eye and then opened up the other one. He could see that the worry had returned to them.

Claire gently brushed the hair away from Nicholas's face, and spoke his name softly. The young boy's eyes fluttered open and he smiled up at his older sister.

"Breakfast?" he asked eagerly. Claire nodded. "Great! I'm starving!"

Claire turned back to Thomas with a concerned frown playing across her full lips. Thomas shook his head solemnly, reflecting her concern as Nicholas darted out of the tent in his pyjamas.

Outside, Father was working on what smelled to Thomas like pancakes. Stepping out of the tent after Claire and approaching the table, Thomas saw that his nose was correct. He also saw a scene that enforced the legitimacy of Father's sudden change in thinking and behaviour, and yet shook Thomas to the core in the face of its normalcy.

Ribs was digging into a bowl of dog food beneath the picnic table as though a meal was not a rare occurrence. Standing in front of the picnic table, Father busied himself over a camp stove, flipping pancakes. He was whistling happily as he performed pastry acrobatics. This show was much to the amusement of Nicholas, who sat eagerly at the table across from Kelly. Kelly's behaviour was the only thing Thomas still found familiar. She sat silently at the table, shoulders rolled forward and hands clasped in her lap, staring off into the trees.

Thomas sat down beside Nicholas as Claire sat on Nick's other side. Claire wrapped her arm around Nicholas protectively. Father smiled at this benevolently. Thom glowered at the man but it went unnoticed; Father had turned his attention back to the frying pan in front of him.

"Did y'all sleep well?" Father asked.

"Very well, thank you," Nicholas replied.

"And the two of you?" Father pressed, glancing at Thomas and Claire in turn.

"Well," Claire replied, her voice cracking slightly.

"No," Thomas replied honestly.

"Why not?"

"Because I've been—" *kidnapped*, Thomas thought, thinking better than to finish the sentence. Father's eyebrows rose in expectation for the rest of the sentence. "...having trouble sleeping," Thomas finished.

"I thought that was it," Father replied knowingly, "a soft boy like you wouldn't be used to roughing it." Thomas caught a glimpse of violence shining in Father's eyes, but it disappeared almost instantly. "Here ya go," he said, serving a single pancake onto each of the plates on the picnic table. "More on the way," he assured the group as he poured more batter into the piping hot pan.

Nicholas snatched up a plastic bottle of syrup on the table and applied a generous helping to his pancake. He then dug in eagerly. Claire started eating slowly and Thomas neglected to eat at all. Father took note of this and glared at Thomas. He could feel Father's venomous stare boring into him. He could also feel his stomach grumbling in protest of his attempted hunger strike.

With the smell of the pancakes wafting up from only a foot and a half away, the temptation was unbearable. Thomas broke, and started eating the pancake, albeit, even more slowly than Claire. Father smiled in a way that looked warm, but somehow exuded cold malevolence, before returning his attention to the freshly cooking pancakes again.

As Father finished up his pancakes, Kelly began to gather up the dishes and wash them in a plastic basin at the opposite end of the picnic table. She cleaned slowly as there was no hurry to finish. Father looked up from his plate and swallowed a mouthful of syrupy pancake.

"I have some new things for the three of you," Father said. He slid a large duffel bag out from underneath the table with his right foot. "Run along and get washed up; we've got a busy day ahead of us, don't we honey?" Father said, directing his last question at Kelly. She nodded, feigning a brief smile. "The shower house is just down the road—" Father pointed left down the camp road, "that-a-way."

Thomas's jaw dropped. *Father is letting us go alone?* He looked at Claire and she looked equally surprised. *This could be it,* Thomas thought. All they had to do was get around the corner, wait to be out of sight, and then make their break for it. Thomas had to think fast and shot a look to Claire. She seemed to understand what he was thinking.

"Let's go guys!" Nicholas interrupted. Hefting the strap of the too-large duffel bag onto his shoulder, he darted off down the road, bag practically dragging in the dirt. Thomas and Claire jumped up from the table and bolted after the young boy, catching up quickly.

"Don't be long now!" Father called after them.

Chapter Forty-Two

A Noted Departure

Oswell recoiled as the taut string of the bow slapped his arm, sending the arrow skittering off course. He dropped the bow and grabbed his arm. The bite of the slap had delivered a sharp but thankfully retreating pain.

"Rookie mistake," Wendell clucked, shaking his head. Darius chuckled, but only briefly as Wendell shot him a hard look.

"I am a rookie!" Oswell complained, ignoring Darius.

"True," Wendell agreed. He picked up Oswell's bow. "Watch," Wendell straightened his arm holding the bow's arch. The bow rested at arm's length. "Do you see the rotation of my arm?"

"Yes," Oswell said, seeing where he had gone wrong. Wendell's arm was not rotated normally to hold the bow. Oswell had gripped the bow with a natural rotation causing the edge of his elbow to get in the way of the bowstring's path. Wendell had only rotated his wrist (and slightly at that) to grip the bow. This turned his inner elbow perpendicular to the ground and kept it turned away from the bowstring's path. The difference in form was almost unobservable, with only about a quarter-inch difference in elbow placement, but clearly that was enough.

Wendell nocked an arrow onto the string, pulled back and let fly. The arrow whipped through the air, thunking into the centre of a target at a hundred feet with deadly speed.

"Now, you try again," Wendell ordered. He handed the bow back to Oswell. Oswell took the bow in hand and rotated his wrist instead of his arm. The difference was only slight, and it produced an unusual strain along his forearm, but he could see immediately that his elbow was out of the way. Oswell glanced over at Wendell and smiled. His teacher smiled back.

Oswell grabbed an arrow and nocked it onto the string. He then stood perpendicular to the target, aligning his right foot towards its centre. Raising the bow, he pointed his forward arm at the centre of the target and began to pull back on the string. The strength required to pull back the bowstring was enormous and Oswell found himself in awe of Wendell once again. The man had pulled the arrow back to his cheek and loosed it almost immediately with startling accuracy.

Oswell had no doubt that Wendell still could have held the position for longer than he had, were it necessary.

Oswell, on the other hand, struggled, and finally let the arrow fly after pulling it back only as far as his chest.

The arrow danced through the air and drove itself into the ground a good thirty feet short of the target. Darius snorted, holding back a laugh. Oswell sighed and looked down at his feet.

"The use of a bow is not only technique," Wendell explained, "strength is key."

Oswell's eyes remained cast down. If he had to get stronger, it would mean more time training, and more time in Myros. He wanted to go home, but remembering Laurence's words, he fought to be patient. He steeled himself and looked back up at Wendell.

"You also seem to have forgotten about another important factor; the arrow falls in flight."

Oswell's eyes brightened up as he realized what Wendell was saying. "Gravity!" Oswell shouted.

"Pardon me?" Wendell asked.

Oswell's brow rose in surprise. *Wendell doesn't know what gravity is?*

"Gravity…" Oswell said again, "it's what keeps us on the ground and what makes you fall from a height. It's a force, and it's why I can't just aim where I want to hit," Oswell thought for a moment. Even Wendell had aimed slightly higher than his intended target. He'd simply needed less room as his arrow had less time to fall. Oswell would need much more; his arrow travelled more slowly.

"I see…" Wendell said slowly. Darius said nothing, although he looked as though he was excited, and deep in thought. The idea of gravity as a force had never occurred to Darius.

"Let me try again," Oswell said. Wendell nodded, as though the request need not have been made.

Oswell set up again and nocked another arrow onto the bowstring. Knowing his limits, he aimed higher this time and didn't struggle to pull back farther than his chest. As soon as he reached it, he twitched his fingers and let the arrow fly. The arrow still danced, and nearly into a branch high above, but it managed to continue in its flight. Finally, it buried itself into the ground a foot in front of the target. The result was considerably more acceptable.

"Excellent," Wendell said, clapping Oswell on the back. Oswell grinned happily at the larger man. At least practicing would be less disheartening. He might actually be able to hit the target a few times.

With training, he would get stronger, and maybe one day, he could do what Wendell could do.

"Should I go again?" Oswell asked.

"That is an excellent idea," Wendell concurred.

Oswell still couldn't get over it. The bird had been so far away, but Wendell had done it.

It was beginning to seem as though Wendell could do anything. Oswell wondered why the people of Numyria needed *him* so badly when they had someone like Wendell Westlake.

He shook that thought from his head and continued eating the lean and gamey flesh off the leg of the pheasant that Wendell had shot and cooked.

"The walls are too high for us to scale them," Darius said.

"Couldn't we use the hole you brought Thom through?" Oswell asked.

"They would expect that," Wendell said.

"It's probably already been filled," Darius added regretfully.

"Besides, what are you going to do once you get inside?" Wendell sucked the meat off of a leg bone.

"Sneak around and find Makkin," Oswell suggested.

"And then what?" Wendell asked.

"Kill him," Darius finished.

"How?" Wendell asked.

"With a knife," Darius sighed.

"Irrelevant, you'll never get close enough to him. He rarely leaves his quarters, and he's got personal guards at every entrance."

"Well I didn't know that," Darius said.

"These are the things we need to know before we start hatching such foolish plans," Wendell lectured.

"We'll think of something," Oswell decided.

"I'm working on something tonight," Wendell informed the pair as he stomped out the fire and wrapped up in a sack what was left of the bird.

"What do you mean?" Oswell asked as he set to gathering the bows while Darius reloaded the quivers with the arrows they had used.

"Getting some new information, hopefully," Wendell replied. His tone implied that he wasn't going to be giving away much more information.

"Can we come?" Oswell asked hopefully.

"Absolutely not," Wendell replied. He looked as though he was ready to counter a complaint from Oswell, but none came. Wendell looked surprised, but then smiled in approval. Oswell was learning to listen. Finally.

"How long will you be gone?" Darius asked.

"That is uncertain, but I hope to return tomorrow if all goes well," Wendell explained.

"Don't think this will be a vacation for the two of you; I fully expect the both of you to continue your training."

"What should we do?" Darius wondered.

"I think the most important thing for the both of you is to get in better shape. Don't worry about practicing; strengthen."

"Like... work out?" Oswell asked.

"If that's what you would like to call it... come to think of it, if Karyn feels up to it, she should join you."

"Okay!" Oswell said. Karyn would be happy to be included, and it would be good for her to have something to focus on. Wendell's suggestion was also an indication that she'd be welcome to stay with them at the Enclave for the foreseeable future. "We'll pump some iron," Oswell decided. Wendell and Darius gave Oswell a confused expression, looked to each other for an explanation, and then simultaneously decided not to pursue an answer to their obvious question. Oswell noticed this and laughed.

"When do you leave?" Darius asked.

"As soon as we get back," Wendell replied.

By the time they got back to the Enclave, it was near dinnertime. None of the three were very hungry because of their late and succulent lunch, but they decided they had better eat something, or they would wake up hungry in the middle of the night.

The trio made a brief stop at the armoury to drop off the bows and quivers, and then found their way back to the main hall. They joined Cicero, Rawlins, Karyn, and Laurence at the table.

Oswell grabbed three plates and offered to fill them for Wendell and Darius. The two complied and Oswell dashed off to the side table on which Laurence and Karyn had placed the spread.

Oswell picked carefully, plating onto each a scoop of smooth mashed yam, along with a bit of roasted pig leg and a hunk of brown bread. It suddenly struck Oswell as unusual as to how the Enclave managed to get the food that they had. He decided that he would make a point to ask Cicero or Laurence about it at another time.

Oswell delivered two plates to his companions and then returned to the side table to grab his own. The food smelled irresistible, and Oswell found himself silently thanking Laurence for being such a good cook. As he sat down, he decided it was silly not to express his gratitude, and so, after taking his first satisfying bite, Oswell thanked

Laurence and Karyn. The resident holy man nodded his head in acceptance of the compliment, but otherwise said nothing. This was primarily due to his mouthful of food. Karyn, on the other hand, slid her chair closer to him and smiled.

"You like it?" she asked.

"I do," Oswell replied.

"What happened to your arm?" she ran her finger along the welt from the bow string.

"Nothing," Oswell snatched his arm away. Karyn looked taken aback.

"Bowstring got him on the follow-through," Darius chuckled, not seeing the exchange as he was becoming intimately involved with his fork and the food on it.

Karyn laughed and put a hand on his shoulder, "We can't all be marksmen."

Oswell felt his face grow hot.

"Don't worry," she said, "I've got your back."

That didn't help.

"Eat up."

By the time Oswell was halfway through his dinner, Wendell had finished. He stood up and strode around the table to Cicero. There, he bent over and whispered something to Cicero. Oswell tried to make out what he said, but couldn't. Cicero nodded, and then stood to embrace Wendell briefly. The pair separated and Wendell left the room without a word.

"He didn't waste any time, did he?" Darius said.

"Nope," Oswell replied.

"Where's he going?" Karyn asked.

Oswell and Darius shrugged.

CHAPTER FORTY-THREE

NOT A FISH

THEY KEPT SMILING. The only ones who stopped were those Thomas decided to address.

"Excuse me," he would say, or "please help," and they would turn away, their smiles gone, replaced by their cold and emotionless backs. In that way, their backs matched their smiles. Even with their backs turned, it seemed as though they were still watching; keeping tabs and always alert. The feature was homologous for all of the campers, and that thought disturbed Thomas. Besides that, Thomas quickly noticed that there were no other children at the campground. Thomas felt his anxiety multiply.

By the time they reached the shower house, Thomas was as unwilling to go inside as Claire. Nicholas was still excited for a shower, and waited impatiently for Thomas to dole out the necessary ingredients. He handed Claire a towel, a bar of soap, and a change of clothes. She didn't move. Thomas then handed a similar supply to Nicholas, and left the last ration in the duffel bag for himself. Without hesitation, Nicholas darted into the men's side of the shower house.

Still, Claire did not move. Thomas could tell why she was worried.

"Can you scream?" He asked, anticipating Claire's worries about going inside alone.

"Yes," she said. Thomas was surprised by how scared she sounded. Usually she seemed stronger. Perhaps it was the way the other campers had looked at them. They almost seemed... hungry. He could imagine how she felt because he felt the exact same way: violated.

"I'm right beside you, and I'll be waiting out here when you're done. Just scream if you need me." Where Claire was weak, Thomas had to be strong, even if it was just putting on a brave face. With every development, Thomas felt less and less capable. He needed Oswell to reassure him again, but even those confidence-inspiring conversations were losing their potency.

Claire hesitated. Thomas could see the fingers on her right hand shaking. The fingers on her left hand were fiercely clenching her towel, turning her knuckles white. Thomas reached out and steadied her shaking hand.

Her fingers were freezing despite the warmth in the air. Looking into her brown eyes, he tried to convey that he would be there for her. Without looking away from his calming gaze, she nodded.

Thomas let go of her hand and she trudged through the door into the women's side of the shower house. Thomas darted into the men's side. If he was to keep his promise, he would need to shower quickly.

In the next stall, Nicholas was humming a tune as he showered. He seemed to be in no particular hurry. Thomas disrobed and stepped into the shower. He eyed the faucets warily, recalling his limited experience from the single time he'd taken a bath on Earth. Turning the red faucet, Thomas was shocked by how cold it was, and automatically assumed he'd turned the wrong faucet.

He turned the blue faucet and found it got even colder. Goosebumps exploded across his body, and all of his hair stood rigidly on end. He shut the blue faucet off and sighed as the water started to warm up. Then he jumped back as it got too hot. Recognizing what he was supposed to do, he winced through the steaming water and flicked the blue faucet back on, balancing the temperature to a comfortable one.

Satisfied, Thomas grabbed his bar of soap and went to the business of cleaning himself. His underarms were humming in a manner altogether unpleasant and different in comparison to the tune Nicholas produced. Thomas spent the majority of his time cleaning them. When he was done, he flipped the faucets off, towelled off incompletely and then threw on his change of clothes. In Nicholas's stall, the boy was still humming.

"Hurry up in there," Thomas said. He stood in front of a mirror and ran his fingers through his hair briefly. Though dissatisfied with the result, it was better than before so he dashed out of the shower house and stood outside, waiting for his two companions. Nicholas had heeded Thomas's order, and appeared first. His hair was a mess, and Thomas did his best to fix that using his fingers as a comb. He looked up as the door to the women's side swung open.

Claire's hair was still wet and tangled. It was pushed back off her shoulder, exposing her slender neck. Her cheeks were flush from the heat of the shower, and her eyes sparkled in a way Thomas had never seen before. For a moment, she'd forgotten where she was, and that moment allowed Thomas to forget as well. She was beautiful.

"You look…" Thomas began.

"Like a mess," Claire finished, brushing her fingers through her hair in the hopes that it might bring about a more organized result. "This is going to be one giant knot if I don't find a real brush," she muttered. Noticing Thomas's stare, she blushed. This only served to add to the colour in her cheeks. Thomas wasn't sure whether she'd blushed because she'd caught him staring at *her*, or because she thought he was staring at her *hair*. The reason suddenly became very important to Thomas, and he too felt warmth spread across his face.

Claire grabbed Nicholas and hugged him tightly. "Look at you," she ran her fingers through his hair in an attempt to fix it. Apparently, Thomas had not done a good enough job.

"Don't worry Nick, we'll get out of this yet," she promised, hugging him again.

"What do ya mean?" Nicholas asked, staring up at his sister confused. Nicholas seemed to think they were just on vacation. Like they weren't kidnapped. Thomas recognized it for what it was: an attempt to cope. Things had been bad, but now they were better. That was good enough for Nicholas; he didn't need to go home, just as long as he was camping. Claire glanced away from her younger brother and focused on Thomas as the pain welled up in her eyes. She too recognized what was happening. Looking into those eyes, Thomas could see that the momentary peace was gone. Thomas mourned for it.

Claire took hold of Nicholas's hand and started dragging him back to the campsite. Thomas hefted the duffel bag onto his shoulder and caught up with the brother and sister. He did his best to ignore the stares of the other campers, and neglected to address any of them this time. Instead, he simply returned their stares, matching them icicle for icicle.

"So what do you kids want to do today?" Father asked when they got back to the campsite.

"Go home," Thomas muttered.

"You *are* home," Father said through gritted teeth. Thomas felt the anger rising up like a smouldering fire being fed. Words in argument began to bubble forth, but a glance to Claire saved him the confrontation. He didn't want to start anything then and there. If anything, Thomas needed to get on Father's good side. If he could lull the man into a false sense of security, Thomas could make things happen. Though the words still circulated in his head and the coal continued to burn, he let the words blow away like smoke off his lips.

"I was thinking we could go out in the lake on the boat," Father suggested.

"I wanna go!" Nicholas agreed as he looked up momentarily from patting Ribs.

"It's settled then," Father decided.

Something else was bubbling up inside Thomas now. This time, it was slightly more tangible: his breakfast.

He sat in the middle of the wide-bottomed boat with an extra paddle clenched tightly in his hands. Claire sat on the bench beside him, her hands stiff on the boat's edge while Nicholas revelled over the prow at the water slipping past beneath them. Kelly sat next to Father at the back of the boat, where he was busy whistling and working the outboard motor's throttle.

If there was one, the god that put him in that boat was a cruel one. Thomas was deathly afraid of the water. He couldn't swim, and that only contributed to his debilitating fear, which had formed years earlier.

Only ten years old, he had been alone, in keeping with tradition. In actual fact, that time, he was less alone than he would have preferred. It was everything he could do just to stay ahead of the band of thieves that pursued him for having the nerve to steal away his share of a job that they'd withheld. When he found the brook he was faced with two choices: One, wade across the river and hope you make it; or two, wait, get caught, and *know* you won't make it.

Although neither of the choices was particularly attractive, at least the first carried a glimmer of hope. He stepped into the running water and breathed a sigh of relief; the current was weak

He waded further, feeling the water rise, first up his legs, then past his belly button, and up to his chest. The current got stronger and the water deeper with each step towards the centre of the brook. When his footing slipped out from under him and the current took him, he didn't even have time to make his peace. He held his breath and watched as the aqueous sky slid by above him. Death, he thought, would be peaceful. He would slip away quietly and almost happily.

When he woke up, he thought he was dead. The man looking down at him was not godly in any way, surprising the limited faith system Thomas had found in those years. His most distinguishing feature was his eyes. Green and youthful despite their deep setting in a wrinkled face.

"Am I dead?" Thomas had asked.

"Nah boy, but lucky ta be alive thassa fact," the man said.

"Where am I?"

"Goffs," the man replied, "ya turned up in my nets downstream from Bankbarrow."

Thomas shook his head and sat up. Goffs was only a short way from Bankbarrow where he'd left with the tail of thieves. The only thing going for him was that the thieves would either think he was dead, or that he'd made it across the river. Either way, they would not be likely to look for him in Goffs. Thieves had better, more profitable things to do. After that brush with death, Thomas had avoided water consistently.

Now, Thomas was gliding over instead of under the water he feared. The only thing between them was a thin aluminum hull. The brook had been over his head, so the lake would certainly be.

He absentmindedly worked the grain of his paddle while Father's commentary echoed in his ears; his voice of authority was far off, as if across the lake and on land. He wished that he too was far off on land, or at least somewhere not in a boat. He would have preferred the old white van they'd started their journey in.

"Loved doing this as a boy," Father reminisced. "Who wants to go swimming?" Father asked.

This gets better and better, Thomas thought.

"I do!" Nicholas volunteered. Father smiled warmly and killed the throttle. The boat drifted to a stop and settled deeper in the water.

Nicholas didn't need any other invitation, he launched out of the boat, rocking it slightly. The young boy hit the water, disappearing for a split second before his life jacket brought him bobbing back to the surface. Ribs followed the boy in. Father looked at the three left in the boat.

"No other takers?" Father asked. Kelly shook her head slowly and Claire avoided eye contact. Father looked pointedly at Thomas. "Not even you, big man?"

"No thanks," Thomas said, trying not to imagine how green he must look. As Nicholas bobbed and laughed in his life jacket, Thomas yearned for his own.

"It's good for you!" Father grabbed Thomas by the shirt and he felt his stomach leap out of his throat. He hit the water hard and immediately began to sink. He flailed about under the water but nothing seemed to help him rise. The water crushed him from all sides and his lungs began to burn. He could hear the muffled sounds of screaming above, and then the distant implosion of the water as an enormous body plunged after him. Rough hands grasped him around the armpits and yanked him out of the depths.

He came up spluttering and locked a steely grip on the side of the boat. The cold aluminum dug into his skin as he hoisted himself out of the water and collapsed in the bottom of the boat, a crumpled, sopping mess. Father followed close behind and stood, dripping with his shirt off.

"What kind of boy doesn't know how to swim?" Father raged. Thomas stared up at the man fearfully.

"I never learned," Thomas spat.

"Useless," Father replied. He turned and dove back into the water, apparently still intent on enjoying a swim for himself. The boat rocked back and forth, close to tipping.

Thomas felt his breakfast make an appearance at the back of his throat. He fought hard, swallowed it back down and grimaced as he felt the acid burn his throat. He watched as Father turned his face into the water and began swimming away in a front crawl. Thomas was struck by the scars that laced back and forth across the man's muscled body as he pulled away from the boat with powerful strokes. He was pleased to see that Father's arm was still bandaged where he had stabbed him. He felt no sympathy for the man; if anything, Thomas would like to add to Father's collection, especially after this most recent assault. As far as Thomas was concerned, one little scar on Father's forearm wasn't enough. Watching Father get smaller and smaller, Thomas hoped the man would keep swimming and never come back. He felt more hopeful with every stroke.

Thomas startled and turned as he heard Claire speak.

"Kelly?" she ventured.

Kelly turned to look at Claire, but said nothing.

"Why are you doing this?" she whispered, throwing a wary glance at Father's receding figure. The man was getting farther away, but Thomas knew that sound carried over water.

Kelly's expression remained hard, staring.

"Do you love him?" she asked.

A tear formed in the crook of Kelly's eye, then rolled down her cheek, hanging on for dear life at the curve of her jaw. She nodded and the tear drop fell.

Claire looked back at Father, shrinking away into the distance. She timed it this time, waiting for his ears to go under. She didn't want Father to hear what she was about to say.

"Are we the first?" she asked. Claire wasn't sure what answer she wanted. Part of her wanted Kelly to say that they were the first, that Father hadn't ruined the lives of countless children before them. Another part of her didn't want Kelly to answer her at all. If they weren't the first, what had happened to the other children?

Kelly blinked then she shook her head, no.

Thomas lost his control and heaved over the side of the boat. Claire on the other hand, huffed, but managed to fight back tears successfully. Where Thomas was weak, she needed to be strong. Thomas dejectedly watched as the partially digested pancakes diffused across the surface of the water. Feeling the urge to retch subside, Thomas reeled himself away from the edge of the boat, breathing hard. He wiped his mouth.

"Ewww! Don't eat that!" Nicholas laughed as Ribs lapped up Thom's leftovers. At that, Thomas felt another wave rise up in him, and leaned over the railing again and added to the smorgasbord.

Off in the distance, Father had turned around and was making his way back to the boat.

Claire hoisted Nicholas out of the water, and helped Ribs into the boat too. The boat rocked minimally. Thomas braced himself, leaning away from Father's entry point as the large man hoisted himself up and sat back down at the back of the boat. Despite Thomas's efforts, the boat was heaving and he had to fight to prevent round three.

"You guys missed out," Father's chest was heaving and the water beaded off his skin. He ripped the motor's ignition cord and the small engine roared to life. A quick yank turned the boat back. Thomas saw where they were headed and leaned in stomach fortified by the prospect of reaching the shore, sweet shore.

CHAPTER FORTY-FOUR

CRACK OF DAWN

Oswell's eyelids parted slightly, sleep reeled them in from completely opening. Through those tired slits, he could see Darius standing in the doorway, tapping his foot on the ground impatiently. Seeing his sleeping companion's eyes open, he grinned.

"About time!" Darius laughed, "You sleep like a Peat'r Bog sloth."

"I sleep like a… a what?" Oswell asked, opening his eyes a little wider, but still with no intention of getting up.

"Peat'r Bog sloth," Darius repeated.

"If you say so…" Oswell replied. He knew enough about sloths to understand what Darius was getting at. Oswell did not like the assertion, but he was too tired to rebut it. It seemed like only yesterday that he had called Grant a sloth. Back when things were normal. Now it was anything but, and the roles were reversed. "What do you want?"

"We need to start training, Wendell's orders."

"Right now?"

"Yes, right now. Karyn's waiting too."

"Give me a minute," Oswell groaned. He reached up and rubbed the crust out of his eyes with the balls of his fists. When he opened them, Darius was right beside his bunk. "What are you—" Oswell felt his mattress upend and found himself face down on the floor, "—

doing?" Oswell finished. He groaned as he pushed the mattress off his back and stood up.

"Let's go," Darius demanded.

"What's the hurry?"

"You've already overslept."

"And Laurence tells me *I* need to be more patient."

"*We're* leaving in three," Darius shrugged, and then left the hut.

"Aw hell," Oswell grumbled. He threw on a new shirt, pulled on his pants, and buckled his belt into place. His knife was secured in its sheath, and he slung the canvas knapsack he'd been provided over his shoulder. He could hear some water sloshing inside the canteen in his pack. He decided he was ready.

Oswell darted out into the morning light, grimacing. The sun was just coming up over the trees. It was early. Oswell frowned at Darius's allegation that he'd overslept.

"It's the crack of dawn!" Oswell grumbled as he caught up with Darius.

"And?"

"How is that oversleeping?"

"It isn't really; I was just ready to go."

"You're pushing your luck. I'm not a morning person."

"You'll get used to it. There isn't much to do in the middle of the night so we make good use of the day." Darius justified.

"Wendell gets plenty of use out of the midnight hours."

"True," Darius admitted, "but what Wendell does isn't our business, unless he sees fit to tell us."

Oswell rolled his eyes at Darius. For someone with such a penchant for invention, Darius did not seem to be very curious about what was going on. That or he'd figured it out already.

"What are we doing today anyway?" Oswell asked.

"Getting you in shape."

"Oh right," Oswell remembered. He was not looking forward to exercise. He was, however, looking forward to a day with Karyn.

"Wendell wants us stronger and faster. Only one way to do that."

Oswell groaned, "Push-ups?"

"Among other things," Darius grinned.

"You boys ready?" Karyn asked, standing beside the ladder. Oswell tried not to stare. She wore a tight-fitted green shirt and brown leggings. Her red hair, gathered into a tight braid, glowed in the sunrise.

"Yup," Darius replied. She kicked the ladder off the ledge and watched it tumble down.

"Let's go!"

"How... much... longer?" Oswell panted.

"Tired?" Darius wheezed.

Oswell collapsed.

"Evidently," Darius noted, and flopped down onto the ground as well. Karyn stopped too, struggling for breath. All three had pushed themselves that morning.

Sweat poured off each of their faces and exposed backs. Their chests rose and fell rapidly, spastically. Oswell pitied the tight wrap around Karyn's chest that she'd revealed as her shirt became too sweaty with the exertion. Oswell had never been so tired in his life, not even after he'd played an entire half of a soccer game without a substitute. Being that tired did not help his game, and he didn't think he was going to be very useful to anyone in his current state either. He was as good as dead.

The trio had spent the entire morning with barely a break. Darius had led Oswell and Karyn through a warm-up that started with an hour long game of tag. With only three people playing, the game was exhausting, but Oswell excelled. Running was something he could always do. Regardless, the game managed to draw the first beads of sweat, even in the cool morning shade of the forest.

After that game, they practiced climbing trees. They would set goals to reach, and then race to get there. Looking back, Oswell was glad they'd done the climbing early on. A fall would have been far more likely if they were as exhausted as they were at the end of the day. Oswell was shocked by Karyn's ability; she won nearly every race.

After their climbing, they took a short break, and then got into a regimen of exercise.

Darius led them through a series of crunches, high jumps, pull ups, and an array of other exercises. They'd just started into their fourth set of push ups when Oswell collapsed.

"I guess we found our limit," Darius decided.

"I guess so," Oswell whispered. Secretly, he was envious that Darius had held out longer than him. He'd only barely outlasted Karyn.

It was just past noon and the warmth of the day was at its peak, though that wasn't saying much. Still, it was warm enough to warrant going shirtless. Even Karyn had stripped down to a small wrap across her chest. If Oswell wasn't so exhausted, he would have been very distracted. His body had never felt so worn out. He was going to be sore.

"We should stretch," Oswell groaned as he picked himself up off the forest floor. Darius agreed; he and Karyn stood up, and joined Oswell in stretching each of the muscles they'd worked. On the bright side, it didn't feel like he'd strained them; there was no pain, simply an unwillingness to function as muscles should.

"Good idea," Darius complimented as they finished their stretch. He sat down and then reclined back comfortably, his hands forming a pillow underneath his head.

"For sure," Karyn agreed, rising from the splits she'd dropped herself into and sat cross legged across from Oswell.

"Thanks," Oswell replied as he reached down and tossed his shirt onto his shoulder and then fished his lunch from his bag. He tore into the piece of dried meat and ripped off a hunk of the hard heel of bread he'd brought along.

"Give me some of that would ya?" Darius grinned, sitting up. He was hungry too. Oswell tossed him the other half of the bread and a second piece of dried meat. Darius started in on his.

"Me too," Karyn pleaded. Oswell laughed and tossed her a share.

Oswell chewed and swallowed slowly. The bread was hard and dry, but was filled with whole grains. He could feel the rough bits of seed and husk on his tongue. It was wholesome, and filled a gap that had evolved from their intense morning. The meat was dry and tough, but it was seasoned nicely. He could taste the salt and pepper easily, but there were a number of other spices that were both unidentifiable and delicious. He decided if he was going to eat tough meat, then this was the way to do it. For the second time that day, Oswell found himself thinking of his friend Grant, his lunch not that far off from Grant's favoured jerky.

He leaned up against a tree and closed his eyes. He hadn't gotten enough sleep. Just a little would be good, Oswell decided, but doing so out in the forest wasn't the brightest of ideas.

Oswell opened his eyes and glanced at Darius. He had finished his lunch long before Oswell, and had returned to his position on his back. His eyes were closed and he had a peaceful look about his face, but Oswell wasn't sure if he was asleep. Not willing to take the chance of both of them falling asleep, Oswell turned his attention to Karyn.

"You're pretty amazing," Oswell said.

"Thanks," Karyn replied. "Father... he taught me a lot."

Oswell looked down at his feet and then back up at Karyn. "You know he'd be proud of you."

"I know," she fumbled with her braid, glancing at Oswell occasionally. "What are your parents like?"

Oswell was slightly caught off guard by the question. He'd been so busy with what Wendell and Cicero had him doing that he'd mostly stopped thinking about home. Thinking about getting home, sure, but home itself had been neglected. His voice cracked before he spoke. "They... they're great. My mom—"

"What's her name?" Karyn asked.

"Monica. She takes really good care of my dad and I. She's definitely got everything going for her; she loves her job, she's got a great husband—".

"And a great son," Karyn added.

"Thanks," Oswell fiddled with a stick in his hands. "Yeah, she's pretty amazing. She knows how to take charge," Oswell laughed, "She literally runs that house..." Oswell glanced up at Karyn, "What was your mom like?"

"Lara," Karyn named her, looking up at the trees, "She was beautiful; the love of my father's life. She was strong, a lot like your mother, I'd bet."

It seemed like they talked for the longest time. Stiffness started to settle into his legs and they both were sure that Darius was sleeping; a timid snore escaped his mouth with every inhalation.

Oswell started to feel drowsy. Karyn's voice and talking about home put him at ease. He was tired, having failed to find a good night of sleep since he'd arrived on Myros. He also couldn't understand how no one else could see that. Everyone seemed to think he was lazy because he didn't wake up with the sun. As far as he was concerned, Oswell had a right to be tired. He'd travelled *more* than a few time zones; he'd travelled between different worlds. His journey brought jet lag to a whole new level.

He leaned back against the tree and let his eyelids fall as Karyn continued to talk. The dark was nice and made the atmosphere seem even more comfortable. Oswell found himself wishing they could go back to the Enclave and enjoy the breeze above the trees. He was just about to suggest they wake Darius and head back when he heard a noise off to his right. His eyes shot open and he immediately focused on Karyn. She stopped talking in mid-sentence. Oswell watched as terror filled her eyes. He jumped up and put his hands on her shoulder.

"Don't make a sound," he whispered. Listening, he heard the sound again. It was faint and coming from far off. Oswell strained to hear what it was. It almost sounded like a swarm of bees, but muffled. With every passing moment, the buzzing got louder.

The realization clicked as the sound came within a recognizable range. *Voices.*

Oswell threw on his shirt. He darted across the short gap between himself and Darius, and clamped his hand over Darius's mouth, then shook him awake.

Darius's eyes opened sleepily, but widened in concern as he found his mouth covered.

Oswell put a finger to his lips and then removed his hand from Darius's mouth. Darius understood and said nothing. Oswell cupped his ear and pointed in the direction of the approaching voices. He then motioned in the other direction. Darius listened for a moment and then nodded in agreement and pulled himself up. He didn't bother with putting on his shirt, simply grabbing his rucksack and darting off into the trees silently. Oswell snatched up his own pack, grabbed Karyn's hand, and followed quickly after him.

The feeling was surreal. He was tired and his muscles were exhausted but the adrenaline pumping through his veins overcame that. He wanted to shout, but he knew that they would hear. He was afraid, but he wanted to fight.

Oswell nearly tripped over Darius as he rounded a tree. Darius grabbed Oswell and reeled both of them in. The voices were still nearby, but the three of them were under cover now, hiding within the thick foliage of a bush.

"Who is it?" Darius whispered.

Oswell frowned and backed down. They would have to sit tight and watch. The voices were too close to run from. They were clearly audible, no longer a muffled buzzing; Oswell could make out nearly every word. Whoever the speakers were, Oswell did not recognize their voices.

The three spies watched from their hidden vantage point as a trio of men wielding spears and wearing ring mail trudged by.

The man in front appeared to be in charge. He was tall, but had an oafish look to his face. The other two men were considerably shorter, but strong despite their fattened bellies. Somehow, each of their faces managed to convey even more stupidity than the first.

Oswell glanced at Darius.

"*Guards,*" Darius mouthed. Karyn's hand tightened around Oswell's as Oswell's eyes widened in recognition; they were indeed wearing the exact same garb as Wilkins, the man Cicero had strangled to death on the night Oswell arrived on Myros.

The guards wandered past their hiding place, talking raucously and paying little attention to where they were going. Oswell and Darius remained silent as the voices faded off to a muffled buzzing again, and then disappeared altogether.

"What was that about?" Darius asked.

"How should I know?" Oswell shot back.

"Of course you wouldn't know... it's just... unusual. Guards from Fletchery rarely patrol the forest. It's too large, and far too easy for people to hide, and for their men to get lost."

Oswell stifled a retort. He didn't like how Darius made him sound like an ignorant fool. He didn't need to be reminded of his ignorance in the area of Numyrian standard procedures. It was annoying. Something clicked and Oswell took a mental note to try not to use his Earthisms in conversation.

"I wonder why they're doing it now," Karyn pondered.

"Maybe they're looking for Cicero and I," Oswell suggested. "They chased us into the forest before, why not come looking for us again?"

Darius looked surprised, "That's a possibility."

Oswell grinned despite himself.

"Regardless, we need to return to the Enclave and inform grandfather at once."

"We'll need to be careful," Oswell said, feeling confident in his reasoning following his level-headed hypothesis, "there could be more guards around."

"Ears and eyes alert," Darius agreed.

He padded off silently along the forest floor Karyn followed closed behind and Oswell took up the rear.

Despite the initial sighting, the three trainees hadn't seen any other guards for at least fifteen minutes. They were making decent time considering the caution they took. Oswell was on edge, ears alert to every sound. Darius seemed to be in a similar state because when they heard two muffled cries of surprise cut short by two consecutive thumps, they stopped on the spot. Oswell arched his eyebrow at Darius who looked to be thinking. Denial seemed to cloud his expression, though it was followed by a sudden look of pride and pleasure, and then a return to denial.

"What was that?" Oswell and Karyn demanded together.

"Nothing," Darius said quickly.

"Liar," Karyn accused.

"Let's go," Darius decided.

"No," Oswell replied, "let's check it out."

Darius tried to protest but Oswell was already trekking off in the direction of the sounds.

The source was closer than he'd expected. He looked up in dumbfounded awe at two unconscious Fletcherian guardsmen hanging by their ankles high above.

"What in the..." Oswell mumbled. He turned to Darius. Darius noticed Oswell's appraisal a moment too late and was unable to hide his prideful grin.

"This has you written all over it," Oswell concluded.

"What?" Darius replied.

"This is your work, isn't it?"

"Of course not."

"You're a terrible liar," Karyn agreed.

"Only with people who know me," Darius defended.

"So it *was* you," Oswell grinned and looked up at the two comatose guardsmen.

"You can't tell anyone!" Darius demanded.

"What, why? What?" Oswell spluttered.

"You can't tell anyone that I did this!"

"Why? This is good!"

"No, it's not good. Wendell would be furious if he found out. These traps... they're not supposed to be active. I just set them up," Darius explained. "I never..." he seemed to think for a moment, "Maybe I did." He grimaced. Oswell arched his brow at the disconnected thoughts.

Oswell had a hard time believing that Darius had forgotten that he had activated the traps. The young man was too sharp. There was only one explanation: there were too many traps to keep track of.

"Are there more of these?" Oswell asked.

"You guys won't tell anyone?" Darius reiterated. He looked for a guarantee from both Karyn and Oswell.

"I won't tell them," Oswell promised. Karyn echoed the response.

"Yes, there are a bunch of them—they're all over the forest. I thought—with the fire system going so well, we might as well have some more security. Couldn't hurt, right?"

"Right," Oswell understood. "Unless Wendell happened upon them before these guys," Oswell motioned to the two men. Darius seemed to go white in the face.

"These have to be the only ones," Darius decided. He searched around the immediate area and after a few minutes, managed to deactivate another half a dozen snares. "That's better."

"Why didn't you tell Wendell?" Oswell asked.

"At first, I wanted it to be a surprise," Darius mumbled, "But after a while, I started wondering what everyone would think. You're right Oz. These things could be dangerous; what if Wendell had fallen into one of them?" Darius shook his head, seemingly annoyed at his own stupidity.

"But he didn't," Karyn said, "and your intentions were good."

"Good intentions don't always breed good results," Darius qualified.

"True," Karyn replied. She glanced back up at the guardsmen again, "What should we do about these guys?" she asked.

"I suppose we should let them down," Darius decided. He untied a knot and lowered one of the men to the ground, then did the same for the other. The two men lay on the forest floor like children down for their afternoon nap. "Let's get out of here before they wake up," Darius said. He seemed to pause for a moment and then returned to the two sleeping men. "Here," he handed Oswell one of the guard's sword and knife.

"Declawing the cats," Oswell observed. Darius nodded and took the matching set from the other guard.

"Good steel is hard to come by," Darius explained, "And Fletcherian steel is among the best."

Oswell hefted the sword in his hand. It wasn't as nice as some of the other swords in the Enclave's armoury, but it would still make a nice addition.

"Come on," Darius urged, striding away from the disarmed guardsmen. Karyn followed after him. Oswell took one last look at the two men. One of them stirred and Oswell took that as his cue. He darted after his companions, sword gripped firmly in his hand.

Oswell helped Darius up from the ladder onto the catwalk. Being back in the Enclave relieved Oswell and the adrenaline subsided instantly. His body felt weak again as the effects of their exercise manifested.

"Come on," Darius said after they deposited their haul in the armoury. He strode off at a brisk pace towards the main hall. Oswell and Karyn followed close behind him. Oswell was interested in finding out what Cicero would have to say.

"Grandfather!" Darius called as they pushed their way through the double doors. Cicero was standing a few feet away, talking to Wendell.

"You're back," Oswell greeted Wendell. He was happy to see that the tall man had returned. If anyone would know how to handle the guards, Wendell would.

"Yes," Wendell replied.

"Yes?" Cicero asked in response to Darius.

"We saw guards patrolling in the forest," Darius said, leaving out the bit about those that were ensnared.

"Wendell just informed me," Cicero replied. Oswell frowned and Darius deflated visibly. Their announcement was redundant.

"Good thing we rushed back here to tell them," Oswell muttered.

"Were you followed?" Wendell demanded.

"No!" Darius said.

"Are you certain?" Wendell pressed.

"Yes!" Darius maintained.

"Okay," Wendell relaxed slightly.

"What's going on?" Oswell demanded, taking his turn to talk. Wendell glanced at Oswell, then to Cicero, and back to Oswell.

"Makkin has stepped up patrols in the forest. They are looking for the Enclave. This means we are going to have to be more careful, and more aware," Wendell explained.

"I think it would be best if the three of you stopped training," Cicero cut in.

"No!" Darius, Oswell, and Karyn said in unison. Oswell was surprised to find Karyn's plea had the most conviction. She obviously valued the opportunity to fight back against the Governyr.

"No," Wendell agreed. "That would only set us back further. They must continue to train, but they must be more careful about how they come and go."

Cicero looked defeated for a moment, but then nodded his agreement. It was natural for a grandfather to worry about his grandson.

"Grab some food and then get some rest. We'll be going into the forest again tonight… all three of you," Wendell said.

Oswell and Darius shared a look, and then smiled in agreement. Apparently the day's excitement had not been enough for either of them. Though Oswell was exhausted, the prospect of the mysterious excursion was enough to pique his interest. Oswell felt Karyn's gaze and glanced her way. She'd sensed their excitement, but there was a question in her eyes.

"Why are you guys so excited?" Karyn asked as they left the main hall, all three feeling full and tired.

"Night training is the best," Oswell explained.

"Agreed," Darius said, "plus, we might get a chance to see what Wendell's been doing."

"What do you think we're going to do?" Oswell asked.

"That's for Wendell to know, and us to find out," Darius replied. Oswell got the distinct feeling that Darius had about as much of a clue as he did, but was trying his best to hide that fact.

"Okay," Oswell grinned.

"See you tonight," Karyn said, ducking into her hut.

"See you tonight," he echoed. He shot Darius a smile and then darted off towards the barracks where he collapsed into bed. A few thoughts fought forward to assert themselves in the middle of his consciousness.

He was starting to feel like he was close; that he would get to go home soon. Oswell batted those thoughts aside, ignoring his eternal optimism. He needed to heed Wendell's instruction for rest. With the spectre of another interrupted night of sleep looming before him, Oswell closed his eyes and drifted off.

CHAPTER FORTY-FIVE

STILL NOT A FISH

HE FELT THE cool metal in his hand. He checked its weight, its edge. He could sense the power accompanying it. The temperature reeled him back in as it quelled the blaze that burned within him. Blood gushed from the huge man's neck, and Thomas was responsible for it. The hot syrup pooled on the ground and took on an inky consistency in the gloom. The man wasn't dead yet, but his very life force gurgled away by the second. Staring down at the dying man, Thomas knew he couldn't wait for the man to die. He wanted to. The man was cruel and Thomas was going to need as much of a head start as he could get if he was going to escape. He turned to run, felt his foot slip in the expanding puddle, and then he, too was on the ground. The ground was hard. Too hard. It didn't make sense. He looked around; the walls, the man drowning in his own blood beside him, Cicero waiting at the prison door impatiently. It was all wrong.

Thom's eyes shot open. A sticky sweat coated his back, having accumulated as he slept. For an instant, the sickly suggestion that it was blood crept across his skin. He reached back and wiped it away. Salty. Wet. Innocuous. Sweat. Thomas sat up in the tent, recognizing the answer he'd been searching for all along. He knew what he had to do.

It had to work because it had worked before. If anything, Thomas was more ready. He'd managed to surprise Father in the past, why not again? This time though, he would aim to kill.

All he needed was a weapon. A knife? A sharp stone might even do. The only question was how to get it, and when to do it. Sooner seemed better than later. *Tonight, while Father sleeps?*

Thomas lay still and held his breath. Nicholas's soft breathing beside him and Claire's, on the other side of the young boy, were all that broke the silence. Peaceful. He listened to the sounds of the night. A cricket here, a rustle there, and amidst that ambient noise was one constant: a far off, rattling breathing. It was slow and explicably ominous. Father was asleep. Thomas shuddered as the rattling inhalations reverberated down his spine.

He sat up slowly without so much as a sound. He was careful not to disturb Claire or Nicholas as he opened the tent zipper. It went up painfully slowly, each click of the teeth barely making a sound. He didn't dare open it more quickly.

He crept from the tent and stood up. Father's familiar breathing still rattled a few feet away. Standing in the grass, Thomas looked up at the sky. The stars were foreign and they looked inexplicably free. They made him feel miniscule. The easiest part of what he hoped to accomplish was finished. It would only get more difficult from here.

Thomas crept forward towards the picnic table and quietly rooted around in the moonlight.

There was nothing to be found; not even a fork, let alone a knife. He fought back a sigh and cast his hands across his head.

He looked longingly back at his own tent, doubting himself. What was he thinking? He couldn't kill Father. The man was huge. There had to be some other way of escaping. He looked down at his feet. Of course, he could run now. He could even wake up Claire and Nicholas, but he couldn't imagine they would get far. They had no food and no water. They had no way of navigating their way to safety. It wouldn't work. They would literally be stumbling through the woods blind. Thomas knew enough about starvation that he would never wish it on Nicholas or Claire. They lived now, at least for the time being. He couldn't guarantee that if he were to spirit them away now. If they were to escape, he needed to be prepared.

Thomas felt relief in his heart at his decision. It was only fleeting, and came from a tiny place that was shrinking of late. It came from his innocence. He did not want to kill. He'd been dealt a bad hand too many times. He'd made choices that corrupted that small part of him, if only to survive. Thomas didn't know what to do with the feeling. He was sure that he had been ready to kill Father tonight. Surely he would have, if he could have. *Wouldn't I?* Now, however, Thomas doubted himself. How had he jumped to such a conclusion so readily? How was it that he had he decided that the only way forward was for Father to die? Would that have made Thomas any better than the monster himself?

Standing beneath the stars, Thomas felt hope. It rose up from beneath his despair and asserted itself in the sparkling evening light. It was hope for himself, because for the first time, he felt as though he was not lost. His humanity was not lost, and his sense of what was good and just had merely been hidden all along. He could do it without death and without violence. He was smart enough, and he could be patient enough.

Thomas looked back at the tent where Nicholas and Claire slept. He could at least start tonight. He crept off into the woods. It wouldn't do any good to steal what he needed from Father. Everything was locked down too tight; Father would notice. Thomas had hopes that the other campers would not be so vigilant.

He decided to start out small, to see what he could get away with. He crept through the trees, superstitiously bypassing the first campsite he came to. That one was too close. At the next campsite he stopped and listened.

A tent trailer sat off to the right and a red minivan sat closer to the gravel road. Two more tents sat on the left. A picnic table, along with a few foldable chairs sat around a dormant fire pit. A cooler sat beside the picnic table. Thomas decided he would start there. He edged his way out of the trees, taking careful steps. Thomas could hear light breathing coming from the tents and trailer; his marks were asleep.

Thomas knelt down in front of the cooler and slowly unlatched the cooler lid; it barely made a noise. He breathed a sigh of relief as he observed the contents. A few bottles of water, at least a dozen assorted cans of juice and soda, all floating in cold iceless water. The bounty was tempting, but he couldn't make it obvious. He also didn't know what to take having only seen such products a few times before.

Water was, at first, an obvious choice. Clean, clear, and hydrating. Thomas quickly identified a few problems with the water. First, there was no way he could take three because there were only five bottles in the cooler. Second, the bottles seemed to be made of flimsy plastic, and probably wouldn't be all that useful outside of refilling. The cans, on the other hand, had a number of benefits. First, they had water in them, but also energy-giving sugar. Second, the metal would be perfect for boiling water, and besides, they were sturdier and more compact. Finally, the metal reminded him of the tray with which he'd taken his first life, only a short time ago. If need be, Thomas could imagine using the cans in a similar way.

He gathered up one bottle of water and three cans of juice. Surveying the cooler, he decided it didn't really look like anything was missing. Thomas doubted that any one person would keep track of what every other person was consuming. The few things missing could easily have disappeared to someone waking up thirsty in the middle of the night. Nothing to be concerned about. Thomas shut the lid carefully without a sound.

With the supplies in tow, he crept back into the woods. He stood there, concealed, listening to the campsite. Light breathing, barely audible. Thomas had slipped in and out without notice, at least so far. He decided that it was enough for the night. He would get a sense of the neighbouring campers' awareness in the morning. It wouldn't do to rob every campsite in the grounds if the alarm were to be raised on first light.

Thomas found his way back to his campsite carefully and quietly. A short way into the woods, he found a large tree and stashed the supplies in a small recess beneath the roots. It would be there when he was ready to escape.

Standing up, he felt freer than he had since being captured by Father. As if that little bit of defiance and those few steps towards recapturing his liberty had created in him a complete cognitive change.

Stepping out of the woods and onto the cleared grass, he felt invincible. For once, things had gone right. He'd been dealt a good hand, and he'd played it spectacularly.

A hand clamped across his mouth, cutting off his voice. A knock to the head was all it took and everything went dark.

When he woke up, he felt the ground hugging him tenderly. No, not ground. Sand; they were at the beach. He opened his eyes to see Father crouched over him, smiling sadistically. The surface of the lake sparkled nearby, its serenity betraying the wickedness alight in the air.

"What were you doing out in the woods?" Father asked.

"None of your business," Thomas spat. Father backhanded him across the face.

"Don't make me ask again."

"I was going to run," Thomas lied.

"Wouldn't have gotten far," Father said. "Why'd you come back? Realize you weren't a match for the woods?"

"That's not why I came back." Thomas continued with the grain of his lie. Father seemed to think for a moment and then laughed.

"What?" Father asked, pausing for a moment. Then he started to nod, "Did you come back for the girl?"

Thomas's face flushed. He'd never intended to leave, but even in the lie he'd constructed, the suggestion that he'd come back solely for Claire made his cheeks redden.

"You're dumber than I thought," Father mused. "Most of them learn to play my game by now."

Thomas didn't understand. Confused, he remained silent.

"What? You don't think the three of you are the first to fall into my game, do you?"

After the confirmation from Kelly, Thomas knew that they weren't, but hearing it from the perpetrator's mouth made it all the more real and all the more frightening. Even with that, he wasn't willing to give Father the satisfaction of thinking he was scared. Thomas set his jaw.

"You call this a game?" Thom's voice was cut by bitter poison as nausea roiled in his throat.

Father looked like he was about to hit him again, but then pulled back and shook his head as though he'd come to a sudden realization.

"I should have done this when I found out they lost him. He don't matter anymore," he said, seemingly to himself. Then his hands were on Thomas. "I'm getting what I wanted anyway," the huge man hefted Thomas up and with a show of his immense strength, hoisted the young man over his head and charged into the water. "Finally," Father laughed, "finally." The water climbed up Father's chest as Thomas fought against his impossible grip. He realized what was happening as Father stopped.

Thomas soared through the air even further into the lake. He splashed down in the water and gasped as his head sunk beneath the surface. In the darkness of night, the water chilled him to the bone. His wild eyes scanned the water, finding it visually impenetrable in every direction but one.

Looking up, he could see one source of light. The wavering moon shrank as Thomas sank. This time, there was no current to carry him away from danger and no kindly old man to fish him from the depths. This time, when it went dark, Thomas Courser knew it would stay that way.

CHAPTER FORTY-SIX

INSIDE MAN

O<small>SWELL</small> <small>COUGHED</small> <small>AND</small> gasped for air as he rolled out of his bed and clutched his chest. He had the sickly feeling of being soaked. Sticky. Just sweat. He'd been sure that he had just drowned; it had been so vivid. Oswell was a good swimmer so he'd never even contemplated drowning before. It was terrifying; like being buried alive, but on a schedule.

"Thom!" Oswell gasped, reaching out with his mind to try and establish a connection with his cosmic twin. Last time he'd woken up like that, Thomas had been kidnapped.

He stood naked in the dark for an eternity. *Thomas!* There was no response. With each passing minute, a stone crawled further up from the depths of his stomach and into his throat. Satisfied, it decided to stay lodged in the most inconvenient place, choking him.

He looked out the window and saw the moon. It looked bigger than it usually did.

The night was late, but he had the sense that he was early to meet Wendell. Whatever Wendell had planned, Oswell had to tell him what had happened first. Wendell could help. He slipped into his gear, cringing at the crusty stink of them. It also didn't help that he hadn't fully dried off from his nightmare. The combination of his clothes' salty veneer with his slippery skin was not a pleasant sensation. Washing his clothes, however, was the last thing on his mind. He rushed out of his hut and down the catwalk to find Wendell.

Standing at the top of the ladder, Wendell was even earlier than Oswell. He looked impressed with Oswell's punctuality, but his smile darkened to a frown as he detected the concern on Oswell's face.

"What is it?" Wendell asked.

"I think... I think Thomas drowned."

"What makes you say that?"

"I had a dream," Oswell replied.

Wendell sized Oswell up, unsure of whether or not to take him seriously. Folding his arms across his chest, he tilted his head to the side, an invitation for Oswell to continue.

"I dreamt that I was drowning," Oswell began. "Last time I had a dream that vivid was when Thomas was taken."

Wendell nodded his head, frowning. "Cicero had mentioned his theories about your connection to Thomas. If you are indeed interpreting your dream correctly, Thomas may very well have drowned."

Oswell stared blankly up at Wendell. They stood in silence.

"I'm sorry; did you want me to reassure you? Did you want me to tell you that he's going to be okay?" Wendell asked.

Oswell stuttered.

"Life has left him without aid, and in a terrible position. It seems as though it has always been that way for him. If Thomas really is in your world, there is nothing I can do for him. There is nothing *you* can do for him. Right now, there are more pressing concerns. You and I are *here*, and that means we need to do what we can, *here*."

Oswell's mouth opened and closed wordlessly, then shut firmly as he set his jaw. He hadn't expected Wendell to be so blunt, but the man was right. He wasn't any use to Thomas, or Claire, or Nicholas. Oswell knew from the start that it was on Thomas to protect them. It wasn't fair that it was on him, but at the same time, it wasn't fair that Oswell had been given the responsibility of fixing the messed up world he had ended up in either. Their cards had been dealt and each of them had to play their hand in the best way they could. Oswell couldn't shake the feeling that he was bluffing his hand.

"We ready?" Darius asked, striding up to the silent pair with a bright-eyed Karyn in tow. Sensing the tension, Darius frowned. "What's going on?"

"I think Thomas is in trouble," Oswell replied.

"What kind of trouble?" Darius asked.

"I think he drowned. But it doesn't matter. Let's do this thing." Oswell kicked the rope ladder off the catwalk and listened as it rustled through the leaves. He heard the distant muffled thump that confirmed the ladder had reached the ground, and then climbed down. Darius followed close behind him.

"What's with you?" Darius whispered as Wendell, far above, pulled the ladder back up.

"Nothing," Oswell said darkly. He wasn't mad, or sad for that matter. He just felt as though the true nature of the world had finally been thrown into sharp contrast for him. Oswell was in a fantasy world, but even it was no fairy tale. Earth was far from it. The world he'd lived in was filled with rapists, murderers, and other depraved and psychotic criminals like the man who'd taken Thomas.

Things needed to change, his world needed to be rescued. The world he was in now was in need of rescue too. However, Oswell couldn't fathom how he was supposed to rescue it. He couldn't see the happy ending. Oswell was along for the ride, just like Thomas. Now —and Oswell was sure of it—Thomas was dead. It was a fantasy to think that Thomas would get out alive. A fantasy to think Nicholas and Claire would either. But what did that mean for Oswell? Would he be next? It seemed as though that would make sense. Whichever twisted entity was in charge of fate at the moment could certainly make it happen. Thomas was a mirror image of Oswell. It would be perfectly poetic for both of them to perish.

Oswell glared up at the trees above him. He could see only patches of sky through the thick forest canopy. He wasn't satisfied with the direction his life was taking. Immediately he thought of Laurence. Choices. He felt a soft hand rest on his arm and he looked to see Karyn gazing at him intently. Oswell could see the support in her eyes. He glanced at Darius, who mirrored a similar sentiment. Oswell looked back up at the stars.

"Damn you," he grumbled. "I'll make my own fate."

Wendell padded softly to the ground in front of Oswell and smiled. Looking into the young man's eyes, he could see that something had changed. There wasn't just blind determination anymore. It wasn't just a means to an end anymore; not just a way for him to get home. It was personal. It was stone-cold resolve and die-hard defiance. Darius couldn't see it, and neither could Karyn, but Wendell did. Oswell had found his motivation. He had to control his fate. Oswell wanted it.

"Let's go," Oswell urged.

"Keep your ears open," Wendell said. "Guards may still be about."

"Are we training with guards around?" Darius asked.

"No," Wendell replied, as though the question was a ridiculous one.

"What then?" Oswell demanded. Wendell shot Oswell a look of disdain, then retracted it almost immediately. Wendell had managed to ignite a fire in the young boy with just a spark. Oswell had fanned the flames on his own. Wendell wasn't about to extinguish it because of a little attitude.

"We're meeting someone," Wendell replied. The way he said it, both Oswell and Darius knew they weren't going to get anything else out of Wendell.

"Who?" Karyn asked.

"Someone," Wendell replied. Karyn screwed up her face and looked to Oswell and Darius for support. They shared a brief look. Oswell shrugged and she pouted her lips. She wasn't yet used to Wendell's brevity. He always held things close to the chest until it was absolutely necessary to reveal them.

Wendell darted off in Fletchery's direction without another word. With the mystery ahead of them, Oswell, Darius, and Karyn hurried after Wendell.

They crept through the woods, following Wendell's lead. Oswell was surprised at how comfortable he felt in the forest. It was dark, but already, he felt as though he was gaining control. It also helped that Wendell was there, guiding the way. Despite his warning, they did not encounter a single patrol. They settled into a steady pace, moving silently and as a unit, when finally, Wendell put up his fist to signal for them to stop. The three trainees did as they were told.

Wendell reached out and gently shook a young tree. It was whippish and tall for its age. Its leaves rustled naturally in the air not far above them. Oswell shot Darius another look, but the other boy just shrugged. He was as lost as Oswell was.

Oswell's ears perked up as he heard footsteps approaching in the distance. Wendell noted Oswell's alertness and smiled to himself. Despite his flaws, the boy was a quick learner.

A man materialized from the shadows. Though his head was full of black hair and he was shorter by a head and slightly more plump, the resemblance was unmistakable. There was the same rugged jaw line, a nose that looked to have been broken in all the same places, and the identical, calculating, stone grey eyes. There was no mistaking Wendell's brother.

There was also no mistaking that he was dressed head to toe in Fletcherian guard's armour.

Wendell and the man embraced briefly, and then he turned to Darius and ruffled his hair.

Apparently the two knew each other. He took a long, slow look at Karyn and Oswell felt himself bristle.

"Who's this?"

"Karyn Alderon," she replied for herself, sticking out a hand. It was shaking. Oswell couldn't tell if it was rage or nerves. The man's armour surely reminded her of the men who'd taken her father's life.

"Nice to meet you," he smiled, taking her hand gently. He didn't seem to pick up on her discomfort. Finally, the man turned to Oswell, looking like he was noticing him for the first time.

"Well I'll be, if it isn't little beggar boy!" the man said too loudly. Wendell gave him a sharp look, and the man seemed to recognize Wendell was right.

"Excuse me?" Oswell whispered.

"Actually, it's not who you think it is," Wendell said.

"No brother; that's him. I remember his face," the man maintained.

"There is more to this than what you can see," Wendell said. "Oswell, this is my younger brother, Watson. Watson, Oswell," Wendell introduced. Oswell extended a hand and shook Watson's. Watson gripped Oswell's firmly, squeezing just a little bit too hard.

"Care to explain?" Watson asked as he released Oswell's hand. "Last time I saw this one he insulted our mother, and then delivered a boot to the family jewels."

"Perhaps Darius would be the best to explain," Wendell suggested. Watson grinned at Darius and nodded.

"You did, didn't ya boy? I didn't think you'd pull it off."

Darius grinned at Watson, his chest seemed to puff out. "The boy *you* saw was Thomas," Darius began, "but, when you turned him away, I got him into the city through the tunnel in the wall." Darius looked at Oswell, "We recruited Thomas to help Cicero escape. We never knew any of the rest of this was going to happen. There was no way to know—it seems like... fate, that he—well, both of you—fit the prophecy."

Darius turned back to Watson, "After we got in, I gave him everything he would need to help Cicero escape. Of course, he didn't know I was feeding him information. He didn't see any of this coming. I got him arrested, and he ended up in the cell with Cicero. Many thanks to you," Darius grinned at Watson. "From there, Cicero and Thomas figured out how to escape, and well... you saw that."

Watson nodded, and chuckled as he recalled the expression of confused recognition on Thom's face as they had dashed past him and he had allowed them to pass.

"But after they left, Grandfather tells me that the guards were hot on their heels, and that it was only the night, and sheer luck that allowed them to escape. When they got into the forest, that's when things started getting weird."

"I'd say that started a while before," Watson said.

"Okay, things started to get really weird. We're going to sound insane, and we don't know how it happened, but... this isn't Thomas Courser. This is not the boy who escaped with Cicero. We think, somehow, Oswell here, switched places with Thomas."

"What do you mean 'switched'?" Watson pressed.

"Well, Oz—he says he is from another world."

Watson choked out a laugh, and then stifled it when he realized that Darius was being serious.

"We think Oswell came to this world, while Thomas ended up in Oswell's."

"And how would that happen? Even if this other world does exist," Watson mocked.

Darius ignored the slight, especially given that the theory was rooted in his father's work, "Once again, we're not sure how exactly. Grandfather has been doing some research, and he thinks it ties into some work that my father was doing before he vanished. It isn't really clear to us at this point, but... it appears that this may have all happened for a reason. Oswell fits Vata's prophecy perfectly."

"Which prophecy?" Watson asked.

"He's been brought here to help us. To get rid of Hallows."

Watson appeared to be thinking for a moment, then turned to Oswell and sized him up.

"I don't see it," he finally said. Oswell bristled at the man for a second time. Watson put up his hands defensively. "That doesn't mean I don't want to see where this goes. If Cicero thinks you've got what it takes, who am I to judge? The man's a genius."

"What can you tell us?" Wendell asked.

"They're increasing patrols in the forest. They want to find the Enclave."

"They've never found it before, they won't find it now," Darius said confidently.

"I've never seen them so organized. It's Jonas, he's got a plan. They're sweeping, and I think they're getting close. They know what to look for; they just need to look hard enough and they'll find it. Makkin is not happy that Cicero got away. Thankfully, he hasn't sent word to the others yet. Probably out of embarrassment. And he knows there will be hell to pay if Hallows finds out. But you're running out of time. What's the plan?"

"We don't know yet," Wendell said. Oswell felt his face go red. He didn't know what they were going to do, but he felt like it was his job to know. He was failing them.

"Well, keep working on it," Watson grunted.

"We are," Wendell guaranteed his brother.

"Good. That's that then," Watson mumbled. He turned to Oswell. "Let's hope you're everything Cicero thinks you are," he then turned to his brother. "You know where I'll be; ready to help when you need it." The pair embraced briefly.

"Soon, brother," Wendell said in farewell.

"We'll see you around too," Watson said, saluting Karyn. She nodded. Darius waved as Watson began to walk away. The man shot Oswell one last curious look over his shoulder and then melted into the shadows.

When he was long gone, Oswell finally spoke. "So what was the point of all that?"

"Watson is our man inside the guard corps," Wendell explained. "He needed to know what we were up to, and he needed to see what we are working with."

"He seems skeptical," Oswell said, somewhat indignantly.

"Well, you'll have to prove him wrong then," Wendell said.

"I guess I will," Oswell agreed. Wendell seemed to think for a moment.

"Let's get back," Wendell decided. "The three of you need your rest. We're back at it tomorrow."

"Even with the guards about?" Karyn asked.

"Even with the guards," Wendell confirmed. With that, he turned and walked away.

CHAPTER FORTY-SEVEN

SAND

H<small>E COULDN'T SEE</small> anything in the dark. His ears hurt like hell. It was a sharp pain, like someone was slowly pushing a needle through his ear drum. It got worse with every second. He sank, and it hurt. It was sequential. Cause and effect. Thomas didn't think it should take so long to drown. *Why am I holding my breath? Why am I delaying the inevitable?* Thomas couldn't tell what was up or what was down. For all he knew, air could be beneath his feet.

"*Thomas?*"

Thomas heard his name, but he certainly couldn't speak. He couldn't even think. He knew it was Oswell. Oswell knew something was wrong; Thomas could hear the concern and the fear in Oswell's voice. It was unusual hearing someone's voice so clearly underwater; it wasn't muffled in the slightest. *Funny...*

"*Thom! You need to protect them!*"

Thomas's mind wandered. It didn't matter what Oswell said. Thomas couldn't protect Claire and Nicholas anymore. He'd tried. He'd failed. He wanted to tell Oswell that he'd done his best, but everything was too distracting. The pain in his ears had ceased its agonizing march forward, but remained unbearable where it stopped. The burning in his lungs threatened to set him ablaze. The darkness occluded his clear thinking and the tickling on his feet was only a minor distraction.

Tickling? Thomas focused on it. His feet tickled. He wiggled his toes, squirming them through a soft mushiness. He probed with his foot and found something else. It was hard. *A rock?* He was on the bottom. He was oriented. He could fight.

Thomas pushed off the rock with his legs and pulled with his arms. Pure instinct, beyond fear; beyond survival even. It was driven by defiance. He rose. The pain in his ear lessened with each passing moment, enough to reassert the urgent burning in his lungs.

When he broke the surface, he gasped and floated there. He didn't know how he was doing it. Kicking his legs, waving his arms. He couldn't have done it two days ago. He couldn't have done it moments ago. But something had grabbed him, and shaken it into him. Oswell's persistence perhaps? Or maybe it was just the luck he had to find his orientation.

Thomas treaded water, gathering his breath on the silky still water of the lake. He was out farther than he'd thought, as if he had drifted out as he sank from where he'd initially hit the water.

Oswell's voice was gone, but it had done the job. Thomas reached out and took his first tentative paddle towards the empty shore. Swimming was awkward and exhausting, but he made it. When he felt the sand beneath his feet, he stopped swimming and marched out of the water, dropping to his knees when he could.

He collapsed on the beach, and there he lay, soaked to the bone, oxygen deprived, and dead tired. Adrenaline had fuelled his last bid at survival, and now it was gone.

Also gone, was Father. Thomas crawled to his knees and dragged himself undercover in the forest bordering the beach. There, he fell asleep.

Without knowing it, Father had given Thomas exactly what he needed: the ability to disappear.

But when he did, he wouldn't be going alone.

CHAPTER FORTY-EIGHT

ENTER SANDMAN

DARIUS THREW HIS arms up in exasperation. "You've got to be kidding me," Darius muttered. "Still hasn't adjusted..."

Oswell heard the grumblings and stirred right before he felt the world turn upside down.

"Get off me!" Oswell shouted as Darius bounced up and down on the mattress that sandwiched him into the floor.

"This happens too often, my friend," Darius stepped off the mattress and let Oswell get up.

"You're telling me," Oswell replied, referring to something completely different.

"I'm up at the same time every day," Darius bragged.

"You have the advantage of having lived here for your entire life. You've adjusted. I'm used to ten hours of sleep a—"

"Ten hours?" Darius said, "Must be nice on Earth, being able to waste all that time."

"Yeah," Oswell agreed, "it is. It doesn't help that you guys have me up all hours of the night."

"We still had six hours!"

"I didn't get that many," Oswell countered. "And I didn't exactly start out with the best track record," he added.

"Well, that's no fault of ours'."

"And it's no fault of mine!" Oswell replied. Darius looked like he was about to press further with his argument, and then decided against it. "As much fun as it is arguing about your slothful lifestyle, we can't waste any more time; Wendell is waiting. To think, he was so proud of your punctuality last night."

Oswell grimaced and decided not to tell Darius that being awake and on time the night before had nothing to do with planning, and everything to do with chance. If Thomas hadn't drowned last night, there was no chance that Oswell would have been up on time in the middle of the night. The mere thought of Thomas sent a bowling ball crashing through his gut. Oswell took a breath at the empty feeling left behind, then put that pocket of regret away. Thomas was gone, he had no time for mourning now.

He gathered up his things, cringing again as he climbed into his gear. He made a mental note to get them cleaned.

"What are we doing anyway?" Oswell asked, squinting as they stepped out into the morning sunlight.

"Training," Darius replied.

"Mornin' Oz," Karyn called out, clapping him on the back. "Gross, you need to clean those," she said screwing up her face at his crusty and stained shirt and pants.

"I know, I know," Oswell replied, feeling the temperature of his face rise. He was saved from having to say anything as they approached Wendell.

"Let's go," Wendell said. The tall man tossed the rope ladder down through the canopy and wordlessly motioned for them to descend. Darius went first.

"Sorry for being late," Oswell apologized. "I didn't get much sleep last night."

Wendell nodded as Karyn climbed onto the ladder. Oswell frowned and then climbed onto the ladder and followed Karyn to the ground.

"Doesn't seem too happy," Karyn said as they congregated below.

"I know," Oswell replied.

"Wonder why," Darius said knowingly.

Wendell hit the ground a few moments later and immediately set off through the trees. Oswell, Karyn, and Darius followed directly after him. It didn't need to be said that they should be quiet.

When they finished for the day, Oswell's fatigue had only multiplied. Despite Wendell's assertions that Oswell was becoming faster and stronger at a rapid pace, Oswell felt like it wasn't answering their ultimate question. Wendell's first lessons on focus and clarity, though practical in principle, were, in fact, completely useless because Oswell simply couldn't put his mind to it. Doing push ups and running about was one thing: mindless endurance. And certainly, the lines of his muscles were more defined, his strength more wiry, and the time to breathlessness later with each day. But, being alert, focused, and skillful was a completely different thing that took a talent Oswell wasn't sure he actually had.

He was barely listening as Rawlins bragged about his glory days over dinner. If the elderly man could be believed, he was quite the swordsman in his youth. He described his great sword *Mathilda*, a giant piece of honed and folded steel with a four foot blade and a bulky handle. With it, he'd fought and won many skirmishes against Outlander raiders in the Far East, beyond Eastwater even, in view of The Ridge. Oswell had a difficult time imagining the frail old man wielding such a weapon, but he tactfully subdued his disbelief, even as Cicero chuckled and attested to the truth of the story.

Oswell turned as he felt a hand grasp his shoulder gently. Laurence was smiling down at him benevolently.

"I'd like for you to come talk with me again," Laurence said. Oswell sighed. If he was going to do anything, he wanted to sleep. He glanced at Wendell and was surprised to see him watching intently. Oswell immediately thought back to what Wendell had said before. Together, Wendell and Laurence could teach Oswell the things that apart they could not.

"Okay," Oswell agreed and stood up. Laurence led Oswell out of the hall and to his hut.

"Thank you for your consideration," Laurence said as Oswell sat down in front of Laurence's desk. "Can I offer you some tea?"

"Yes, please," Oswell replied. Laurence nodded and started busying himself over a brazier, boiling some water. He sat down behind his desk as the tea steeped.

"Wendell tells me you have been making great strides, but become increasingly weary every day."

"Well, that's no surprise. They don't let me get enough sleep!" Oswell exclaimed, letting his frustration pour out. "I haven't gotten a full night's sleep since I got here."

Laurence put his hands up to calm his ward. He'd sought no quarrel in the statement. He appraised the young man for a few moments, and then stood up. Oswell slumped back in his chair as Laurence poured the tea. He placed a cup in front of Oswell and then sat down with a cup of his own.

"I will not contest that circumstances have required you to have less sleep than you are ordinarily used to, but *they* don't let you get enough sleep?"

"*They* don't," Oswell grumbled as he sipped on his tea.

"What about you?"

"What do you mean me?" Oswell asked.

"Perhaps you aren't using your time as well as you could," Laurence proposed.

"Are you telling me that I don't know how to sleep?" Oswell laughed.

"More accurately, I'm telling you that you don't know how to get to sleep. I'm not saying that's your fault—I'm sure you have a lot on your mind: Thomas, Claire, Nicholas, your parents…"

"Why *shouldn't* I worry about them?"

Laurence sighed and folded his fingers in front of him. "Please do not mistake me for a creature without compassion," he began, "but there is a time, and there is a place. Right now, is not the time, and right here is not the place."

"I can't just forget them!"

"And I don't expect you to, but what I hoped is that by now, you would have recognized that the world is not under your control. For your own sake, you need to understand that you will do your best, and despite those best efforts, things may not work out exactly as you hope... I do not mean to be pessimistic."

"You're coming off that way," Oswell grumbled.

"Do you truly believe that you can be all things for all people?" Laurence asked calmly.

Oswell stared at Laurence.

"You cannot believe that. There is only One who can do that, and because He can, He mustn't."

Oswell started to roll his eyes, but thought better of the disrespect. Instead, he locked his gaze on the Deacon. *Does he really think that I'll start to believe in his god? That I'll believe in Myr?*

"What's your point?" Oswell asked.

"I am giving you justification to relax, to unwind. It does you no good to worry the way that you do. If you can relax, and let go, you will sleep easier. You'll have better rest, which will have you back, working at full capacity," Laurence explained.

"I don't disagree with you," Oswell replied, "but where am I going to get the time? I'm still sitting on a huge debt."

Laurence nodded. "I've spoken with Wendell. You have the day tomorrow. I want you to go and relax. Don't think, just relax..." Laurence searched around, and then grabbed a book. 'Here, read this, it'll keep your mind off of everything else."

Oswell took the book and looked at the cover. He was relieved to see that it wasn't a religious title, *The History of the Teton Dynasty*. Laurence, at least, knew when not to press his luck.

"Sounds boring," Oswell said.

"It *is* history," Laurence replied, "if anything will put you to sleep, that will," he chuckled.

Oswell cracked a grin, "Thanks Laurence."

"My pleasure," Laurence replied. "Now go get some sleep."

Oswell nodded and left the hut. Laurence hadn't undersold the power of the history book. Even with Oswell's uncomfortable straw mattress, the tome had a formidable effect. That night, Oswell fell asleep faster than he had in months.

CHAPTER FORTY-NINE

PLAN OF ATTACK

THOMAS WAS HAPPY with the point; thoroughly charred and meticulously worked. It was hard, and sharp. It was long and sturdy. It was deadly.

It was only the third time he'd fire hardened a spear. With it in his hands, he felt safer, and he felt powerful. The spear was a simple tool, but it was exactly what he needed. It was about five feet in length; not so long that it would be ungainly, but certainly long enough to impale Father at more than an arm's length.

Even with that advantage, Thomas still wasn't sure if he would be able to kill the man. Not in his physical ability—with the right kind of surprise, it would be more than possible—but morally. Could he kill again? Killing didn't sit right with Thomas. There were still times he would think back to the guard whose neck he'd slit, and feel remorse. It had been necessary, Thomas thought, but that justification still did not give him much peace.

What would killing Father mean for Thomas? Would that make him just as bad as Father? Thomas was sure that the man had killed many in the past—*children* at that—and he was also certain that Claire and Nicholas would be next. Father had already tried to do away with him; Thomas imagined it was only a matter of time until Claire and Nicholas followed after. Next year, the cycle would continue and a few more unfortunate children would be caught in the wake of Father's sadistic obsession. That fact, in itself made Thomas feel that killing Father was justified. A preventative measure. A necessary evil. *Father needs to die. Doesn't he?*

Thomas gazed at his reflection in the tiny pool of clear water. Soul searching, Thomas found that, at least physically, he was unrecognizable. His hair was a tangle with only the slightest hint of his natural blonde showing through. His face was considerably worse, though intentionally. His bruises were obscured by mud, smeared across his face. It served to keep the flies away and as camouflage. He'd stained his clothes with grass and mud as well. Unmoving, he was practically invisible.

Comfortable was something he would not be, but comfort was a luxury he wasn't particularly accustomed to in the first place.

He swirled at the water with the butt of his newly minted spear, dispelling the image of the alien boy before him. It was true that he was a different person. Circumstance had made sure of that.

Thomas had always been that way; he wasn't static, he was malleable. He evolved every day, changing to suit his needs for survival. The metamorphosis he'd experienced of late was the most dramatic of his short life. Perhaps it wasn't for him to decide whether killing Father would change him. The only choice he had left to make was survive or perish. Surviving without Nicholas and Claire was out of the question, so the debate over Father's mortality was becoming particularly one-sided.

Thomas crept through the forest carefully and quietly. His main advantage was that Father thought that he was dead; it wouldn't do him in any good to give that away by being clumsy. What he was attempting would probably be the second riskiest endeavour involved in the escape (followed close behind by actually nabbing Nicholas and Claire and making the escape). Of course, Thomas was continually improving his familiarity with risky situations. He wasn't in it for the thrill, it was a camaraderie born of necessity, and an unfortunate one at that.

The sun began its descent as he settled in to observe Father's campsite. The pseudo-family sat at the picnic table, eating dinner. Father's face was one of happy bliss, completely unaffected by his recent act of homicide. Nicholas was not altogether bothered, more interested in his meal. Kelly, as usual, had a blank look about her. But Thom's heart went out to Claire; her eyes were puffy from crying and desperate with concern. He also detected the hint of another kind of desperation in her eyes. *That won't do.* He would have to tell her that he was still alive before she did anything she would regret, or anything that could mess up his plans. Thomas would have to wait for the darkness, and he would also have to be careful. He would go in and out without a sound, quickly. He wouldn't be caught this time, and if he was, then Father's fate would be decided for him on the point of a spear.

Thomas sat and watched as the group wound down for the night. Claire went in for bed early while Father and Kelly sat around the fire with Nicholas, who fought to keep his eyes open. Father finally suggested Nicholas go to bed, and the young boy did as he was told.

Father poured water over the dying flames and the fire went out with a hiss. Thom's eyes adjusted rapidly to the change in illumination. He watched as Father and Kelly retreated into their tent. The sounds of settling in drifted through the night air and then faded off into silence as their creators fell asleep.

Thomas waited in complete silence for ages. He hadn't moved in any appreciable way, and felt as though he were disconnected from his body. He was a pair of eyes growing out of the underbrush.

The moon had travelled halfway across the sky by the time he decided to move. He started with his fingertips and toes, wiggling them. Then slowly, he readied the rest of his body for action. He crept out of the underbrush with minute movements. After clearing the brush, he stood up and crept across the campsite, careful to avoid any debris that could trip him or make a noise.

At Claire's tent, he quietly lifted the zipper as he'd done only the night before. It rose, tooth by tooth noiselessly. Thomas was calm, and after waiting all day, taking his time with the zipper was far more bearable than the last time. When it was open enough for him to get into the tent without a sound, he slipped inside and took a shallow breath.

Nicholas was sound asleep, face down in the pillow and snoring softly. Claire was curled up in her sleeping bag. She looked like a ball. Underneath the covers, he knew she had her knees pulled up to her chest. Her face wasn't peaceful anymore. She looked like an artist had painted a permanent grimace onto her once smiling face. Thomas watched her in pain for a few moments and then placed his hand over her mouth and gently shook her awake.

Her eyes darted open like she'd only been barely unconscious. Thomas held his hand over her mouth and held one of his fingers up to his own mouth telling her to be quiet. He watched her eyes as they first conveyed fear, then confusion, then relief, and then back to confusion. Thomas also detected a hint of anger on the tail end of it. He removed his hand from her mouth, but kept his own finger across his own lips.

Claire didn't say a word; she simply reached up, moved his finger away from his lips and kissed him. Thomas was shocked as her soft lips pressed against his, which froze.

She pulled away from him and he stared at her in silent shock, blushing. She smiled and then frowned and then punched him in the shoulder. It didn't hurt him. He leaned in, placing his mouth right beside her ear.

"I'm sorry," he breathed.

"I thought you were dead," she breathed back. "I didn't know what he did to you."

"He tried to drown me, came damn close too."

"Oh my God," Claire mouthed.

"I'm okay," Thomas said, "If anything, this is just what we needed."

Claire pulled away from him again and surveyed him pointedly, her brow a knot.

"Claire, he thinks I'm *dead*. Only way he could have given me a bigger advantage is if he handed me a knife and offered me his neck." Claire's eyes got bigger as she began to recognize what Thomas was saying. Thomas nodded, "I'm going to get you and Nicholas out of here."

"When?" she asked.

"I need another day. I'm going to steal some food, and try to find a map."

Claire nodded, agreeing that it was a good idea, "Get a compass too, otherwise we'll be flying blind."

"A compass?"

"It points North, so we'll know what direction we're going," she paused, sensing that Thomas still wasn't following, "They're round and usually have a red needle on them that spins to point North. There should be markings for North, West, East, and South."

"Okay," Thomas replied. Claire fought to bring a smile to her face. "I know it will be hard, but try to get as much sleep as possible tonight, and make sure you and Nick are in bed early tomorrow. We're going to run for as long as we can." Thomas seemed to think for a moment, "And you're going to have to keep acting sad for Father, he can't know anything has changed," Thomas realized.

Claire nodded again, but then it seemed that a thought crossed her mind. She leaned forward and breathed ever so slightly, "Are you going to kill him?"

"I haven't decided yet," Thomas admitted. Killing Father made the most sense for an unhampered escape and also promised to ensure safety for any unknown future victims.

However, if killing Father put himself, Claire, or Nicholas in any immediate danger, then the man would live. Thom's main concern was that he wasn't sure he could successfully kill the giant man. Would it be better to slip away in the middle of the night and get a head start, or try to kill the man in his sleep and risk failure? Thomas wasn't certain. He would have to adapt to the situation.

"I have to go," Thomas said. Claire nodded and pulled him in for another kiss. Thomas responded this time, kissing her back gently, and then pulling away. This time, it was her turn to blush. "I'll be back tomorrow night. Same time. Be ready to go."

Claire nodded and Thomas backed away. He slipped out of the tent and listened intently to Father's breathing. It was regular. Thomas hefted the spear in his hand and melted into the woods, a smile on his face for the first time in days.

Chapter Fifty

PEAT'R BOG SLOTH

Oswell ambled down the street through Fletchery. He wasn't a human, but a giant sloth about the size of a man. Considering Darius's description, Oswell was in the form of an oft mentioned Peat'r Bog sloth. Oswell looked almost comical, with a meek and unintelligent look on his sloth face as he lazily made his rounds through the unusually quiet town. Oswell became slowly indignant about the comparison Darius had drawn.

He watched as people shuttered their windows and locked their doors as he passed by. Guards gave the salute, showing what seemed to be undue respect and deference for such an unassuming and benign creature. Why would anyone be afraid of a sloth that couldn't hurt them, and why would the guards treat him with such esteem?

Oswell observed the guards as he meandered by. Every salute was the same: rigid and practiced, as if satisfying some sort of duty. Oswell looked even closer, watching their eyes. After every salute, the guards' eyes would flit away from him for a moment as if to confirm with a higher authority that their duty had been fulfilled correctly. Oswell followed the glances and finally noticed a tall, dark, and unassuming shadow, striding beside him. Oswell couldn't see the man's face, but everything about the spectre exuded malevolent energy. Oswell couldn't believe he hadn't noticed it before. He pondered it for a moment, absorbing the power of the shadowy figure. Perhaps the spectacle of the sloth had been too distracting. It was all too obvious now. They did not respect the sloth; they appeased the shadow.

Oswell sat up in his bed, wide awake. "That's it!" he raced out of the barracks, across the Enclave, into the main hall, and finally burst through the trapdoor into Cicero's study.

"Welcome," Cicero smiled, fingers steepled in front of him on the large desk. He looked like he was expecting the visit. Oswell stuttered, taken aback by Cicero's preparedness. He gathered himself and then strode forward and placed his hands on Cicero's desk.

"What is it?" Cicero asked.

"I figured out how to beat Makkin," Oswell replied.

Cicero smiled, pleasantly surprised, "Go on."

"I just had a dream," Oswell started, and Cicero leaned in. Oswell bristled at the interest, unsure if it was genuine or whether he was simply being humoured. "Listen, I know it's just a dream, but hear me out. I saw a Peat'r Bog Sloth—well, a giant sloth, I don't know what a Peat'r Bog Sloth looks like—walking through Fletchery," Oswell began.

Cicero nodded.

"Everyone was afraid of the sloth, it seemed. The people were hiding in their homes and the guards were saluting carefully," Oswell took a breath. "But really, it wasn't the sloth they were saluting!"

"No?" Cicero asked.

"They were saluting a... a shadow beside the sloth. It was pure... evil..."

"Vorley," Cicero mused.

"Exactly!" Oswell replied. "Makkin is useless, we've seen that. Vorley does all the dirty work for him. It's not Makkin they respect; it's Vorley."

Cicero nodded, thinking pensively.

"We shouldn't be going after Makkin, we should be going after Vorley. We need to target the trunk of the tree, not the top, if we want to bring the whole thing down."

"Get rid of Vorley, and Makkin's world will collapse all around him," Cicero agreed.

"Exactly."

"Excellent work Oswell," Cicero congratulated. "We may have something here, however, it raises similar issues. Why should Vorley be easier to assassinate than Makkin?"

"Let's get the others and get a plan together!" Oswell said.

Cicero shook his head. "The idea will still be there in the morning," he paused. "Get some sleep, and we will start planning in the morning."

Oswell was itching. He wanted to get it done, and he wanted to get it done now. The sooner he got home the better. Cicero seemed to sense this in Oswell's fidgeting.

"Remember Laurence's lessons: relaxation, humility, *patience*," Cicero stroked his thin white beard.

Oswell sighed, recognizing that Cicero was correct. As usual. "We're going to fix this," Oswell said. He turned and disappeared through the hatch in the floor.

Cicero smiled mischievously as the trap door shut. He waited a moment and then roused Bartimaeus. The bird gave a decidedly displeasured eye to Cicero, but stretched its wings nonetheless.

"Fetch Wendell," Cicero said. The bird alit from its perch and disappeared through the window. Cicero sat down with a familiar book and waited.

Wendell pushed his way up into the office. He hadn't been asleep, but questioning what the man did in the late of night was something Cicero had long stopped asking.

"You called," Wendell said, letting Bartimaeus step from his perch on Wendell's shoulder back onto his stand.

"It's happening. Oswell's seen it, in a dream."

Wendell raised his hand to his brow and shook his head. "Seen what?"

"You know what he's seen," Cicero said.

"Vorley?" Wendell asked.

Cicero smiled.

"So what?" Wendell replied. "We figured that out months ago."

"After how much thinking? How much observation?" Cicero asked, not looking for an answer. "He's solved a problem in a span of days that took us months to unravel."

"It's different for him."

"Precisely."

"I mean that he has fresh eyes, and he knows everything we know already," Wendell sighed.

"I do not think that is all there is to it," Cicero replied.

"Is that so?" Wendell asked.

"You've seen the first five lines, but you've not seen the second."

"There's more?"

"Yes," Cicero said. He flipped open the book sitting on his desk, the *Oraculo Vata*.

"That book is—"

"Quiet," Cicero commanded. He read off the five short lines.

"What others ponder, days on days,
The travelled one, asleep he sees,
A careful path into the fray,
The thoughts they share will set them free,
Salvation in a golden way."

Cicero looked up from the text. Wendell looked surprised.

"You didn't show me that one."

"I wanted to be sure," Cicero said. "This can't be coincidence."

"Perhaps not, but the fact remains," Wendell shook his head, "when we tried that last time, we lost you."

"I know," Cicero replied.

CHAPTER FIFTY-ONE

WISH LIST

H E STOPPED AT a different campsite this time; he didn't want to hit the same one as before. The occupants of the two tents were silent and sound asleep. Thomas crept forward and quietly dug through the first cooler he found. He retrieved another bottle of water and collected a few granola bars from the picnic table that had been left unopened. It was a good haul, and it would be unnoticeable that anything was missing. That was exactly what he needed to maintain his present non-existence in the mind of Father.

Thomas robbed four more campsites that night, taking bits and pieces of food where he could find them. By the end of the night, he'd amassed an impressive collection. Bottles of water, cans of juice and soda, granola bars, bags of potato chips and boxes of crackers. He hoped he hadn't gone too far in stealing an old and empty duffel bag from outside one of the tents. He needed something to carry all the food and supplies in.

He shook his head at the pile nonetheless, not fully satisfied. Thomas was used to not eating much. He would get by. Claire was old enough to be able to tough through it, even if it would be difficult. Thom's real concern was for Nicholas. Having a grumpy, stubborn, and hungry six year old along for the ride would be a serious disadvantage. The food he'd collected would only last for a few days, and that would be if they were disciplined. Thomas would have to do some hunting or they would have to find their way back to civilization quickly. More quickly than Thomas could hope.

Thomas felt the anxiety building. So many things could go wrong. Of course the alternative—doing nothing—was worse. If he failed, at least he could say he tried.

Thomas stuffed the duffel bag into the hollow in the tree he'd first hidden his stash in, and then stood up. He hefted his spear in his hands and turned in the direction of the campsite office. He only needed two more things: a compass and a map. Without them, they would simply be wandering through the forest, hoping to find help or salvation. He couldn't risk it.

He was still amazed by the way the forest and campground simply shut down for the night. The usual noises of nature were present, though muted, and scarcely more than breathing could be heard coming from each campsite. Everyone was always early to bed, and Thomas had yet to see any other children, or even signs of them. Something about Cahill Campground was truly unusual. Of course, that was obvious if a man could be welcomed back every year with a new cohort of unfamiliar children. Thomas knew that the other campers were in on the plan; that they were part of Father's game. The way the other campers had watched the three children when they'd arrived, like holy objects, it was eerie, and it didn't sit right with him. They needed to get out of there as quickly as possible.

Thomas remembered how far they'd driven from any sign of civilization before reaching Cahill Campground. He was certain that he couldn't rely on anyone else in the campground to help them. It would be a long trek, but Thomas would push himself, and he would push his charges. He wasn't going to let nature take what Father so dearly desired. No, Thomas would deliver his new friends to safety and he would put an end to the twisted cycle Father had concocted over the years. The police would be most interested to know what had been going on at Cahill Campground.

Thomas crept from the trees towards the camp office. The building looked like it had been vacated for the night. A small porch light illuminated the front of the building, but otherwise, the rooms inside, and the grounds surrounding the office were dark. Thomas hugged the wooden border as he circled around to the back of the building away from the lighted porch.

He dashed across the open space and knelt beside the foundation. There, he lay down his spear and stood up on the tips of his toes to peer into the dark window. The room was crowded with junk. Finding his way through that mess would be risky. He tried the window anyway, it budged, but he left it closed.

He slunk along the wall of the building and peered through the next window. This opened onto the main office. It was more organized, and also looked to contain general goods for sale. It would be the jackpot. He tried the window, but the lock caught. He cursed under his breath. Thomas took another look through the locked window and spotted the door that would lead from the cluttered back room. It was slightly ajar.

He would just need to be careful.

Thomas returned to the first window, pushed it the rest of the way up, and then carefully hoisted himself into the room. Illuminated solely by moonlight filtering through the open window, shadows formed the bulk of the room's contents. He slowly slid his feet along the floor, afraid to lift them for fear of moving too quickly and knocking something over. It was a tight squeeze with counters on either side of him stacked precariously with paper. On top of these stacks were blobs of knick knacks (or toys?) that he couldn't make out in the darkness. His curiosity got the better of him as the moonlight filtering through the open window alit to a rag doll, its colours moon-bleached and faded with age.

His eye flitted to a photograph beneath the doll, sitting on the top of the stack. A girl no older than Nicholas stood with her hands hidden behind her back, standing beside the arched climbing structure at the centre of the camp's playground. The film was grainy, but even in it, Thomas could see the forced strain of her smile, and the sadness in her eyes. Instantly, he knew who she was. Not in the personal sense, but in their shared experience. He put the photograph back down and carefully placed the doll back on top of it.

It seemed to take an eternity to safely traverse the mess. He breathed a sigh of relief as he opened the door into the front of the office. Standing before him was a plethora of goods; certainly more than he could hope to carry. The thought sobered him, and reminded him that he still had to keep his presence unknown. If he was to take anything, it would have to be unnoticeable.

He crept up and down the aisles, eyeing the food hungrily. It wouldn't do to steal much more because he could only carry so much. He elected to grab three assorted cans of soup, out of countless. He was sure to take them from the back of the shelves. He reluctantly passed by a hatchet sitting on the office desk, as it appeared to be frequently used, and was the only one in the store. Finally, he gathered up a box of matches, a small compass, and a folded map. He observed the map briefly, finding that the whole area looked unrecognizable to him. Of course, it was only the second time he'd seen such a map. He was fairly certain that he'd identified the lake that Father had tried to drown him in, and by that token, the campsite. He could see other signs of civilization on the map, but decided it would be better to leave Claire to interpret it. With that, he folded the map and stuffed it into his shirt.

Thomas's ears perked up as he heard the crunch of gravel outside the office. His heart stopped as he realized someone was coming. Thomas tip toed across the office and back into the cluttered room.

Travelling towards the light of the open window, his path was better illuminated. He slunk across the room quickly. He needed to get out. Besides, he didn't have time to waste. Hearing the telltale tinkle of keys, he heaved himself over the window sill and dropped to the ground with a soft thump.

Turning around, he immediately slid the window shut as the front door to the campground office swung open with a creaking noise. Thomas hugged the building wall, partly hiding and partly steadying his rampaging heart. A light went on in the main office. He heard some shuffling inside and listened intently.

"Bastard questions *me* when I take all the risks?" Flynn's voice, Father's voice, was gravelly and unmistakeable. Thom's heart stopped dead in its raging. How close had he come to being discovered? And why was Father awake in the middle of the night, storming about the campground with a ferocity no different from the heart beating in his chest?

The light went off and the front door swung open and closed again. Thomas crept around the corner and watched as Flynn's feet crunched gravel into the distance, away from the porch light and down the camp's main gravel road. Thom's curiosity spurred him on. *Who's questioning him?* The other campers had been next to deferential with the monster of a man, and now one had ignited his ire?

Thom's grip tightened around his spear and he slipped back into the shadows behind the building. He looked at his haul, then shook his head. It would have to wait. His feet padded through the grass quickly and he melted into the forest, tracking Flynn silently as the man continued down the gravel path.

He took a side road, and Thomas hesitated yet again. He'd not been to this part of the campground before. His nimble feet picked their way through the underbrush, barely making a sound, and he stopped as the light around him intensified.

"Are ye ready?" Flynn grumbled.

"Not yet," another man, a camper Thomas hadn't yet encountered replied. Tall and weedy, almost bookish. There was a hint of familiarity about him, though Thomas was certain he did not know him.

"What's taking so long?"

"We were readying for three."

"He lost the third, that's not on me," Flynn shot back.

"Nevertheless. It changes the ritual. We can't know what two will bring. We've only ever done one at a time."

"I *know* that," Flynn said.

His patience was worn thin. Thomas would have grinned at the inconvenience he'd caused him, if not for the cold stillness gathering in his gut at what he'd just heard. *A ritual?*

"It will be ready in time," Flynn formed the statement rather than posing it as a question.

"Just need another day. We will still be ready for the new moon."

"It had better be."

"We cannot rush this. You want it to work this time, right?"

"Of course, after last year, we need this. *He* demands it."

"Then let us do it right," the man replied.

Flynn grunted and turned away from the bookish man. Left in the dim light, the man busied himself with the preparations. A small platform sat in the middle of the clearing. Extinguished lanterns surrounded the platform, and two wicker bodies, roughly the shape and size of Claire and Nicholas stood on the platform. Thom's eyes alit to a third wicker body, burning in a nearby campfire, and he felt heat rise at the back of his neck.

Thomas watched the bookish man reorganize the space, dread climbing in his heart with each passing moment as his mind pieced together exactly what he was preparing for. Its intent was clear to Thomas, even if its motivation was not. Who could possibly make demands of Father?

Finally, the man retired. He extinguished the remaining lights, poured water over the partially burned effigy of Thomas, and then trod off into the darkness, leaving Thomas under the cover of leaves and stars.

Okay to breathe, Thomas took in a deep one, grabbed his spear and slowly circled back to the camp office. There, he gathered his haul and dashed back off into the woods. When he found his stash, he put the food away. Starved from the active night, he allowed himself one of the granola bars he'd collected.

As he chewed on the dry grains, he too chewed over what he'd seen. The ritual was one clearly intended for them. Nothing could explain what it was for or what it entailed, but the deeply malevolent energy of the space, of the campground, of its inhabitants, offered many sinister intentions satisfied by a single recurring event. Whatever it was they had planned hadn't worked the year before. There was an urgency to it. The only silver lining was the interruption he'd created by going ahead and dying. He had that at least.

HOME FIELD
ADVANTAGE

W ENDELL SHOOK HIS head. "No, that raises the same problems we had before," Wendell said. "A full on assault isn't going to be any easier just because we have a different target."

Oswell cast his eyes down, reddening. He'd gotten a good rest, and woken up filled with dreams of battle and glory.

"It was never going to be a full on assault," Cicero said calmly, though it did nothing to make Oswell feel any better about his boldness. Darius was nodding absently in agreement.

When they'd all gathered in the main hall that morning, everyone knew something had happened, but only Cicero, Wendell, and Oswell were aware of the latest development. Cicero had given Oswell the opportunity to tell the group about his dream, and explain what he thought it meant.

Wendell expressed a certain annoyance, though Oswell didn't know that Wendell had been prepped. Karyn had given Oswell an appreciative look that warmed his heart. Laurence merely smiled contentedly, and Rawlins slept. Darius had remained silent throughout Oswell's proposal, and remained silent through the ensuing discussion. He was paying attention, but only shallowly; he looked to be deep in thought, almost as if he had something to say, but couldn't decide whether to express it or not.

"Okay, you're right," Oswell finally conceded.

"We need a way to get at Vorley," Wendell started. "Let's just lay out what we know."

"We know that Vorley is Makkin's right hand man," Oswell said.

"Yes," Wendell confirmed.

"We're certain it's Vorley, not Makkin, that keeps Fletchery running the way it does," Oswell added.

"Yes."

"So far as I've seen, Vorley carries out all of Makkin's dirty work," Oswell said.

"That is accurate."

"Is there anything Makkin *does* do?" Oswell asked as an adjunct.

"He signs all decrees, acts as judge... and jury, reports to the Vice and Archlords of the Hallows Court..." Cicero began.

"How often?" Oswell asked, his brain getting into the thick of a thought.

"There's no way to tell," Cicero mused.

"How often does anyone from Myria come to visit?" Oswell asked, deciding it was the more pertinent question.

"Rarely. They don't really care what happens here as long as we keep feeding them the spoils of our toils," Wendell replied.

"Right, so would I be right in saying that if we try anything, and we pull it off, there's a good chance Hallows won't find out about it?" Oswell asked.

"Word travels," Laurence said, "though it does travel more slowly here than it does in Myria."

"So you'll have a window," Oswell said.

"Of time? I would imagine, but why?" Wendell asked.

"If you're going to get rid of Makkin, you might as well try to get rid of the other Governyr, take the whole continent," Oswell said.

Wendell laughed at the boldness and simplicity of the statement. "He's right."

"Be a lot easier without this Hallows guy breathing down our necks. Without my *considerable* skills, you guys will need all the time you can get," Oswell laughed, feeling euphoric at the thought of finally going home.

"We're getting ahead of ourselves," Darius interrupted. Everyone turned to look at Darius. "We can dream about taking back Numyria, but we haven't even figured out how to get rid of Makkin."

"Well, do you have any ideas?" Oswell asked.

"No," Darius muttered. Oswell sized up his friend. He'd told him not to say anything, but it was their only hope.

"I have an idea," Oswell said. Darius began to slowly shake his head, then stopped as his grandfather noticed.

"What is it then?" Wendell asked.

"Where are we right now?" Oswell began.

"The Enclave," Karyn replied.

"The forest," Oswell corrected impatiently. "We know this forest intimately. Wendell is right, a full on assault is not going to work. It was never going to work. There are just too many of them and too few of us," Oswell explained.

"Exactly," Wendell agreed. "Good to see you're finally thinking."

Oswell chose to ignore the sleight. "This forest is enormous, and to those unfamiliar with it, it could be a damn near death trap," Oswell continued, "and that's just from getting lost. We could make it a lot scarier."

Darius sat straight up in his chair and shot the fieriest of eyes at Oswell. Karyn perked up, Wendell started to nod, and Cicero stroked his chin.

"Darius," Oswell said, "stop being a fool. Tell them."

Darius felt all of the eyes in the room shift to him. Karyn and Oswell both smiled at him widely.

"What is he saying?" Wendell asked Darius.

The young man stammered, began, and then stopped again. Wendell growled and Darius started properly. "I'll need all of your help, but we can turn this forest into a living Abyssys for Fletchery's guards."

"And then we just draw them in," Karyn smiled.

"Nothing like playing with a home field advantage," Oswell smirked. The others eyed Oswell curiously for a moment before deciphering what that particular Earthism meant.

"Then all we need to do is single out Vorley and take him in," Wendell smiled.

"Where are we going to find the time to do this?" Laurence asked, injecting a voice of reason into the dialogue. "The guards are getting closer to finding us here every day."

"The fire extinguishing system hasn't been my only extracurricular project," Darius said proudly.

Wendell rounded on Darius and grunted in surprise, the vocalization a demanding inquisition more than anything. Cicero guffawed.

"Explain," Cicero said, having a difficult time hiding his smirk.

"Well, I figured with the extinguishing system going so smoothly, it would make sense for us to have some other defences in place," Darius said as he scratched the back of his head. "I've been working on some traps for a few months now."

"You should have told me," Wendell growled. "What if one of us fell into your traps? Foolish boy!" As head of security, it was slightly more than an oversight that he didn't know everything available to protect them.

"Whoa," Darius put his hands up. "I wouldn't go that far... none of them are active yet. I've only laid down the infrastructure."

Oswell quickly squelched the rise in his eyebrows, not wanting to give his friend's carelessness away, and shot Karyn a knowing glance. Darius's eyes widened at Oswell as if to say, "Not a word," before turning back to a red-faced Wendell. Oswell was taken aback by Darius's bald-faced lie, but he let it go.

Wendell was still bristly, though his expression seemed to have softened slightly. Cicero had a gleeful smile and Laurence was outright laughing. Oswell stifled his own laughter, which set Karyn to laughing.

It wasn't often that Wendell lost his composure.

"You're going to need to tell us where these traps are," Wendell grumbled. Oswell could tell them where one of the traps was, but not all of them.

"I'll go grab the map," Darius said. He stood up and jogged out of the main hall. Oswell was sure he heard Darius sarcastically mutter, "Foolish boy," as he left.

"That one has too much spare time," Wendell grumbled.

"I thought security was *your* job?" Oswell asked Wendell.

Wendell scowled.

"Can't be complaining about him being productive during his spare time. The guy's brilliant," Oswell laughed. "He's like a modern Da Vinci," he paused, "Actually, not modern. A young Da Vinci," he corrected.

"Who is Da Vinci?" Laurence asked.

"A famous inventor in my world. He was Italian or something and he came up with a bunch of inventions way before his time. He had plans for catapults–"

"We have those," Laurence interjected.

"–and helicopters and gliders and robots," Oswell added.

"We don't have... those; what is a 'robot'?" Laurence asked.

"It's like an automated machine that does work," Oswell explained. "Like; we have robots that build our cars for us."

"Cars...?" Laurence asked through squinted eyelids. He'd contracted a headache.

Oswell laughed. "I've learned a lot about your world, but I guess I haven't told you guys much about mine," he realized.

"I'm sure Darius would be most interested to hear about some of these grand inventions," Cicero decided.

"What grand inventions?" Darius asked as he re-entered the main hall.

"It seems Oswell has some knowledge of engineering that the two of you may be able to make good use of," Cicero explained.

"I wouldn't call myself an expert," Oswell qualified.

"No, the expert would be me," Darius grinned.

"Interesting that we should overlook such an advantage," Cicero pondered. "We may have to explore the feasibility of your Da Vinci inventions once we have disposed of Makkin."

Oswell nodded. If he was going to be stuck on Myros for the time being, he might as well contribute some of the knowledge of Earth. It would have to be awfully rudimentary, but sometimes, all that was needed was the idea; there would be many ways to make it work.

Oswell imagined himself riding towards Fletchery inside an armoured tank. Of course, the effort to make such a machine would be next to impossible with what they had available. The most limited resource of all was time. They would not have long until the guards stumbled upon the Enclave.

"The map, then," Wendell urged.

"Indeed," Darius complied, spreading the map out on the table. "Here *we* are," Darius pointed to an unmarked spot on the map. Wendell smiled. Better that the Enclave remained unmarked, should the map fall into the wrong hands. The map itself was larger than Oswell had expected. To him, it was still practically unreadable. He didn't know the forest's landscape as well as any of the others in the room. Cicero, Laurence, Wendell, and Darius all seemed to have a solid grasp. Rawlins was still asleep. He at least found kinship with Karyn. They stood close together pretending to know what they were looking at.

"As you can see, I've set up a rudimentary network," Darius pointed out a number of symbols on the map. "Each symbol represents a different kind of trap—I really got creative with some of them," he said. "The traps are localized mostly between the Enclave and Fletchery; west and north-west of here, there are none."

"What kind of traps do you have?" Wendell asked, motioning to the ambiguous symbols.

"The spade is a spiked pit," Darius began, "they're covered over. Only about four feet deep with two foot spikes; it's probably not going to kill anyone, but it will certainly put them out of commission."

Oswell thought Darius was underselling the lethality of the trap. *Two foot spikes?*

Wendell nodded, motioning to the next.

"The squares are foot holes. Each square represents a field of about ten of them. Foot goes through a latch, but the latch doesn't open the other way. They'll be stuck there until someone digs them out, or they rip their own feet off," Darius explained. "I'm proud of those little darlings."

"And the circles?" Wendell asked.

"Those are your run of the mill hunting snares, scaled up to man-size. You step on one of those and you're going to be upside down, thirty feet off the ground in a split second."

Oswell smiled at Karyn knowingly.

"What about this one?" Karyn asked, pointing to a symbol unlike any other on the map.

"Oh, that was just a fun little experiment for me. The other traps are easy enough for one man to set, but if you will all indulge me, I would like to set that one up as well." Darius grinned.

"What is it?" Oswell asked.

"It's trip wire activated," Darius illustrated with his hands, "there's a big gap between two trees; could probably fit ten men abreast. We'll have to lay some bait to pull that many in... We'll figure something out," he paused thinking.

"What does the trip wire activate?" Oswell prompted.

"Oh, it releases a fifteen foot log from about twenty feet up—swings down and obliterates anything in its path. That'll take a few of us to hoist up there," Darius explained.

"Your grandson is quite the mastermind," Laurence said to Cicero.

"It would seem he is," Cicero agreed. Darius beamed.

"So... we've got traps," Oswell started, "now we need to lure Vorley out into the forest, which will mean he's accompanied by his men. With the traps going off, there will be complete confusion. We nab Vorley in the middle of the pandemonium, and get rid of him."

"Exactly," Wendell and Darius echoed.

"How exactly do we make sure Vorley comes with the men?" Oswell asked.

"We'll need to give him a good incentive," Darius said.

"What's a good incentive?" Oswell asked.

"Me," Cicero said.

"No!" Darius shouted.

"It *should* be me," Cicero reiterated. Darius's distress was palpable. He clearly had something else in mind. Oswell had only known Darius for a short time. Though their relationship had been competitive at first, Oswell had grown to enjoy Darius's company. Their shared competitive nature became less of an annoyance and more of a comfort for Oswell. It reminded him of Grant and provided him an opportunity to really push himself. On top of that, Darius was a lot like Oswell in other ways: defensive, witty, and perhaps a little over confident. Oswell knew how dear Cicero was to Darius. And rightly so, now that Oswell knew the circumstances of his father's disappearance.

"I'll do it," Oswell interjected before Cicero could get too attached to the idea. Darius perked up at this.

"No," it was Cicero's turn to deny the proposal.

"I can do it," Oswell said. "You say that's why I'm here: to help you," Oswell fortified his offer. He didn't notice the brief look shared between Cicero and Wendell. "Besides, you're an old man, and I'm faster than you," he grinned. Cicero failed to respond, though it looked like there was a certain pride in his eyes.

"Yes," Darius agreed, "and you were the last one seen with Cicero. He's not going to leave it up to his troops to capture you. You *have* to know where Cicero is. He'll want you. He'll lead the hunt," Darius laughed excitedly.

"I should let Watson know," Wendell decided. "He can help; we'll make sure he is the one to spot you outside the city, and then notify Vorley."

"And then what?" Oswell asked.

"When you see Vorley on the walls, you need to reel him in. Then, you run," Wendell said, "you'll guide them through the whole gamut until Vorley's either trapped or alone."

"How will I know where to go?"

"We don't need any of you falling into any of my traps. Let me give all of you the tour; Oswell, you can practice." Darius grinned, "Come on, we've got a lot of work to do."

Rawlins snored in his chair as everyone filed out of the hall after Darius.

The sun had started its slow descent and Oswell was tired of setting traps. Starting with the traps closest to the Enclave, they had moved outward from there in a direct path through which they would lead their pursuers. They worked as a team, removing the safeguards Darius had built into the traps, and then concealing them in light brush to make them invisible.

Oswell's mind turned in awe at the sheer scope of the project. Darius must have truly been at it for months. The engineering was simple and ingenious. Oswell marvelled at the foot traps—like miniature bear traps, but without the need for a spring. The spiked pits were as nasty as Oswell imagined and he pre-emptively pitied any guard that was going to fall into one. He still wasn't sure what kind of material Darius had woven the snares out of, but they were nearly invisible—they spent a large majority of their time just trying to find the inactive snares that Darius had left behind—but wickedly strong. Finally, with the combined strength of all five rebels, they managed to hoist the gigantic log high into the trees. That trap was set nearest to Fletchery. It would be a devastating opening blow to Oswell's pursuers.

As soon as the log was secured, Wendell darted off in the direction of Fletchery to tell his younger brother of the plan.

"Let's walk through this one more time," Darius suggested. "First, you'll run through here. Be *sure* to jump the trip wire," Darius said, motioning to the strand stretching between two trees about twenty feet apart.

"Right," Oswell agreed, "and don't look back."

Darius nodded, "You're going to keep running straight and when you see the crossed trees, you've come to a foot trap field."

"Run straight down the middle to avoid them," Oswell answered before Darius could ask the question.

"Precisely;" Darius grinned, "should thin the herd nicely."

"Then there's a pair of spiked pits: just go around them. Then another foot trap field; same deal as before."

"Correct. What's after those?" Darius asked.

"Snares. We've got a whole array of them. Start from the rock and run straight, I won't hit one."

"Yes. After that?"

"Two more foot trap fields."

"Good," Darius smiled. "I think you have it." He sighed almost regretfully, "it's a shame we won't get to use all of the traps. I suppose there are only so many guards to dispose of."

"Wendell, Darius, Karyn, and I will be running alongside you, in the trees," Cicero said. "We'll be right there if you get into any trouble."

"And if Vorley gets caught up, we'll grab him while you lead on," Darius continued. "Once we've got him, we'll get rid of any other guards, and then get back to the Enclave.

"Okay," Oswell said, feeling like it was a good plan.

"Foolproof," Darius smirked.

"Let's hope so," Oswell replied. He frowned up at the huge tree suspended high above them. "You mind if we *walk* through this one more time?"

"We'd better," Karyn agreed.

Darius sighed, "Very well."

"Thanks," Oswell said.

"First, you jump the trip wire..."

- *CHAPTER FIFTY-THREE* -

THANK YOU

THOMAS'S EYES PARTED, opening to see the golden glow of the summer sunset filtering through the forest canopy. He felt well rested, but a nagging voice at the back of his mind pessimistically reminded him that it didn't matter how well rested he was, it wouldn't be enough for what lay ahead. Meanwhile, something else was talking too. His stomach grumbled angrily.

"I know, I know," Thomas mumbled to himself. He looked at his handcrafted spear and decided he had time to find something; it would be a few hours until Father went to sleep.

Besides, he needed to make sure he was still capable of hunting because he wasn't sure how long the food he'd pilfered would last. If he managed to steal Nicholas and Claire away, cooking himself a caught meal beforehand would be a perfect proof of concept that they could survive the intervening time between escape and help.

Thomas stretched as he stood up. "This is more difficult than I remember," he chuckled to himself. He then walked slowly away from the bed he had slept in for the last time.

It took him nearly half an hour to spot something beyond the tiny, flittering birds that populated the trees. The prized target was a fat squirrel. Unlike Thomas, it seemed to be enjoying his summer. The squirrel watched Thomas out of the corner of his eye as though the boy was an oddity, but not really a threat. Thomas crept closer, stopping when he felt he was within a good range. He hoisted the spear into a throwing position, took aim and let it fly.

It clattered off the branch on which the squirrel had been sitting, and the squirrel bolted.

"Damn," he cursed, though secretly pleased. The spear flew straight and fast. Thomas had no further doubts that it would be deadly if necessary. With the failure behind him, he gathered up his spear and set off to try again.

Another hour later, deep in the forest, he was sitting happily beside a small fire, watching a slightly less fat, but no less appetizing squirrel roast on a spit.

"That really wasn't *too* difficult," he mused to himself as he deftly picked chunks of meat off the piping hot carcass, trying not to burn himself. There wasn't much on the skeleton, but the meat was sweet, tender, and juicy. He sucked the grease off his fingers when the fragile bones were picked clean, and then stomped out the fire. The sun had just disappeared, leaving Thomas in the darkness of twilight.

By the light of the moon, he returned to his supply stash and double checked the duffel bag he'd stolen to see what he'd collected. His inventory included a box of matches, his compass and map, five bottles of water, six cans of juice and soda, four granola bars, a bag of potato chips, and two boxes of crackers. He packed each item in carefully such that they would not jostle about while he was moving. He then hefted the bag onto his shoulder and heard the chip bag crinkle. He groaned. It was too loud, he decided, too much of a liability. He was about to throw out the calorie-rich food when he came up with an idea.

He opened up one of the boxes of crackers and pulled the bag out of the box. The bag containing the crackers was a light plastic, and barely made a noise when crinkled. Thomas cracked open the bag of potato chips, poured them into the cardboard box, and then carefully rolled up the crinkly bag and stuffed it into the remaining space in the box. He sealed the box, gave it a shake and, satisfied, put the box back into the duffel bag. He wasn't sure why he kept the potato chip bag, other than it felt wrong to waste it. He also would have felt strangely incomplete if he'd left his makeshift home with even a single trace to suggest his prior occupancy.

Thomas kicked apart his bed, grabbed his spear, took one last survey of the space, and then turned towards Father's campsite.

A few minutes later, he carefully laid down the duffel bag, and silently went prone beside it with a concealed viewpoint on the campsite.

Father's face was flushed and mouth turned into a snarl. Kelly grimaced with pain as she clutched her right side, but was otherwise silent. Thomas frowned when he saw Claire crying. His fingers gripped tighter on the spear. Thomas couldn't tell if she was truly upset, or just acting convincingly as he'd suggested. Tears also streaked down Nick's cheeks, where he sat on the ground with his arms wrapped around Ribs.

Despite the tension in the group, Thomas couldn't discern what had gone wrong. He did hope, however, that with the lack of conversation, the group would be to bed sooner rather than later. In an attempt to figure out what had happened Thomas started to observe the rest of the campsite. Nothing else seemed to be amiss. The dinner plates were washed and stacked nicely on the picnic table, and nothing, besides himself of course, was absent. Before he could identify anything else, Thomas startled, but remained silent, as Father started to speak.

"Would you get away from that goddamn animal?" He growled at Nicholas.

Nicholas simply sobbed and shook his head. Father scowled and stood up. He took two steps towards Nicholas before stopping. Kelly stood in his way. Thomas's jaw dropped.

"I thought you already learned your lesson," Father said. Thom's eyes shot to the hand on Kelly's side.

"Leave 'im alone," she whimpered. Thomas couldn't believe it. Those were the first words he'd really heard Kelly speak with any strength; certainly the first words she seemed to have spoken of her own volition.

Father backhanded her across the face and she fell to the ground, sobbing. Claire stepped forward and pulled Nicholas away from the dog on the ground. That's when he saw it.

Recognition struck him as he spotted the hatchet from the office the night before, buried in Ribs' neck.

Thomas felt a fire burn up in his gut. In the back of his mind, he knew all along that Father did sick things. He did them to children, he did them to women, and he did them to animals.

This, however, was the first time he'd really seen him do something with such finality; the first time he'd seen him take a life. Ribs was innocent and good, and now he was dead. It felt like a great stone was lodged in Thomas's throat. He wanted to cry, but he couldn't. Father had done terrible things. Not just to Ribs, but to every child who'd crossed his path, and even to Kelly. The enormity of Father's crimes manifested themselves for Thomas in the murder of that one, faithful animal. Thomas was gripped by an intense desire to kill Father where he stood for all that he'd done.

"Don't," Thomas heard a voice whisper.

Oswell? Thomas asked, reaching out immediately. There was no answer. *Don't?* Thomas thought. A moment later, he was glad he hadn't revealed himself.

"To hell with the three of you," Father barked. "I gotta take a leak," and with that, he turned towards the road, paused, and then looked back. "I want all of you in bed by the time I get back. And guess what sweetie? It's your turn," he added, pointing at Claire before he stomped off in the direction of the men's wash house. He disappeared around the corner.

Thom's mind spun. *Claire's turn.* He watched as Claire looked frantically into the trees.

He reached for his spear, hands shaking and failing to grasp the wood. His knees were weak as he tried to pull himself up. *Not now,* he thought, as sheer panic rushed up inside him. The nausea in his stomach doubled as his body quivered, paralyzed, he fell back to the ground. *Not now,* he thought again, more forcefully this time. He didn't have time for such diversions any longer. Not worrying over whether he could pull this off. Not perseverating on his inadequacy and his past failures. Not playing the part of the victim. There was no time at all. He lashed out at the panic gripping his mind and his body. *You don't control me!*

His mind reeled as it took control with the very decision. The shaking stopped, his stomach quieted, and the strength flowed back into his body. He grabbed his spear, hands steady now, and stepped out of cover into the campsite. Kelly spotted him and stared with her mouth opening and closing silently as though she'd seen a ghost.

"Don't scream," Thomas ordered, levelling the spear in her direction. "I'm taking them, and we're leaving," Thomas turned to Claire and Nicholas, "Come."

Claire and Nicholas immediately ran to his side. Kelly shook her head, "He'll kill me."

"He killed me," Thomas replied. "He's going to kill them, and you know what sick things he has planned," he thought for a split second. "Kelly, I saw what you did for Nicholas," Thomas put a hand on the boy's head. "You love him, and you don't want anything to happen to him. This is the only way. I'm taking him, and I'm taking Claire."

Kelly's eyes flitted to the young boy standing beside Thomas. Tears welled in her eyes, part love, part pain. The pain seemed more real than any other pain she'd felt before, and it was worse than anything Father could do to her. She did love Nicholas, and it was time to put an end to Father's twisted cycle. Kelly stopped shaking her head.

"You keep 'im alive," she ordered.

Thomas nodded. A tension bled out of his shoulders.

"Thank you," Thomas said, he turned to go, guiding Claire and Nicholas away, then paused and turned back. He knelt down beside the dog and gave Ribs a last pat between the ears. "Thank you, old boy. I'm sorry," he ripped the hatchet out of the dog's neck and wiped the blood off on the grass before turning back to Claire and Nicholas. "Let's go," he nodded, grabbing Nicholas by the hand. They darted into the woods, Claire on his heels.

Thomas scooped up the duffel bag as they ran past it.

"No stopping until I say so," he commanded. Claire nodded and Nicholas cried as he ran beside him.

Thomas wasn't sure exactly *how* long they ran before he heard it, but it wasn't *very* long. The coming night was rent by a roar of anger and followed by a desperate cry for help that was cut off by a shriek. Thomas didn't know if Kelly was dead, but he hoped for her sake that she was. Father would be after them.

He tossed Claire the duffel bag and hoisted Nicholas over his shoulder. They had to move; Father was on the way.

CHAPTER FIFTY-FOUR

HOOK, LINE, AND SINKER

EVERYONE LOOKED UP from their bowl of stew as Wendell strode into the main hall. "Everything is in place," he said. "Now Vorley just has to take the bait."

They'd just finished eating an early dinner: a feast of rabbit stew with root vegetables accompanied by a heel of day old bread with butter. Oswell had never gone into battle before, but he was working under the assumption that the last meal before was supposed to be a good one (it possibly being the last meal ever, after all).

Darius was jittery with nerves. After setting down a spoon that had vibrated throughout dinner, he'd stood up from the table and started to pace around the room. His lips moved wordlessly as though he were going over everything in his mind, reassuring himself. Oswell was strangely confident. He glanced at Laurence and took a moment to assess his resolution. He wasn't afraid, and he didn't feel cocky. No, he wasn't overconfident. Oswell simply knew what he had to do, and was ready to do it. The plan sounded like it should work. The only wild card was whether Vorley would rise to the occasion and join the pursuit. Oswell had designs of his own in that department.

"When will Watson take watch?" Darius asked, speaking for the first time since he'd finished eating.

"He starts his shift at six o'clock. It gives us about three hours of sunlight to reel Vorley and his men into the woods," Wendell replied.

"You'll want to be in the forest before it gets dark," Darius directed at Oswell. "We don't need you tripping any wires or missing any cues."

"We'll be waiting, in case anything goes wrong," Wendell said. "Better we take more of a risk than you. You're the one running the gauntlet."

"Won't they see you?"

"We'll be camouflaged," Wendell assured him. "Ghosts."

Oswell frowned. He hoped their camouflage was good. Taking a peek outside, he glanced at the sun. "Let's get the ball rolling then," Oswell said.

"Are you sure you're ready?" Laurence asked.

"Pretty sure. Let's do it before I convince myself otherwise," he chuckled. Laurence furrowed his brow, but then nodded his head. It wouldn't do any good to sow seeds of doubt this late.

"Come," Wendell said, motioning for Oswell to follow him. Oswell took a step towards him, but felt a strong hand grip his shoulder, holding him back. He turned to look at Cicero.

"Thank you for your help," Cicero said. His eyes amplified the warmth in his smile.

"Good luck boy," Rawlins added from across the room. "I'll hold down the fort. Can't wait ta see the look on ol' Vorley's face when *he's* the one in shackles."

"Thanks," Oswell said, finding that he'd finally begun to like the eccentric old man.

"Be safe!" Karyn hurried up to him and took hold of his hand. He squeezed hers and then shrugged. She nodded, knowing that he would try.

Oswell turned and followed Wendell out the door.

"All you need to do is get their attention," Wendell reiterated as he and Oswell stood on the edge of the forest. "Watson will be on the wall. When you see Vorley, you need to give them a chance to decide to go after you. Watson'll do his best to encourage Vorley to chase. He'll drop his spear when Vorley's committed. That's your cue to run."

Oswell nodded.

"How do you feel?" Wendell asked, eyeing the distance between the forest and Fletchery.

"Good," Oswell replied.

"You'll have to get well and good into the tenements for them to be able to see you," Wendell pointed to the hill on which they'd stopped to surveil Fletchery. "You're going to have to run like a quarter horse, Oswell. When they come after you, they *will* be mounted. It'll take them a few minutes to muster the horses; that will be your head start."

"Let's hope it's enough of one," Oswell felt the nervous beating of his heart accelerate minutely.

"It will be," Wendell said.

"It will be," Oswell repeated. *I can do it.*

"Are you ready?" Wendell asked.

"Ready as I'll ever be."

"Well then, see you shortly," Wendell smiled and clapped him on the back. "Good luck."

Oswell half-smiled back before Wendell melted into the trees. Oswell immediately gave himself a once-over.

He'd fashioned a pair of shorts out of old pants he'd found at the Enclave. A small knife sat comfortably within its sheath, fastened to his belt. Oswell hoped he wouldn't have to use it because it wouldn't be much use in a fight regardless. Otherwise, he carried nothing else. He touched his toes and held them for a minute, and then dragged his feet up one at a time behind him. His legs felt limber. He jumped up and down and breathed in and out, pumping himself up.

"Good to go," he told himself, more to deceive himself than for any other reason. "Good-to-go, good-to-go, good-to-go." He took his first step out of the woods and set off at a brisk walk towards Fletchery.

Oswell stopped on the outskirts of Fletchery's slums. Butterflies roiled in his stomach and threatened to burst up through his throat and out of his mouth. He'd gotten increasingly nervous with each step towards Fletchery. He couldn't believe how close he was to the town. It was going to be a long run back to the forest.

A peasant eyed the young boy with some suspicion. Oswell nodded to the man and then proceeded deeper into the shantytown until he found a suitable hut. A quick glance around was his only precaution before he clambered onto the roof and secured a clear view of the city's defences.

He scanned the walls and spotted two guards lining them. One of the guards immediately fixed his attention on Oswell while the other seemed to remain oblivious. Oswell waved to the guard. Oswell recognized Watson by his long black hair, height and build. Even from this distance, he could see the wide smile on his face. Oswell stopped waving and waited.

He watched as Watson called the other guard over to him. The man followed Watson's pointing and finally seemed to spot him. The two men conversed for a moment before the other guard hurried away, leaving Watson alone on the wall.

"He's fetching Vorley," Oswell narrated. Watson waved, confirming Oswell's observation.

The intervening minutes were agonizing. He started pacing back and forth on the top of the roof, fighting the urge to run. He couldn't sit to calm himself down; he simply kept his eyes glued to the top of the battlements.

"Finally," he whispered as he spotted the tall and unmistakable figure of Jonas Vorley stride onto the battlements beside Watson. Watching from on far, he put his plan into action, wishing he knew what was being said on the wall.

"Syr, that *is* 'im, ain't he?" Watson asked.

"It would appear so," Vorley mused, appraising the golden-haired boy standing on a tiny square of roof in the middle of the poor quarter. "Why haven't you dispatched a guard to collect him?"

"We thought we should notify you first, syr," Watson replied.

"For Myr's sake, you are all *completely* incompetent," Vorley paused and squinted at the young man, who'd stopped pacing and changed position. "What is that he's doing?"

Watson expertly fought back a grin as he too squinted at Oswell and recognized Oswell's taunt. "Syr, it appears that he's... uh... he's exposing his rear end... syr." Watson said.

"What is the meaning of this?" Vorley growled.

"I'm not entirely certain, syr, but it's awfully offensive. He didn't start doing that 'til you got here, syr," Watson said. He watched as Vorley's face puckered in pure anger.

"Bring him in!" Vorley exploded.

"Syr?" Watson asked gesturing to the young man's moon, "He's done *that* for you, syr."

Vorley growled again, "Send word to the stable, I want to be a part of the greeting party." He turned to follow the other guard that had just rushed off, then paused as Watson fumbled his spear to the ground. "Pick that up, fool, and come with me."

"Syr, he's running," Watson said as he picked up his spear. Vorley's face hardened further.

"Stop wasting time then!"

"Of course, syr," Watson hurried after Vorley.

Acer Makkin motioned for one of his servants to fill his cup. One did so dutifully, careful not to spill a drop. If there was one thing Makkin hated more than the Numyrian scum he was forced to give audience to on a daily basis, it was the waste of good wine. At least wine made such dreadful interaction bearable. He scowled and took a long draught of the rich red drink.

The wine was passable, but he eagerly anticipated the next shipment from Saosin's cellars. The Emperyr rewarded him well for his devotion through the war years and his continued loyalty. Few were so lucky to enjoy such splendid grace. Acer enjoyed his seat as Governyr of Northern Numyria, and with that, his unrivalled authority within its borders. Such authority and power came with other gifts. Riches, wine, food, women—materials he appreciated in that particular order.

Makkin looked up from his meal as a breathless page burst into the room.

"This had better be good," Makkin growled. He hated to be interrupted with business when he was eating. Actually, he hated to be interrupted with most business, regardless of what he was doing. That was what he paid Jonas Vorley for.

"Apologies, your honour," the page rasped.

"Granted," Makkin said. "Get on with it."

"*Syr*, one of the fugitives—he has appeared outside the town walls."

"Nagel?" Makkin demanded, a spark of malevolence flashed across his eyes.

"No, your honour, the boy."

"Blast it. That will have to do. Bring him to me."

"Apologies again syr, we do not have him in custody," the page explained. Makkin noted this and a smile flickered across his face before melting into the slag of his impotent rage.

"What do you mean?"

"Syr, he fled almost immediately after he appeared."

"And you did not catch him?" Makkin fumed.

"No, m'lord. Sherryf Vorley is personally leading the hunt for him. He is headed for the forest, but they should be close behind him on horseback."

"Yes, they should be!" Makkin said. If his men let the boy slip through their fingers again, more than one man would be held responsible this time. Evidently the example he'd set with the prison warden who'd haplessly allowed their escape, was motivation enough.

"Quite right, your honour," the page said. He continued to stand awkwardly in front of Makkin, who seemed to have lost interest in his supper. It wasn't often that he lost his appetite. He was, however, frustrated, and eyeing a serving girl hungrily.

"Do not disturb me until he is captured. You are dismissed," Makkin grumbled as he beckoned the serving girl closer.

The butterflies had settled. They fluttered away as he watched from between his legs as an upside down Vorley exploded in anger. He hadn't thought there was a clearer way to concisely express exactly what he thought of Vorley. He'd had a pleasant little laugh as he danced on the top of the roof with his shorts around his ankles. However, Oswell's laughter stopped the moment Watson's spear slipped from his hand—the decided upon signal that Vorley had committed to the chase—and he leaped from the roof.

Now he was running hard. He knew he was going to have a head start, but he didn't have much of one. His feet pounded the grass and he felt like a leaf in the wind as he sailed over the hills towards the forest. Each step was mechanical and yet organic. Oswell was a living, breathing machine.

In, and out, he thought, feeling his lungs expand with every influx of air, and contract with a whoosh only a second later. He had a smile on his face. Running was something he could do, something he could always do.

He'd covered over half the distance between the edge of the slums and the forest. Still, he hadn't missed a beat. Glancing over his shoulder, he watched a veritable herd of mounted riders burst from the edge of town into full sprint across the fields. Oswell picked up the pace. He wouldn't look back again.

The forest rushed up in front of him as Vorley and his guards closed the distance between them. He could hear the men yelling and the pounding of hooves behind him. "No arrows," yelled Vorley, "he is no use to us dead!" Oswell's mind briefly touched on the oversight that he could have been cut down by an arrow at any moment, but his thoughts couldn't linger.

Oswell spotted the subtle mark on one of the trees—his entry point—and forced himself to run faster.

He broke the tree line and almost immediately heard the whinnying of horses as they denied the guards their mounted pursuit into the darkening trees.

"On me!" Vorley shouted, a mix of frustration and annoyance flavouring his words. He'd been so close to making the easy capture. Too close to quit now.

Oswell smiled as he heard the sound of at least fifty men trampling into the forest at a run.

He made no attempt to hide his movement, shouting and whooping; he wanted them to know exactly where he was. He deftly hopped the first trip wire. Ten seconds later, Oswell heard the sickening crunch of a two ton log swing into the thick of Vorley's men.

"Keep going!" Vorley shouted, leaping over the dozen broken men at his feet without pause. He could still see flickers of the golden boy ahead, but worse were his catcalls. So many terms unrecognizable, aside from the repugnant tone with which they were hurled. They would capture him and extract his knowledge of Cicero Nagel by any means necessary. Putting down the rebellion once and for all would be his final great task, thought Vorley. With that accomplished, Hallows would be unable to withhold the authority Vorley so clearly deserved over the North. Finally, the Governyrship would cede from the lumbering fool called Acer Makkin to a man with the appropriate skills to keep his subjects in line. As he pushed his men forward, Vorley's mind whirled with the possibilities. Success was at hand. Of course, he would relish in the painstaking extraction the information he needed. He hoped that the boy would be difficult to break. Vorley's lips curled up in pleasure at the thought.

He followed closely after his men, who surged on through the trees without fail. Stupid though they were, they knew how to follow orders. He had taught them that much at least. They knew the price of disobedience.

Darius and Karyn hurried alongside the rushing guardsmen. They were practically invisible and moving nimbly and silently. Darius was surprised by how comfortable Karyn was in the forest after such a short period of training. She moved like a seasoned hunter, quite unlike the despondent girl they'd found in Thane's Hollow. On the other side of the rushing guardsmen, Darius knew Cicero and Wendell were also closely shadowing Fletchery's force. If only Vorley knew.

A guard drifted in front of them from the main crowd and Karyn quickly dispatched him with a viciously blunt attack to the man's head. Her face was ablaze with violence (or vengeance?), something Darius had never seen before. The guard dropped, dead or unconscious, where he stood. Neither Darius nor Karyn paused to check.

Darius perked up as he heard the sounds of men crying out in surprise. They'd reached the first foot trap fields. He allowed a small smile on his lips as he listened to Vorley urging the men on, only to find they were completely immobilized.

"We're losing him!" Vorley growled, leaving his trapped men behind. They still had over half their men left. "Whatever you do, do not stop!" He commanded.

Darius was pleased; Vorley's rage and obsession had consumed the better part of his tactical thinking.

He listened as two more guardsmen cried out in surprise, their voices replaced by screams of pain as they fell into the spiked pits. The cries of fear only multiplied as another half dozen trapped their feet in the following foot trap field. Their numbers were dwindling but they pushed on, following Vorley's barking commands.

Darius knocked a guard unconscious as the man crossed his path and then Karyn eliminated another immediately after. The guardsmen were starting to peel off, not interested in being the next one to fall into a trap.

Ahead, Oswell's legs burned with a recognizable urgency, but instinct and adrenaline carried him through. He'd fallen into a careful rhythm long ago; one foot in front of the other, careful not to trip on any roots or outcrops. Looking to his side, he was shocked by a face he didn't expect to see.

The face was focused but strained, tired but defiant, and startlingly familiar. Even more startling to see was the young boy draped over his shoulder, and the girl sprinting alongside them.

"Thomas?" Oswell panted. The trio paid Oswell no mind. Similarly, Oswell paid no mind to where he was running. His voice caught in his throat as he felt a snare tighten around his ankle and the world turn upside down before he watched it go black.

When Oswell opened his eyes, he fought back a cry of surprise. Ten feet away from him, Vorley hung by his ankle, unconscious. Five other guards were similarly ensnared.

Looking down, he watched four hazy shrubs gather beneath him.

"You weren't supposed to fall into the trap yourself!" Darius complained, shaking his head.

"Get him down," Wendell ordered. Oswell felt himself jolt towards the ground and then stop abruptly a foot lower. A splitting headache told him of the whack he'd taken to his head as he was upended by the snare. He puked and felt some of it catch in his hair.

"Gently, please," Oswell moaned. He felt himself lower more slowly this time, and then lay on the forest floor breathing deeply.

"What happened?" Karyn asked.

"Thomas..." Oswell groaned, pulling himself up into a sitting position and rubbing his ankle.

"Thomas?" Darius asked.

"I saw Thomas," Oswell explained. "He's still alive."

"That's why they kept running," Cicero realized, "they still had a blonde boy to chase."

"Nicholas and Claire were with him," Oswell added. Oswell couldn't believe the development. He'd been sure that Thomas was dead. Even alive, Oswell had been doubtful that Thomas could have successfully rescued Claire and Nicholas. Now, Thomas had proven him wrong on both counts.

"An apparition," Cicero hypothesized. *Probably the closest he has come to crossing back over,* Cicero thought, deciding not to say it out loud.

"We can talk about this later," Wendell said. "We need to get this bastard off the line before the other guards realize they're chasing a ghost."

CHAPTER FIFTY-FIVE

GETAWAY

FOR THE SAKE of his exhausted body, they'd slowed down. Nothing Thomas had seen in Father, as yet, suggested that he was a seasoned tracker. Thomas believed they had put enough distance between them and their warden. If they moved slowly, and didn't leave any obvious clues indicating their direction, they could stay invisible. They had to.

Thomas listened the second time he heard the voice. The first time, he'd ignored it as an unnecessary distraction during the height of their flight. A few minutes later, however, he heard it again, as they carefully picked their way through the trees, trying not to leave a trail. This was proving to be more difficult than planned with a cranky, terrified six year old in tow.

"Thomas," Oswell said.

What? Thomas replied. He didn't have time to be talking. Their escape required all of his focus.

"You just saved my ass," Oswell said.

Saved your... ass? Thomas asked, incredulous.

"You just appeared here, and the guards started chasing you instead of me!" Oswell explained. Thomas didn't know what to say. He certainly hadn't saved Oswell intentionally, not that he wouldn't have had he been given the option. *"I... I saw Nicholas and Claire with you."*

Thomas furrowed his brow, *Yes, they're with me.*

"You've escaped then?" Oswell asked.

We have, Thomas replied.

"Good. Thank God, no..." Oswell seemed to pause. *"Thank you."*

Of course, Thomas said.

"You keep at it. Get them to safety. I'm saving your world; you save mine," Oswell said, chuckling lightly. The statement was so absurd. Oswell never would have imagined saying something like that. As much as he liked to think he was special, he never thought of himself as a hero. He did, however, feel confident applying the term to his look-alike, especially after managing to rise from the dead and escape with his two friends safely.

You know I'm doing everything I can, Thomas replied.

"I know."

Thomas nodded his answer, forgetting that Oswell wouldn't get that. Oswell made no effort to talk beyond that. Thomas had more important things to deal with.

"Here," Thomas said, handing Claire the hatchet. "If he finds us, and I'm out of the picture, I want you to put it right here," Thomas motioned to his shin. "He won't expect it. It isn't going to kill him, but he will *not* be walking after that."

Claire didn't like the idea of Thomas being out of the picture, nor could she imagine how that would happen. Nonetheless, she nodded as she handed the duffel bag back over to Thomas.

He hefted the strap onto his shoulder. It was considerably less heavy than Nicholas. Claire held the hatchet in one hand and Nick's hand in the other. A stark contrast existed between the innocent terror of the crying child and the understated malevolence of the blood-stained axe.

"We need to keep moving; get oriented," Thomas decided. They wouldn't be sleeping for a while. In fact, Thomas wanted to go until he collapsed, but realistically, he knew that there were limits to Nicholas's, and even Claire's endurance.

"What have you got in the bag?" Claire asked.

"Water, juice, food, matches, a map, and a compass."

Claire looked surprised but pleased.

"You'll have to do the navigating, when we get a chance. I've no idea how to use the map and compass together."

"I'll teach you," Claire replied. Thomas smiled and then set himself to the task at hand: they needed to get as far away from Father as possible, as quietly as possible, and eventually establish a direction in which to travel.

Thomas stopped and knelt down to eye level with the little boy.

"We're going to need you to be quiet, Nicholas. I need you to be strong for your sister and stop crying," Thomas said. "This is our chance to get you both home to your parents."

Claire stopped a few steps ahead. Nicholas sniffled and then his mask of tears was replaced by a stern grimace. "Good man," Thomas patted the boy on the chest. "Let's move."

- CHAPTER FIFTY-SIX -

FREE FALLING

OSWELL SMILED BENEVOLENTLY. "Wakey, wakey," he said. Jonas Vorley hung upside down by his ankle, his head six feet off the ground and his hands tied behind his back.

"Release me immediately!" Vorley hissed as he regained his senses. He cast his wild gaze around, memorizing the face of each captor.

"I don't think so," Oswell poked Vorley in the forehead. "You're coming with us."

"Let him down," Wendell said. Darius did as he was told, lowering the man to the ground. Wendell levelled his sword at Vorley's neck. "You are a captive of the Numyrian Independence Front. We are arresting you on our vested authority for crimes against the good people of Numyria."

"You have the right to remain silent," Oswell said. "Anything you say or do can and will be held against you in a court of law." Wendell, Darius, Karyn, and Cicero simultaneously appraised Oswell. "I always wanted to say that," he replied sheepishly in response to the inquisition.

"He doesn't have the right to remain silent," Darius said. "If we want him to talk, we'll make him."

"Oh," Oswell replied, rubbing the back of his head. "Sorry there, Jo-Jo; guess I was wrong," Oswell smirked as their captive brightened further in anger at the boy's naming.

"Enough," Cicero said. "Let's get him back to the Enclave before we're discovered."

"Wait. Why don't we just kill him?" Oswell asked.

Cicero looked at Oswell, surprised, meeting the young man's eyes. When Oswell urged an answer, Cicero understood the seriousness (and validity) of Oswell's question. "This man has been fighting to undermine the Independence Front for years." While Wendell kept his sword levelled on Vorley, Cicero guided Oswell a short distance away. Darius, Karyn, and Laurence joined them in a small circle as Cicero lowered his voice to a whisper. "He has plans in place that could threaten us even after his death. If we have the chance, we cannot throw away this opportunity."

"Okay," Oswell replied, mollified by the frank response.

"Onwards," Cicero said.

The group nodded their agreement and Wendell forcibly lifted Vorley up onto his feet and gripped him firmly by the arm.

"You will pay for this with your lives," Vorley warned.

"We already have been," Cicero said, "a long line of lives, I need not remind you of Maryam Leegra, or Warr Willim... certainly you remember Grian Barnicke."

Vorley struggled against his bonds.

"There are others. You will answer for them," Cicero turned, the righteous justice on his face palpable in the air.

"That was easy," Watson said as he emerged from the trees and strode up to the group.

"You there! Release me!" Vorley shouted.

"I don't think so," Watson replied, scratching behind his ear.

"Turncoat!" Vorley growled. Watson seemed to contemplate the accusation for the moment.

"I suppose that's accurate," he nodded. Watson grabbed Vorley by the other arm. "Shall we, brother?"

The two men shoved Vorley forward and the group started back to the Enclave.

"What about the other guards?" Oswell asked, motioning to the men high above still trapped in their snares.

"I'll come back and lower them later. Might do them good to have the extra blood in their head; could make 'em smarter," Darius chuckled.

Vorley fumed as he was pushed and prodded through the forest towards the Enclave.

He'd cursed them loudly for the first minute until Wendell became disenchanted with the vulgarities and stuffed a gag into the man's mouth. Everyone was much happier with the silence.

It also reduced the likelihood of any remaining guards finding them. Although the six fighters were prepared for an attack, it was one that never came.

Oswell was pleased at his comfort in the forest as they approached safety. The trees didn't all look the same anymore; certain ones stood out, acting as landmarks that could guide him to the Enclave. He stopped along with the others beneath the entrance.

Wendell let out a high pitched whistle, repeating it twice more. A moment later the rope ladder dropped out of the canopy. Oswell observed Vorley. The man was shocked by the appearance of the ladder. Apparently, the guardsmen were not looking for the Enclave above the trees. They'd been safer than they thought.

"Darius, Karyn, send down the cage," Wendell ordered. Karyn leapt onto the ladder and scampered up with ease. Darius followed. They'd done it enough times that it had become second nature. A minute later, Oswell watched as a wooden cage parted the branches above and descended towards them.

Wendell and Watson shoved Vorley into the cage and locked it behind him. Meanwhile, Cicero climbed onto the ladder and disappeared into the canopy.

"I'll help reel him up," Watson volunteered. "Been ages since I've gone up this thing," he grumbled as he found his footing on the ladder and started to climb. When he'd disappeared above, Oswell turned to Wendell.

"I can't believe it worked!" Oswell enthused.

"That was only the first step," Wendell said. "We'll see if your theory is correct in a few short days." Oswell hoped he'd been right. He couldn't imagine the people respecting Acer Makkin without the threat of his Sherryf.

"Look at him," Oswell gestured to Vorley, whose eyes bulged out of his head with fury. "He sees what we've done. I'll put ten to one odds that I'm right." They watched as the cage lifted off the ground and started its slow rise.

"I cannot take that bet," Wendell laughed. "Go," he said, motioning to the ladder. Oswell felt a rising in his heart. Safe above the tree tops, their mission would be complete.

He started climbing the ladder. He didn't feel Wendell climb onto the ladder behind him, but knowing the man, he would probably climb up by other means. Oswell took a peek, and unsurprised, saw Wendell clambering his way up a nearby tree. Oswell had never met a more capable man. What *was* surprising to Oswell, however, was Thom's capability. He was amazed that Thomas had managed to escape from the kidnapper with Claire and Nicholas. Cicero had not exaggerated the boy's resourcefulness and tenacity. Of course, Oswell would be happy to take up the job of rescuing his friends, just as soon as he could fulfill the prophecy, return independence to the North, and get back to Earth.

Oswell hoisted himself up onto the catwalk and started reeling in the ladder as the others continued to crank the cage up into the trees. He finished reeling in the ladder as the cage came to a rest beside the catwalk. Vorley was sitting in the middle of the cage, uncomfortable with the height perhaps more than with his captivity.

"How was the ride?" Watson taunted, unlatching the cage and grabbing Vorley roughly. He dragged Vorley out of the cage as Oswell secured the ladder with a few knots.

"Oh—!" Watson cried out as Vorley lashed out with his feet, delivering a resounding kick to Watson's knee. The man crumpled where he stood and Vorley dashed past him towards Oswell, eyes ablaze with frenzy.

"Oz!" Karyn cried.

Oswell turned too late and felt the tall man crash into him. The next thing he felt was the railing sliding across his back as he upended over it and then the sickening weightlessness of falling.

- CHAPTER FIFTY-SEVEN -

A NEW WAY

THE SUN WAS setting on the horizon when Claire stopped in her tracks and grabbed ahold of Thomas's arm.

"Yes?"

"I think I see a landmark," Claire grabbed Thomas's hand and pulled him a few steps closer, then pointed off into the distance. They were standing at the edge of a cliff, something that Thomas wasn't very happy about. It was as good as a corner if they got backed onto it, with the exception that there would remain one final route of escape.

Thom's gaze followed her finger and picked out what she saw in the growing shadows of the distant forest. He was shocked that she'd seen it in the first place. It looked to be some sort of tiny village, abandoned and heavily overgrown.

"Is it even on the map?" Thomas wondered. He dropped the duffel bag and pulled the map out of it. Unfolding it, he scanned over the unfamiliar cartography. Claire knelt down beside him and joined in the search while Nicholas dropped rocks off the cliff.

"Is that it?" Claire asked, pointing to a faint line on the map that randomly terminated in the middle of nowhere. She looked up and scanned the forest, unable to see an indication of the highway the tiny road was connected to.

"I don't think so... but it's better than sitting up here," Thomas decided. "We'll take a look." He folded up the map and packed it away. "Let's find a way down from here."

They veered off to the left, following the cliff down. When they finally reached the bottom, they'd properly descended into the darkness of night, however, beams of moonlight allowed him to make out the forest floor. Thomas thought it would be best if they continue to push on into the night. Finding civilization would mean they were that much safer from Father. They made a best guess at the direction that the village was in and set off for it.

"This must be it," Thomas said, an hour later, as they pushed through a rotting wooden fence and stepped into the overgrown clearing. A chill trickled across his body at the eeriness of decayed civilization in the dark of night. The village consisted of only five buildings, all of which were wooden and didn't appear to have been used in decades. No immediate safety would be found in this particular vestige of civilization. Across the small clearing, Thomas saw a path leading off into the woods. Just like the buildings, the entrance to the path was heavily overgrown. Even with the obstruction, Thomas could tell that the path was just that: a path. It certainly wasn't a logging road, which Claire had suggested.

"I don't think that's the road," Claire agreed, disappointed that they had not actually found a reference point.

"It's okay," Thomas said. "We'll rest here and eat before we keep moving." Nicholas perked up at the mention of food; he'd been complaining about being hungry for the past hour. Thomas also felt the familiar pull of hunger, though for him, it was a less formidable sensation.

"Should we set up inside?" Claire asked.

Thomas was about to say no, but then a quick appraisal of his companions made him falter. Claire's shoulders drooped with exhaustion, and Nicholas had been dragging his feet and blinking long since they stopped running. "Yes, inside will do," he said.

"Cool!" Nicholas exclaimed. "Sorry," he whispered as he received a glare from Thomas. "Which one?" the boy asked.

"Whichever you like," Thomas figured it wouldn't hurt to let the boy have some choice in this nightmare.

"This one," Nicholas decided. He started to walk up to one of the buildings, but stopped as Thomas put a hand on his shoulder, restraining him.

"Let me check it out first," Thomas stepped past Nicholas and approached the door. Grabbing the handle, he tugged on it. It didn't budge. He pulled on it again without result.

"Locked?" he mused to himself, *or seized?* "Hatchet," Thomas said. Claire put the hatchet in Thom's hand. He wound back and then delivered a blow to the wood of the door between the handle and the doorframe. He heard something shift. This time, when he pulled on the handle, the lock yielded and the door opened.

Thomas was half expecting to find something surprising inside the house—why else would it be locked? His expectations were wrong, however, as he stepped inside the one room hut. The contents were cast in darkness, illuminated only by the scarce moonlight filtering through the windows. There was a fireplace on one of the walls, a desk against another, and a small table with two benches in the middle of the room. The roof was in reasonably good condition, as were the floors, though the boards creaked as he walked across them. Satisfied, Thomas turned and invited the siblings into the room.

"Wow..." Nicholas gushed, rushing over to the fireplace.

"Better than roughing it," Thomas decided.

"This isn't roughing it?" Claire laughed.

"For me it's not," Thomas joined in, laughing genuinely for the first time in a long while. Claire smiled and gave Thomas a hug. Thomas hugged her back, and then reeled Nicholas into the hug as well. "Now, who's hungry?"

"Me!" Nicholas said, "I mean, me," he whispered. Thomas smiled in spite of himself and then dug through the duffel bag, retrieving the box he'd poured the potato chips into.

"Do you like these?" Thomas asked, taking a chip for himself.

"Mmmhmmm," Nicholas smiled, grabbing a handful from the box. Claire reached in next and grabbed a few chips for herself.

"I'm going to see if the other cabins are as empty as this one," Thomas decided as he brushed some salt off his hands and onto his pants. "Get comfortable, but I think it's best we leave no trace, no fires," he decided. Claire agreed. The heat of the day hadn't yet leached out of the hut as it were.

The first house Thomas checked was outfitted similarly to the one they'd already opened. Thomas did a quick once over before leaving. In the second house, Thomas found an old pot. It wasn't too heavy, and Thomas decided it would be perfect for boiling water.

The third house was slightly bigger than the others, and locked. Thomas levelled his hatchet at the frame and swung. With a thunk, Thomas buried the hatchet in the wood, heard a crack, and then pulled open the door.

This time, Thomas had reason to be surprised. The hut, though just as old and unused on the outside, appeared to have been used more recently. The floors were swept, with only a thin layer of dust covering them. In the first room, Thomas found a table with an unlit gas lantern on it. In the fireplace, there were still pieces of blackened logs, though dust had settled onto them and magnified their petrified look. Thomas could clearly see papers scattered on the desk.

There wasn't much to the scribbling; at least Thomas couldn't discern anything from them. They were written in a language he only recognized by a few words on signs he'd seen shortly after crossing the border. *French?*

Unfortunately, that also meant he couldn't read them.

Leaving the desk, he eyed the second door in the room that he'd ignored at first. Just as the cabin was the only one to indicate any signs of prior habitation, it was also the only one with two rooms. Thomas grabbed the handle and slowly opened the door. Creeping into the room, Thomas stared in muter terror at its sole occupant. A desiccated corpse rested on a wooden bed frame. The bones were arranged in such a way that it looked like the person had simply faded away in their sleep with no one to tend to them.

Thomas shook his head in sympathy and avoided the bed. Instead, he investigated the dresser across the room. The first drawer contained ragged, moth eaten clothes. Thomas shut the drawer immediately.

The next drawer had a browned, unsealed envelope filled with slips of paper not much larger than Thomas's hand. Thomas had never seen paper money before, but he marvelled at the intricacy of the design. If it was money, it had to be valuable, so Thomas grabbed the envelope and stuffed it into his pocket.

Inside the last drawer was another piece of paper, much larger, and rolled up. Thomas pulled it out of the drawer and carefully unrolled it. Immediately, he recognized it as a map.

Thomas slid the drawer shut and rushed out to the table in the other room. There, he gently spread the map out and examined it. Just as he'd hoped, there was an indication on the map, a red circle. In this small hunting retreat, it could mean only one thing: showing him exactly where they were. He identified a few other landmarks: lakes, and rivers. It was just what they needed.

Thomas dashed out of the house and burst into the first one to find Nicholas and Claire playing a game on the floor.

"We're playing rock-paper-scissors, I keep winning," Nicholas gloated.

"What is it?" Claire asked, sensing the excitement in Thomas's face.

Thomas held up the rolled paper, "I found a map."

"We already have a map."

"This is an old one."

"Why do we need an old map?"

"This place is on it."

Claire's eyes widened as she realized what he was getting at. She pulled the newer map out of the duffel bag and unfolded it on the table as Thomas weighed down the corners of the old one. He pointed out natural landmarks on the two maps and then put his finger down on a blank spot of the new map.

"We're right here," he said, triumphant.

"Nicky, pass me the compass," Claire ordered. The boy dug through the duffel bag and handed it to his sister. She placed it down on the map. "We go southeast... there... that's the closest town to us," Claire pointed to a settled area on the new map.

"Good," Thomas felt the wind drift out of them as the way forward was found. The sense of disorientation that had clouded and amplified his every anxiety seemed to melt away. Of course, they still had miles to go through wild northern Canadian forest, but at least they knew where they were going.

"Let's go now!" Nicholas exclaimed. Though Thomas was tempted, he knew better.

"No, you need to rest," Thomas said. "We all need to rest. We've got a long road ahead of us," he reminded the young boy as much as he reminded himself, "but we'll face it together."

As the siblings settled into a position of semi-comfort on the hard wooden floor, Thomas folded his arms across his chest and slid into a seated position against the door. Claire motioned for him to join them, and he merely shook his head. Claire's face furrowed at the rebuff, an expression wrought with equal measures of concern and confusion. He shook his head again, for he was where he belonged. With them, yet separate. He wasn't one of them, not of this world. Here, he had one job, and that was to get them to safety. He would do it. Brought across time and worlds by no other means possible than divine intervention, he was their protector—their protector as *they* made their crossing in the woods.

Chapter Fifty-Eight

Another Way

O SWELL FELT A calloused hand wrap around his wrist and, a split second later, as he came to a brief and jarring halt, the agonizing pain of his shoulder dislocating. The resounding snap of a tree branch breaking took the brakes off his descent and he felt himself falling again.

Squinting through his tears upward, he identified the face connected to the hand around his wrist. Wendell grabbed another branch, this one bending, but failing to break. The pair dangled from it by Wendell's one arm. The sickening thud of a body hitting the ground resonated far below.

Wendell hauled himself up onto the branch and then reeled Oswell in, apologizing with his eyes for the pain. When Oswell sat down on the branch beside Wendell, he breathed deeply and motioned with his head towards his shoulder. Wendell nodded and jerked the joint back into its socket.

"Goddamn it!" Oswell cried, wincing. "How did you—"

"Luck, I'd say," Wendell replied. Oswell couldn't believe it; he simply stared wide eyed at his saviour. "I've got him!" Wendell called up into the trees. "Darius, Karyn! Get down there and see if Vorley's still alive!"

"He's dead," Oswell predicted, though it didn't take a post-graduate physicist to make that calculation. Wendell nodded, agreeing. It would have been a quick death. Something the man did not deserve.

"Toss a rope down!" Wendell shouted upwards again. A rope dropped through the branches a few feet away. Wendell stood on the branch and climbed to grab it where it had tangled on another branch. Meanwhile, Oswell did his best not to look down. Falling had become an all too-real possibility. Wendell yanked the rope down and sat back down beside Oswell. "I'm going to tie you in."

Wendell lifted Oswell's legs one at a time and looped the rope around them, then tied a knot around his waist. He handed over the rest of the rope for him to hold on to.

"Comfortable?" Wendell asked. Oswell shifted in the makeshift harness.

"The boys are in the same room," Oswell nodded. Wendell understood his meaning and chuckled.

"Bring him up!" Wendell called.

Oswell lifted through the tree branches and sighed with relief as he was hoisted over the railing and onto the catwalk. Cicero stood Oswell up and grabbed him by the shoulders. Cicero's expression was one of deep concern. Oswell winced as the elder's hand grasped his injured shoulder.

"I'm okay," Oswell said. Seeing Oswell's pain, Cicero moved his hand and smiled before nodding once. He had thought the boy was gone. It would have been his fault for getting him caught up in it all.

"He's dead!" Darius's muffled voice shouted up from below. "We're going to bring him up! Lower the cage!"

Watson looked both ashamed and in pain as he limped over to the winch and set it loose. The cage rushed down through the trees. A minute later, Darius and Karyn climbed off the ladder onto the catwalk.

Karyn dashed forward and wrapped her arms around him. Oswell winced, but the feeling of her warmth pressing against him was enough to make it worth it.

"I... I thought..." her tears filled in the blanks.

"I'm okay," he replied. "It's fine," he planted a kiss on her forehead and she beamed, burying her face in his neck.

"Thought we lost you," Darius said.

"It's all good, I'm okay," Oswell replied.

Darius appraised Oswell. "You're tougher than I thought you were," he decided, smiling. Oswell grinned back and Darius shook his head in disbelief. He then turned to help Watson crank up the cage.

"Heavier this time around," Watson complained. The cage rose through the trees with Wendell riding on top of it and the broken body of Jonas Vorley inside. The man looked far less menacing in his inanimate state, though Oswell still found his face unsettling.

"Take two?" Oswell mused as they opened up the cage door and hauled the body out.

"Where are we going to put him?"

"I'll take care of it," Laurence said, "Darius, help me?" Darius nodded and helped Laurence carry the body towards Laurence's hut.

"Well, that could have ended better," Oswell laughed.

"It could have ended worse," Cicero said darkly.

"Oh lighten up old man, I'm alive, remember?" Oswell replied, trying to improve the spirits.

"We can take solace in that," Cicero agreed. "Though, now we must tread carefully, until we find some other way to root out Vorley's remaining plans."

"We'll figure it out," Oswell said confidently. "Now, what's next?"

"I hold up my end of the bargain," Watson replied.

"What's that?" Oswell asked.

Watson grinned.

Makkin heard violent banging on his door and shot up in bed as quickly as his puffy body could manage. Before he could roll out of the sheets, the door caved in and Makkin struggled to cover himself as his guardsmen burst into the room. The serving girl occupying his bed, concerned more for her safety than modesty, fled the room uncovered, and disappeared amongst the ranks of armed men spilling through the door.

"What is the meaning of this?" Makkin bellowed. He fully intended to have the head of whoever was responsible for this trespass and have it mounted on a spike above the town walls.

"Serjant Watson Westlake, at your service," a confident man strode forward. He had the look of a warrior with stone cold grey eyes, a shock of black hair, and the swagger of a leader. Makkin would enjoy making an example of him. "I'm here to place you under arrest for murder, political corruption, and suppression of the faith on the authority of the Numyrian Independence Front." The smile on Makkin's face disappeared.

"Where is Vorley?" he demanded.

"Dead," Watson replied, "and good riddance. I'll be in charge in your absence. Men, apprehend the Governyr."

"You will all be had for treason," Makkin warned feebly as two guards stepped forward and grasped him roughly by the arms.

"I think not," the serjant replied. "You'll answer for the crimes you've perpetrated against the people of Fletchery and Numyria. Take him to the dungeon."

Makkin's eyes widened as he was prodded towards the door. How quickly the walls had fallen down around him.

Take Me Home

WATSON BURST INTO the main hall smiling widely. "It's done," he proclaimed. "We've got him in custody."

"What happened?" Oswell asked. Watson had left less than a day ago to take Fletchery.

"So, Oswell was right," Cicero said, pleased.

"They came to my side immediately when I told them Vorley was dead," Watson replied.

"The guards?" Oswell asked.

"Yes, seems neither of them were particularly loved, but only Vorley was feared. Fletchery is ours," Watson confirmed. "Oh, and Makkin is enjoying the same hospitality you enjoyed, Cicero."

"Excellent. Laurence and Rawlins, you will hold the Enclave," Cicero commanded. "We make for Fletchery."

Oswell smiled widely.

"Wait," Oswell paused, "can we...?"

"Of course, we owe you that much," Cicero replied. "Gather your belongings, I will come with you. He shot a glance to Wendell and Darius.

"We'll go on ahead," Wendell said. The brothers and Darius left the main hall together.

Oswell hurried out of the hall after the trio, and then split off from them to the barracks. He gathered the few things he'd come to Myros with and put them in the canvas sack he'd been given. His flashlight, his pocket knife, and the filthy shirt he'd never gotten around to washing. So little physical evidence of his origins. He stood at the door with his bag and took one last look around the barracks. It felt like a second home to him already. The bland but solid walls offered refuge from the storm of a new world. The sturdy, empty bunks stood guard around his single occupied one. The light filtered through the handful of windows and a gentle treetop breeze drifted through the same, keeping the room fresh. It was nothing like his true home, and though it was different, it had somehow indeed become something akin to a home. He would miss it, but he was ready to go back to where he belonged.

He shut the door behind him as he left and found Cicero waiting patiently beside Laurence, Rawlins, and Karyn. Darius, Wendell, and Watson stood off to the side. Watson tapped his foot impatiently. Darius's eyes flitted back and forth, conflicted in his sadness to see his new friend depart, but happy that their plan had worked and that Oswell was getting what he wanted. Wendell's face was softened by pride, though he did not seem altogether affected by Oswell's imminent departure. Karyn's face was one of confusion. Oswell took in all of these expressions, but ultimately lingered on Karyn's.

"What's going on Oswell?" she asked.

Oswell tried to speak, but his voice cracked and no words issued forth.

"Oz?" she said again.

"I couldn't—I can't stay here forever—I need to go home," he said, words finding their way through his cracking voice. He hadn't anticipated this particular complication, though it had been plain to see in every tender moment they'd shared. It wasn't like they were dating, but it didn't take a psychologist to tell that she liked him. Hell, *he* liked her too, but that didn't mean he belonged on Myros. His family was back home, his friends, his memories, the years—though powerful, his history couldn't be reversed by a summer of new memories, new friends, and the promise of love.

"You're leaving?" she asked.

"He doesn't belong here," Cicero said, saving him. "He belongs on Earth."

"Who are you to say that? He's here for a reason. We've said that all along. It wasn't just to serve you and your war. He made a promise… a promise to my father," Karyn shouted. "Oz… don't go."

Oswell felt his heart break at Reg's mention. He had promised to keep her safe. If anything, he'd done nothing of the sort over the days and weeks, but certainly now she was in safe hands. He hoped, at least, he'd helped to create a Numyria where she would thrive, and above all, be safe.

"Laurence, can you," Cicero motioned towards Karyn. Laurence seemed to say no, but then placed a hand on Karyn's shoulder at Cicero's unspoken insistence. She shrugged out of his grasp. Laurence leaned over and whispered something in her ear. Oswell watched tears well in her eyes, but fail to fall. She stared at Laurence and then nodded, sending the tears coursing down her cheeks. She stole one last glance at Oswell—one loaded with betrayal and disbelief—and then walked away. Oswell felt his heart follow her.

Without a second thought, so did his feet. No sound of protest arose from the men waiting behind him as he hurried after Karyn. He caught up with her as she slammed the door to her quarters in his face.

"Karyn," Oswell said.

"Go away, it's what you wanted anyway," Karyn replied.

"It's not like that," Oswell rested his forehead against the solid wooden door. "Let me in, please."

"No."

"Please?"

A laboured sigh sounded on the other side of the door and then it opened.

"Thank you," Oswell said, stepping inside. He appraised Karyn, arms folded and appraising him right back. Her eyes were red, and cheeks still streaked with her tears. He stared at her for a long time.

"What do you want?" Karyn finally said, wiping the wet from her cheeks furiously.

"I want you to understand why I have to do this," Oswell replied.

"I do understand," Karyn said. "Go."

Oswell tried not to show his frustration and fought with himself not to leave. She was hurt, and he didn't want to hurt her more. He wondered if simply leaving would be easier for both of them. Dragging it out was agony.

"Karyn, it's not that I don't *want* to be here, it's that I'm not *supposed* to be here."

"How do you know?"

"This isn't my home! My parents aren't here, my friends aren't here... my friends need me!"

"Your friends are *here* too. *These* people need you here," Karyn couldn't look at Oswell. "*I* need you here."

Oswell felt whatever was left of his heart shatter at those words. The fragments urged him to stay with promises of self-repair, while his yearning for home demanded that he go. A tear rolled down his cheek as he faced his conflict alone.

Suddenly, Karyn was on him, hugging him so tightly he could barely breathe. His heart seemed to mend piece-by-shattered-piece with every second that she held him. He held her back, taking in the scent of her crimson hair, revelling in the feel of her body against his.

You cannot stay, his mind reminded him.

I know.

Oswell pulled away from Karyn and held her at arm's length. His body rebelled as it realized what he was about to do.

"I'm torn between two worlds. In every moment, I think about my mom and my dad worried to death about what's happened to me. They must think I'm dead. And yet I'm not, but the worst part is that even if I do get back to Earth, I'm not safe, I might still be dead. If I stay, I could die here, they'll never know, even if Thomas does get Claire and Nicholas to safety. Even if they get through the woods in one piece, my mom and dad won't have me back. I never even got to say goodbye to them, I snuck away, I was so awful…" he sobbed even as he kept Karyn at a distance with his arms, even as she tried to break through and wrap him in the hug that he so desperately needed. "Karyn, they raised me, they're my blood, they deserve to have me back. I'm sorry, I have to try."

Karyn didn't attempt to hold back her tears this time. She let them flow freely. Oswell watched them cascade down her cheeks, taking a path beaten by those who'd gone before, and as each drop hit the floor, he felt the stitched-together pieces of his heart unravel and drift down after them. His heart belonged with her, but his obligations belonged elsewhere.

"Go then," Karyn choked, betrayal still written across her face, even if it was infinitesimally softened by the real pain wracking his body. He'd hurt her more than he had before, perhaps more than anyone or anything could have. His promise to her father, to Reg, was broken.

"Good bye," he said at the door. She didn't respond. His voice tried to produce three more words—words that spoke the truth of how he felt for her in that moment—but, he knew that those words would form the tip of a blade, driving home more pain for the both of them. He closed the door behind him, words and feelings unsaid.

Walking back to the rest of the men was the longest walk of his life. He put on a strong face and stood in front of them. He rubbed the back of his hand on his nose to stop it from running, and failed to feel embarrassed in front of the others.

Laurence stepped forward. "Take this," he said, dropping a satchel full of food into Oswell's arms. "I know you're not going into the best of conditions."

"Thanks," Oswell choked out and stuffed the food into his pack.

Laurence nodded and backed away.

"Yer a good kid," Rawlins said, "I'll write a song 'bout ya."

"Better be a good one," Oswell laughed, though it sounded phoney with the emotional crack in his voice. "Do me a favour and make me sound taller than I am."

Watson stepped in front of Oswell, looking somewhat uncomfortable as he grasped Oswell's shoulder. "Good luck, beggar boy," he said, smiling. Oswell shook the man's hand.

"Good luck with Fletchery," Oswell replied.

"Don't forget—" Wendell stepped forward.

"Respect, relaxed, ready," Oswell replied.

"And stay focused, for Myr's sake," Wendell added. "You've got what it takes to get your friends home."

Oswell nodded to Wendell, thanking him for the vote of confidence. He then turned to Darius.

"As annoying as you were, I'm glad you were here to help us," Darius said, wrapping up the younger teenager in an embrace. Oswell was going to miss him, and he was surprised to find there was capacity for the ache in his chest to deepen.

"Ditto," Oswell said, smiling forcefully at the jab. Sensing Darius's lack of recognition, he continued, "It means, 'same to you,' dummy," Oswell explained. Darius laughed. Oswell couldn't.

"I don't mean to make this hard on you, but really?" Darius said, he tilted his head towards Karyn's hut, "You're going to leave *that* behind?"

"If there was any other way," Oswell said, "I'd do it."

"Stay," Darius pleaded.

"I have to go," Oswell said, "I'm sorry. Keep her out of trouble."

"I will," Darius said solemnly, sensing that there was no further point in argument.

Finally, Oswell looked at Cicero. The older man's intelligent eyes flitted to the side and the pair strode off to the ladder wordlessly. Oswell went first and descended towards the ground. He chose not to look back; it was too hard. He would miss them all.

"You think this will work?" Oswell asked as they touched down on the forest floor.

"No guarantees," Cicero said. "Follow me."

Oswell readjusted the straps on his shoulders and followed after the older man. They walked for the better part of an hour before Cicero stopped abruptly.

"I think this is close to where it happened," Cicero mused.

"What do I do?" Oswell asked.

"This is not an exact science by any means, you'll be the first person I try to send back across a dimensional rift," Cicero started. "I would start by connecting with Thomas."

Oswell nodded and closed his eyes.

"Wait," Cicero said.

"What is it?" Oswell asked, opening his eyes. The older man pulled a ring off of his finger and held it out to Oswell. Oswell took it and examined it.

"It belonged to my brother Mathias. I'd like you to have it. To remind you of your great strength, and what you did here."

Oswell slipped the ring onto his middle finger and stepped forward to embrace the man.

"We thank you for your help, Oswell."

Oswell smiled, thinking back through the short time he'd been on Myros, and how much he'd changed in that time. He was stronger (by half), more patient (by far), and wiser (perhaps). "It was my pleasure," he replied. He then stepped away from the older man and closed his eyes.

Thomas, Oswell thought, reaching out. He felt the forest fade away from him as he descended into silence. A different forest rushed up to greet him, pausing only inches away. He watched as though he were shifted in space and time, neither here nor there, but simply slightly out of phase.

Before him, Thomas led Nicholas by the hand and Claire walked at his side. Sweat glistened on Thomas's brow and the three travellers wore matching expressions of exertion. They were on the long walk.

Thomas, Oswell repeated, pushing forward. Thomas appeared to pay no mind. He was oblivious to Oswell's presence, focused single-mindedly on the task at hand. Thomas was him, perhaps thinner, but set firmly to the task he'd been assigned—a task assigned by Oswell, and perhaps by something or someone with greater designs.

Oswell's mind faltered as he followed the trio. Who was he to think he'd be any better at this than Thomas? And what would Thomas be coming back to? A world changed by Oswell's actions? Would there be a place for him? Oswell shook his head, of course there would be, Cicero loved Thomas. Though he'd been abstracted from the puzzle, he'd fit right into the place where Oswell had carved out a niche. The worlds had to be set right.

Remembering how he'd changed places in the first place, Oswell picked up his pace as he followed and angled towards Thomas and then canted into a sprint towards the young man.

A wayward force crashed into his body and Oswell felt himself tumble sideways. When he opened his eyes, he felt the ground caressing his back as he looked up at the forest canopy above him. Claire's voice cried out in surprise and as Oswell struggled to pull himself up, he saw a shadow, or vapour of Thomas clambering to his feet as Claire helped him up. The vision faded.

"It didn't work," Cicero observed.

Oswell balled his fists and drove them into his closed eyes in frustration. He groaned and sat up. He'd been close to crossing back over, he felt it. Thomas had been right there, but something had stopped him from completing the transition. What, exactly, had stopped him, Oswell wasn't sure, but the interference had thrown the both of them apart.

"No," he agreed. "Cicero, how'm I going to get home?"

The older man said nothing, electing instead to sit down beside the younger man. Oswell sat in silence, waiting for Cicero to reply. The older man remained silent. It seemed like it had been an eon when he finally spoke.

"You were brought here for a reason," Cicero began, speaking slowly. "You came here with a purpose, unbeknownst to you. We assumed it was for you to rid us of Makkin, but..." Cicero paused again, "It would appear Myr has greater designs for you."

"But..." Oswell started.

"One will come, memory astray,
When darkness, death, and sin are found
In hallowed lands of black and grey.
Our world despairs, but hope's in bound,
Salvation in a golden way," Cicero recited the prophecy. "There may yet be more expected of you. Myr has grand designs, and it would seem," Cicero paused, "He has great and dire things in store for Oswell Wallace."

ABOUT THE AUTHOR

J. R. McConnery is a paediatrician by day (and often by night) and an author by night (and often by day). He lives in Toronto, Ontario with his wife, Cara. When he isn't dancing around sneezing children or writing, he likes reading, cooking, and following politics. *A Crossing in the Woods* is the first novel in *The Courser & Wallace Chronicles*.

PREVIEW

If you enjoyed
A Crossing in the Woods,
look out for

A FEAR OF
ALL DEFIANCE

Book Two in The Courser & Wallace Chronicles

by J.R. McConnery

- CHAPTER ONE -

WELCOME BACK

THE ARROWHEAD RIVER cut a swath through the hills, taking the
path of least resistance as it shouldered its way southward. In the distance, a small city sat comfortably in a large clearing, surrounded by
the poor districts outside its formidable walls. The walls were foreboding, shooting a lance of trepidation through him as though they
warned him of what he must face. Perhaps it wasn't the wall, after all,
maybe it was just him.

"Oswell," Cicero said. Oswell looked up at the man. Cicero tilted
his head in Fletchery's direction. Oswell nodded. Despite his apprehension about seeing Karyn, he also felt a certain excitement building
as they began to walk to Fletchery. The rest of the crew had left for
Fletchery early that morning, with pressing matters to address while
Cicero supervised Oswell's attempt to burst his way back to Earth. A
clash of emotions warred within him; he was disappointed to have
failed in returning home, but he was also excited to share in the glory
of the rebellion's success.   He didn't know how to feel. Days ago,
Fletchery was a town in which he and Cicero were wanted fugitives.
Murderers. Now, they would arrive as heroes. Only in his dreams and
childhood adventures, had he ever been a hero.

It started with whispers. Walking the road, people eyed Cicero and
Oswell, staring with wonder, whispering under their breath, but do-

ing little beyond that. As they continued on, Oswell started to hear Cicero's name, and even his own. Word had travelled fast.

Glancing over his shoulder, Oswell noticed that they had acquired a retinue. The majority were children, though more and more adults inserted themselves into the throng. He did his best to keep his composure, despite the growing pride welling in his chest.

Cicero stopped and Oswell shored up beside him as one brave child, a girl no older than ten with unruly blonde hair stepped out in front of them.

"Yer them fugitives, ain'tcha?"

Cicero smiled as the girl's father snatched her up.

"My apologies, m'lord."

"Do not apologize," Cicero said, "her curiosity will take her far."

The girl's father reddened in the face and put her back on the ground. Cicero stepped forward and crouched to take the little girl's hands in his.

"Indeed, we are them fugitives," Cicero said. The girl's cheeks reddened. "What is your name?"

"Lana," the girl replied. Her father coughed behind her, "Weydryn, Lana Wydryn," she tacked on.

"It is wonderful to meet you Lana, tell me, you do not seem to be afraid of us. Why? Everyone else seems to be."

"'Cause you done rid us of that old, fat, horrible man. The both of ya did," she looked at Oswell shyly.

"That is correct, Lana, and why is that good?"

"You've freed us, syr."

Cicero smiled and nodded. He stood and surveyed the crowd that had gathered around them.

"I know that you are afraid. Afraid of what we have done. Afraid of what we will do. Afraid for what the future now holds. With change comes fear, but I assure you, my people, the change we are approaching is great. I will not try to dissuade you from fear, for that would be misleading. There is still much to fear."

Oswell thought about cutting in, but decided against it. He couldn't tell where Cicero was going with his speech, but if he knew Cicero at all, it had to be going somewhere.

"You will have fear for your lives," he looked at Lana's father pointedly, "fear for your children's lives. For what we have done is high treason. But I ask you this: mere days ago, what kind of life did you live?"

"'Twas a prison," one man amongst the crowd mumbled.

"Aye," another voice echoed.

"I cannot disagree," Cicero said. "You are the people who work the fields and the forests. You build the tables in our homes and put the food on those tables. You are the very backbone of this great nation, and what reward do you see for it?"

"Nothing!" someone shouted.

"Worse," Cicero said. "You get a life in chains. Chains forged by Saosin Hallows." The crowd gasped at the accusation, but silence returned as Cicero raised his hands. "He has taken your freedom of religion. He has taken away your freedom to thrive and to prosper. Is there anything he has not taken?"

"Our lives?"

"And what kind of life is that?" Cicero asked.

Silence fell over the crowd, which by now, seemed to consist of everyone outside the walls of Fletchery. Every labourer, every child, every merchant.

"We have come to give you liberty," Cicero said. "To give you the freedom... the life that your hearts desire. No, the life that your hearts *deserve*."

The people stared at him. Oswell could feel a thousand eyes flickering from Cicero, to him, and back to Cicero again. It seemed as though they were collectively weighing the truth of Cicero's words. In moments, it seemed that they had all come to the same conclusion. They began to kneel.

Cicero raised his hands yet again before even a single knee could touch the ground.

"Do not kneel before us. We do not ask for your worship, we ask only for your support. There is much work to be done. Our future," Cicero gestured around, "relies on all of us, and in that, we are all equal!" If he had not won them over before, he had them with his final words.

A cheer erupted from the crowd as people rose to their feet. They rushed forward and clamoured around Cicero and Oswell. Oswell felt loving hands caress him before stronger hands bore him up and onto the shoulders of many. Looking across the sea of hands, he saw Cicero receiving similar treatment. The throng shifted in the direction of Fletchery's main gate.

Oswell grinned at Wendell and Watson as they shook their heads in amusement.

"Couldn't have just walked in?"

"Don't ask *me*, that was Cicero's doing," Oswell replied.

"It was the people's doing," Cicero corrected.

Oswell felt high on the righteousness that Cicero exuded. He felt like he had finally done something meaningful in his life. He'd done good things in the past. Babysat Nicholas and Ella for free. Intervened in the occasional schoolyard fight. Hugged Helen, the girl he'd known for years but never really talked to, because she was being bullied. But never in his life had he ever done something so significant. So profound and important. He'd literally freed an entire city from oppression, all because one man thought that a vague prophecy indicated that he was the one that was destined to do so.

"They love the both of you," Watson said. "It will be a powerful tool."

Wendell placed a hand on his shoulder and brought Oswell back to Earth. "I take it that you were not able to return home to your world? You still have work to do here?"

"It would seem so." Oswell replied solemnly.

Oswell and Cicero followed the brothers to a long meeting hall with a grand table running down its centre. It seemed that the entirety of the Numyrian Independence Front was there, and the movement was growing. He looked around, but Karyn's face was not in the crowd. A small part of him was relieved.

Oswell stood, feeling the energy flowing through him. He paced up and down the length of the room ignoring the eyes that followed him. He had too much energy to sit still, which was unusual, given the events of the past few days. Everything had happened so fast. He paused at the head of the table and finally appraised the men sitting along it.

Watson and Wendell sat to one side of the table, both giving him an identical look of amused interest. Laurence sat quietly, observing Oswell with a measure of sympathy. Oswell met eyes with him only briefly, not prepared to feel the sadness at what his failure to return home actually meant. He huffed and turned in the room.

On the other side of the table, Cicero's eyes sparkled as he enjoyed the vigour lighting up Oswell's face. Another man that Oswell had not yet met, Ganavan Shea, looked on with a mix of hopeful curiosity and careful doubt.

Ganavan Shea was a short, unimposing man of middling age. Though balding, a few wisps of hair still traversed the widening space on the top of his head, while simultaneously fighting off an encroaching grey. The thick hair of his sideburns had not fared so well, being well peppered. Despite his generally unimpressive stature, his face was handsome and his eyes were filled with an unmistakably sharp intelligence.

Oswell only knew Ganavan by the few words Cicero had offered as they had approached Fletchery. He was a former councillor that had served on the Fletcherian Town Assembly. Upon the installation of Acer Makkin years before, his services had been deemed unnecessary. Without putting up a fight, he'd faded into the fold and integrated himself, for the sake of survival, back into his former trade as a merchant. There, he'd served for fruitless years, paying taxes into the very machine that had unseated him. Needless to say, he was happy to see Acer Makkin go.

Oswell felt the men watching him grow impatient as he stood before them. He had, before him, two options.

The easy route would be to remember that he was only fifteen years old (not even, he realized, his birthday was in a few weeks), and that a fifteen year old couldn't do anything (despite the mounting evidence to suggest otherwise) to help people. Everything so far had been a fluke and he was crazy. So crazy, in fact, to think that he could get lucky and survive much longer trying to do the things he was doing.

The more difficult route, the scarier route, would be to accept the chance he'd been given, the directive (however vague) to help the people of Numyria achieve their independence and their freedom. Everything he'd done so far had worked out, after all.

Oswell glanced at Cicero, who was smiling patiently. Oswell's eyes then flitted to Ganavan, whose expression was slowly shifting away from hopeful curiosity in the direction of less careful doubt. In that growing doubt, Oswell had his answer, for he was a stubborn young man, and any doubt other than self-doubt was the greatest motivation a stubborn young man could find.

"What's next?" he finally said.

FOR RELEASE IN 2020

www.ingramcontent.com/pod-product-compliance
Lightning Source LLC
Chambersburg PA
CBHW030540260626

47157CB00006B/2122